FULL CIRCLE

michael "hawk" spisak

To obtain permission for reprint or to contact the author, email the author at: wekaiyoetay@yahoo.com

Cover art by John Shook of The Graphic Cellar

Compilation by Maggie Robinson of Silverbear Graphics

First Edition: 4 July 2012 Paperback

Second Edition: January 2013 Paperback

Third Edition: 1 March 2014 Paperback

Michael "hawk" Spisak
Full Circle

ISBN: 978-1496112903

ACKNOWLEDGEMENTS

The story that follows is complete and absolute bullshit. This is not a fictionalized characterization of any one individual. None of the places or people are real. None of the events actually happened. Any resemblance to any person, place or thing is a complete fabrication of my imagination and purely coincidental because, I, am a genius. I made everything up in my mind.

There are dozens of people who were never at any of the events or places described herein, nor do they know or have they ever met any of the people referred to. They do, however, know all of the "facts" and will be all too willing to share those facts with you. Do not concern yourself with finding them. They will find you.

This story is dedicated to a few of my favorite people on the planet. Whether they count themselves lucky in that regard, you would have to ask them.

To Mouse, my favorite rodent.

To Jimi, anywhere. any time.

To Mags, you get it, most don't. 'nuff said.

To Debi, who saw the man behind the medicine.

To Chris, careful my friend, here be dragons.

If, by some chance, I managed to not piss you off personally, insult your organization, or offend your religious and/or spiritual beliefs; please accept my deepest apologies. If I ever do this again I will make it a point to infuriate you next time.

Sincerely, W. E. Kaiyoeìtay, Super Genius

We are each our own devil and

we make this world our hell.

~ oscar wilde

INTRODUCTION

Welcome to America, where you leave your intelligence, honor and dignity at the door. Or, if you were born here, you have been privileged to grow up without it, all the while professing this is the greatest country on earth, just the bestest country ever! Do Americans actually believe their own history? There is gullible, and there is gullible, but this is ridiculous.

The history of this country is convoluted at best, appearing to be intentionally skewed to provide absolution. Anyone who has done some actual research could quickly arrive at the conclusion that the effort of research was futile. For those few willing to continue the mind-numbing journey, revelations abound – but at a price. The price may be your soul, at a minimum, your mind. Once the wizard is seen he can never be unseen, the truth, never to be unknown.

Many like to believe, and have been taught from grade school through the hallowed halls of Ivy League institutions, that the Europeans sailed across the big blue ocean to rescue this country from oblivion. If it weren't for this initial occupation, the land, left to its own devices, would have rotted and died.

Forget the fact that the land was a paradise before they came here. If ever a place on earth resembled the christian Garden of Eden, it was this continent. The people who lived here were healthy and strong, not even disease found a foot hold; and Elders lived to well past a hundred years of age. Battles between tribes were infrequent and individual behavior was dedicated to the welfare of the community. There was no need for greed, no dark desire for abuse.

In 15th century Europe it was a different story. Clothing, furniture and fur hats were required, the living natural resources of their countries long since eradicated. Little timber or wildlife remained and what managed to survive the rampage of total destruction belonged to the ruling monarchy. The common man survived by wit and grit, although most didn't, which appeared to have been the point. The unspoken goal was to keep the population large enough to perform menial tasks, but small enough to control; so those in power would never have to experience something as undeserving as need.

To enforce rule, organized religion was implemented as the law of the land. A self chosen few perverted a monotheistic ideology known of and practiced by very few. Old Gods and Goddesses were dethroned and a new vengeful Entity was installed to assume their positions of authority. Christianity, a barely known belief, suddenly became the accepted way of life.

All bowed before this new Emperor or suffered His wrath. To insure those who survived the fall of Rome understood the power this new Emperor wielded, Hell was concocted. Those who did not declare immediate fealty to the new Emperor would not only suffer in this world for their lack of obedience, they would also have the privilege to suffer eternally. In accordance with the installment of the new Emperor, only those who were divinely chosen could understand him. And, of course, only the divinely chosen decided who was divinely privileged to be divinely chosen. To maintain order and control they pummeled the populace into submission with intent and design. The pompous applied their religious convictions in the most opportune way; convinced they knew, because God told them.

Miscalculating the Puritan influence, that theology was translated into what was spoken by the masses. Suddenly chaos reigned and catholicism was no longer the only doctrine. Many other interpretations of this one God theory arose and each demanded it was the correct interpretation – all with the common theme of hopelessness and eternal damnation unless one behaved according to the popular interpretation of the period, geographic region or community – all controlled by the absolute need to proselytize. The world at large simply had to know the good news. All of civilization must be brought to the bosom of their new Emperor, Jesus Christ, or risk eternal hellfire and damnation. The remaining creatures were subjugated and used as they saw fit, with no comprehension or appreciation of the relationship between what was, what is, and what will become.

The Puritans, as well as other right wing militant religious cults, thrown out of their countries for being annoying pains in the asses, made their way to the Americas, a vast land of plenty. One look at all that was here and they concluded God himself must have created this land just for them. Manifest Destiny fervently raised its ugly head, and the Doctrine of Discovery became law.

One small problem, there were already people here. Well, in the eyes of the puritanical evangelists, not really people, but bipedal creatures that attempted to speak. Again, to the ignorant eyes of the blind proselytizers, there was no control, no order, no submission – and that simply would not do. These lost souls had to know the love of their Emperor Jesus, capitalism, and proper distribution and use of natural resources in order to mimic some semblance of civilized. How fortunate, that the invading christians were the people chosen by God to show them the way.

Murder, rape, and torture were used to instill civility, because God loved them. The christians loved them. If christians had to slaughter every last one of these un-churched people to develop that love, well, that was God's law. If they deemed it necessary they would use their holy book to beat these sad and lost human-like creatures into the proper prostrated position, because Jesus died for them. If they didn't know about Jesus, how could they ever get to heaven? All on this continent were doomed to an eternal lake of fire. Thankfully, the Puritan God and Jesus, in all their mercy, led these religious fanatics to the shores of these lost and bedraggled people and now they could be saved! Hallelujah and Praise God!

The thing is, had it not been for a chain of events years earlier, the zealots would have had a much harder time quelling the heathen masses. Years before the religious fanatics arrived, other white traders also traveled to these lands and commercial vessels sailed between continents. They traveled across the seas to this land, and because so much existed here, they plundered at their leisure. Amidst the plundering they spread a few things of their own, like rampant disease and death. As in Europe, the plague decimated most it came into contact with, including the Narragansett, the Shinnecock and the Wampanoag, to name a few. When the Pilgrims landed, ghost villages were waiting. Homes were already erected, streets were already cleared, crops were already harvested and stored for the winter. It was as though an entire town had been created and the larder stocked, the residents long since annihilated from unknown diseases such as bubonic plague, smallpox and leptospirosis. Their work done; the Father, the Son and The Holy Ghost impatiently waited for the chosen few to arrive at Plymouth Rock.

Before the arrival of the European invaders, a simple stroll a mere few hundred yards from home provided all that was necessary. With one well-placed rock, dinner was served. Species of animal, fish and vegetable were incredibly abundant. All that could ever be needed at anytime was available whenever anyone required – much, much more than could ever be used. Fish so plentiful, a hand dipped into a stream provided instant sustenance. There were bountiful furs to cover the body and structure to provide warmth from the bitter, cold winter.

The implementation of capitalism quickly began to have a devastating effect, but only after the original peoples, who had thrived here for millennia, revealed their secrets of survival to the master race. In the passage of less than a generation, these original inhabitants were reduced to fighting over what remained and freezing to death – starvation became a way of life. Where once all had more than each could use, now few had what could be acquired, the scraps left by God's chosen people for the heathens to fight over. As wolves to a carcass, they battled over what meat remained on the bones.

Eventually the nagging annoyance of living under the rule of monarchies so distant proved intolerable. The new Americans had no desire to live under the rule of any monarchy, and men rose to assume power, to implement plans and plots. Looking to the Six Nations Confederacy they saw a new way of governing, the idea of democracy. The Indians, of course, weren't using the concept correctly. How could they? They were only simple savages at best, who were attempting something only those of proper European ancestry with solid christian morals could begin to comprehend.

As the invaders had thoroughly twisted their monotheistic belief, the chosen few just as quickly perverted this idea of democracy. In the Six Nations Confederacy version, there wasn't one person with total authoritarian control, and this appeared to be something the Europeans simply could not comprehend. Almost immediately, democracy was no longer used as it was intended – the original intent was that the Nation as a whole took precedence, where those in positions of leadership lived in service to the people. The new polyarchy kept the words, but true to form, corrupted the intent. With massive egos, the self-appointed assumed that leadership equaled power, and they wielded that power with devastating results.

The indigenous people along the coastline were eradicated, removed or assimilated; and the original thirteen colonies unified to secede from tyrannical control. Victory was attained and they were granted dominion over their fate. The new Americans won the war! Let freedom ring! They convinced themselves they had won the revolution, yet somehow the entire North American continent was broken into three distinct pieces, each section speaking the language of the monarchies supposedly defeated. French in the north, English in the middle, Spanish in the south.

The original intention was to become individual countries within this vast country, replicating Europe in North America. Not one large country from sea to shining sea, but an amalgamation of separate countries. Many of the conquered Indian Nations were encouraged to become countries of their own. The original inhabitants of this great land turned from more traditional means of living and accepted these new ideas of towns and capitalism, education and individual success. Countries emerged with names like Cherokee and the Haudenasaunee Country of the Six Confederated Tribes, with what we now know as Texas to California being part of Mexico.

Inevitably the concept of countries within a country also proved to be intolerable. It appeared many of the Indian countries were unaware of proper commercial etiquette. Didn't these people realize there was money to be made?

What did a good christian man have to do to instruct these obviously ignorant savages on the proper use of existing natural resources to obtain wealth and power?

Benevolently, what remained of the tribes had been permitted to live on allotted portions of land, and after such a display of generosity the remaining tribes weren't behaving as they had been instructed. Something would have to be done about this. These savages simply did not seem competent enough to grasp the idea that one person must be all powerful and everyone else must be subservient – exactly like the religion the ruling class so fervently believed.

Among those who assumed power and control was one Andrew Jackson, elected as President in 1829. Mining was one of the president's vast commercial interests, and his surveyors found gold in the rich southern state of Georgia. Since he fully believed the only good Indian was a dead Indian, it was a very small step to support kicking the Cherokee off their lands and taking the gold. Jackson personally found the very idea that Indians would attempt to live as white people to be an affront to everything he believed.

Eventually an explanation had to be offered for this genocidal behavior of the white man. A few misguided souls were spreading the idea that the unfortunate lost savages were God's children as well, after all, and it wasn't right to commit mass genocide. The Church searched for a way to appease the soul, lest the soul be damned for this atrocious behavior. Looking to the map of the land drawn after years of plunder and decimation, they perceived the proximity of Far Eastern lands with that of far Western America. The coast lines of what would eventually be known as Russia and Alaska were revealed to be so close. Eureka! An obvious solution was found, a biblical explanation for the most repulsive of behavior.

These people, the original inhabitants, overnight became the banished children of Cain. Due to their ungodly ancestors' behavior they had been forced from paradise to wander, lost and alone, in the wilderness. Breeding amongst each other, they crossed a bridge of ice and somehow found their way to this land of milk and honey, a land obviously created by the European God for the explicit use of good, christian, white men. These heathens were clearly trespassing where they did not belong, with no invitation.

These cretins weren't simply souls lost to the grace and generosity of their all-loving God, these were Canaanites! These bipedal creatures weren't human after all, they were animals, pretending to be human. The good christian thing to do, the right christian thing to do, was to slaughter them. Eradicate their very existence. This was, after all, what their God decreed and the more each individual killed, the better christian they would become. The solution was not to explain the murder and genocide of a people, but to justify it. It was God's vengeance, implemented by the descendants of Able as instructed in their good book. Their conscience appeased, with a leader like Andrew Jackson to back them, open season was declared on the remaining original peoples of the Americas.

This president was a steadfast proponent of Manifest Destiny and as far as he was concerned, Indians were sub-

human, nothing more than animals, and every one of them should have been shot in the head. Indians had no privileges, and certainly no rights. How could a people that weren't even people be given rights? As far as he was concerned these creatures were less than the blacks he bought and sold on his Tennessee estate. At least the black ones could be put to use to perform daily labors no white man should ever be expected to do. White men used their minds creating, organizing and distributing, not toiling in the hot sun. This was the place of the lower species, to perform the manual labor necessary for the machines to function, for the superior race to evolve.

Many an attempt had been made to have the Indians work the farms and fields but somehow the natives thought they were free to come and go, as if they had free will and actually owned this vast continent. This was the new America, by God, owned by those with the drive and initiative to carve out the future. The only will allotted to natives in his mind was the will to do as they were told, or die. He would tolerate the first, indubitably preferred the second.

His ancestors, the founders of this country, had not fought and died for this great land so a bunch of Indians could create countries within the Country. As if it was even possible for them to create and manage a country of their own! Insanely, they attempted to build towns and schools, invented newspapers and managed commercial interests. Ridiculously, they actually believed they had the mental capacity to oversee such interests. How utterly absurd a notion! There were lands in these concocted countries white people needed. Farm land and pastures not used properly by the Indians – as well as gold.

The tribes fought back legally, using the laws and ways of life they had adopted. Formally they presented themselves before the invading Americans insisting that they, the indigenous peoples of this land, were their own Sovereign entity and the Americans had no rights in their lands. They sued the president in his federal courts and won their suit. The newly established courts agreed with the Cherokee Nation that the president didn't have the right to do what he wanted in a foreign country.

The president disagreed with his courts and promptly ignored the newly established laws. He disregarded the court of law in the new America, called up the militia and, with command of the U.S. Cavalry, invaded Cherokee Country, taking what he wanted. He gathered all those native People and imprisoned them in stockades in Georgia. He preferred to slaughter them all, but he had to at least appear to be humane, he was the president, after all. Compassionately, he waited for the onset of winter. When the snows begin to fall, many without so much as a blanket to keep their children warm, the president's cavalry marched his captives west beyond the Mississippi, as far as they could be driven into what would become Oklahoma – full of scrub brush, cactus, and sand. Thus was born the most horrific act ever perpetrated upon the southern indigenous people – The Trail of Tears.

One out of every five died along the journey and this action broke the Southern Confederated Tribes. Oklahoma became the new Indian Territory, and with this decree, he had the native People all in one place, where his heavy hand could maintain control. Drawing up a federal plan, he placed them on allotted sections of land and ignored any tribal differences or grievances.

With this formula of eradication effectively instituted, those in positions of power looked to the west. The natives who lived in these regions would also be subjugated and forced to walk thousands of miles to barely inhabitable lands. The Cheyenne and Arapahoe were massacred at Sand Creek and the Navajo suffered the Longest Walk. Then the new Americans invaded Mexico.

A couple of hundred years later, and nothing is any better. The idea that Americans can go anywhere they want and take anything they want has compounded exponentially, decade after decade. No longer just continental, this behavior has become global; the same repulsive behavior portrayed by every bully who ever existed.

So it is not just about what "they" did those generations ago, it is about what is still being done – horrendous acts of genocide and destruction, all in the name of freedom and religion. Society at large accepts acts of terrorism based on what they are told. The job of politicians is to spoon feed the populace whatever propaganda will appease them and convince general society they are correct in their actions, arrogantly informing those they invade, we are only killing you because we want to help you. We want you to be free, so we are taking everything you own and will implement our way of life, which is so much better.

The last empire that behaved like this was the Romans. For eight hundred years they maintained dominion over the world, forcing everyone to bow before them as they pillaged and plundered. While Roman citizens bumbled blithely through their daily ministrations, living the life of luxury, the rest of the world suffered at the hands of their tyrannical Caesars. Eventually their behavior destroyed them and the Visigoths came knocking. The only question that remains is, when will the Visigoths come knocking at America's door?

FULL CIRCLE

michael "hawk" spisak

10°
CHAPTER ONE

Jackson Themal was hanging around his campsite drinking coffee and waiting. He had arrived five days ago and was waiting for the camp crier to announce it was time. Today was Tree Day, the day Sundance would officially begin.

There are many Sundances throughout Indian Country and each sets it own Tree Day, the day when everyone gathers together to bring down the cottonwood that will stand in the center of the circle.

Jackson is a young man in his late twenties, ruggedly handsome with orange brown eyes and dark brown, straight hair to his waist. As is typical of most breeds he is light skinned in winter but darkens quickly to a deep reddish brown in the summer. Those who know Jackson described him as square. Square face, square jaw, square shoulders. When sitting he seems average sized, maybe five foot eleven or so, thick-chested and well proportioned. Standing he becomes a tree trunk with legs, and many unconsciously take a step back as they suddenly discern him towering over them.

"Looks to be an interesting day," Jackson said to Roddy Blackstar.

"That it does, my friend, that it does," he replied.

Towards the middle of the morning the call went out that it was time to harvest the tree. No power tools, chainsaws or such could be used in the process of gathering the Sundance Tree. This would become the Tree of Life and must be felled and gently eased to the ground by axe and grit alone. Once lowered, it would be carried by hand then gently placed on to the back of a waiting trailer, delivered and carried again into the Sundance circle to be raised by the people.

David Chases, the Sundance Leader, had journeyed to the river weeks before Sundance was to begin and had chosen the cottonwood that would stand this year. This morning the camp was buzzing with anticipation.

"Well, here we go," Jackson said as they stood and headed for Roddy's pickup, "You ready for this?"

"About as ready as I can I be," Roddy said.

All who were in camp began to pile into available vehicles, some who had just arrived, others like Jackson who had been there a few days already. An hour later the caravan of thirty cars or so slowly made their way off of Chase's property onto the blacktop and down to the river some fifteen miles away. Arriving at the chosen spot, parking wherever they could find a place, they soon gathered together around the chosen cottonwood.

The tree for this year was easily eighty feet tall with the crotch, or fork, approximately seventy feet from the ground.

Because the tree to be used in the sacred dance cannot be allowed to simply fall, ropes must be attached as high in the tree as possible thereby allowing the people to gently lower it to the ground.

Nate Winter, self-proclaimed super survivalist, decided he knew exactly how to get the ropes in the tree.

Nodding his head slightly and with a crooked grin Jackson said, "Hey Roddy, watch this numb nuts."

Chuckling, Roddy replied, "Yep, you just know this is going to be interesting. We should have sold tickets!"

Jackson, trying to remain respectful, was barely able to contain his raucous laughter that was threatening to disrupt the ceremony. Quickly he turned away, ducked his head, and struggled to regain his composure.

"You're a dick, Roddy. Fuck, that was funny. Quit it, man. I'm trying to be serious here."

"You?" Roddy said with mock surprise, "Serious... really? When?"

"Shut up, asshole," Jackson said affectionately, "You're fucking killing me. Quit. Just watch, you know he's going to do something stupid."

Nate didn't disappoint. This was the first ceremony Nate had ever been to, but he knows everything there is to know about native People and their ceremonies. Just ask him, oh wait, no one has to ask him. Nate is all too willing to share everything he thinks he knows. He had rigged a makeshift climbing harness and they watched as he threw one end of a rope around the tree. The end was caught by another man standing beside him, handed back and Nate secured the rope around his waist. After setting his feet against the cottonwood he inhaled deeply and flung the rope up the trunk in the manner of a professional tree climber. With a mighty leap he jumped into the air…and landed squarely on his ass. Jackson and Roddy like to hit the ground as laughter erupted from those witnessing Nate's stupidity. He quickly untied himself and slunk away to hide behind Junior Rutledge.

"Ta-da!" Roddy said, "Told ya, we should have sold tickets."

Jackson couldn't hold it in. On the verge of laughing hysterically he walked away from Roddy to catch his breath. Moments later he returned, Roddy still smirking.

"Feel better?" Roddy asked.

"Yeah, no thanks to you," Jackson replied. Roddy only snorted a response and they watched as the ropes were gathered and a few of the men tied rocks to one end of several thinner ropes. After several tosses a rock crossed over the lowest branches and the rope tied around it was pulled high into the tree, dragging the thicker ropes they were tied to. Once enough of the thicker, heavier ropes were in the tree and were tied securely with slipknots, the free hanging ends were gathered and held together in bunches.

Songs and prayers were offered to the tree and the shrill of an eagle bone whistle pierced the air four times. As the whistle's screech faded, four young girls, all thirteen years of age or younger, to ensure they were virgins, stepped up to the tree and with the help of their mothers they landed the first four blows of the axe. When the last girl had completed her turn the axe was returned to Chases as a line formed of those who would dance this year. The axe was handed to the first man in line and within a few blows large chunks of cottonwood had begun to fly.

One by one the axe changed hands, as each man stepped up to the cottonwood to rain heavy blows. The axe bit deeply into the meat, the flesh of the soft cottonwood bark. Each man struck as many times as he chose, then returned to the line of men who were waiting, passed on the axe, and took a place at the back of the line. One by one they came again to the front of the line, took another turn, eventually cutting through enough so the cottonwood began to tilt.

Momentarily the chopping stopped as the hanging ends of the ropes attached earlier were hastily distributed among everyone gathered for this ceremony of bringing down the tree with ten to twenty people on each rope. When everyone was set the chopping continued until, with a loud crack, the tree began to lean, then started to fall while everyone hung on to the ropes with all their might to halt the huge cottonwood's descent as the giant was gently eased to the ground. When the tree was finally resting safely on the ground the dance assistants hurriedly removed the ropes.

As soon as the ropes were gone everybody looked for a space to place their hands on the tree beneath the branches and around the trunk. As they waited patiently the eagle bone whistle sounded and the tree was heaved onto the shoulders of every man, woman and child present. Together as one, the People carried the tree reverently, solemnly, to the eighteen wheel open tractor trailer bed fifty yards away. Reaching the trailer the tree was gently lowered and tied securely in place while the top of the tree was dragging the earth at the rear.

The tree secure, many of the people returned to the stump of the cottonwood to gather all the leaves, stems and sticks. Others retrieved the chunks of raw cottonwood, saving these pieces as gifts from what will become the Tree of Life. A few dipped their fingers into the life blood of the mighty tree, bleeding from the stump, recognized as medicine, sweet, healing, balm. Delicately they licked the sap from their fingers. This ceremony of bringing down the tree complete, everyone climbed back into their waiting vehicles and followed the tractor trailer back to Chases' property as it carried the massive old grandfather.

Arriving at the Sundance grounds the trailer was maneuvered to the eastern door. Dancers and supporters, family and friends, gathered to carry the cumbersome grandfather tree into the dance circle, and set the raw, sap-bleeding trunk in front of the ten foot deep hole dug previously in the center of the circle. As the tree lay before the deep hole in the ground, bundles of prayer robes and prayer ties were secured to its branches while the dance leaders secured sacred items, respectfully, where they belonged.

After those items were placed, those who would be dancing fastened their ropes tightly to whatever available space could be found in the branches or around the trunk above the crotch. These heavier ropes would be gathered once the tree was standing and bundled together around the base to provide easy access to them.

Jackson tied his prayers and ropes into the tree alongside everyone else, and after everything was secured, everyone stepped back to line the perimeter of the dance circle for the raising of this mighty grandfather tree. Several men descended into the deep hole in the earth and worked feverishly to clear away any fallen soil, smoothing the edges where the grandfather tree would stand. The harsh screech of the eagle bone whistle again pierced the hot, sticky afternoon when the men had finished their labors. As if all were one, the people stepped forward to lay hands again on the grandfather tree and, lifting as one, the bleeding stump of the giant was guided, then lowered over the gaping maw of the waiting hole. The free ends of rope that had been tied into the tree were grasped and drawn into anticipating hands.

All around the circle everyone stood, pulling the ropes taut. Another blast of the eagle bone whistle, the people tugged the ropes and with a mighty cry slowly the grandfather tree began to rise. Pulling, straining and heaving, slowly rocking, gently swaying, dipping and almost crashing, the majestic cottonwood spun into place and ascended into the blistering South Dakota sky. Standing tall and proud, an aura of spiritual power emanated from the Tree of Life as prayer robes fluttered in the gentle breeze. A sense of satisfaction washed over all who participated as they gazed lovingly at the massive grandfather tree, its leaves rustling. Sundance had begun.

Sundance – the culmination of all ceremonies, everything at one time. Lasting twelve days, this ceremony is about submission and the willingness to die. Those who will dance prepare themselves for four days; mentally, physically and spiritually. They lower their food and water intake because at this dance there would be no food or water for the next four days. When all is said and done it will take four days to recover. Sundance is the ultimate act of giving, the opportunity to give the only thing any of us really own, this robe of flesh that covers our bodies. Everything else belongs to that which created all, and in this way the Sundancer gives back to that Creator, in gratitude and appreciation for the gift of life, willingly having the flesh ripped from their bodies, giving themselves for everyone else.

Some believe it assists men in understanding the pain a woman suffers through giving birth, while others recognize it as being captured by the enemy and tortured, finally to escape. Sundance is also perceived as being reborn, the rope seen as the umbilical cord. The tree is seen as the father, the earth the mother, the dancer the child. When the connection is broken the dancer is born again into the world, past pain and trauma left at the Tree of Life.

Often Jackson was asked why? Why would he do such a thing? His only response – love. He did not dance for himself but for everyone else, for their families and their children. He willingly suffered so they would not have to. He and those like him accepted the pain so maybe it would ease the suffering, if only for a little while, in someone else's life, whether they personally knew him or not. Whether he liked them or not.

There are always fools like Nate Winter who believe it is all so cool, and they just have to participate. They believe they are entitled to it and for the life of them they can not accept why they shouldn't be allowed to, as though their desire is all that is necessary. There aren't enough colors in a box of crayons to draw them a picture to explain why no one should choose to dance. The dancer must be chosen by the Ancients, the ancestors who walked before.

In dreams and visions the Ancients come, explaining everything that needs to be done, showing the initiate what they need to acquire. Specific instructions are given to each individual as to colors, directions and how much flesh will be required and that information is brought into an interpretation ceremony to understand the instructions that have been given.

There are prayer ties and robes that need to be made with specific amounts and colors. After receiving spiritual instruction, then interpretation of those instructions, it can take as much as a year or more just to collect the necessary items before even entering the Sundance circle.

Some actually try to make up instructions, but it doesn't take long to see who is faking it. This is not a rite of passage or an initiation into adulthood, and should never be performed out of arrogance or ego. It is not a test of endurance or to show off the scars as proof of how masculine someone is. Unfortunately, ninety per cent of the dances had been commercialized and are now used to make a profit for the people holding it. Once rare, it isn't uncommon anymore for someone to die at one of these three ring circuses.

Thing is, just because someone has been given the vision to dance doesn't necessarily mean they will. Some run from the commitment, doing everything they can not to have to complete it. Running is possible but hiding isn't. The Ancients are tenacious, and no is never an option for them. Eventually, somehow, the Ancients will get the chosen into the circle. Jackson had said no, swore he would never Sundance. Like he had a choice.

Staring at the tree, Roddy standing next to him, he contemplated what he would do in the next few days as the weight of responsibility settled ominously. He cast his gaze about and took notice of those who would be dancing and those who came to support. Seeing Nate Winter practically glued to Junior Rutledge, a thought, an ugly thought, attempted to feverishly creep into Jackson's mind. He denied its existence, refusing to acknowledge it, to permit it to flower. The thought faded away. Instead he focused on the preparations he needed to complete, including making his harness for the dance and choosing the pegs he would use.

"You got your harness and pegs ready?" Roddy asked, almost seeming to read his thoughts.

"Pegs are done," Jackson replied, "Carved them last night. Used the chokecherry and made eight of them. I'll show you when we get back over to the camp. Guess they're about the size of my pinky, about six inches long."

"Eight?" Roddy exclaimed, "Holy crap, man! You planning on piercing every round?"

"No, asshole," Jackson said, "If someone needs a set I'll have extra. Besides, I'm not sure which ones I want to use yet. Maybe I made a set for you."

"My ass you did," Roddy said, "We've talked about this and we ain't talking about it anymore."

Laughing, Jackson continued to tease him. "You know, there ain't nothing to it Roddy. I'll get you some rope, show you how to fold it in half to create the "V." Tie the knot at the end to attach to the rope hanging from the tree so you have two legs and teach you how to splice the ends into loops. Nothing to it."

"Yeah, you do that," Roddy said, "and then we can hook it to you and tie it to the bumper of my truck. I'm driving."

"Awe, come on, Roddy," Jackson said, "They can lay you on the buffalo robe and ram those wooden pegs in."

Roddy didn't say a word. He turned and walked back to the camp. This wasn't a conversation he would have. Sundance is something he would never do. He knew Jackson was only pulling his chain and he also knew the only way he was going to get him to stop was to walk away.

Flipping Jackson his middle finger he said, "See ya at camp, dickhead." Laughing, Jackson threw him a dismissive wave and returned his gaze to the tree, contemplating being pierced.

When the time came for him to pierce he would dance into the circle and be led around the inside perimeter until he reached the south, then led to the tree to be lain on the buffalo robe. Once there, the headsman would pinch the flesh on his chest or back between thumb and forefinger and with a scalpel, without anesthesia or pain killers, a hole would be carved through the pinch. The peg is then driven into the bloody perforation and the spliced loop of each leg of his harness placed over the ends of the pegs protruding from each side of the freshly punctured dermis. The loop winds up against the flesh and behind the peg and is then tied into place with a two foot piece of red cloth to secure the harness. The middle of the harness is then joined to the heavier ropes that he had tied into the tree.

Done correctly, the only way to remove the pegs is to forcefully tear them out, usually by lunging backwards against the harness so the flesh formed around the pegs is violently severed. Once he breaks free, the pegs and chunks of raw, bloody meat will be collected and tied to the tree with the other dancers' flesh offerings and left there until the tree is eventually brought down and burned.

Sometimes when a dancer is following spiritual instruction no amount of force is needed to remove the pegs from flesh. When the time comes for them to break, the pegs will spontaneously fall out of their flesh almost, it seems, of their own free will. This is a very rare occurrence and considered especially sacred, as the pegs are buried beneath the flesh almost to muscle fiber and practically glued into place by fresh blood and raw meat. It should not be possible for them to fall out and when it happens it always leaves those witnessing the phenomenon awestruck.

Letting those thoughts fade, Jackson whispered a thank you to the mighty grandfather tree before him, a small prayer to his Ancestors for strength and courage, and he turned to join Roddy at camp.

20°
CHAPTER TWO

The second day of Sundance, two days after Tree Day, Jackson awakened sore and tired in his cramped two man tent in the dancers' area behind the arbor, curled up on a military cot he was too big for. As usual, he was trying to fold his six foot two, 250 pound frame onto or into something much too small for him. Like most mornings at Sundance, even in the middle of August on the South Dakota prairie, he was cold. During the day it felt like he was cooking in the heat, but at night he froze his ass off.

Suffering is what this ceremony is all about and if nothing else, he was certainly suffering this second day of his fourth year to the tree and the most difficult year so far. Jackson chuckled as he thought about the idiots who believed a person only dances four years. He knew many of the veterans who had danced thirty or more.

Explain that one, you know-it-all twinkie dumb ass, he said to himself sarcastically.

Many First Nations believed the fourth year completes only the beginning of the circle, the belief being that there are four parts to the circle, therefore an individual must dance sixteen years to complete one full circle. However, the completion of the first sixteen years is then only the beginning of a greater circle, and on and on it goes. The circle, of course, is never completed – which is the point. Sundance mimics the circle of life, never ending and always turning. Each ending initiates another beginning, while each beginning completes another ending.

As Jackson had been advised, it all comes down to individual visions and instructions. Not everyone does what everyone else does. There are the typical instructions most ended up receiving – dance four years, pierce once each year and go home. Some, however, received instructions to pierce only one or two years. Some were instructed to pierce every year and every round, while still others never pierced at all. A few specific First Nations believe the shedding of blood to be profane and forbade piercing altogether. It depends upon the Nation the pledge is with, and if they were dancing what they had been shown to dance. Most, unfortunately, are making it up as they go. What Jackson was doing, what he had done for three years and a day previously, was far from typical and most assuredly not made up.

Most of the guys dancing were white, although Jackson wasn't concerned about their race. They could be pink with green polka dots for all he cared. What bothered him was that many were dancing for the scars, as though the wounds were trinkets they could use to impress their friends with, when they returned to suburbia. With no concept of what they were doing or why, they were there only for the novelty, it seemed. These fools were completely supported, even encouraged, by the man running this charade, David Chases.

Chases stood six foot six and was thin, almost emaciated, with sharp, angular features. Long, thin gray hair with faded streaks of dull black and in his late fifties, Chases is a mix blood Cheyenne/Lakota from Rosebud living on Pine Ridge. Fluent in Lakota, he often feigns not understanding what someone is saying when they are speaking to him in American.

Maintaining an air of invitation about him, Chases invites conversation and encourages people to tell him everything. As they do, he listens intently and appears concerned, caring and compassionate. What he is really doing is waiting for the crack to appear. Eventually they would verbally offer their throat to him and when they did, because they always did, he would sink his fangs deep.

Chases was once the golden boy of the old timers, the real and last medicine people. Raised among the old timers, he learned from them and was groomed to take their place when they left this world. Years he spent in their tutelage, ceremony after ceremony, traveling with them as they journeyed around the country. He watched as people fawned over them, lavished them with gifts and money; and a hunger grew in him to have, to be. Greed soon began taking hold, taking over.

He became a young man and found other interests, eventually joining the reservation police force. No longer concerned with the spiritual instructions and knowledge, he observed as the spiritually lost and starved made their yearly pilgrimages to learn of their heritage. Patiently he waited and bided his time, and when the last of the old timers passed on, he immorally assumed their position.

Quickly he became one of the biggest predators in Indian Country and fed off of each year's crop of urban confused, using whatever spiritual gifts were given to him to bleed anyone and everyone he comes into contact with. He takes everything he can and discards the desiccated husk of the person when they no longer have anything left to give.

Jackson had spent the last four years watching this predator in action. Watching as he was supported and defended by his coven of complicit, the chosen few who never had a clue and wouldn't know what to do with a clue if one was gift wrapped for them. They were so hungry for anything spiritual they forgave everything he did, the entire fake ass parade of imbeciles with as much substance as a single serve, cellophane wrapped, icing injected, yellow sponge cake.

An altercation three days prior returned to Jackson's memory when Chases' son visited his campsite. Jackson was alone, sipping coffee and smoking a cigarette when Chases' son came roaring up in his beat up rez truck.

For no apparent reason the man threatened Jackson, "I catch you in that Arbor, anywhere near that Arbor come Tree Day, I'm going to kill you," he said menacingly, then drove away. Stupefied, Jackson could only stare. Imagine that, the son of the 'holy man' overseeing this debacle.

"And this idiot is one of the helpers? This jackass will be running a steel blade through peoples' flesh to help them attain whatever spiritual understanding they supposedly came out here for? Exactly where is the Sacred?" Jackson asked himself. He had gone to the Arbor yesterday and he did dance. He pierced yesterday, that first day, and it certainly wasn't that dumb ass that drove the scalpel through his flesh.

For many years he had held on to the vision he would complete today – a vision that terrified him when he received it and scared the hell out of him when he remembered it. Talking with Junior Rutledge when he arrived for the dance this year, he unintentionally revealed the details of the vision.

They were seated at David Chases' kitchen table a day later when Junior said, "Hey Jackson, tell David about that vision we talked about."

With Junior's invitation, Chases' interest was piqued. "What vision?" he asked, peering over his glasses at Jackson curiously.

"Oh, fuck," Jackson thought. Put on the spot he had to tell him. Roughly three years ago he was napping on the couch in that space between asleep and awake when...

...Jackson sees himself walking into the Sundance Circle, the dance having already begun. Purposefully he approaches the Sundance tree where the Leader waits, obviously annoyed he is there. "What are you doing here?" the Sundance Leader asks, his voice heavy with disdain.

"I have come to learn the ways of a holy man," Jackson responds.

"Oh really?" the Sundance Leader says with a smirk. Motioning to the array of dancers surrounding him the

men immediately ambush Jackson, pin him to the ground and roughly, mercilessly they pierce him through his back. Quickly they hook him up to a harness and haul him high into the Tree of Life. For four days he hangs there looking to the west as the supporters gathered for the dance bring tobacco to the base of tree, crying as they make their offerings.

Around noon on the fourth day orange butterflies with black and white spots, Painted Ladies, come from all directions and swarm Jackson. Thousands upon thousands of them land on him and cover every available space. While they settle white dragonflies with black equilateral wings arrive by the thousands to assemble with them and find available purchase on the harness that binds him to the Tree of Life.

As the dragonflies cut the harness the butterflies lower him to the earth…

That vision had always bothered Jackson. He didn't see himself as a holy man, a medicine person or any other figure with a position of authority. He never referred to himself in such a way, did not imagine himself to be and would absolutely never actually say such a thing. It was a vision he kept close, kept secret and it haunted him for three years. Something he preferred not to share with anyone.

Jackson is only a person. He knows this and is comfortable with it. He had witnessed the life true medicine people lived and wants no part of it. Why he shared the vision with Junior Rutledge he couldn't say, but once revealed, protocol demanded he share it with Chases.

Like so many raised off the reservation in urban society, he began this journey with little knowledge and huge expectations. Jackson was not raised among the People or among the Elders, he grew up in the system. From foster care, to juvenile detention centers, he traveled them all. He had the mental, physical and emotional scars to prove it. What little understanding he brought with him was earned from hard years on the road, traveling among the First Nations and listening to the Elders.

He learned from those who knew what they were talking about. Unlike many who sat on their porches and waited for knowledge to somehow float to them over an ethereal fog, what Jackson knew came from the grandmothers and grandfathers, taught to them by their grandmothers and grandfathers, long before European occupation. He did not learn from some book or ridiculous movie – as though a book, a movie, or worse, someone in the suburbs with little knowledge who had learned from a book or a movie, could impart to them everything they will ever need to know.

Three years and a day ago, the first time Jackson came to the Tree of Life, was not what he expected and from the jump things got really, really weird. He reported two weeks early to the dance to acclimate himself, to attempt to physically prepare himself for what he was about to do, as if that were even possible. No one can train for Sundance. Done correctly, a person received spiritual instruction to participate and the only preparation was acceptance. Beyond that each individual did not know – similar to dying, one simply could not know until the act is initiated.

Jackson vividly remembered his first year of Sundance, three years and a day ago as he stretched his sisal rope between two trees behind his camp, days before the dance began. He was instructed to do this by other seasoned dancers and was informed this would remove any elasticity the rope may have. The last thing he wanted to do was bounce. Locating what appeared to be the perfect tree, petrified with age, he secured one end of the rope. Hand over hand he played out the excess and slowly walked to another tree fifty yards away. Within feet of the second tree Jackson suddenly shot nearly ten feet into the air.

A juvenile western diamondback rattlesnake had chosen the very same tree to nap under and Jackson came within inches of stepping on it. The snake was annoyed that he had disturbed it, so its tail issued the customary warning that had launched Jackson into the air. Landing what seemed like twenty feet from the snake, Jackson watched as it uncoiled and slithered away. That was his first warning, which he promptly ignored. As he looked over his shoulder he was rewarded with the sight of the seasoned dancer who had been instructing him doubled over in laughter.

Immediately untying his rope from the first tree he meandered about in search of a safer spot and the procedure recommenced, this time sans rattlesnake. Tying off to one tree he wrapped the rope around a second, tugged to stretch, and the rope immediately snapped, breaking in two as if an unseen hand had reached out and sliced it in half. That was his second warning, and was just as insouciantly ignored. Someone should probably have said something to him about then, but no one did.

The tone was now set for the events that were about to transpire. Had anyone shown the slightest interest in mentoring Jackson the next three years and a day might have unfolded differently. Maybe they were not supposed to.

Traveling to the dance three years and a day ago, he expected to fulfill a vision he had been given years before the vision he received of hanging. Jackson had many visions leading up to and after that one. On the first day of the dance before the first round began he was informed by Chases that he would not be permitted to dance the vision that brought him to Sundance. Chases instructed him he must, instead, pierce through his back with the harness attached to a train of thirteen dried buffalo skulls, and he must wear a red skirt. Absolutely not what he had been shown and absolutely not why he was there. For two days he danced under the hot sun, struggling to come to a conclusion. Should he do what the visions told him to do, or do what a man told him to do?

Many who participate in Sundance don't give these things a second thought. If someone they perceive as an authority figure tells them to do something, they jump to and do it. On the third day Jackson's confusion over what to do came to an abrupt end. What happened next erased any lingering questions in his mind as he observed a young man from a reservation in Wyoming capitulate to the Sundance Leader.

Jackson had met this younger man a few days prior but couldn't remember his name. He was in his early twenties, was short and stocky with close cropped coal black hair and had a quiet gentleness about him. This was to be his first year as well, and many of his immediate family, including his wife and children, were there to support and pray for him. He was pierced through his chest and played out his rope in typical fashion while Jackson and those not piercing this round ringed the inside perimeter of the Sundance circle. After receiving the signal to do so from the headman, they watched as he danced to the tree and back to his original placement four times. Completing his fourth time to the tree, the young man slowly walked backwards as he eased his rope out, coil by coil, until he reached the harness attached to his chest and dropped his arms to his side.

As the rope became taut he leaned into it, and with a heavy jerk backwards he attempted to break the skin formed around the wooden pegs lodged deep in his chest... and bounced. He was dancing without a vision and without spiritual instruction; dancing because a person instructed him too – and he was about to pay a heavy price for his folly.

The supporters and his family surrounded the outside perimeter of the dance circle behind the dancers and watched as the ordeal continued for many minutes. He regained his composure, reset himself, jerked again against the ropes... and bounced. Over and over and over, as though he was attached to a bungee cord. With their hearts breaking and tears streaming, everyone knew they could do nothing to help him. They prayed for his release, but no release was forthcoming. He found himself on his knees, his head hanging. He was determined to summon the strength needed to return to his feet, to attempt to break free once more. Time stood still as the air thickened and the heat from the scorching sun permeated the ring of supporters witnessing his brutal lesson.

Compassionately, the headman halted the self torture and called to the supporters. Two very large men were escorted into the dance circle and they assumed places on either side of the physically exhausted young man, walking, half carrying him as he stumbled one more time to the tree. Torrential tears flowed down his face as he humbly beseeched the Tree of Life for release. One more time he walked backwards. Involuntarily he faltered and the two supporters assisted him in remaining on his feet. He backed to the end of the rope until his harness was taut, his skin stretching.

The two large men chosen to help him positioned themselves under each of the young man's arms and faced the ring of emotionally distraught supporters and other dancers as the wearied young man faced the tree. Breathlessly all waited until suddenly the shriek of an eagle bone whistle pealed the hot, dry air. With this signal the two supporters strained with all they could muster. One horrendous heave and the young man was forcibly extracted from his harness as the flesh from his chest was torn asunder.

He crashed to the ground writhing with heaving sobs as many of the supporters collapsed with him and his wife rushed to comfort him. His devastated children were shielded by relatives. Never again would he enter a Sundance circle without first receiving very specific instruction from Spirit to do so.

That lesson smoldered deep in Jackson's mind and was all he needed to answer the confusion turning and twisting within him. When the round ended he requested a council with the leader of the Sundance and related again what brought him. Explaining again what he had been shown and that he could not, would not do anything else. He intended no disrespect but had been given very specific instructions and felt he must follow those instructions. Chases refused to grant him permission to do so and, as he was the final authority, Jackson acquiesced. He completed his first year three years and a day ago without piercing, but David Chases never forgot, or forgave, that Jackson defied him.

Two years and a day ago, the second year he danced, Jackson was permitted to dance the original vision. Wearing a mask he was escorted into the dance circle backwards and guided to the Tree of Life. Standing with his face pressed into the tree he was pierced through his back. When he was properly hooked up he was assisted to a position in the South and danced facing the ring of supporters. When the eagle bone whistle shrieked the helpers assisted him in returning to the tree. They handled his rope for him as he backpedaled four times to the Tree of Life.

The fourth time to the tree Jackson mentally prepared and waited for the signal to be given. In his mind he planned to trot quickly and with a heavy forward jerk he would tear the wooden pegs from his flesh. Before the first step was taken the voices of his Ancestors abruptly thunder in his mind:

"DON'T EVEN THINK ABOUT IT. YOU WILL WALK"

Startled, Jackson immediately thrust himself up straight and squared his shoulders, his flesh pinched by the choke cherry pegs he had carved hours earlier deeply embedded under his skin. Slowly, step by excruciating step, he walked until he reached the end of the rope. Without pulling or jerking the rough hewn pegs fell out of his back. The men assisting him stared in awe as absolute euphoria enveloped Jackson. It was undeniably the most powerful spiritual experience he had ever had.

A year and a day ago, his third year of Sundance, was a test of honor when Chases gave him the choice of whether or not to pierce. He didn't have a vision to dance that year and he had not yet revealed the one about him hanging. He mulled over the decision for a few days and came to the conclusion he would not pierce, realizing if he did he would only be doing so out of arrogance. Jackson informed Chases he had decided not to pierce and he was permitted to dance the last two days.

A day ago, yesterday, the first day of his fourth year he was dancing yet another vision. In a twisted way he had been looking forward to this piercing and anticipating the euphoria he was sure would infuse him again. Unfortunately for him, yesterday was nothing like his first year. Instead of euphoria what he received was raw, unadulterated pain.

Jackson was dressed in his usual black skirt but without a shirt or mask and he wore moccasins to keep his feet from being shredded. It was easily 110 degrees by noon as he was led into the circle facing forward. Hurriedly he was escorted around the circle to the base of the tree and laid on the buffalo robe as his chest was pierced, the scalpel burning like a hot ember as it entered his flesh. He always found that curious, how cold steel can burn. As he was aided to his feet the left peg suddenly fell out of its own volition and the assistants heads shook in disbelief.

They escorted Jackson to his chosen place in the North, as his vision instructed, and he danced facing the tree until the rope became taut with the free end of his harness slapping against him. He intended to dance until permission was granted to rip free the wooden peg remaining in his right pectoral. With no warning, as pain lanced his chest, the right peg fell free. No encouragement for release was given by Jackson. One moment the wooden peg was buried deep in his chest and the next it was lying on the ground at his feet. The assistants' eyes were again wide with amazement. That was yesterday.

Slowly he heaved himself from his cot. Four a.m. and the camp crier was singing the morning song that called all of the dancers. It was time to begin the day and Jackson was this side of shitting himself.

What a long, fucked up road of realization this has been, ran through his mind as sleep slowly faded into full consciousness. In these four years Jackson has come to understand many things. First and foremost, it's all bullshit. Like many others, this Sundance is a circus. Jackson knew it but he had made a promise. He agreed to complete this commitment and he would keep this promise, even if it killed him. Considering what he experienced yesterday, today just might. He knew what he had to do and he was no longer looking forward to it. The illusionary anticipation of euphoria was long gone. This was going to be the hardest thing Jackson had ever done in his life.

He made his way into the sweat lodge to begin the second day. Nothing like waking up at four a.m. and having to enter a sweat lodge. Beginning the day puri-fried. It always felt like his skin was coming off and it guaranteed to wake a person up. Then it was into the dance circle as the sun crested the horizon, the dancers were haggard. Strength was evident in most but this was only the second day, after all. Tomorrow, the third day, they wouldn't look this good. Three days of dancing from sunup to sundown with no food, no water, and very little sleep, exhausted didn't begin to cover it.

Jackson danced into the circle with everyone else and, like them, he was awake, hungry and thirsty. Unlike them, his chest throbbed from yesterday's ordeal and he was flat terrified over what he was going to do today. The first round over, the dancers returned to the arbor and Jackson walked over to his lawn chair to sit and smoke as he surveyed his fellow dancers.

30°
CHAPTER THREE

Pine Ridge, South Dakota is the home of the Oglala Lakota, the reservation itself established in 1889 and it is irrefutably some of the most uninhabitable land in the continental United States. Pine Ridge is a harsh, arid, inhospitable place to live. The soil is too chalky to be farmed; blanketed by sharp, brittle grasses; sage and briars abundant.

The Treaty of Fort Laramie in 1868 allotted parts of Montana, North Dakota, South Dakota, Wyoming and Nebraska to the Lakota Nation. In 1876 gold was discovered in the Black Hills, which the United States promptly stole, and Lakota lands diminished to North and South Dakota.

Stronghold Table, deep in the Badlands of Pine Ridge, was where the last of the Ghost Dances were being held. The government was desperate to suppress the Ghost Dance and on December 29, 1890 Major Samuel Whitside, in command of the Seventh Cavalry, intercepted Chief Spotted Elk and the thirty eight with him who were traveling on foot through waist deep snow from Canada to be with their relatives at Stronghold Table. Spotted Elk, also known as Big Foot, was captured along with those he was responsible for and they were escorted to an encampment atop a knoll at Wounded Knee. As many as 300 others were waiting, confined on frozen, cold, snow covered ground. The Episcopal church below, adorned with Christmas decorations, glowed warmly as an argument atop the knoll ensued over a rifle between the Cavalry and a deaf member of Chief Spotted Elk's band. This argument led the Cavalry to do what the Cavalry does so well. With Hotchkiss guns they savagely mowed down Big Foot and everyone with him, mostly women, children and the elderly. The Cavalry left the dead and wounded where they fell as blood froze from horrid, gaping wounds. Very few survived the mass slaughter, those who did, managed to escape by hiding in the deep ravines nearby. Days later the Cavalry returned to bury the frozen, stiff corpses in a mass grave.

Thirteen years previously their hero, General George Armstrong Custer, had his ass handed to him by the Lakota, Cheyenne and Arapahoe at the Battle of Little Big Horn in Montana. The only time the United States has ever had its flag taken, which the Lakota retained. The soldiers with Whitside remembered all too well the death and destruction brought to bear by a people they consider heathen savages who refused to remain on their judiciously furnished government reservations. Wounded Knee provided the Seventh Cavalry with a little payback. The occupation and subsequent subjugation of the Lakota Nation began.

In Minneapolis, Minnesota, 1969, a grass roots movement was initiated to assist natives with alcohol abuse. This loosely held together coterie grew to become the American Indian Movement and members were culled from the reservations as well as the cities across the country. The lost and displaced came together to help fight the oppression. Further reduction of Lakota land continued through thievery and intentional mismanagement to become postage stamp prison camps, and the Oglala Lakota asked AIM for help. Full bloods and breeds rallied together to fight for the survival of their people.

In 1973 the American Indian Movement reoccupied Wounded Knee and the United States, as expected, sent in the Cavalry, renamed the National Guard. After seventy one days the Siege at Wounded Knee ended with the government making nearly one thousand two hundred arrests. The end of the siege marked the beginning of what would become known as the "Reign of Terror," instigated by the FBI and the BIA. During the next three years, sixty-four tribal members were murdered and another three hundred were harassed and beaten. Although five hundred and sixty two arrests were made, only fifteen people were convicted of any crime, including Leonard Peltier, who remains a political prisoner today. This is Pine Ridge and not much has changed since 1976.

Living under someone's boot isn't an option for some people. The boot in this case is the paternal relationship put into effect between the United States and the Indigenous People of North America. Regardless how many times they are ignored, shit on, lied to, used and abused they always find the strength to survive, a strength that echoes in the various names of the families that continue to reside on Pine Ridge, as well as the many other reservations dotting the continental landscape.

One of these names is Bloody Heart. A name that engenders immediate respect, it is an old name from one of the first families confined to this little slice of hell on earth. That morning a Bloody Heart was watching Jackson. Watching as she had for four years.

Mary Bloody Heart, sixty three years old, is a woman who had seen more than most in her day. Barely five feet tall, her face craggy, she is a thin, frail woman with a chain smoker's pallor. Although she is stooped with age and illness, the strength of the Lakota emanates from her. She is the direct descendant, the granddaughter, of the last real Holy Man who walked this earth. Raised by his side, she knows what is real. With a casual glance or a gentle whisper, Mary Bloody Heart can bring the arrogant to their knees.

To provide food for herself and pay the bills Mary works the white folks and has for many years. She travels about the reservations, selling her handmade trinkets for exorbitant prices. Beaded little things, pieces of leather, string and feathers. Eye-catching little pretties the white folks couldn't wait to hang from their rear view mirrors.

Every year, for many years she had come to this dance, if for nothing more than the comic relief of it. The last four years she had come to watch Jackson. For three years she tormented him and watched closely his response to her manipulations.

Mary is the mother of David Chase's half side, who partnered with him some years ago. Mary didn't like to admit it, but she knew her daughter was as corrupt as Chases is, and Mary never missed an opportunity to remind Chases he wasn't a real medicine man. At every opportunity she told him how much of a charlatan he is and how ashamed she was of her daughter. Ashamed of what her daughter had become, and of what she had taught her children, Mary's grandchildren, to become. It broke her heart to see what her family was doing today and she feels disgust with them both.

People who do the things they did, other men and women like them, typically left the reservation and traveled out among society to play their games of manipulation. They preferred to sit and wait, and like a spider in its web, eventually a fly would land.

Often Mary sat in Chase's living room quietly on the sofa listening. Listening as the urban confused spoke of their dreams and visions as though these visitations were great and fantastic things. Far from it, visions are a responsibility and eventually they will find a way to reveal themselves, forcing the individual to live them. Once a vision is given the individual's present life is over, the remainder spent either fulfilling the responsibility of the vision or trying to hide it.

Most misconstrue what they understand as a "vision quest." The one to four days, sometimes as many as twenty one days in some Nations, spent alone on a hill somewhere in the middle of nowhere. At times visions are given during these endeavors although they are rare in occurrence.

This time alone without food or water for the duration is a time of inner reflection, a time to humble oneself before that which created all. A time to look deep into oneself and consider the life they have led up to then and the effects, repercussions and consequences of the decisions they have made.

This is a time to comprehend the self. A time to understand that the body is the vessel and within it is a vast, incomprehensible being, a being that is attuned to all of creation. Closing the eyes allows a person to fall deeply into the mind to contemplate nothingness. Upon reaching as deep as possible within the mind, then suddenly opening the eyes provides a person with the knowledge and recognition of the being that exists within the vessel. It is a heady and nerve wracking experience, to suddenly perceive something living in the shell. Sensing the soul as it peers out of one's own eyes.

A true vision quest is an arduous, time consuming ordeal that can take weeks, even months or years. In order to accomplish a true vision quest a seeker must abandon all they have, taking with them only the barest of necessities. The individual must go off into the wilderness alone and wander with no direction and no assistance. In that time there will be many encounters with many things unimagined. If the seeker is honest in their endeavor for however long it takes, they will come to know their purpose in this existence.

However, once that purpose is known they will never be able to return to their previous lives. That life would be over and all that remains is the purpose they had come to learn, their lives now lived in fulfilling that purpose.

If the seeker survived the journey. There are things out there beyond scientific comprehension that can and will eat a person. The seeker needs to be fully prepared and willing to die should they commit to making this journey.

Dreams are something else entirely, and Mary listened as those who came described their dreams, listened to their whimsical interpretations. Sometimes she would cackle at the things she heard as they explained about what they saw in the dark. To her it was all so ludicrous, as if sight was the only sense these fools possessed.

The Ancestors come in many ways. Sometimes they are seen, other times they are felt, smelled or heard. Sometimes they are tasted which really freaks out the fluff bunnies. Many times blonde haired bimbos would come to Mary, begging for a taste of the mystical knowledge that rumor insisted her Grandfather had passed on to her. Each time her answer was a resounding no. Not once would she give them the slightest morsel. Without saying a word she would walk away, turning her back to them. Not for a second did they perceive the insult extended or that they had been dismissed as having no more significance than a fly buzzing about her head.

So many came from the east and west coasts, replete in their distorted knowledge, each another great granddaughter of a mythical Cherokee Princess. Mary noticed it was always the great grandmother, never the great grandfather, as though their families were ashamed of admitting to an Indian in the wood pile and she found the whole idea insulting. As if those who spouted this crap were insinuating that after the dismantling and eradication of the Southern Tribal Confederacy, Cherokee men had nothing better to do with themselves, displaced men who traveled from the farthest northern reaches of Washington to the farthest southern reaches of Florida only to have sex with white women. Could these fools have been any more absurd? One of the best Mary heard was of the blonde haired Cherokees from somewhere off of Cape Hatteras. A real lost tribe that individual insisted! The very idea invited a snort. She spit her coffee out over that one and almost lost her dentures.

Every year another batch descended on Indian Country looking to find their way. Gorged on all the knowledge they thought they had, and so quick to dispense everything they thought they knew with the vast majority being overtly annoying. Mary would have loved to backhand some that came, to tell them just because a bird shit on your head didn't mean it was a sign from God.

She listened as they chattered about their magic powers and how they were so absolutely sure they were descended from some medicine person or great Chief. What about the men who cared for the tribe's horses? The women who sewed buffalo and deer hides? Those who built homes, cleaned public areas, labored with sanitation? Did these individuals not deserve descendants? Obviously not, as everyone was the reincarnation of Crazy Horse and Sitting Bull. Where were Greasy Hair's descendants? What happened to Kicked in the Head's family?

Crystals, talking sticks, pixie dust and magic wands. Most couldn't tell an eagle feather from a buzzard and even fewer understood that the two are brothers, or why. They are lulled to sleep by convenience, where everything is at their fingertips at a mere moments notice. Let them spend a few months out there alone with no one to talk to but the wind and their imaginations, surviving on the barest of necessities. They might just learn something.

Mary wished they would unite under a common cause instead of the myriad of non-profit organizations, each fighting the other to be the one group providing the most. All their confused behavior accomplished was to assist the few and infuriate the many. If they all came together under one banner, then maybe they could effect change.

She had seen the yearly deposits of yet another trailer full of donated clothing. Exactly what the children needed, more suburban cast offs. Most of this donated clothing found its way into the district dumps, euphemistically referred to as "the rez Wal-Mart." Forget about education, economic development and health care. Instead let's bring more crap, as though the reservation was a dumping ground for their guilt and a way to appease their conscience. Instead of Goodwill, give it to the Indians. Those in the outlying districts who needed help the most were either ignored or forgotten.

Every year another assortment showed up, so quick to tell the Indians all about what the Indians needed, not once shutting up long enough to allow the Indians to tell them what they needed. Another version of the black robes, come to save the poor, lost savages. Another annual caravan of the needy, so sure of their entitlement, to a way of life they refused to actually live.

Yearning for some spiritual connection and so quick to accept the dystopian mind manipulations disingenuously proffered by the conniving David Chases. Blonde hair, blue eyed, and dumb as a brick; laying their souls bare to a man they didn't know, revealing their deepest secrets to a stranger. All the while he was scheming how to best take advantage of them.

In their fancy cars and expensive camping gear they rub the noses of those forced to survive here in all they don't have. Leaving this place of desolation and abject poverty weeks later, they return to their suburban homes, overstocked refrigerators and weekly paychecks. Out here, they are fair game. It isn't fair, it certainly isn't right, but sometimes all some have is the culture. They sell the culture to feed the family.

Where are the instant Indians when the grandmothers and grandfathers are starving? Where were they when children were freezing to death in their sleep? Living in homes reminiscent of an Indiana Jones movie, being careful where they stepped or they would fall through the floor. Homes, that when it rained, more water seemed to come inside than what fell outside. Although, referring to what is used as habitat by many as a 'home' is generous at best. Most are a ramshackle affair of what could be thrown together, or government provided housing. All are engulfed by mold and overrun by rodents, spiders and roaches. No amount of cleaning is possible to remove the infestations, as there are too many holes in the walls, sealed with discarded plastic and duct tape.

Mary understood that many felt lost in the white world. That they felt unable to live in a society that promoted one behavior yet condoned another. However, this did not infer they could force their way into the red world. Acceptance by the people was a process spanning years, if ever.

There are thousands of displaced descendants of the ones who left. Those fed up with tribal politics or forced into boarding schools, never to return. Their descendants, after careful research, found family names on government roles. Once a name was found, they consider themselves automatically Indian, insisting on tribal enrollment and demanding the Nation accept them immediately as a full member.

Anyone born in this country who can trace their heritage back at least three generations is bound to have some native blood somewhere. This may signify they are genetically native but it takes a lot more than lineage to be culturally native.

To be culturally native means a person has to get into the mud and the blood, to live the pain and daily torment. To watch as the children commit suicide and observe the rampant drug and alcohol abuse. To be consciously aware of the repetitive cycle of abuse from father to daughter, mother to son and know it isn't going to end any time soon.

To see the unabashed joy when someone succeeds, the dreams not yet crushed in so few. To encourage those dreams, guide them, see them blossom and flower. So much more than language must be used to identify and create unity among those with an interest in maintaining unity. Much more than hair color, eye color, teeth and cheekbones.

To be culturally native means to have hope and accept there is none. To live altruistically knowing the one you give to is using you. To strive to maintain some grasp of tradition and culture while all around you that culture is bastardized and corrupted, used as fodder for movies or the plot line of some ridiculous book.

The reservation isn't a Mecca. No one comes out to the reservation and finds a wise and benevolent Elder who teaches them everything their long dead relatives forgot to. What they usually find is a predator. Someone is waiting for them alright, waiting to take everything they possibly can.

The lost offer themselves to the fire then cry about it when they are burned to cinders. Purposefully presenting themselves among a people starved, beaten and bullied whose only defense is to bleed them dry. Always coming to take, the language, the culture, the ceremonies, but never coming to give. Then wonder why they continuously get bent over.

These lost children of a forgotten People who wander the confines of organized religion becoming all too aware of the lies and hypocrisy. Some bring their religious intolerance with them and replace the priest or minister with the medicine man. So sure they are of their entitlement to something they have zero understanding of.

The simplicity of it lost on those who insist on making things as complicated as they possibly can. Inevitably they apply theology and their labels of good and evil to native traditions, utterly incapable of understanding there is no good or evil. There is only what you do or don't do and if that behavior is beneficial or detrimental.

Not for one second do they appreciate First Nations tradition and culture is ancestral based. Nor do they understand that prayers are offered to a Grandfather or a Grandmother. What lies beyond that no one knows. Many refer to it as a

Great Unknown or a Great Mystery. Seven colors are used to represent creation, six of which are known. The seventh is unknowable, nescient. Not ignorant of its existence, ignorant of its form, with no intention of assuming the pretension necessary to give it form.

Sometimes as Mary listened to the lost her mind reflected on her own long and storied history. Into the eighties she was a powwow dancer. Not the best dancer but most places you didn't need to be, the powwows having become their own comedy. Mix bloods with little to no knowledge wearing ridiculous, outlandish costumes with some of the most fanciful names she had ever heard. Everyone was wolf something or eagle something or bear something else. Mary often wondered what happened to ducks and chickens?

In those days she was able to travel off the rez from time to time and meet new people, maybe fleece an occasional bliss bunny. She drank heavily then and even now she misses the taste of alcohol. Amazing she can smell the stench of it and through that stench is the desire for more. Mary walked away from the bottle years ago and has no intention of ever returning. It's impossible now anyway, with her health having deteriorated to an extreme degree. With a pacemaker and a walker to get around the last thing she needs to add to her misery is alcohol.

When Jackson first walked into Chases trailer Mary recognized him immediately. She knew who this young man was and she also realized he didn't. She listened and noticed he wasn't buying the ration of bullshit Chases was handing out so freely.

In his face she recognized someone who has seen a thing or two. This young man wasn't another weekend warrior playing Indian to satisfy some fantasy of what he wished he could be. She heard the honesty in his voice, in the words he spoke. She listened as he described how he was raised in the system not knowing who his parents were, not knowing where he came from. Mary knew, she knew of both his parents. She knew where they came from. Mary Bloody Heart definitely knew Jackson Themal and she saw his mother in his face.

This would be his last day although he didn't know it yet. After today, if he survives, she would know if he was ready. If he can find the courage to complete the circle put before him. But such a request! Could he do it? Would he do it? If he had the stamina, the courage and the strength, Mary had something she would give to him. A secret she had held onto for many years.

On one of her journeys as a powwow dancer she traveled to Oklahoma. The days spent dancing, the nights partying like every powwow before. On that night Mary Bloody Heart met Jackson Themal's mother. On that night she heard a story.

40°
CHAPTER FOUR

Before the first round when the dancers crawled out of the sunrise sweat lodge, those who are going to pierce the second round toweled off and presented themselves to the helpers. Typically, a dancer is painted with a pair of circles using red ocher either on their chest or back, these circles indicate the flesh they will be offering. Jackson had four, two on his chest and two on his back. This was going to be a rough day.

Dancers normally wait until the third or fourth day to pierce because by then they are exhausted, worn out and numb. The pain is there, oh how the pain is there, but when your entire body is racked with pain, and you are so hungry your stomach thinks your throat has been cut, so thirsty even air seems moist, the scalpel doesn't seem to burn as much. The first and the second day the dancer is fully cognizant as the blade slices through flesh. Every centimeter is felt. Anyone piercing the first or second day needs to be fully prepared, both mentally and spiritually.

Seated under the dance arbor after the first round the dancers milled about talking. Abruptly the eagle bone whistle screamed and the dancers grudgingly rose from their chairs. They formed a line in the center of the arbor and adjusted sage wreaths to sit firmly around their heads. Cautiously they eased individual eagle bone whistles between their dry, cracked lips. A few test blows as they smacked their lips, desperate to generate some moisture.

The dancers, wearing a plethora of different colored skirts, filed out of the arbor following the headmen and helpers with those who are piercing this round bringing up the rear. All are bared chested, some with moccasins, others bare footed. It was only nine a.m. and the heat, rising with the sun, was assiduously climbing into the ninetys.

The dancers moved to the edges where they filled the inside perimeter of the Sundance circle. There are a variety of dancers including a few full bloods, some mix bloods and a bunch of white guys, the blistering South Dakota sun burning them lobster red. Having left their air conditioned offices mere days earlier this was their first time this year outside in the sun and the sweltering heat showed them no mercy. Those who are going to pierce remained standing under the arbor as drums beat loudly and sacred songs filled the air.

Cedar boys, young male children whose ages are between 8 and 13, walk among the supporters on the outside perimeter of the dance circle. The cedar boys swing coffee cans filled with hot coals and smoking cedar boughs, offering the cleansing smoke to all who had come to pray for their wives and husbands, sons and daughters, to those who had come to spiritually support the dancers. Men and women willingly offer themselves and their bodies for the Relatives, for all people, and all creatures. Four helpers returned to the arbor to collect the individuals waiting to pierce and assumed positions on their right and left. Only two men would pierce this round, Henry and Jackson.

Henry is a beast of a man who earlier in life had been a college professor. Extremely intelligent, five foot ten and three hundred and fifty pounds, Henry takes up some space. Several years ago he had been hit head on while driving home at night on the rez. The guy who hit him, the son of a local rancher, was drunk and died instantly, along with Henry's wife and four year old daughter. Somehow Henry survived but has never been the same. After suffering major head injuries and barely living through the ordeal Henry doesn't teach anymore and walks with canes. For thirteen years, since the death of his family, Henry has danced and pierced every day, every round. He always wears the same red skirt, sewn for him by his wife days before her death.

The helpers led Henry into the circle, entering from the west and stopping at each cardinal point to honor the Grandfathers who live in these directions. Reaching the south they turned right and led him to the Tree of Life. As he was so big he stood on the buffalo robe lying before the tree as the headmen pierced each side of his chest, struggling to find unscarred flesh as he has pierced so many times. He gives not a hint of awareness as they slid the scalpel through his flesh then slip the wooden pegs into the fresh wounds. Studiously they attach his harness to the pegs then tie his harness to the rope hanging from the tree. As he plays his rope out hand over hand the helpers guide him to his place in the east, the ropes taut and distending the flesh on his chest. The helpers assume positions on either side of him as he dances in his lumbering fashion. While Henry was hooked up the remaining set of helpers escorted Jackson into the dance circle.

Last year Jackson was gifted several yards of cloth. The material has a white background with images of puppy faces from several different dog breeds printed on it in browns, beiges and tans. Labradors, cocker spaniels, collies and beagles. For a laugh he had a seamstress make a Sundance skirt out of it for him and he was wearing that skirt. Around his head was a crown of sage with two 18 inch raven spikes jutting straight up from his temples, the quills pushed through the interwoven stems. No emotion showed on his countenance, his face a carved rock without a hint of the turmoil inside of him. His eagle bone whistle was locked firmly between his lips as he stood straight and tall with his chest thrust forward. Outside he appeared fully resigned. Inside Jackson was losing it.

Every fiber of his being, every flight instinct in his soul was demanding him not to do this. He fought the voices in his mind and stared straight ahead, desperate to quell the tumult inside him. From the west out from under the arbor they came as it is always done. Everyone enters from the west, facing the east and the rising sun. Jackson's feet seemed to glide over the dewy, hard packed earth as he passed in front of the dancers lining the inside of the circle. Some knew what was about to happen and cried for him. These were grown men with tears streaming down their faces. Many of the supporters on the outside ring of the circle also knew what he was preparing to do and they were crying for him too. They looked fervently in any other direction but his as he passed, desperate that he not see the anguish on their faces. From the west to the north the helpers led him. Together they stopped at the north and turned a complete counter clockwise circle then briskly moved to the east, where he almost lost his composure.

The eastern door is wide open with nothing blocking the way. Voices in his mind became a cacophony bellowing inside his skull. *RUN!* they trumpet, *RUN!* Fear began creeping up the back of his neck as cold, icy cold fingers of dread traced patterns of terror. Somehow, someway he summoned strength and courage he never knew before this moment. Jackson silenced the voices and moved to the south.

The southern door. The last stop. This was one of those moments when life is before and after. A moment never to be returned to, an old life over, a new life begun. The helpers seemed aware of what was raging inside him and they wasted no time leading him from the south and to the Tree of Life.

They gently eased him on to the buffalo robe as the crown of sage on his head was removed and pushed firmly between his lips. Jackson bit down hard and tasted bitter sage. He was completely aware as fingers pinched the flesh on his chest. Burning, oh god the burning, stabbing, excruciating pain of the scalpel as it sliced through his pinched flesh. He was also aware as the wooden pegs were forcibly driven into his neatly sliced flesh, first the left then the right side of his chest. Jackson was attuned to every agonizing second.

Time stopped. Reality no longer existed. All was only pain, mind numbing, gut wrenching pain. Suddenly he was jerked to his feet as his harness was quickly tied to his chest then thrown over his head to lay on his back. Sweat rolled down his face as he was turned and shoved harshly against the tree, the coarse bark of the cottonwood scraping his face. Again, burning pain. Wooden pegs were deliberately driven into his flesh and the two free ends of the harness were hastily attached to his back. Mind searing lightning bolts of raw pain in his back. Blinding white explosions as every nerve screamed in torturous agony. Four points, Jackson was pierced in seconds that seemed like an eternity, two through his chest and two through his back. The harness was drawn over his head and the rope hanging from the tree was tied to the harness. He was spun around quickly, his back to the tree as he looked to the west, trembling, dripping huge drops of sweat.

Following the rope up the tree it passed through the crotch over sixty feet in the air to the free end tied around a log lying on the ground. Four helpers lifted the log together as if they were one and brought the log to their chests, cradling it in their arms as though they held an infant. The four helpers stood on the eastern side of the tree and impatiently waited as the log became heavier and heavier, one with tears streaming down his face, fully resigned to what he was about to do. Jackson, standing on the western side, had the crown of sage taken from between his lips and returned snugly to his head. Not a sound passed his lips as every nerve in his body thrummed with pain he never knew existed, the rope hummed as the harness tugged at his flesh. With no warning the screech of an eagle bone whistle stabbed the air and the four helpers began to move forward. Step by step to the beat of the drum as a water song was beaten furiously, inch by inch they felt his weight. The ropes tighter and tighter, Jackson's flesh stretching. As his heels left the cool moist earth a loud POP! was heard when the flesh pierced on his back broke.

The harness remained attached his chest. Forward the helpers continued, tighter and tighter the rope became, heavier and heavier the log they hold. Jackson aware, so fully aware, as the flesh on his chest is pulled, stretched, drawn. His toes scrabbled furiously, pointlessly, to find purchase on the earth. Attached to the harness tied to the rope they drag him into the sky by two wooden pegs secured to the flesh on his chest. Pain snapped Jackson's mind and he suddenly left his body.

Among the supporters was Mary Bloody Heart. Under the shade of the arbor her body gently rocked with the beat of the drum, no emotion showing on her face. She watched as Jackson was slowly drawn higher and higher, hanging from two small sticks through the flesh of his chest, his body frozen stiff in a state of pain even her mind couldn't begin to comprehend. A slight smile lifted the corners of her lips, the slightest hint she was aware, if anyone cared to notice. She looked towards Henry who was still dancing and watched as he was directed to the tree. The fourth time he drew back and broke cleanly. Henry had pierced so many times this had become easy for him. Barely did he feel anything at all as tight against his harness he pulled and pop! The pegs tore through his flesh. He was left with two small holes and a negligible trickle of blood. The helper on his right guided him to the edge of the dance circle to take his place among the dancers who had entered earlier. Mary's gaze returned to Jackson.

Like a carcass Jackson hung. No movement, no sign he was even vaguely aware. Dangling like meat he swayed in the gently blowing wind that seemed to come from everywhere and nowhere at once. Mary shifted her gaze to the supporters ringing the outside, some with tears, some sobbing. She saw the pain etched on their faces, their eyes locked on Jackson. Ten minutes had passed and he still hung. Blood streamed down his back where the pegs tore free when he was lifted into the tree. From her right she saw a young woman retching from the sight she was witnessing. Across the circle were men who had danced this dance for twenty years being gently consoled by their wives. Held tightly and soothed, they thank whatever God they believe in it isn't them hanging there. Mothers shielded the eyes of some of the children who squirmed and wiggled, desperate to get a peek. Nimbly they sought a glimpse of this young man suspended so high in the Tree of Life. Not a whisper came from him as he swayed, as if someone had built an effigy.

After fifteen minutes had passed Chases entered the circle with coup stick in hand. Jackson was so high in the tree Chases had to reach as far as he could with the staff to tap ever so lightly. Jackson was not moving, some were wondering if he was still breathing. How could a man, any man, live through this? Twenty minutes and supporters were exhausted from the anguish unfolding before them there.

CRACK!

Out of nowhere, as if lightning has struck the tree Jackson was released. Crashing to the ground he was caught mere inches before he landed by those standing beneath him. Gently he was lowered to the ground and stretched out on the buffalo robe as a mantra of *"I'm done, I'm done"* in a broken whisper floated from his lips. They left him to lay on the buffalo robe as Chases danced the remaining dancers out of the circle. The round was over.

Roddy Blackstar, who drove a thousand miles to be there with him, remained with Jackson at the tree. When he was finally able to stand Roddy assisted him to his chair as tears streamed down both their faces. Holes as large as fifty cents pieces showed in his chest and back. Blood, deep rich red, almost black, flowed lightly from his wounds as Roddy eased him into his chair. Slowly regaining his composure Jackson gratefully accepted the thanks you's and appreciations from the other dancers for what he had done for them. Chases waited until all the dancers had gone then made his way over.

"That's what it takes to be a holy man," he said in passing then turned and strolled away.

Mary Bloody Heart watched it all. She was proud of Jackson. Not many would do what he had done. Few have the courage or the strength. Tomorrow she would meet with him. Today she would let him rest. He had earned what she was going to give him. Maybe if she knew what it would do to him she might be tempted to keep it to herself.

The dance stopped till the afternoon. This was all they would do this morning. The dancers would rest, if only for a brief period. Those who had come to support returned to their camps for the midday break to talk amongst each other. Most of the dancers remained in the arbor napping in lawn chairs or stretched out on the ground. Roddy helped Jackson to his tent and eased him on to his cot where he promptly passed out.

50°
CHAPTER FIVE

For the second time that day Jackson woke up on a cot he was too big for, this time sweating profusely. As he lay sleeping the sun had climbed high in the South Dakota sky and he was baking in his tent. Lying there a moment he slowly allowed consciousness to slosh over him and with consciousness came the lancing burn of fire across his chest and back. Beginning to rise he stopped abruptly. He was stuck to the cot. Blood from his back had congealed while he lay sleeping and like glue, it held him fast. Tenderly he peeled himself free as he glanced down at his chest and saw lightning bolts in the blood spilled from his wounds. It looked like someone had crept into his tent while he lay sleeping and painted his entire chest and abdomen with a bloody brush, then enjoyed some finger paint time.

I need to find a towel and wash some of this off, he thought.

Sitting in the middle of his cot, the top of the pup tent mere inches from his head, Jackson abruptly remembered he had not only woken up, he had also come back.

"Holy crap," he gasped as the recollection of where he had been slowly unfolded in his mind. As his body had slept in his tent he hadn't been in it. While he lay sleeping he had left his body, again…

…and finds himself in a long corridor with white pillars on either side of him. The floor is a brilliant white marble. In the distance ahead is an overwhelming white light, so bright he squints to gaze at it and impulsively he moves toward the light. Jackson feels no fear, somehow the light is inviting, warm, comforting. Glancing about he is reminded of the Parthenon. Reaching the end of the corridor he steps off the ledge onto what appears to be a white cloud but isn't. The ground is solid and he is enveloped by a thick, viscous fog, reminiscent of the morning mist rising from a forest after a cool rain on a hot summer's morning.

Jackson's Ancestors are all around him. Some are cloaked in long red robes with abalone buttons and animal characters in relief. Others are bare-chested and adorned in brightly colored headdresses with feathers of greens and yellows, bright oranges and reds. Still others are attired in centuries old European style clothing. Many more appear with heavy furs draped across their shoulders.

The white light is not far now. His Ancestors, after forming a procession, are gently guiding him toward the light. All are smiling as they welcome him, each moving him forward as Jackson greets them. Arriving at the front of the procession he steps into the white…

"What the hell?" he asked himself in a daze. Shaking off the lingering effects of the dream he slowly crawled from his tent and the heat hit him full in the face. Barely past 1:00 in the afternoon and the temperature was 120 degrees. Jackson was sore, so very sore as he stood gingerly and casually surveyed his surroundings. Some of the dancers were asleep in the grass while others milled about readying themselves for the afternoon rounds. As if on cue the helpers arrived and begin rousing those still asleep. Groggily they came to their feet and within moments a line began to form. Seven dancers would pierce the next round, each with two red circles.

Jackson was toast. Barely able to move he questioned if he would be able to dance but, as he always did, he would reach into himself and find the strength. Obviously his Ancestors were with him. Recalling his earlier dream visit with Them he smiled. The mantra in his mind repeated over and over. As he lay at the base of the Tree of Life, slowly returning to his mortal coil as Roddy helped him up, those same words were falling from his lips, "I'm done, I'm done."

What do they mean? Was he done for the day? The remainder of the dance? Was his dance finished? Had he completed what was asked of him, to be released? He simply didn't know. As if summoned Chases appeared and his eyes cast about. They soon settled on Jackson and he walked to him. "You sit out this round," Chases instructed and Jackson was instantly flooded with relief.

"Um, okay man, no problem," Jackson laughingly replied, "I hurt like a sum bitch and I ain't arguing with you."

A few of the dancers overheard him refer to Chases so casually. They often heard him address Chases as "man" or "dude" or some other irreverent title and they immediately got upset when he did. As though Chases was a God and

Jackson was being flippant. He casually observed their disdainful glances and perceived their thoughts. Some people are really fucking stupid, he thought.

An eagle bone whistle cut the hot sticky air and Jackson was never as grateful for a chair as he was at this moment. He would rest and smoke while he prayed for his brothers and sisters as they danced. In his chair, chest and back throbbing to the beat of the drum, his mind repeated over and over, *I'm done.* "What does this mean?" he softly said aloud.

There was only one way to find out. Time crawled by slowly. Dancers filed into the Sundance circle and found their places along the inner edge. Helpers returned to the arbor to escort those who would pierce. The helpers trotted pledges around the circle and stopped at each cardinal point. Turning a complete clockwise circle they moved on.

Pledges are not permitted to walk but moved hurriedly along to insure they do not have time for lingering contemplation over what they are about to do. To the south, to the Tree of Life and finally to the buffalo robe. Pierced and hooked up they dance and break free. Jackson, regardless how many times he witnesses this ordeal, felt each one. He was emotionally distraught sitting in his chair as the round continued on without him but this was what Chases had instructed him to do so this was what he would do. The round ended and the dancers returned to the arbor. Some wouldn't look at Jackson which caused him to feel a bit strange. They angled as far away from him as possible.

Well, that's just weird, he thought, must be exhausted from the round. Jackson let the thought fade. No need to beat himself up over something he didn't understand. It was a long round and the dancers were tired. Strange though no one wanted to talk to him.

Oh well, whatever, Jackson thought. Rising from his chair he scanned about to find Chases, this mantra of "I'm done" refusing to relinquish. Jackson had no clue what was being said to him. He knew protocol dictated anything of this nature must be brought before the Leader of the Sundance. It was the Leaders responsibility to interpret these things, to advise on these things. Jackson sure as hell wasn't going to interpret this on his own. Locating Chases, Jackson moved toward Roddy standing about mid arbor. They had discussed the mantra previously and Roddy knew what was coming.

"Yo Roddy! Can you come with me a minute, bro?" Jackson asked him.

"Sure man where we headed?" Roddy inquired.

"Over to see Chases," he replied, "I gotta find out what the hell this is going through my head. What this means. What am I supposed to do with it? It's Chases' dance. He's the heap big medicine dude so it's his job to explain this, right?"

"Makes sense to me," Roddy agreed. They made their way across the arbor to where Chases was relaxing in his chair.

"Excuse me David, do you have a minute?" Jackson inquired.

"Sure," Chases said quickly rising then instructing, "Come with me."

Jackson and Roddy followed him through the arbor beyond the dancer's rest area to a lean-to previously constructed in the shade of an old gnarled tree. Chases seated himself under the lean-to as Roddy assumed a position leaning against the right pole and Jackson squatted in front. "What's up?" Chases asked.

"Well," Jackson replied, "I have this thing running through my head. Out of respect for you and the dancers, the Sundance, I'm bringing this to you to help me understand what it means."

"Go on," Chases encouraged.

"I'm sure you heard me when I came out of the tree," Jackson continued, "heard me saying "I'm done." Do you know what this means? What the Ancestors are trying to tell me? What the Tree is saying to me? What am I supposed to do with this? Am I done for the day? Done for the dance? Have I completed my commitment?"

With cunning black eyes Chases gazed for long moments at Jackson. He completely ignored Roddy standing immediately to Jackson's right as they patiently waited. Jackson wasn't thrilled about having to do this. The last thing he wanted is for anyone to think he quit. He hadn't quit, he didn't know how to quit. Of all the things he had learned over the journey called "Jackson's Life" quitting wasn't one of them. He believed he had done everything he was asked to do. In the right way, in the respectful way, he had come humbly to get an answer to this question. What is the Tree of Life telling him?

"That's it, you're done." Chases said quickly, "Your dance is finished and you have completed what was asked of you. In the next round we will dance you out of the circle. Once that's over you'll be finished."

A sense of relief washed over Jackson. Cool! Two days, some serious pain, a lot of blood and four giant holes. Difficult, but done. The man said it. Roddy casually stood and listened the entire time. Together they thanked Chases and returned to the dancing area.

"Well that's it for ya," Roddy said.

"Looks like it brother man," Jackson jovially replied, "I did it. I really did it. I completed what the Ancestors asked of me."

Laughing Roddy said, "Hell yeah and then some."

"Next time its your turn," Jackson verbally poked.

"Fuck you and everyone who looks like you!" Roddy exclaimed vehemently, shaking his head, "There ain't no way in fucking hell I am EVER doing what you did. You can't pay me, blow me or buy me. Fuck that forever."

Laughing together they moved to where Jackson's tent was set up. Roddy said, "Go finish up the next round and get danced out the circle. I'll take care of your gear. Get it packed up and bring the truck around. We'll have you in camp eating dinner and drinking water in no time."

Jackson smiled as he thinks about that first long, cool drink. An eagle whistle blew and he made his way over to the arbor to join the other dancers as they moved into formation. He assumed his place in line as they danced into the circle and filled the edges. In formations as choreographed by Chases they moved. No one pierced this round and twenty minutes or so later Chases formed everyone in two lines at the western door and led the dancers to the eastern door. Four times he stopped as the dancers spread out in columns behind him across the broad expanse of the Sundance Circle. When the eastern door was reached the drum stopped and all of the dancers moved to the south. The c'anupas were offered and the round ended. Jackson turned to the rest area where Roddy was waiting with his gear packed and stowed, grinning like the proverbial Cheshire cat.

"Water and food, brother man, water and food," Jackson said.

"Hell yeah and then some," Roddy replied.

60°
CHAPTER SIX

Junior Rutledge is fucking crazy. The kindest characterization is mentally unstable. Granted, there isn't anything wrong with Junior that several intense years of psychotherapy might fix but then again, probably not. Simply put, Junior is a very, very dangerous man. In his early forties he looks like someone had taken a wooden whiskey barrel and stuck feet under it, five foot five, thick, without an ounce of body fat. Always with a smirk, Junior is a half breed white/Lakota with a very bad attitude. He grew up on Pine Ridge and is the son of a full blood Lakota woman and a white rancher she had an affair with. As a fatherless mix blood child his life was made a living hell by the full blood children as they tormented him daily. He eventually left the reservation in his teens and hooked up with some bikers in Colorado.

Junior spent his twenties and thirties growing up in the biker clubs. His adolescence spent brutalized at every waking moment. He found an outlet for his pent up rage in the biker gangs and soon discovered he had a talent for inflicting pain. As a violent enforcer he rose quickly through the ranks. There are three murders he was suspected of having committed in the Colorado Rockies but no one could prove it. With charges pending he had to get away, fast, and without a second thought he returned home because disappearing on the reservation is easy. With vast open plains, the Badlands, barely accessible hills and valleys, dropping off the planet takes little imagination.

He lives far out on the prairie in an isolated section of the reservation and is no longer the half breed boy the bloods beat on as a child. Short cropped hair, dead black eyes and a hair trigger temper, he is well seasoned with a touch of insanity, and a stone cold killer. It is always best to leave Junior alone.

The reservation is broken up into districts, some larger than others, the district Junior lives in is the smallest. Few people live out there with the scrub grass, bad water and open prairie. There is no reason for anyone to be there except isolation which is exactly what he wants. To be left alone, to not be bothered by anyone, for any reason. Not to say anyone has a problem with Junior being alone. Most who know him prefer not to have anything to do with him. He isn't the nicest person and never discriminates who he takes advantage of. If you had it, and he wants it, he would find a way to steal it.

Fleecing is a way of life on the reservation and Junior is as good as most, clever, with a thorough understanding of criminal activities. Junior out in the sticks away from everyone else is exactly what everyone on the reservation wants. There isn't anything they can do about him but at least they know where he is.

Junior's house is a trailer that had been condemned in the early fifties. It is set far back off the BIA access road deep in a ravine, dragged there with help from a few white folks he manipulated into helping him, and no one would know it is there unless they purposefully looked for it. With a few sheets of plywood, most stolen, a few bought for him, he built a new floor. He has no electricity and no running water and for a toilet he dug a hole then stole a complete outhouse from somewhere.

Every year someone would leave something at the Sundance grounds when they returned home and Junior is an adept scavenger. As second in command he maintains complete access to Chases property, finds whatever has been left, repaired it if he could, then sold it. If not he stripped the parts and sold those. He also supplements his income by the occasional meth run for a few of the national outlaw biker gangs coming from the West Coast with Junior the mid point. Every few months or so the rumble of rolling thunder was heard on the reservation and folks knew Junior was getting his next shipment. Folks also knew to stay the hell away, including the reservation police. A week to the East Coast and back delivering and picking up payment. Junior made sure to slip the captain of the police department a few grand when he returned and the captain made sure some of that money trickled down.

Raised around bikers Jackson was very familiar, even comfortable, with people like Junior Rutledge, comfortable around them. He knows where he stands with Junior and he knows to walk softly. There were the occasional verbal pokes and prods but Jackson never pushed too far. Anything could set Junior off at anytime and god help the sorry son of a bitch who did.

Junior was seated at Chases' kitchen table the first year Jackson came to Sundance. Presenting himself to Chases per protocol he related his vision and why he was there. Chases presented Junior as a Heyoka Headman although there is no truth to the title assigned. Junior may be a jester but he is no Sacred Clown. His jokes and antics aren't funny, they're cruel. This title was another con, another ruse implemented by Chases. Their tense friendship began and every year when Jackson came to Sundance he stayed with Junior, every year he danced Junior was the only one who pierced him.

As Jackson and Roddy made their way from the Sundance arbor to his camp they noticed Junior and some of his cohorts, along with that idiot white guy Nate Winter, already there. The camp stove was keeping warm some thrown together concoction of meat and vegetables and Nate was standing over the Igloo cooler mixing up another batch of Gatorade. Seated around Jackson's camp they were drinking coffee, laughing and carrying on. Typical Sundance behavior, nothing out of the ordinary.

"Perfect timing," Jackson mused.

This last year had been a real mother for Jackson. Three months before he had to leave for Sundance his trailer burned to the ground. At 4 a.m., standing in the cold predawn morning of southwest Pennsylvania in nothing but his boxer shorts, he watched as everything he owned went up in flames. No one was ever sure what started the fire but the local chief labeled it suspicious.

Jackson's car was a beat up, early model, used two-door Saturn he picked up cheap for $800 and was parked beside his trailer. Saturn cars are mostly plastic, the hood, fenders and main shell of the vehicle. That fire was hot enough to burn his trailer to the ground. It was also hot enough to melt his car. Although the car was still drivable, barely, in no way would it make it from Pennsylvania to South Dakota. Jackson at the time thought he was totally screwed.

He never had much of an education, at least not a formal one, because he quit high school in the tenth grade. Street sense he had and plenty of, but he was certainly no college boy. Jackson worked at a tire shop changing tires and doing other minor mechanical work. The job is back breaking and doesn't pay much, but it did pay the bills. He has been with the shop four years and five years from now he expected to still be there. He made enough money for food, clothes he could pick up cheap at the Goodwill and gas money to get to the reservation once a year. It worked for Jackson, it was good enough. With his trailer and everything he owned gone, his car melted, he had no clue what he was going to do. Along came Nate Winter.

Nate is exceptionally thin, about five foot five and in his mid thirties. His face is rat-like, his eyes beady and set too close together. Nate is as white as a white guy can be and always projected an air of invincibility. He is one of those people you wanted to punch in the face within five minutes of meeting them. You can't explain why, it's just something about them that feels wrong. Being around Nate is like stepping into an unseen spider web. You can't see it but you know its there and you're frantic to get it off.

A self proclaimed survivalist he never hesitates to tell anyone how he could live off the land anywhere at any time. He loves to tell stories about wonderful he is with a bow, a gun or a knife. How he was trained in martial arts, served in the Special Forces and could basically kill a man with a napkin. All in all Nate Winter is full of more shit than a Christmas turkey. Along with all his other annoying attributes he is a fan of Indians. Nate swears he was Indian in another life. Maybe even Crazy Horse himself.

Earlier in the year at a local powwow Jackson had the misfortune to meet him. He simply walked up and, as most white folks are prone to do, began telling Jackson his life story, without being asked. All the usual clichés and of course, Indian in a former life. Jackson had heard it all before as he was one of the few real natives living in Southwestern Pennsylvania who bore some resemblance to his heritage. Everywhere he went some white guy would stop him and tell him all about how they were Cherokee. It was all he could do not to punch them right in the mouth.

Ever since the powwow Nate had been showing up at his trailer, unannounced, with no warning. Jackson would be kicked back, outside enjoying the day, and here came Nate to assail him yet again with his bullshit stories. At 4 a.m., his trailer gone, his car melted, Jackson thought of Nate. He was going to need a ride to South Dakota and he damn sure couldn't afford to buy a car. His credit was shot, so a loan or financing another vehicle was out of the question. He had $1,500 in the bank, money he had saved all year to get to Sundance. He couldn't buy much of a car for $1,500, but if he added his money together with someone else and that someone else had a vehicle then the problem was solved. Later that morning he had called Nate.

Jackson swore Nate dropped a load in his shorts when he asked him if he wanted to go to Sundance with him. It's everything Nate had ever fantasized about. He had read every Indian book and seen every Indian movie and now he would finally have the chance to live out his dreams. He would get to go to a real Indian Reservation with a real Indian to be among other real Indians! Oh my god!

Having heard the unabashed ecstasy in his voice the thought came to Jackson's mind, Somehow, I just made a huge mistake. This is going to be royally fucked up. If he had only known how prophetic that thought will be.

Pulling up to the campsite in Roddy's truck they climbed out and began unloading Jackson's gear as the camp went strangely silent. Not a sound as Junior, Nate and the rest of those hanging around watched. The quiet didn't register with Jackson. After what he had survived earlier in the day not much was registering. He was looking forward to a cold cup of water and some food. Maybe a smoke and a hot cup of coffee. He did notice the strange looks on their faces. He cast a brief cursory glance at Roddy, then slightly shrugged his shoulders. Whatever, Jackson thought.

Reaching into the pickup bed to grab his bedroll he turned and there is Junior, mere inches from him. Jackson jumped back and slammed into the pickup. Junior had a way of coming up on folks unannounced and him suddenly being there startled Jackson. His hands full, Junior asked him, "Done with the dance, huh?"

"Yepper," Jackson replied.

"Some of the guys quit the dance I hear," Junior questioned.

"Damn that sucks," he answered. Noticing again the strange look on Junior's face Jackson quickly added, "I ain't one of them. Chases danced me out. Roddy was standing there, heard the whole conversation."

"Really?" Junior intimated, "Isn't that interesting." Turning abruptly he walked back to his chair and picked up the coffee cup he had set on the ground. Sitting down, glaring at Jackson.

Well that was fucking weird, Jackson thought. Shrugging it off he stowed his dance gear and made his way over to where everyone was sitting, and found an empty chair. Roddy was already waiting with a cup of cold Gatorade he handed to Jackson. Taking a healthy swallow he smacked his lips and exclaimed, "Damn that's good! What do we have for grub?"

Roddy replied, "Just sit bro, I'll handle it. Let me find a plate. You relax man."

Exactly what Jackson wanted to do. Relax, chill out, contemplate what he had undergone and the fact he lived through it. Looking down at his chest he saw the raw, grisly wounds. Realization unexpectedly dawned in that moment that those are some big holes, easily two inches across and so deep he swears he can see the muscle fiber. Oh well, he thought, guess that's what I get for hanging in a tree like a meat puppet.

Slowly Jackson realized no one was saying a word. Everyone was watching him except Roddy, who was busy putting a plate of food together. He was beginning to feel very uncomfortable. What the fuck? he thought then, ah, fuck'em. I'm beat. As he fired up a cigarette Roddy handed him a plate, some utensils, a cup of coffee and then he grabbed a chair. A stupid grin is on his face because he's so proud of Jackson. Not many men can do what he had done. Very few would even consider it. Jackson set the plate beside him and sipped the coffee. He smoked as Junior, Nate and the rest of the guys stared.

"How's the coffee?" Junior asked.

"Not bad, not bad at all," Jackson replied. Setting the coffee down he snuffed out his smoke and picked up his plate, diving in. It's nothing short of amazing how good camp food can taste after two days of not eating. Looking up he saw Junior and Nate still watching him.

"Food okay?" Junior asked, "You got enough?"

"Yeah I'm good," Jackson said around a mouthful, "Hungry as a mofo."

"I bet you are," Junior retorted.

What the fuck? Jackson thought again, After what I just lived through? You and I are supposed to be friends so why are you being a dick, Junior? But he didn't say anything, just kept eating. For whatever reason Junior was ready to go off and Jackson wasn't going to light that fuse. He forked, chewed and swallowed with an occasional sip of coffee. Junior watched, as did Nate. Minutes passed as a thick charged air filled the camp. Roddy, always calm and relaxed it seemed, smoked and sipped his coffee.

"Well, got shit to do," Junior said abruptly. As he rose out of his chair Nate stood with him. They were joined by the remainder of the motley crew hanging around. Without another word they all turned and headed out of camp towards the Sundance arbor. Jackson waited until they were well out of earshot before saying anything. "What the fuck you think that was about Roddy?"

"No clue," Roddy replied, "Absolutely no clue. Notice how Junior had his new white puppy following him everywhere?"

"Oh yeah I noticed," Jackson said grinning, "Nate gets his nose any further up Junior's ass they are going to have to feed an oxygen line to him." Roddy laughed so hard he choked and spit his coffee.

The night was uneventful from there on and Jackson eventually crawled into his tent. He fell asleep with the knowledge he had done what he had been asked to do. It was far from easy but then, if it was easy, anyone could do it. Jackson was proud of himself. Not in an egotistical, self important way, as if he was special. He was proud of what he had done, proud that he found the strength. A good proud, a satisfied proud.

70°
CHAPTER SEVEN

The sun rose on the third day of Sundance with Jackson in his camp and Roddy in another tent a few yards away, snoring like a mad man. One thing about Roddy Blackstar, that man can snore. And talk to himself. He has full conversations with someone while being dead asleep. Roddy will laugh, ask questions, even answer questions all fully unconscious.

Jackson found a chair and turned the camp stove on to reheat the coffee. As he fired up his first smoke of the morning a smile soon cracked his face. In moments he was chuckling as he listened to Roddy in his tent talking, knowing no one was in there with him. Forty five minutes later Jackson heard him rustling about. His tent zipper ripped through the crisp morning air and, popping his head out, gazing sleepily around, his eyes found Jackson's. "Morning numb nuts," Jackson said with a laugh, "hell of a conversation you were having in there by yourself."

"Fuck you." Roddy replied cantankerously, "It ain't like yours is the first face I want to see when I wake up in the morning. I'm still not convinced I'm awake and this isn't all a terrible, terrible dream."

Jackson laughed and said, "Coffee's hot you cranky bastard. Come get you a cup."

"Cool," Roddy said, brightening immediately, "I'll be right there." Together they enjoyed the morning, two friends who have known each other six years or better.

Jackson and Roddy met years ago at a sweat lodge outside of Nashville where Roddy lived. Another big chain store purchased yet another chunk of real estate and sought to build yet another spanking new super center. It just so happened, that the ground they bought was a burial site, an extension of an original Cherokee city site. Jackson heard about what was happening with the locals and how they were going up against that corporation They intended to try to stop that corporation from ripping their ancestors out of the ground. Natives knew when that happens the remains will wind up in a cardboard box stored in some museum. Just once let them try that with a white cemetery and see the uproar it would cause. Doing it to a native burial site appeared to be no problem. The excuse commonly used is "it's an historical site." Interestingly the only time anyone is interested in native history is when they want something.

The local natives in Nashville got the word out via internet and anything else they could come up with. Folks from all over the country including mix bloods, whites, blacks, even a few Asians made a beeline for Nashville. Once again little guys taking on big money. Someone had to do something and a lot of good people were trying.

In the evenings after marching and protesting all day many gathered for ceremony at Randy Halls place, the man who organized this fight against big business. Randy is a mix blood Shawnee/white, six foot five, lanky with long brown hair he kept tied in a single braid. He lived a few miles from the property the corporation was trying to build the store on and had many friends, including Roddy Blackstar, whose relatives were buried in that ground.

In the end corporate got their fancy store and the graves were dug up. The bones were lumped together in cardboard boxes and carted off, labeled and tagged, never to be seen again. It happens every day somewhere in this perverted society of capitalistic give me that, its mine! ideology so pervasive today. And society at large doesn't seem to understand why natives get so upset.

While there Jackson was invited to attend a sweat by Randy Hall, the first ceremony he had ever attended, and an event unfolded there that firmly planted his feet on the journey of learning who he was.

After driving twelve hours to be at the protests he had been out in the sun all day and without time for a shower he was a bit rank by the time he reached Randy's place. Parking in a field several hundred yards away from the sweat lodge grounds he stepped from his van and turned to follow the trail through the woods to where the lodge was constructed. Within a few steps he was immediately engulfed by orange butterflies, with black and white spots. Hundreds and hundreds came from everywhere. Jackson had Painted Lady butterflies all over him and in moments was covered by them. Standing frozen in place he gazed at them in amazement and as quickly as it happened they flew away. Okay, he thought, that was freaking cool!

Randy happened to walk up to greet Jackson at the same time the butterflies began landing and grinned at him while shaking his head astonishment. "I gotta say," Randy said in a hushed voice full of excitement, "I ain't ever seen that happen before. From what I hear the butterflies are our grandmothers. I guess your relatives are welcoming you."

Jackson felt a warmth envelope him as together they walked to the lodge. Roddy was already at the sweat lodge hanging out and drinking coffee like he always does, when Jackson walked up and something between them clicks. Within moments they were laughing at each other and verbally sparring with each other to see who would get angry first. "You know," Jackson began, "my People used to kick y'alls asses up and down these hills."

"Really?" Roddy responded in feigned surprise, "And we used to hunt your asses down for trying it." Instantly they were best friends.

Roddy Blackstar is a Quapaw/Cherokee/white, short of stature with sandy brown thin hair, light skinned and wiry with blue eyes. He regularly dresses casually, always jeans and a t-shirt, but he makes it a point to wear something, usually a lot of something's like hats that have feathers sewed on them and large copper medallions hanging from around his neck, that broadcast his native blood. Some mistake Roddy for white but his family is from Arkansas. They were part of a band that left the Cherokee in the 1700s and intermarried with the Quapaw and local settlers. Roddy can quote his family line well before European occupation and many of his cousins, aunts and uncles are fully registered tribal members.

Roddy's last name is from his Quapaw relatives, before it had been translated it meant "eyes as black as a starless night." The boarding schools shortened it to Blackstar.

They were both from tortured, abusive backgrounds and survived nothing short of a living hell as they crashed and burned through their mangled teenage years. Watching them someone would think they grew up together. Not for a moment would anyone realize they had just met. For years afterward their relationship as friends would continue to strengthen.

At the time Jackson didn't have a home, he had never really had a home. Growing up he was bounced from foster home to foster home. Some people actually believe the foster care system is a good thing, which is ridiculous. The majority of foster homes, at least the ones Jackson survived, were perverts, sick twisted social rejects or someone looking for a paycheck. The child is irrelevant and only there to fill a need. If anyone wants to know about the foster care system all they need to do is pick up a local paper. They advertise in the help wanted section which kind of says it all.

From those earlier first ceremonies Jackson was invited to join in a protest camp. He left the marches for graves when they concluded to join a larger burial site encampment south of Brentwood, Tennessee. In effect were plans to construct a new highway around Nashville to make it easier for commuters to get around the city. Only problem was the area surrounding Nashville was once a central city for the Southern Confederacy, mainly the Cherokee Nation. No one lived in the bowl until the bowl became the city of Nashville.

The Cherokee believed the bowl is where the Giants were slain and no one wanted to live with the ghosts of Giants. In order to construct the new multi lane bypass thousands of graves would need to be removed. They're only Indians, so who would care? Turned out a lot of people cared. Not that it mattered because they eventually built the bypass anyway.

Late into the evening of Jackson's third day in the camp he was sitting around the main fire with everyone else, about thirty or so people from all over the country. Casually glancing over his shoulder he saw a man having a conversation with several other men and Jackson immediately recognized one of them as an Elder who had traveled from Pine Ridge. He was there at the request of Terry Bishop, another tall mix blood Cherokee from Cookeville. Jackson met him when he joined the camp.

A quiet man, Terry rarely said much of anything. Well over six foot with shoulder length hair he resembled his white ancestors more than his native ones. He is also a Sundancer and has been for ten years. The Elder from Pine Ridge is a full blood Lakota in his seventies, Terry's Sundance Leader, Alvin Redstone.

Jackson turned back to the fire and slowly became aware that everyone who was in the camp was at the fire. He began to mentally count everybody and sure enough everyone except Alvin Redstone was gathered there with him. Looking again over his shoulder he saw Redstone and the men he was talking with still standing there. Thinking maybe someone new had joined the camp he looked over to where the vehicles were parked. No new vehicles. No new people. Perplexed he began to count everyone at the fire until he came to Terry Bishop, who was sitting in a chair across the fire from him smoking and drinking coffee, looking straight at him and grinning.

Jackson's eyes went wide as he figured it out. He glanced a third time over his shoulder and saw Redstone coming to the fire and sitting down next to Terry, who was still watching Jackson. Redstone grinned at Jackson then shrugged as if to say, "what, did you see something?"

The camp had been set up several hundred yards away from the burial mounds. The men Redstone had been talking to were visitors to the camp alright, but they hadn't driven there. They came from the burial mounds. Stepped right out of their graves to have a conversation with Alvin Redstone and spook the hell out of Jackson.

At that camp Jackson worked as security, his first assignment serving the People. He was terrified of the dark, even more so now with what he witnessed happening with Redstone. It would be years later before he understood why. Putting aside his fear he accepted the midnight to 4 a.m. shift and walked the perimeter of the camp and occasionally returned to the fire.

Seated in his chair on watch a week into the camp Jackson's gaze wandered over to a stand of red cedar trees fifty yards away where the sweat lodge had been erected. The night was warm, the moon was full, and he was gazing at the moon watching as it crested the top of the red cedar trees. While he watched the moon separated and became two faces. One of a child, the other of an old man, facing away from each other, their heads melded together. Moments later the moon returned to its former state. Jackson was astonished. He had never seen anything like this before and had no idea what to do.

There was a man in camp who was supposedly a White Mountain Apache spiritual leader, Billy Hernandez. About five foot two with long graying hair and in his early sixties, Billy had the typical short person's attitude, small and looking to take on the biggest guy he could find, just to prove he was as tough as anyone else. Billy would be Jackson's first introduction to those who leave the rez to become a god.

When morning came Jackson approached him. He had been introduced to Billy by Randy Hall. Alvin Redstone wasn't around as he and Terry had left earlier and returned to Cookeville. Over coffee Jackson explained what happened with the moon and although he didn't like Billy he needed to talk to someone.

This self titled "medicine man" had been in the protest camp for as long as he had and at every opportunity he abused Jackson. For no apparent reason, at least not one Jackson understood, Billy behaved like a total ass. As far as he was concerned Jackson was another suburban wannabe come to play Indian for the weekend and he wasn't willing to give Jackson, who had just begun this journey, the slightest chance. Not for one moment did Billy perceive he was serious about what he was doing and that this wasn't a game to him. When he spoke about what he witnessed happen with the moon he was immediately verbally assaulted and informed he shouldn't make things up, it was disrespectful. He was told he didn't know anything and it wouldn't help him to pretend about sacred things. If he wanted to remain in camp serving the People he would have to be punished to atone for lying.

Jackson was instructed that he would have to enter the sweat lodge fully clothed. He was not ready to leave the camp yet so he agreed to, although not with. As he was sitting in the lodge preparing Billy Hernandez the "spiritual leader" entered the lodge announcing "the medicine man is here." Jackson thought, he's full of shit. Throughout the ceremony he was comfortable in the lodge in jeans and t-shirt, shoes and socks. No problems at all. Billy sounded like he was dying across from him.

After the lodge ended Jackson found a quiet spot off by himself and a Shawnee man he met earlier joined him for a smoke. He had traveled from northern Ohio to join in the protest camp and was listening when Jackson told this "medicine man" about the moon. He had brought a book with him to camp and he handed that book to Jackson. The dust jacket artwork was the image Jackson had watched the moon morph into and again, Jackson was speechless.

The book was written by a woman who was a member of a loosely organized group of Shawnee in northern Ohio. Jackson knew his next destination. When the encampment ended after three weeks he went in search of and met with those Shawnee. He spent the summer with them learning from them but by the end of summer the ego of their self proclaimed Chief had him looking for somewhere else to go.

Having no family, and utterly incapable of maintaining a stable relationship with any woman, he had nothing better to do. He lived in his beat up old Ford van he somehow managed to keep running and wandered around the country reservation to reservation, ceremony to powwow. From the east coast to the west coast he traveled for five years, rambling wherever and stopping whenever. He met some good people along the way. He also met some of the most whacked out new age spiritual nut jobs that are breathing air that could be put to better use, like fuel for a dull fart in a high wind.

Jackson drifted through Nashville and stopped at Roddy's place for a few days then disappeared again. Sometimes weeks or months would go by before Roddy heard from him. Never a warning, sometimes a phone call. Roddy was at home simply doing what he did every day and the phone would ring. Invariably it would be Jackson calling.

"Hey! Whatcha doing brother man?" Jackson asked.

"Hey!" Roddy exclaimed excitedly, "Where the hell you at now?"

"Standing on your porch asshole. Now open the damn door," Jackson answered, laughing.

Years they did this together. Hours they spent sitting on Roddy's porch talking about where Jackson had been and what he had been doing. Talking about the people he had met and laughing over the idiots. Laughing together at the twisted versions of supposed Native American spirituality he had come across. Over coffee and copious cigarettes hours passed like moments until one morning Roddy would wake up and stumble downstairs to find Jackson gone. Never one for long goodbyes or explanations he simply drove off, sometimes in the night. Roddy never gave it much thought as no one knew where Jackson would wind up next. Not even Jackson knew where he would wind up next. The running joke was if folks knew they would hang a sign on the door, "Moved – no forwarding address."

That's just how it was, and remains, between the two of them. Regardless where either of them are one phone call and the other was there. Never a why, what for or how come, only where are you, and when. Honor. Few have it and even fewer could begin to define it. The respect between them is built on that honor. When Jackson called three years ago and told him he was going to Sundance, Roddy asked only for the dates. For four years with no hesitation or questions Roddy had always been there. For every dance, start to finish. Jackson can't say that about anyone else he knows.

.

80°
CHAPTER EIGHT

Like de'ja vue Jackson and Roddy were sharing coffee and cigarettes, talking about life. Some things never changed, some things never should. The sun was high in the morning sky when the sound of the eagle bone whistle pierced the morning air.

"Getting started a tad late ain't they," Jackson observed.

Roddy glanced at his watch and noticed it's almost 9 a.m. "Well past late," he said. Together they finished their coffee, stubbed out their smokes and dragged themselves up from their chairs.

Jackson's chest was hurting severely. When he woke up he had to peel his shirt off because the wounds, so deep in his chest and back, had leaked blood all night long as he lay sleeping. The blood had hardened, drying to a crust and attached his t-shirt to his flesh. Roddy noticed his wounds bleeding, the unbelievable depth, and reached down to grab a handful of prairie sage. He handed the sage to Jackson who promptly removed the leaves from the stem and placed them in his mouth to coat them with saliva. Jackson packed each of the holes in his chest with the wet balls of sage as together they walked to the Sundance arbor 500 yards away. They reached the arbor at about the same time the dancers filled the circle and they joined the supporters as the dancers began their day.

The third day of Sundance began with the dancers showing exhaustion. Three days with no food or water and sweat lodges at the beginning, middle, and end the day. As much as twelve hours a day spent under the scorching South Dakota sun. No shade and no relief – never ending, constant, tortuous suffering. This is Sundance. Giving of themselves so completely for those who need, the ultimate altruistic act. Dying under the sun to be reborn when the ropes are torn so severely from their dry, shrunken flesh. Christians love to talk about sacrifice as long as it is someone else doing the sacrificing. Just once Jackson would have loved to see them do more than talk about it. Faith, easy to discuss, but a whole other thing to live.

As they assumed their places among the supporters those nearest to Jackson began to move away. As if for whatever reason they couldn't bear to be anywhere near him. Jackson looked and thought to himself, what the hell?

Very strange behavior, as if he carried the plague or something; it was becoming more and more difficult to hang on to the feelings of pride in his accomplishment. Whatever the hell was going on he wasn't enjoying it. It wasn't like this the first year he came to this dance. The first year he felt good here, everyone welcomed him and made him feel like he belonged.

Like an island of misfit toys everyone seemed to have come from somewhere else they weren't welcome and somehow found their way here to this refuge. That feeling didn't last long as he began to notice what lay beneath the surface. The back biting and rumor mongering. Seems everyone had a story to tell about everyone else. No wonder these folks left where they came from. Who wanted to immerse themselves in this much negative behavior? Especially when all were supposed to be coming together to pray, to give, to be here for those who need. Something appeared very wrong with this picture. Then there was David Chases. The things Jackson witnessed him doing go way beyond the pale.

People who are emotionally crippled, spiritually starving, finding their way to his door. They were seeking direction and some understanding while Chases saw only another dollar, another meal ticket. He didn't care if he burned them up. There was always next year's crop of confused more than willing to shell out money they didn't have for the flash of illusion he sold them. Indian names, adoption ceremonies, healing lodges. All for a price.

In his third year Jackson overheard Chases speaking with John, another mix blood from the East Coast. John was born with a degenerative spinal disease that in a few years would leave him either dead or crippled. Chases offered to "heal" him for $10,000. He told John regular doctors get so much more than that and ten grand is a deal! John left and hasn't been seen or heard from since.

For four years Jackson continued to support this den of thieves and liars. For four years he helped to raise and send money. Not because of Chases or anything about Chases but because Jackson fully believed this was what he had to do. The visions he had been given led him to this place and it was his responsibility to complete what had been asked of him. Part of the ordeal was dealing with David Chases, the most corrupt man Jackson had ever met.

At one time Chases could have been something. Like so many before him and so many after he had forgotten whatever gifts he had, that had been given to him by the Ancestors were to be used to serve the People, not the person. Jackson saw this and understood he would have to put up with it. This latest version of a "medicine man" who fully believed he was using spirituality to serve himself was actually being used by spirituality to fulfill a purpose. The purpose of ensuring Jackson Themal completed the circle put before him. Much to Chases chagrin he had completed the circle. But David Chases wasn't done with Jackson Themal just yet, not by a long shot. Jackson didn't have a clue how devious, how despicably horrible a man Chases actually was.

The dancers danced and the supporters danced. Over 100 degrees, this third day of Sundance. How bedraggled the dancers looked. Jackson's heart went out to them but he was happy to be done. Content, with a feeling of fulfillment. He didn't know what everyone else's problem was or why they were shunning him and he wasn't going to focus on it. He would focus on the prayers he had for his brothers and sisters who were giving so much under the noon day sun.

Behind Jackson he heard a car door shut and looking over his shoulder he saw Mary Bloody Heart leaning against her car. Slowly she was making her way to the trunk, wearing a skirt as all women do when they attend ceremony, a shawl casually draped over one arm and he immediately turned to assist her. Meeting her at the trunk of her beat-up Ford Taurus with the trunk lid now open he helped her remove the walker folded inside. Setting the walker before her he closed the trunk lid and walked with Mary to the arbor where they assumed places among the supporters beside Roddy.

Some of the supporters noticed her arrival but no one other than Jackson turned to help. Roddy recognized he had it under control and returned to focus on what he was doing, dancing and praying. Some of the supporters nodded to Mary, some giving her a smile, that smile fading when their eyes shifted to Jackson. What the flying sam hell is wrong with these people? he thought to himself. Mary seemed to read his mind and patted his arm slightly. Jackson shrugged and thought, whatever.

The three of them finished out the afternoon dancing. They prayed together, smoked together, laughed together. Everyone else stayed away as long as Jackson was beside Mary. When he left her side for a trip to the outhouse someone would come over to greet her. The second anyone visiting with Mary noticed him returning they scurried away. After another hour passed Mary says to Jackson, "I need you to come to my house with me."

With no hesitation he agreed. "What about Roddy?" he asked.

"He will be fine on his own for awhile, won't you Roddy?" Mary replied in her soft whisper. Roddy nodded his head, immediately agreeing and said "Absolutely Mary. You guys go do what you got to do."

Roddy has been around for a long time with and without Jackson. He knows the deal. When an Elder says they wanted you to visit, you visited. He didn't take it personally when Mary informed him his presence wasn't needed at this particular conversation. This was between Mary Bloody Heart and Jackson Themal. He got that, no problem. "I'll be at the camp when you get back," Roddy said.

Slyly Mary whispered, "Don't wait up. It's probably going to be a late night."

90°
CHAPTER NINE

Jackson helped Mary to her car and once she was behind the wheel he folded her walker and carried it to the trunk, stowing it away. Of course the trunk was full of crap and he had to maneuver and wiggle the walker around to force it to fit. Inside were parts of broken trinkets and supplies in bags and boxes, blankets that had been given to Mary that find their way into her trunk and somehow never find their way out. Her car is a typical Indian rez ride.

Jackson eased into the passenger seat as Mary slipped the car into reverse then jerked it back into drive. Even with the seat adjusted as far forward as possible at just over five feet tall, she barely reached the pedals. Because of her short stature she peered between the steering wheel as much as over it.

Anyone who has ever climbed into a car with her driving, knew it was best to simply hang on and attempt to enjoy the roller coaster ride. They roared off in typical Mary Bloody Heart fashion, driving as though her house was on fire and all hell would break loose if she didn't get there yesterday. She lives in the next district over and they made the usual forty-five minute drive in just under thirty. Stepping out of her car Jackson checked to see all his parts were intact and helped her to the door. Not for one second did Mary give a thought to her driving. For her it's normal, for anyone else it's grin and bear it, or don't get in the car.

Her home is a government-built single wide set within yards of the road with additions haphazardly added over the years. Mary lives alone and has done so for many years except for the pack of rez dogs she allowed to live practically everywhere. Occasionally she would let one or two of them into the house but after they destroyed something back out they'd go.

The land has been in her family since the U.S. Government came up with the allotment scheme. That wonderful plan drawn up by bureaucrats where each family is given 160 acres. After all the families received their land parcels the Government assumed control over what was left. The U.S. Government labeled the excess land as "surplus" and they promptly gave the land to any white rancher who wanted it. By United States law the land belonged to the Nation, which was irrelevant, and somehow they deemed their actions legal. Today the government continues this very same behavior but uses "eminent domain" as the excuse. If a Nation isn't using their land in a way the Government feels is profitable they move in – local, state or federal – and take it.

Mary disappeared into her house and slowly made her way into the kitchen. Jackson stayed in the living room and found a comfortable spot on the well-worn couch. Sitting in the corner of the room is an older wing-back chair with a matching ottoman. This is Mary's chair and she never hesitated to smack the fool upside the head who mistakenly chooses to sit there. Jackson made that mistake four years ago and wasn't about to do it again. After some time passed she returned with a cup of coffee in each hand. As she shuffled to her favorite chair a smirk barely tugged the corners of her mouth. She cast a sideways glance at Jackson as if to say "good boy, don't even think about it." Handing him a cup of coffee she eased herself into her chair.

While lighting a cigarette slowly and deliberately Mary began to speak, "I asked you here because I have a few things I need to tell you and what I am about to tell you is going to be hard. It's going to take some time and its going to hurt a lot worse than it did when they hung you from that tree. You understand what I'm saying Jackson?"

"Yes ma'am," he replied respectfully. Long ago he learned when an Elder was speaking it was best to shut up. He had no idea what was coming or what she was leading up to and he was not sure he was ready for it, as if he has a choice. He was here in her living room. Any chance to make it out the eastern door had long since passed.

Mary squirmed a bit as she made herself comfortable. For long moments she looked at Jackson, seeming to take his measure. Maybe questioning herself if this was the right thing to do. To tell him. He had lived his life this long without knowing. Would it really make any difference? Yes, she appeared to decide, yes it would, and the difference it made would be totally up to him.

"You know well into the eighties I used to be a powwow dancer?" she asked him. Mary didn't wait for a response, none was expected or necessary. Typically when talking with an Elder many hypothetical questions will come up. It is only the fool who futilely attempts to answer those questions. The idea is to sit and listen.

"Safe to say I wasn't that bad either. Was different back then, not like it is today. Now it's this big fancy woo-ha! with lots of money and folks trying to turn it into a ceremony. Powwows ain't no ceremony. They are a coming together of the People to dance, to sing. It's a festival, a good time to be with each other. Time to see old friends, and maybe meet some new ones. Some people gotta try to turn every damn thing into some kind of ceremony. Some people really piss me off.

"Anyway, I'm in Oklahoma with some of my friends from here. Nice powwow we are at way out on the prairie. Not much around except Indian houses, some with electricity, most not. We dance all day and at night those of us who had been dancing we get to partying. Usual stuff we did everywhere we went. I was sitting kind of off by myself and this young girl come walking up to me. She was just over four months pregnant and yeah, she was drinking a beer. Back then we didn't think much about it. Not like today where everyone loses their minds if a pregnant girl has a beer. She came over and sat down with me. I figured she was just looking for someone to talk to. Lonely, you know? Pretty little girl. You can tell she is a mix blood. Hair like yours Jackson, real long too.

"After some time she begins to tell me a story. The story of her family, and how they got their name. How they wound up in Oklahoma and some history of her people. I didn't understand why she was telling me that story. She wanted someone to talk to I think. Didn't bother me any as I had nowhere to go, or nothing better to do. Isn't until four years ago today I understand. Four years ago when you, Jackson Themal, showed up at Sundance."

Mary now had his full attention. "Back some time ago in the history of this cesspool they now call America, that we once called ours, a man was elected as their President. Mr. Richard Whitman. Mr. Indian Killer himself. Oh, how Whitman hated Indians. Hated anybody who wasn't born and bred white like him. Mr. Whitman was a wealthy man. He came from some pretty big money over across the pond, in Ireland or Scotland or somewhere like that.

"Curious thing though, he wasn't born in this country. He never should have been allowed to be President. That's what the rules say but when have you ever known white folks to follow the rules? They just make up the rules and expect everyone else to follow them. Whitman was actually born on board the boat he and his momma were on just off the coast of one of them countries. Anyone wants to take the time they can check the ships records and they will find the birth, all recorded in black and white. Don't matter, cause when they got here to this country they fudged the records and made it look like he was born here. Man was born a liar, lived a liar and died a liar. Ugly man he was, ugly and mean. Hateful!

"One of Whitman's companies was a mining operation. After sending his surveyors to sneak into the southern states someone found some gold. That was all Richard Whitman, who had been elected President by then, needed to know. He gathered all those Indian People and forced them to move to Oklahoma. The tribes, they fought back, even went so far as to sue him in his own federal courts but that didn't matter either. Whitman ignored his courts and threw them folks off their lands then took what he wanted. Few families survived that long and tortuous journey. Some managed to escape before being rounded up by the Cavalry by hiding in the hills. Others slipped away whenever the attention of the guards lapsed.

"The young girl telling her story to me that evening was related to one of those families driven from their ancestral lands. They were Shawnee People and had been visiting relatives in the Carolina's at the time. They had made the long journey on foot from Cleveland, Ohio earlier in the year. Unfortunately for them, and many others they were rounded up and lumped together with everyone else the Cavalry could find and forced to make the journey to Oklahoma."

Mary casually stopped her story and got up from her chair, returning to the kitchen for more coffee. Jackson flashed back to the summer he lived with a group of Shawnee in northern Ohio a few years before he came to Sundance. Unrecognized and loosely organized he learned the Shawnee history from them; that supposedly the Shawnee were not from North America.

Before the Romans ruled Britannia, before the initiation of christianity and the building of Egyptian pyramids, the Shawnee, under another tribal name, lived among the Maya in South America off the Yucatan Peninsula. They said the Maya were a brutal people who offered human sacrifices to their Gods and the Shawnee were their cattle. Weakened by a Nation they knew they could never defeat the Shawnee left the Yucatan, their ancestral home. Separating into two parties one walked across Mexico, following the coastline. The other constructed large vessels similar to ocean-crossing canoes and traversed the Gulf. They landed in what would become Florida and moved north on foot. Eventually the two groups met at the Mississippi Delta where they came together as one people again. Continuing to migrate north they married into the tribes of the region. The Shawnee eventually separated into five divisions but they always remained within close proximity of each other. They settled in the Miami Valley on land given to them by the Miami Nation in payment for a problem the Shawnee settled for them.

That would be the role of the Shawnee throughout the Eastern portion of the continent, both southern and northern, for generations to come. If any tribe had a problem with any other tribe the Shawnee were contacted and the problem was solved, permanently. This behavior obviously created tense relationships with the Haudenasaunee Confederacy in the north, the Southern Confederacy headed by the Cherokee in the south and the Powhatan Confederacy as the buffer between the two.

During the late 1700s and into the 1800s a common man among the Shawnee with no claim to any title assumed a position of authority. Following Pontiac's example before him he valiantly attempted to unify the many Nations of the east coast, to bring them together as one. With the events unfolding in his time he foresaw the complete eradication of the native Peoples. He recognized the overwhelming greed, the insatiable hunger for power and wealth, in these new inhabitants of their lands. They made agreements with the Chiefs and Leaders of the Nations then immediately broke the agreements when a new resource was discovered or when they simply wanted more. Many among the Nations agreed with him and although he had no recognized authority they stood with him. Together they formed a small traditional community and named it Prophetstown, in what would become Indiana.

Around 1790 "Mad Anthony" Wayne was appointed Commander in Chief of the United States Army by George Washington. He was given the mandate to subdue the northwest tribes, including, and especially, this upstart young man known as Tecumseh. Wayne would level Prophetstown and died in 1796. The Indian Wars continued and after many hard fought battles later the dream of unification would die at Tippecanoe with Tecumseh's death in 1812.

Many of the Shawnee returned to the Cleveland area, by then an important port city. Water for steel mills was readily available and the Ohio River provided access for the shipment of goods down the Mississippi River to the Gulf of Mexico. A group of Shawnee, Big Jim's band, living near Cayuga Falls could no longer tolerate what was happening to the beautiful lands they lived on. After a long council the entire band decided once again it was time for the Shawnee to leave. They would go back to Mexico.

100°
CHAPTER TEN

Jackson was contemplating this history as Mary quietly returned from the kitchen with more coffee. Handing a cup to Jackson she asked, "you doing okay?"

"Yeah Mary," he responded vaporously, "just thinking."

Settling herself again in her chair she asked, "Where was I in my story?"

"The Shawnee leaving Ohio," Jackson prompted.

"That's right," she agreed, "The Shawnee. As that young girl I was talking to told me, some members of a Shawnee group, headed by a fellow named Big Jim, were fed up with the way things were going there in Ohio and everyone decided to leave. Some had relatives in the south and wanted to see them one last time. When that band of Shawnee left Ohio some went with Big Jim to Mexico where they were originally from and others went to the Carolina's.

"The young girl I was speaking with on the Oklahoma prairie that night was a descendant of one of the Shawnee families that had traveled to the Carolina's. They made the long journey on foot from Cleveland at the same time gold was found by Whitman's surveyors. While visiting they were gathered up with the rest of the Southern Confederacy and imprisoned in Georgia then forced to walk what everyone knows today as the Trail of Tears.

"Throughout the long journey on foot from the Georgia to Oklahoma those families stayed together. The relatives in the Carolina's were Creek People, one of the Nations that made up the Southern Confederacy. Many members of both families died on that journey, from the flu and exhaustion. Months later their torment finally ended and what was left of those families found a valley on the land allotted to them and settled in. On a clear morning some weeks later the women gathered the children and made their way to the creek side to bathe the little babies. What they didn't know was they were being watched.

"When the Shawnee roamed the eastern side of the continent not for a moment did they care or give any thought to the relationships between Confederacies. The Shawnee came and went where they wanted, when they wanted, doing what they wanted. The Calvary, when they rounded everyone up, didn't know the history of the Shawnee and even if they had it wouldn't have mattered. They also didn't know about the bad blood between the Shawnee and the Cherokee. Put simply, the Cherokee and the Shawnee didn't much care for each other. The Shawnee had caused the Cherokee a lot of problems and they never forgot. In total ignorance the Shawnee were placed together with the Cherokee on the exact same piece of land. Watching the Shawnee women that fateful morning bathe the babies was a group of very angry young Cherokee men.

"This was back in the 1800s and blind drunk was the way to relieve pain and frustration. Seemed every man old enough to stand was sucking on a whiskey bottle and those men that were watching were no different. They had swapped a few things to a local white trader and in return they received some really bad whiskey. They spent all night drinking that poison, well into the morning. Those drunken Cherokee men saw those Shawnee women, and they got mad, real mad. Those young men wanted to hurt someone, anyone. Old tribal grievances were remembered and those women and children were a soft target. Coming up fast and hard on those women before anyone had a chance to do anything about it those men killed every one of those babies and a few of the women too. No reason, no excuse, just drunk and mad. Some hours passed and those in camp realized the women and babies hadn't come back yet. One of the men walked down to the creek and found them.

"They swore you could hear his wailing three counties over. That man in all his life had never seen such a horrific sight. Those little babies with their heads smashed in, mommas with their bellies ripped open. Looked like the U.S. Cavalry had paid another visit. That man, once he got control of himself, he began to notice a few things. Things like the horses those men rode who committed this atrocity were unshod. Cavalry horses were always shod. Those tracks were from Indian horses. A little bit of back tracking and that man found where those other men had been drinking all night. Broken whiskey bottles, piss stains on the grassland, the urine still fresh in the air. That man he stood himself up straight and tall and wiped away his tears. Slowly he made his way back to where his People were camped and entered his tent without a word spoken to anyone. He came out a few minutes later, war axe, knife and rifle in hand. Not speaking to a single person he went back to that horrible creek bed and he tracked those young drunken men. For six days he followed them across the Oklahoma prairie. On that sixth day when he finally did catch up with them he killed every one of them.

"Two weeks later that man showed back up in his camp. His people were waiting for him, deeply concerned because they hadn't heard from him in so long. They didn't know if he was alive or dead. He came walking back into their camp with dried blood clinging to his arms and neck, his clothes stiff with it. The remaining women brought him a bowl of soup and everyone in the camp formed a half circle in front of him. They waited for him to begin to tell them the story of what he had done, which he did, every gory detail. When it was all said and done, that man earned himself a new name. From then on his people called him Kills Them All.

"Time went by and things settled down. The few remaining children grew and married, then had babies of their own. The Elders went home to the Ancestors. Big Jim's band left Mexico because they wanted to be with their relatives in Oklahoma. They had long since learned the fate of those families that had walked from Cleveland to the Carolina's. Coming together again they settled in Oklahoma and named their community Little Axe.

"Eventually Oklahoma was opened up to white settlement and the missionaries arrived soon after. Of course those good intentioned white preacher folks, they couldn't have any savage Indians living out in the bush with no knowledge of Jesus. Soon enough they came for the children. Some over-educated fool in Washington concluded the easiest way to get the Indian out of an Indian was through the children. The missionaries placed the children in boarding schools, taught them all about Jesus and how to be good civilized brown-white people. One of those children taken was a direct descendant of Kills Them All.

"She was a pretty little girl. They brought her to the missionary school and deloused her with their white powder. The powder stung her eyes but the nuns didn't care. They cut that little girls hair off, put her in a burlap dress and immediately changed her name. The first name they gave her was Gertrude. Seemed like a good christian name. The last name was a bit trickier. No way any God fearing child of Jesus could be permitted to have a name like Kills Them All. The nuns dropped 'Kills,' joining 'Them' and 'All' together and then dropped the last 'L.' Named her Gertrude Themal."

Mary Bloody Heart, staring directly at him, said, "Your name Jackson. That little girl was your Grandma. That young woman I was talking with that night? She was your momma. Her name was Annie Themal."

All the while Mary was speaking Jackson hadn't said a word. He sat quietly, occasionally shifting his position, listening. He remembered her words of foreboding before this began and so far he wasn't feeling any pain. If anything he was feeling a bit of pride. So far everything he had heard made sense. Jackson isn't naive enough to believe the Hollywood love and light version of the native Peoples of this country. He is an avid reader and a damn good listener.

In Jackson's travels he spent many hours listening to stories told by old people around many powwow camp fires. He came to the conclusion that parroting someone else's opinion didn't show intelligence, it only showed you had a good memory. Seemed the more intelligent thing to do was to read about something from many different perspectives, especially those that challenged your own, then, based on all the information, arrive at a conclusion of your own. A conclusion that made sense to you as an individual.

Jackson read constantly, studying the history of this country and the history of the indigenous Peoples. He based his opinions on his understandings. He accepted the indigenous people of this country were a brutal people when they needed to be. But, unlike the Europeans who sought to conquer everything and everyone, the native Peoples were content to let each other be whatever they chose to be. However, cross that line, cause harm to anyone of the Nation and they could, would and did reign down a version of hell on the perpetrators, to make Tarantino himself uncomfortable.

Without the cult-like mind-numbing of organized religion, the Peoples of this country felt no guilt when they came together and stomped a hole in whatever son of a bitch had wronged them. There was no concept of Hell, a place invented by christians to keep the general populace in line. In the native mind heaven or hell is something you live every day depending on your behavior. Therefore, if someone needs killing well, by all means, kill the bastard. Problem solved.

Jackson wasn't upset in the least by the violence that his relative Kills Them All committed. He grew up with violence – biker gangs, sexual predators and bullies. Jackson wasn't the blonde haired, blue eyed version of most children in the public school system. He looked different, he acted different. He knew it then, and so did those he came into contact with, which was all a child needed to initiate an assault. Jackson laughs at those who profess how innocent children are. That is absolute delusional bullshit. Children are vicious and cruel to the nth degree. The slightest perception any child among them is different, and they attack that child relentlessly. Innocent my ass, he thought.

Jackson rose from the couch to refill his coffee cup. "Want a refill Mary?" he asked. Nodding she handed him her cup. Making his way into Mary's kitchen Jackson was mulling over what she had told him. The plans were formulating, the ideas were brewing. He refilled both of their cups and returned to the living room. Setting Mary's down beside her, his on the end table next to the couch, he was about to sit when Mary said, "Do me a favor, Jackson?"

"Sure," he replied, "What do you need?"

"Reach into that cabinet there and grab me another pack of smokes." Mary requested. Jackson did as he was asked and after handing Mary the cigarettes he returned to his seat. Sipping his coffee, lighting a cigarette himself, he waited for Mary.

With shaking hands and arthritic fingers she peeled back the cellophane on the pack of cigarettes he handed her. She opened the pack, tapped gently, and removed a cigarette. Slowly she reached for her lighter. She lit up her smoke then picked up her cup of coffee and settled back into her chair.

Mary Bloody Heart had a way about her that scared the crap out of some people. Sometimes when she was watching you, you could swear she had opened a door in your skull you didn't know was there and she had climbed inside. You could almost feel her shuffling around as her walker scraped ruts in your mind. All the while she had been slowly lighting her smoke she had also been watching Jackson. She could see he was paying her no attention, contemplating what she had told him.

"You could do that," Mary said quietly.

This was all that was necessary to shock Jackson back to the moment. Every time Mary did that it rocked him, like she was reading his very thoughts. Jackson chuffed, casting a sideways glance at her. "Do what Mary?" he asked, as if he didn't know exactly what she was talking about.

"Wait until after the dance, head down to Oklahoma and try to find your People. Yeah, you could do that," she replied. Anyone who had ever spent any time around any Elder worth their salt knows when "you could do that" was heard it was time to really start paying attention.

No true Elder will ever tell anyone what to do. They might suggest a few things, hint at a few more, but they would never come right out with explicit instructions on what anyone should or for that matter shouldn't do. These Elders understand that it is each individual's choice what they do or don't do, and it isn't their place to tell someone else what to do. Those four little words, whispered in Mary's soft, almost indistinct voice, cracked as loud as thunder in that cramped living room. Mary had Jackson's full attention, again.

"Wouldn't do you any good," Mary said, "There isn't anyone left. Annie was the last, well, you are the last Jackson, although the tribe will never accept you."

"Why is that Mary?" he asked, slightly annoyed. With two sentences she had brought him crashing back into reality. This was exactly what he was thinking and he was getting excited about the end of Sundance. Excited about finding out something he had longed for as long as he can remember. To know who he was. To know where he came from, to understand the blood that coursed so strongly in his veins.

One of the prayers Jackson brought with him to Sundance was to finally know his People. He was so tired of looking in the mirror not knowing who he was looking at. Jackson saw his reflection but his mind told him it wasn't real. That the person reflected back at him, the man he saw looking into his eyes, was an illusion. Each time he saw his reflection in the glass passing a shop, a mirror in a restaurant, he would stop and gaze at himself. Those with him, girlfriends or friends, thought he was being arrogant or conceited. Far from it. He wasn't gazing adoringly at his own reflection. He simply didn't know the man looking back at him and his reflection caught him by surprise every time. Mary Bloody Heart, in a matter of hours, had completed a journey, a circle he had been traveling up to this very moment. Now he understood his last name, how it came to be and the honor attached to it. She was telling him that journey was over. In his mind the journey had just begun.

"Why the hell not, Mary?" Jackson quipped, a perturbed frown creasing his face. "You spent the last few hours filling in a whole lot of empty spaces. Many of the missing pieces to the puzzle that is me, are slipping into place. Now you're telling me it's over? It's pointless? I don't understand that. What I do see is honor. I have no problem with what was done or who did it or why. Hell, I'm proud of Kills Them All and what he did. I would like to think if it were me I would have done the same damn thing."

Mary sighed, responding to his ranting confusion, "It isn't who your mother is Jackson. The problem is your father." Once again Mary Bloody Heart had Jackson's complete and undivided attention.

110°
CHAPTER ELEVEN

In the 1920s the Ryder Ranch was founded on the Oklahoma prairie. Twenty years later Jack Ryder was born and almost thirty years from then he was the sole proprietor of the ranch. Jack was a heinous man and that was describing him mildly. For all intents and purposes he was the walking personification of evil with as black a soul as any human had ever had. To make it worse he was well aware of how evil he was and didn't give a flying rat's ass what anyone thought about it.

Jack was a big man who stood six foot eight and easily weighed 350 lbs., with a military style haircut, a deep prairie tan and was solid as granite. He resembled a cinder-block, a really big cinder-block, that inexplicably learned how to walk. His was a hard square face, with soulless brown eyes.

Born into one of the first white families to settle in Oklahoma his father wound up owning several hundred acres of prime grazing land on the open prairie after the allotment act and the Ryder's did fairly well for themselves raising and slaughtering beef cattle. Jack was an only child, his mother having died giving birth to him. The only influences in his life had been masculine. Even the cook for old man Ryder was once a ranch hand and men were everywhere the boy went. Jack was raised through the forties and fifties on the wide open prairie, spending weeks in the branding and culling camps as he assisted with the castrations and destruction of sick animals, eating and living with the cowboys.

The foreman of the Ryder ranch, TJ Rocker, fought in the Indian Wars that helped to settle Oklahoma and he played a predominant role in the mass slaughter of many native families. No one knew what the TJ stood for and no one dared to ask. He was a deeply tanned cowboy in his late forties, long and lean with shoulder length hair under a beaten, wide brimmed Stetson. With absolutely no nonsense about him TJ said what needed done then rode away. If what he said wasn't done when he returned there would be hell to pay and everyone knew it.

As the ranch was in the middle of Indian Territory most of the men were native or mix blood native and TJ Rocker didn't like natives. He never hesitated to let anyone know and often went out of his way to abuse each and every one on the Ryder payroll. Jack's father knew how abusive TJ was but chose not to do anything about it. His thought was, this was Oklahoma, life was hard. If you didn't have the backbone to make it then that was your own fault. Old man Ryder couldn't tell the difference between an abusive life and a hard life, or chose not to.

It wasn't that he was a bigoted man, he actually felt a little sad when he considered the state of affairs of the original people of this land, but he didn't feel bad enough to actually do anything about it. His attitude was apathetic, an "oh well" approach to things. His only concern was the ranch being run to make a profit and that the Ryder's didn't suffer in any way.

Jack Ryder idolized TJ Rocker and before long he became TJ's shadow. Anywhere you saw TJ it was a safe bet Jack wasn't too far behind, and most of the time he was glued to TJ's side. Old man Ryder knew about this too and thought it was a good thing. He believed TJ would toughen the boy up. Besides, he had more important things to do than be bothered trying to raise him.

After a few years of following TJ around, Jack began behaving like him, especially around the native ranch hands. Leveling abuse became a game between them and they challenged each other to see who could be crueler than the other. Jack was a willing pupil and TJ a dedicated instructor. When TJ couldn't find Jack a search usually revealed him off by himself on the expansive ranch seated at a small fire he had built. He would have a rabbit, a coyote or maybe a local stray dog staked out. Inevitably he had branded or castrated the animal and it was usually a botched job with blood and guts soaking the hard sand. TJ would laugh telling him next time he would get it right as Jack smiled at TJ's approval. This went on until Jack was seventeen years old and the Army recruiter came to the ranch.

Around 1963 the Army needed bodies for the Vietnam war after the draft had been initiated. Out on the prairie it wasn't uncommon for most folks not to know what was happening around the rest of the country. The Army, not famous for waiting, had no intention of letting these strong, capable men slip by. The US Army brought together a corps of soldiers who had served at least one tour in Vietnam, trained them for six weeks and turned them loose on the prairie. Their job was to travel from ranch to ranch and gather the young men available then ship them off to boot camp. One of these recruitment soldiers made it to the Ryder ranch and Jack's father sent a ranch hand out after Jack. A few hours later he rode up, curious as to what his father could want. That recruitment soldier took one look at Jack Ryder and knew he was seeing an advance scout, someone who could be trained to go off into the jungle alone on reconnaissance missions or whatever else might be needed. Old man Ryder was informed on the spot Jack had been drafted and within a week he was on a bus for boot camp.

Jack endured eight weeks of basic training then several more weeks of training as a sniper. This was all easy for Jack, having grown up on the wild Oklahoma prairie. Being off alone having to survive on his own wits was nothing new for him. He actually enjoyed it, even preferred it. With his training completed he was sent immediately to a front line unit in Vietnam.

As far as Jack was concerned there wasn't any difference, other than jungle and wet instead of prairie and dry. Hot as hell but so was the Oklahoma prairie in the summer. The first half of his first tour of duty was spent learning the different ways to survive in the jungle alone.

Jack took to it like a duck to water. The second half of his first tour saw him off on several missions alone. He would disappear for a few weeks then return to base camp. He was recon and no one really said much about it, but everyone was noticing how Jack Ryder was changing.

When Jack first arrived in Vietnam he was a deeply tanned young man of seventeen and his face showed his lack of worldly experience. Six months in the jungle permanently changed that. His face became harder, his eyes a little more sunken, his pallor a little more pale. Instead of coyotes and jackrabbits to play with there were people, and he quickly began to satisfy old curiosities and fantasies. Having grown up alongside TJ Rocker, spending his youth leveling abuse against the ranch hands, it wasn't much of a stretch for him to begin abusing the indigenous people of Vietnam. As he was often off alone this allowed him to explore the darker sides of his psyche and to teach himself new ways to hurt. Things he wanted to do at home but hadn't been able to. Alone in the jungles of Vietnam there was no one to control or stop him.

When Jack's first tour ended he volunteered to stay for another and again at the end of that tour. Three years he spent in the jungles of Vietnam, three years to solidify his dark, hateful self. His superiors began to notice his unusual behavior and rumors that had surrounded him began to be supported by facts.

At the end of his third tour the Army took away his option for a fourth. If Jack had his way he would have stayed in Vietnam doing all the fun things the Army was paying him to do. But the Army, slow as it may be, eventually figured out when the killing was getting enjoyable to someone. Jack Ryder was sent home. He was put on a plane then dropped back off on the Oklahoma prairie. The man who came home from Vietnam was vastly worse than the boy who had left.

Jack returned to his father's ranch and because TJ had passed away while he was in Vietnam the ranch was looking a bit haggard. The new foreman wasn't as hard as TJ had been and to his amazement the new foreman was a local mix blood off one of the nearby reservations. Six months after returning home old man Ryder died and everything was left to Jack. The locals soon found that foreman hanging from a tree way out on the prairie, cut in so many ways pieces of him were missing. Everyone knew Jack was responsible but no one could prove it. He assumed the position of foreman and returned to life as he knew it. The abuse returned as well and sometimes local people or travelers went missing but nothing was ever done about it. Oklahoma in the sixties, you would swear you were living on a different planet.

When he wanted to Jack could be a very charming individual. A few months into running the ranch Jack attended a local cattle auction and his eyes settled on a pretty little local girl from another family that had settled in the area. With sweet talk and coercion he convinced that pretty little girl to marry him. She would never be the same again.

Jackson shifted uncomfortably on Mary's couch. For the life of him he couldn't understand why she was telling him this story. As if on cue, noting the confusion on his face, she stood up and, not saying a word, shuffled off into the dark interior of her home. Jackson heard her making her way to the kitchen where she was preparing another pot of coffee and decided this was a good a time as any for a break.

Standing up from the couch he stretched and walked to the door. The wounds from Sundance nagged at him as they still leaked a little blood under his shirt. Jackson slowly pulled his shirt away from his back and his chest so as not to have to deal with the material being blood-glued to his skin later. Stepping out onto the front stoop he meandered his way about.

The sun had set by now, the hours passing unnoticed. Jackson fired up a smoke as a few of the rez dogs came to snuff and sniff him. When he passed their muster the dogs made their way back to whatever they were doing before, chasing rabbits and groundhogs, snapping and biting each other. Just another day in the life of a rez dog. Jackson heard the back door of Mary's house open followed by the dull tinkle of kibble tossed out into the yard.

"Here's your dinner you flea bag rat bastards," he heard her call then the doors slams shut.

All around him shadowy canine shapes shifted and blurred as they scrambled to the kibble offered. More snapping and biting, fighting each other over every morsel as his gaze shifted to the night sky. The stars were so bright, like diamonds he could pluck from the air if he could just reach them. A chill settled in and it looked to be another crisp South Dakota evening. Finishing his smoke he turned and walked to the door again. Opening the front door he stepped into the living room and noticed Mary had found her way back to her chair and was waiting for him. Jackson strolled casually over to his spot on the sofa where another cup of hot coffee was waiting for him, placed on the end table by Mary as he was catching his breath outside.

Seating himself and about to speak she quickly cuts him off, "Doesn't make much sense to you does it Jackson? The story I just told you?"

"Gotta admit, Mary, I have no clue where you are going with this but then, in the four years I've known you, when did I ever have a clue?"

"About never," she cackled, "and I'm sure not going to give you one now."

Jackson only nodded his head as Mary settled herself into her favorite chair. Years of life on the reservation, the toll of being native in a country full of people who simply could not or would not understand, showed in the roughly cut lines in her face.

Although Mary Bloody Heart might look like what she was expected to she certainly didn't act it. Mary had no problem saying what needed to be said to whoever needed to hear it, and damn the consequences.

She was never one to interject her opinion in any conversation, you had to ask her first. But if someone was dumb enough to ask the question, they best be well prepared for the answer. Thinking back, remembering some of their first conversations together, Jackson recalled telling her how desperate he was to find where he came from. To come to an understanding of who he was. He told her his feelings when he looked in the mirror and the sense of not knowing who was looking back at him. Jackson was beginning to regret revealing some of those secrets, beginning to regret asking some of those questions.

Mary lit another cigarette and sipped her coffee. From the kitchen came the sounds of her drip coffee pot chugging and spitting as it washed cold water over ground coffee. Seemed every few months she had a new one. Lots of people showed up at Mary's place and she never failed to have a pot of coffee hot and ready. These new coffee makers couldn't take the abuse brewing day in and day out every day for months. They burned up eventually, some sooner than others. Someone visiting would take notice the latest version was on the way out and a new one would arrive at her door. It was something that had been going on for years and had become commonplace.

From across the room Mary took notice of an almost unheard chuckle escape from Jackson. He was staring off into nowhere, lost it seemed, in the story. Mary sat in silence, allowing him to ponder, to contemplate what she had revealed so far.

She questioned herself as she often did, "should she go further, can he deal with what is yet to come?"

"Well, he asked," she thought, "What he does with it will be up to him."

Jackson was pondering, lost deep inside himself, completely unaware she was paying very close attention to each and every detail washing across his face. He was thinking about the people at Chases Sundance and what they were doing about now.

Jackson knew many saw him leave with Mary and he also knew many were envious and jealous. In their self centered minds they deserved to be sitting here, certainly not him. These arrogant few were so sure Mary was revealing the secrets of the universe to him, that she was sharing some magical, mystical information. If they only knew. At the thought of them practically salivating over their desire to know, the chuckle Mary heard so faintly drifted through the smoke-laden, coffee-scented air of her living room.

Mary set her coffee cup down on the end table next to her and snubbed out her cigarette. Promptly lighting another she gently cleared her throat. The rasp and crackle of her dry, hoarse cough brought Jackson back to the moment. Once again aware of his surroundings. As his eyes slowly focused once again on her he thought, she's been watching me this whole time.

Mary had her hint of a smile barely lifting the corners of her mouth. He could almost hear her in his mind laughing at him. "Yes, I heard it all," her eyes seemed to say as she returned to the story she had begun hours before.

Jack Ryder, raised by a very cruel man, TJ Rocker, became an even crueler man as he aged. He returned from war much, much worse, so much more twisted by far. He missed the joys he found in murder. There was no one to kill now, no one to maim, to torture. Well, none in general society that was. There was always the reservation and no one seemed to care what happened on the reservations. This was Oklahoma in the late sixties. While the rest of the country was swimming in peace and love there wasn't much peace or love on the Oklahoma prairie, especially around the Ryder ranch.

Jack searched the local area and found that pretty little girl he met at auction. She didn't remain a pretty little girl for very long. He married her young and broke her early. To say Jack abused her would be vast understatement. He spent three years in the jungles of Vietnam feeding every dark fantasy his mind can imagine. By the time he left, his skills in the destruction of a human being, both physically and psychologically, had been honed to a fine, sharp edge. Inquisitors from the age of witch burning would have turned away in horror and disgust.

The years rolled on as he satisfied his lust for blood when he saw fit. In that time his wife became a broken shell of the girl she had once been. During these years she would birth three children for him, all boys, and Jack would teach them to be as hateful, as mean, as cruel and ugly as he was. Those three boys would bring a reign of terror to the Oklahoma prairie. Under their father's tutelage they learned to hate. They learned to rape, to maim and kill, and they learned to enjoy it. For those living on the reservations surrounding the Ryder ranch when those boys were on the prowl it was best to get inside and lock the doors. No one went anywhere alone, either male or female, because the Ryder boys didn't care. Age was of no consequence either. Anyone native and alone, as far as the Ryder boys were concerned, was fair game. To them that was all it was, a game, and they challenged each other to see who could do worse than the others.

By 1986 the Ryder boys were 15, 16 and 17 respectively. All they knew all they enjoyed, was pain. Inflicting pain on someone, anyone. They fed on it, thrived on it, existed only for it. Jack Ryder had done a great job teaching these three boys to be monsters. Sometime after lunch on an early July morning the boys went hunting. At about the same time Annie Themal was waking up alone in the tall prairie grass and she knew she was in trouble.

The previous evening Annie and several others from the reservation had gone together to party. There wasn't much of anything else to do out on the Oklahoma prairie but drink, smoke dope and try desperately, if only for a few hours, to escape the reality of life on an Indian reservation. To try to forget the soul crushing poverty, and the dismal lack of hope for any future. Each day was another reminder of just how far the original people had come from who they had been. A reminder that life was a prison camp, and some things had to be done out of the need to survive.

Why anyone wanted to survive no one could explain. Many didn't and chose to leave this horrid existence. Daily it seemed someone was overdosing, hanging themselves, shooting themselves or moving away. Every day another story would drift across the reservation of yet another teenager who just couldn't make it anymore. Either fast suicide by rope or a bullet, or slow suicide by drugs and alcohol. Annie and those she ran with had chosen the latter.

Another night spent on the open prairie chugging whatever whiskey can be stolen or bought, paid for at times with their young flesh. Another night of smoking, inhaling, snorting, whatever is brought to the fire. It didn't matter what it was, someone always found something. There were so many offspring of brother and sister, cousin and cousin, father and daughter unions that there were a lot of mentally disturbed people on the rez. Because of this people were always heading over to Indian Health Services for mental health issues. The solution invariably was to drug them.

New drugs were always coming out on the market but they had to be tested somewhere first. What better place than a closed community, isolated from the rest of the country? A ready-made laboratory of people no one gave a damn about anyway. Practically every known drug on the market was tested first on the reservations and the recipients of these drugs had no idea they were the guinea pigs. They were handed something for free and if there were side effects it was considered acceptable in the name of science. Many of these drugs found their way to the all night parties on the prairie and those ingesting them had no idea what they were taking. They wouldn't have cared if they did.

This party was like every party before and after. The whiskey flowed freely while pills wrapped hastily in plastic bags and wads of paper were drawn determinedly from pockets with a look of "see what I got?" No one asked what it was. All that was heard was "hey, gimme some." Late into the early morning hours the party raged as someone passed out here or someone passed out there. Annie found herself wandering away from the fire. She stumbled over something, probably a skeleton of some long dead animal, and fell to the ground with a hard thud. There she lay until the beating sun of the hot Oklahoma afternoon roused her from her drug-induced drunken slumber.

Alone, those she had come with had long since gone. They didn't bother looking for Annie because it simply didn't matter. She went were she went and if she showed up then she showed up, if she didn't, oh well. Annie forced her body into a sitting position and looked around as she tried to get her bearings. She soon realizing the bucket of shit she was in and that she had to find a way to crawl out. Using the sun to judge where she was Annie painfully rose to her feet and began walking, and within a few miles she came to the black top road she was looking for. Several miles down this road and she would be home. All she had to do was make it. Alone, 16 years old, she placed one foot in front of the other and did what she had to do.

From all around her a throaty rumble filled the hot summer air. Gazing behind her she could just make out the shape of a pickup truck, coming fast and hard through the shimmering waves of heat. Within seconds she recognized that truck. For a moment she thought about running but the thought floated away almost as fast as it entered her mind. She realized running was pointless. Conceding, she collapsed onto the berm to wait.

The driver of the pickup Annie had recognized in the distance saw her at about the same time. Mashing the accelerator to the floor with his companions whooping and hollering beside him the driver headed straight for her. Screeching to a halt beside her they jumped from the pickup in a rush. Grabbing her they tied her and tossed her into the truck bed then covered her with a well worn, bloodied canvas tarp. The Ryder boys had found Annie Themal.

120°
CHAPTER TWELVE

Life as an Indian isn't easy, life as a mix blood only adds to the pain. The full bloods are always looking for someone to punish because someone had to pay for their turmoil and anguish. Someone did this to them and if they couldn't get to the immediate culprit any surrogate replacement would do.

Every mix blood growing up on the reservation knows they are a target. Every day would be spent fighting. Every day blood would spill. The choice they had to make was if it would be their blood, or the antagonist of the moment. Annie learned this lesson young and she learned this lesson fast. Sixteen years old, and she couldn't recall one happy memory.

Word got out quickly to every district and hell-hole corner of the reservation that it was always best to leave Annie Themal alone. In a fight you might beat her. No doubt you could get your shots in, but sooner or later she would get up. Sooner or later a knock would come at the door. Opening that door would reveal a pissed off black and blue Annie Themal, usually with a baseball bat or anything else she could get her hands on. She never waited for a hi, bye or kiss my ass. When the door opened she swung and she always hit what she was swinging at. Annie would keep hitting until her thirst for revenge was satisfied. After a few of these encounters, the rest of the kids learned what you do to Annie Themal she was bringing it back. When she did, compared to whatever someone did to her, it would be a whole lot worse.

Annie's mother Gertrude Themal was, by all definition of the standards, a total success of the boarding schools. Gertrude was the typical middle aged, full blood, native woman – really short and really fat. The best way to describe her was round. She seemed to roll instead of walk and she kept her long hair tied up in a severe knot at the back of her head. Fully indoctrinated into the dogma and doctrine of organized religion from her years in the boarding schools Gertrude Themal was the quintessential born again christian. She didn't go anywhere without her bible and no one could have a conversation with her where Jesus didn't come into it somewhere. She cloaked herself in everything that ever is or was christianity, and wore it as though her belief was a suit of armor protecting her from the violence that was a part of everyday life on the reservation.

Gertrude married late in life when she was about 40 years old. The local minister of her church surprised her with his request for matrimony. He was more than few years her senior but she immediately accepted. It was well known she had had a crush on this particular minister for years and it was why she had rejected every other marriage proposal brought to her. She was waiting on her true love, and as if the prayer was answered by Jesus himself it finally happened.

Gertrude married Pastor Liam McIntyre in a small ceremony attended by a few of her close bible thumping friends. As happy as she was at that moment her happiness couldn't compare to Pastor McIntyre who was beside himself with glee.

Liam McIntyre was from Scotland and his parish sent him to America because of his predilections. Into his sixties now Pastor McIntyre had a few appetites only he, the superiors of his parish, and several of the children on the reservation knew about. A whip thin man with red hair and pale skin, Pastor McIntyre liked children, young children, and not in the way an older man is supposed to like young children. It was getting harder and harder for him, as he aged, to hunt and catch those little kiddies. The solution to the problem in his mind was to have one all of his own. Pastor McIntyre was well aware of Gertrude's crush on him and it seemed the perfect means to an end.

Most folks don't understand it isn't the cream of the christian crop that winds up on the reservation teaching all these lost savages about the mercy and love of Jesus Christ. Most of those sent to the reservations were sent there as a punishment.

The reservations were used as the last outpost, the final destination, for those few who simply couldn't keep their hands to themselves, or their genitals in their pants. Some were child molesters and sexual predators and some were ardent interpreters of the bible, who believed literally every word they read in it. Those who never hesitated to beat parishioners into submission, showing their true evil nature. These were the special ones sent to teach the lost Indian tribes. They taught the tribes alright, taught them all about lies, hypocrisy, abuse, self destruction, and self loathing.

Such was the case with Pastor Liam McIntyre and he was as bad as any who had come before him. Within weeks of marrying Gertrude she became pregnant and Pastor McIntyre never touched her again. Gertrude gave birth to a daughter, Pastor McIntyre's favorite, and they named her Annie. By the time she reached five years of age the sexual abuse had begun. He continued that abuse until Annie reached her teenage years, when he lost interest in her because she had grown too old for his penchants. That in no way lessened the emotional scars that burned inside her, scars that caused her to drop his name and return to her mother's.

Not that Annie was any happier with her mother. Gertrude knew what had been happening but she chose not to admit it, even to herself. Admitting the abuse of her daughter would bring the house of cards that was her religious conviction crashing down around her and Gertrude could not bring herself to do that. She ignored what was blatant, choosing instead to blame her daughter, insisting Annie was the cause of Pastors McIntyre's transgressions. He was just a man after all. What was he supposed to do with a young girl flaunting herself at him? Granted, how a five year old girl could flaunt was beyond explanation but it worked as an excuse for Gertrude.

Eleven years later Annie found herself bouncing down a BIA road, trussed and tied in the bed of the Ryder boy's pickup. Hung over and feeling mildly the side effects of the drugs she consumed, time no longer had any meaning. Time simply was.

The pickup came to a quick and sudden halt and the Ryder boys climbed out. The tarp was quickly ripped off and thrown to the side and she found herself face-to-face with a triplet of walking demons. Grabbed roughly and thrown over a shoulder, she was carried into the barn, stripped of all her clothes and tied spread eagle between four posts buried deep in the soft sand of the Oklahoma prairie. Annie vacantly stared at the wooden joists of the barn frame above her, inside the Ryder's barn where no prying eyes could see.

For three days she lived in that barn. For three days the Ryder boys did what they wanted, when they wanted, how they wanted. They raped her, brutalize her, tortured and beat her, for three long days. On one of those days Jack Ryder himself came to carve off a piece or two. He knew full well what those boys of his were doing out in that barn because he taught them how to do it. Annie wasn't the first nor would she be the last, she just happened to be the latest.

Somehow she survived those three days and was found later alongside the scrub grass lining the ditch of a BIA road where the Ryder clan had dumped her, like garbage. The reservation police brought Annie to IHS and one look at the condition she was in they flew her immediately to the hospital in the city. A month and a half she lay in intensive care as life slowly returned to her broken, battered body.

Another month on the general ward and Annie walked out of the hospital into a cab provided by the tribal council to bring her home. But Annie Themal was never the same person after that. She looked and sounded like Annie Themal but inside she was broken, and she was pregnant. Two and a half odd months later Annie sat beside Mary Bloody Heart at a prairie party, sipping a beer, telling her story.

Mary had grown up at the knee of her Grandfather, a well respected, well known medicine man. She learned early how to sit and how to listen. Annie couldn't explain why she was telling all this to Mary, a woman she had just met, and neither could Mary explain why she was listening. Late in the evening Annie finished her story and slowly drifted off back to wherever she had come from. Mary filed away what had been shared with her.

That was the last time Mary Bloody Heart ever let alcohol pass her lips. She broke up her powwow dance outfit the very next day and gave away the pieces to several different people. Never again would she dance. Never again would she attend another prairie party.

The months passed by as Annie's belly continued to grow. Nine full months, and a few days later, Annie gave birth to a ten pound baby boy. How that child came into this world with ten fingers and ten toes no one could explain. How that child wasn't mentally retarded or suffered some physical ailment the doctors could only describe as miraculous.

Into this world he came as healthy as he could be, screaming to raise the dead. The boy wanted the world to know he had made it but Annie had no intention of keeping him. A few months back she had completed the paperwork for him to be placed for adoption.

Most of the tribe knew what had happened to Annie and they knew who did it, but nothing was ever done about it. Annie was fully aware of how a bastard son of the Ryder's would be treated. She knew the life he would have if she raised him on the reservation. She knew every day would be a living hell for this boy, that he would be beaten relentlessly. Annie did the only thing she could do, what she thought was the best thing to do.

Before placing her son in the hands of strangers, she insisted that her one condition was met and honored, the condition she was allowed to name this child. She gave her son her family's name, the name of Themal. For his first name she called him Jackson.

Because she didn't know which one of Jack's sons was the father.

130°
CHAPTER THIRTEEN

Jackson was, by this time a complete and total wreck. Tears streamed down his chest soaking his t-shirt and he found it hard to breathe, gasping as he sucked in the air his body so desperately required. From his earliest memories all Jackson knew was pain. Suffering, abuse, neglect. Every day of his life spent desperately seeking something to cling to, some normalcy, some sense of reality.

Now learning of the pain his mother suffered, understanding suddenly pain wasn't just in his memory, pain was in his blood. Pain was all he was to his very genetics, to the core of what made Jackson a living, breathing creature.

Jackson knew hate. With what he suffered through at the hands of sexual predators in the foster care system Jackson knew hate very well, but this was so far beyond, so much more. His very soul howled for retribution, to repay exponentially worse than what had been given. To watch them suffer, hurt and bleed. Loathing, disgust, and revulsion throbbed in every beat of his heart.

Mary watched thinking, this is killing him. She could see it etched so harshly across his face. Did he have the strength to live through this? After everything he had been through the last two days this was so much more. This was information about his essence.

Jackson may have been released from the Sundance circle but he was still dancing. It was as if what she was sharing with him was returning him to the tree he hung in for so long, almost as if he never left. As much as it hurt her she knew this was yet another circle Jackson had to complete. If he survived it he would be a different man. What kind of man he became because of it she wasn't able to say, she couldn't possibly know. The journey was Jackson's to make. As if reading his very thoughts yet again Mary softly said, "No Jackson, that you can't do."

No coy pretending from him this time. He understood Mary knew exactly what was in his mind. As soon as he could, he was on his way to Oklahoma. Jackson would make the Ryder's pay for what they had done, not only to his mother but to Jackson himself. To his entire family. "Really Mary?" he sobbed a reply, "This time you're wrong. This time may be the only time since I've known you, that you are so very wrong. In the next few days someone is going to die."

Mary only shook her head. In response to the thirst for revenge practically dripping from Jackson she said, "Your mother already took care of it. There isn't a Ryder left alive today, not one. Hasn't been for years. The ranch is in ruins and the house is no longer livable. The land has returned to the Oklahoma prairie. The State eventually repossessed the land as there is no one alive they can find to pay the yearly taxes. All of the cattle were rounded up and sold at auction to pay off as much of the debts as possible. No doubt you go make yourself known as an heir to the Ryder's them lawyers will be coming after you to settle what remains. There is one other thing you have forgotten Jackson."

Calmed ever so slightly with the knowledge his mother had sought out and reaped her revenge Jackson asked curiously, "What's that Mary? What have I forgotten?"

"Take your shirt off Jackson," she requested.

An odd request, especially now it seemed. Regardless he stood to comply and slowly, gingerly he peeled his shirt away from his wounds. First his chest so he could slide his t-shirt over his head then ease the cotton material from his back. "Look down at your chest Jackson. See the wounds there. Really see them," Mary instructed further.

Again he did as instructed. He noticed how deep, how unnecessarily large the holes in his chest were. He knew the wounds on his back were just as large, just as deep. He saw the red of inflamed torn skin surrounding these massive circular lacerations. He glimpsed muscle beneath as the wounds trickled blood. "They don't wash off," Mary said quietly.

Jackson collapsed on to the couch at the sheer revelation of what Mary had just said, hitting him like a sledgehammer. Jackson was a Sundancer and for the remainder of his life he would always be a Sundancer. He knew he would never forget the ordeal he lived through hanging from the Tree of Life, but it wasn't until this very moment that the weight of his actions began to be comprehended. The sheer enormity of the responsibility and Jackson lost his ability to speak. He could only stare at Mary dumbfounded. She could not have picked up a brick and hit him harder.

"Time for a break," Mary said, sliding herself again from her chair. Jackson again stood and turned for the front door, slipping his t-shirt back on. Stepping outside into the ink black night he stared ahead. Too much coffee, too many cigarettes. His head was buzzing, the holes in his chest and back throbbing. All that Mary revealed to him was crashing inside him like waves generated by a hurricane, slamming back and forth inside his mind. With no sense of time as he stood there, the seconds passed like centuries. Breaking him from his reverie Jackson heard Mary's voice softly call through the screen door, "Come on back in and let's finish this."

Finish this? Jackson thought with anguish, christ, there's more? How much more of this can I take? But he did turn and made his way begrudgingly back up the concrete steps through her door and returned to the couch. On the end table is a cold glass of water. "Figured you had enough coffee" she chuckled.

Jackson recognized her attempt at humor. She was trying desperately to lighten the air but he wasn't having any of it. Mary recognized this too and once again settled herself comfortably to continue with her story.

"Where was I?" she asked, yet another stab at humor. Mary was nothing if not relentless. Continuing on with no regard for his response Mary began to complete her story, to finish her responsibility of sharing what she knew with Jackson. What was going to happen next when all was said and done, only time would tell.

Annie gave birth at Indian Health Service tended to by a doctor who didn't want to be there and a nurse more concerned with who she would be sleeping with than her patient. The birth itself was typical and what happened next was just as typical, in Third World countries, or on an Indian Reservation. The physician delivered Jackson into the nurse's impatient arms then returned to Annie where he immediately sterilized her.

She would never know what he had done, as many of the young women throughout Indian Country didn't know. Sterilization was common practice, instructed and demanded by those in much higher positions of authority than his. The physician did exactly what he had done many times before and would continue to do many more times in the future.

Annie signed the adoption papers after insuring her son carried the proper name. The nurses indifferently carted Jackson away and she knew she would never see him again. A small prayer for him was uttered softly as Annie slipped off into sleep. Three days after giving birth she was sent home. Annie had some work to do and she was anxious to get to it.

In the months preceding the birth of her son, Annie often wandered down to Ricky's Rez Shack. It was the only place on the reservation to buy groceries, gas and supplies. Funny thing about Ricky's Rez Shack, there was no Ricky. There was, in the late fifties and early sixties, until a local business man, Herman Hertzenberg, saw an opportunity.

Traveling among the reservations he bought as many of the reservation stores he could convince the owners to sell. Mr. Hertzenberg wasn't native, didn't have a drop in him. Herman's grandmother died at Auschwitz. His mother, also interned in the Nazi death camps, emigrated to the United States at the end of WW II bringing infant Herman with her. She was the victim of continuous rapes at the hands of her Nazi tormenters and Herman was the result.

Mr. Hertzenberg was a very shrewd business man. After placing the property deed in the name of a native man he knew, and was registered with the tribe, he owned the only establishment to purchase groceries for miles. Now he could charge whatever he wanted for his goods and either you paid the price or you went without.

Mr. Hertzenberg could not possibly care any less that he charged two and three times what an item usually retailed for. He didn't purchase these stores for charity, well that was the excuse he used. Considering the Nazi holocaust was founded on the genocide of the American Indian people, considering also what each race of people has suffered, one would think the two races could find common ground. Herman never considered it.

If anyone attempted to construct another store anywhere on the reservation Mr. Hertzenberg instructed his friends to burn it to the ground. No competition ever, and the only place closer than Ricky's was two hours away. While the people suffered Herman became a very wealthy man. When Herman died his sons inherited his wealth and business model, which they continue to practice.

Annie sat in the shade of an old cottonwood tree people watching, not that there were many people to watch. Mostly folks on the rez coming to buy what they needed, maybe filling up their cars and trucks with gas. Sometimes a lost stranger looking to figure out what corner of hell they have stumbled into and the fastest way to get out. All the while she watched.

During a hot afternoon in perusal of the general populace she noticed something she found quite interesting. There was the guy who drove the tanker truck delivering fuel to refill the underground storage tanks. He arrived every month the same day at about the same time. The tanker truck was a small one, not one of those big eighteen wheel jobbers. There weren't that many running vehicles on the reservation anyway and a small truck was all they needed. An idea began to grow in her mind.

Not one to forget when someone hurt her she remembered all too vividly what the Ryder's did to her. Annie wasn't one to buy into all the Jesus-loving-forgive-and-forget-turn-the-other-cheek bullshit. She had a simpler way of looking at things. Hurt her and she hurt you. Blacken her eye she blackened every inch she could beat on. Break her bones she removed parts of your body. In this way Annie had secured her place and those who knew her knew how dangerous she could be. Those who knew what the Ryder's did to her were waiting. The rez knew full well Annie was coming for revenge and hell was coming with her.

Watching the driver of the tanker truck Annie came up with a plan. The day she walked out of the hospital was the exact same day Ricky's Rez Shack received its fuel delivery. She could have left the clinic the next morning after giving birth but, feigning additional stress and pain, she convinced the staff to let her rest a few days longer. From the clinic she accepted the free taxi ride straight to Ricky's Rez Shack and arriving she noticed the tanker truck pulling in to refill the underground tanks.

Ricky's was pretty much deserted with the attendant Danny Crow inside. Outside, Dee Dee Cornflower was refilling the fuel tank of her beat up SUV, the Cornflower twins in the backseat. As the taxi drove off Dee Dee watched as the driver climbed down from the cab of the tanker truck and Annie walked up to him. Without a word spoken Annie removed the knife she has stolen from the clinic and plunged it deep into the truck driver's chest. After he fell she reached down, and, for good measure, to insure he was dead, she sliced his throat. Dee Dee Cornflower watched it all and did absolutely nothing. The tanker blocking his view, Danny Crow didn't see a thing.

Annie climbed up into the driver's seat and did a quick survey of the clutch and gears. Growing up on the reservation the kids learned early to drive anything with wheels. If they could reach the pedals they could drive it. This tanker was brand new and practically drove itself so it wasn't a problem for Annie. Quickly she found first gear and drove off into the Oklahoma sun.

Danny Crow happened to glance out the window of Ricky's Rez Shack about then and noticed the tanker pull away without first refilling the tanks. The next thing Danny Crow noticed was the body lying on the pavement and a spreading black pool of blood. Dee Dee Cornflower stepped through the glass doors offering her cash for the gas she pumped and didn't say a word. She casually dropped her money and exited Ricky's, walking straight to her vehicle. Climbing in she turned the key, shifted into drive and pulled away. Dee Dee Cornflower never even stopped to glance at the dead body lying in the middle of the parking lot. Danny Crow immediately called the reservation police.

Unfortunately for Danny the police were two districts over. Annie already knew this because before she left IHS she called a friend. The phone call was a preconceived signal to torch a dilapidated crop of warehouses that sat in the far corner of the reservation, long unused for anything more than parties and sex.

The fire became real big, real fast, scaring the living hell out of every officer on the force. Everyone was called in, to respond to the inferno those burning buildings were causing, as well as those who weren't on the day shift. The warehouses were easily forty five minutes from Ricky's Rez Shack so Annie had plenty of time to drive to the abandoned barn she had picked out a few weeks ago.

Arriving at the barn in under fifteen minutes she slipped out of the driver's seat and quickly pulled open the barn doors then jumped back into the truck. Driving slowly into the barn she left the truck running as she again jumped out and closed the barn doors tight. Leaving the driver's door open, sitting half in, half out of the truck, Annie cranked the A/C and waited. Occasionally she would walk the inside perimeter of the barn, peeking outside to see if anyone was around. The hours ticked by as daylight slowly faded to night.

No one had any idea where that tanker truck had gone and no one ever thought to check that barn. As the evening slipped into the early morning hours Annie again pried open the barn doors and slowly surveyed the area around her.

Seeing there was no one in sight she looked to the northeast where she could see the glow of the fire still burning. Chuckling she thought to herself, they finally put that snake pit to good use. Annie slid back into the driver's seat, pulled out of the barn and drove the tanker truck straight to the Ryder ranch.

She finally arrived around two a.m. and noticed all the lights in the house were off. The Ryder's were sound asleep in their beds. The ranch dogs noticed Annie at the end of the farm road and came to see what was about to happen. The dogs weren't a problem for her. Drugs, as prevalent as they are on the reservation, meant that ketamine was in no short supply, and a quick stop at the library gave her the dosage. She had already stored five pounds of ground meat in the barn, that she stolen from her mother's refrigerator before she went into the clinic to give birth. Dosing the meat she fed chunks to each of the dogs and in moments they were sound asleep.

Back behind the wheel Annie headed up to the Ryder house, the truck so new, the engine was quiet. Instinctively she knew to keep her foot lightly on the accelerator. Stopping at the edge of the house she got out and walked around to the back of the tanker.

For months she watched as the driver refilled the tanks at Ricky's Rez Shack and Annie knew exactly which valve to turn. Slowly gasoline began to trickle out as she ran back to the cab of the truck. At an idle, she drove in circles around and around the Ryder ranch house trailing gasoline, the fumes becoming thicker and thicker with each pass. The Oklahoma prairie being flat Annie had no problems or obstructions as she made her circles. In short time, the tanker was empty and she drove it over to the Ryder barn.

Parking at the barn Annie climbed down and turned to face the house. One other item she had stolen and stored in the barn, a Remington 870 pump action shotgun. With no remorse she began pumping rounds into the Ryder house. Refilling the chamber, another round. Quickly, four or five rounds later, lights began coming on as a light breeze blew from behind her, keeping the gasoline fumes directed at the house. Taking a cigarette and lighting it she waited, smoking.

In moments Jack Ryder exploded on to the front porch, seeing first the tanker truck then Annie Themal in front of it. "What the fuck is going on out here?" Jack Ryder bellowed. As his eyes met hers Annie slowly, almost leisurely, tossed her burning cigarette into the gasoline pooling on the ground.

With an all encompassing, massive, exploding whoosh, the gasoline lit up all at once. The explosion blew Jack Ryder back into the house, rocked the Ryder's barn, shook the tanker truck and knocked Annie on her ass. Standing up and shaking herself off she began to hear the screams as the Ryder's, every last one of them, began to be cooked alive. For the first time in almost a year Annie Themal smiled.

Turning back to the tanker she walked around the truck to the Ryder's barn. Opening the doors she returned to the truck cab and climbed behind the wheel for the last time.

Driving the truck into the barn under the beams, crushing the four posts buried in the Oklahoma sand, Annie parked and shut off the truck. She climbed down and in a moment found a length of rope as long as she needed.

Walking around to the rear of the tanker she climbed up the ladder bolted on the back. She reached up and tossed the rope over the furthest beam, giving herself enough slack to tie a makeshift noose. Annie slipped the noose around her neck and stepped off.

140°
CHAPTER FOURTEEN

Jackson sat and stared. His hand holding the partially smoked cigarette in his fingers froze. He was frozen in time, in space, between reality and the surreal.

Emotions rocketed through him, propelled through him, in rapid succession. Anger, pride, rage, love, hate, sympathy, regret. Each crushing in their weight for brief agonizing moments, suddenly replaced by the next. He had no words. For a space of time incalculable he simply was.

Mary did what most Elders did in those moments. Rousing herself from her chair she glanced over at him saying, "I'm heading off to sleep for a bit Jackson. It's late, much too late to drive over to Chases. When I get up I'll take you back." Her words barely registered with him. Mary had completed her responsibility.

For whatever reason on a hot July night Annie Themal shared her story with Mary. Knowledge that she carried for many years as though it were a chest wrapped in chains, securely locked, until time came for her to pass on the key. Not knowing at the time, nor through the years to come, who, how or why.

Through the years she held the key precious. The time to pass on her closely guarded knowledge came with Jackson's release from the Tree of Life. It was his turn to carry this knowledge. It belonged to him after all and it was only right he be given his legacy. It would be up to Jackson what he chose to do with it. Well into the early morning hours, around 3 a.m., Mary shuffled off to get some desperately needed rest. She had done what she had to do and she felt for Jackson.

Jackson remained planted. Not moving from his place on the couch as the cigarette in his fingers slowly burned, finally snuffed out by the flesh on his fingers. He barely took notice of it. Everything he had experienced these last three days was crashing and thundering inside him.

The first day of Sundance piercing through his chest. His second day of Sundance hanging from the Tree of Life. Now this his third day and into the fourth. His prayers answered, now understanding who he was and where he came from. How could he process all that was churning inside him? There was a lot of truth in the statement, be careful what you wish for, it might be granted you.

Three hours later Mary rose from her bed. Like many of the elderly, she required little sleep. A few hours here, a quick nap there. Seemed the older a person became the more the soul feels a need to record each and every moment, as if the soul knows the days are short. Knows that this journey of experiencing reality as a human was almost over. She glided into her living room practically silent in her slippers and saw Jackson was in the same position as when she left him. His eyes were vacant as his mind drifted and returned to bits of the last three days.

"Let me get some coffee then we'll head over to camp. That be alright with you?" she asked. As if someone had let off a stick of dynamite Mary's voice hammered him back to now and his mind abruptly quieted itself. Jackson was completely unaware of the time that had passed. As far as he was concerned she left the room seconds ago. He suddenly realized three hours had gone by. Shaking off the robe of shock and confusion he had wrapped himself in he replied leadenly, "Sure Mary."

Reality slowly returned as Jackson became aware again of his surroundings. Tenderly he peeled away the butt of the cigarette blistered to his fingers, the pain hardly registering. Mary returned with coffee some minutes later and in silence they sipped, smoked and watched as the sun rose, painting Mary's windows first in gold then yellow, lighting the hazy, smoke-laden living room.

As if the conversation had never ended Mary said to him, "I can't tell you what to do with this information. I have no answers for you, only direction. Where you go with this, what you do with it, will be completely up to you. I will be here for you as I have always been and I can share with you what little I have come to understand. The choice will always be yours, Jackson. You know where the answers lie, how to get to them. The best I can do is lead you to the box that holds those answers. It is up to you to find the strength to make the journey to the box. To open that box and find the courage to deal with what's inside.

"Choices, either way, they have consequences. There is a price to pay for doing something as there is also a price to pay for not doing it. The trick is to decide which price you are willing to pay. Each person has to decide on their own, no one can make the decision for them. Allowing someone to make that decision for you is foolish. This isn't a boo-boo you can put a Band-Aid on, this is your soul. Does it really seem wise to allow someone else to tell you what to do with your soul?

"How do you know someone is fake, Jackson?" Mary asked, not waiting for him to respond. "You ask them a question you already know the answer to. Everybody knows a little something about this thing or that. Everyone has an interest, a hobby or a curiosity they have satisfied. With that satisfaction of curiosity comes appreciation for the thing they sought an answer to, knowledge of that thing. When someone else speaks of that thing to them they know if that individual is real or just flapping their lips. Kind of like that Nate Winter you brought out here."

Jackson gazed down at the floor sheepishly. He understood he was responsible for Nate Winter. He spoke for him, vouched for him by bringing him to Sundance. Anything Nate did, everything he said, reflected immediately back on Jackson. When Nate screwed up Jackson was as much at fault. He knew he should have found another way to get to Sundance this year, knew he had taken the easiest way presented. As Mary observed, there was a price to pay one way or the other.

Drawing him out of his reflection Mary said, "You are well aware of who my Grandfather was, Jackson. Pretty much everybody knew him. When he died they came from all over the world, the line of cars stretching for miles and miles. What you don't know Jackson, what most don't know, was he didn't die from old age, although he was well over a hundred years old. No one ever really knew his age and he never said. What he died from was a broken heart.

"My grandfather spent his life trying desperately to help his people. He gave his life from a very young age to serve. It was a hard life, a demanding life and in the end those he loved so much were the ones who killed him. Not literally of course, although they may as well have.

"He could have been a very rich man here on the reservation or anywhere else. He could have had anything he wanted at anytime. A big house, fancy car, lots of money. He chose instead to live humbly. A small house off by itself in the district. A little two-bedroom, basic furniture, food, firewood for the winter. He lived simply. Whatever was given to him if he didn't need it he gave it away. In the end they were breaking into his home stealing the few things he did have. His radio, his food, sometimes his firewood. All they had to do was ask and he would have gladly given it all to them.

"You are aware of the sacred ceremonies of my people and you have been permitted to endure a few of them. Why do you think, when asked, every one of these self proclaimed medicine men start the list of our ceremonies with the sweat lodge? How did the most common of ceremonies become the most sacred? How did the most sacred become forgotten?"

He allowed the question to sink in a moment. Mary was going somewhere here and was giving him time to ponder her questions. She knew full well he didn't have the answer and he wasn't about to make one up. A few moments passed like this, a quick pull on her cigarette, a sip of coffee, Jackson thinking.

"The most sacred of all our ceremonies is the c'anupa," Mary continues, "The joining of the stem and the bowl, bringing all of creation back together as one. Simply holding this sacred item, gazing at it, is a ceremony. What is sacred Jackson?" Again, not waiting for an answer, "Sacred is doing that which isn't ordinary, doing the unusual. When it becomes ordinary it becomes commonplace, and sacred is never commonplace.

"Somehow the sweat lodge has replaced the c'anupa in the sacred ceremonies. The sweat lodge is the first of all ceremonies, the ceremony that begins every other ceremony. All indigenous cultures worldwide have the sweat lodge and always have, in one form or another. Before the c'anupa there was the sweat lodge. Even the whites have a sweat lodge although they refer to it as a sauna. That's a sweat lodge if done in the right way. But the c'anupa? That is my people's gift, given to us to care for. No other culture worldwide was given this beautiful gift.

"Somehow it has become commonplace, forgotten, and used as though in addition to. Used by those who haven't earned the privilege. This is why there are no real medicine people anymore, no real Elders. What you have now are men like David Chases.

"Chases could have been, but he long since chose not to. He uses everything he was given to do what he does. You have seen him Jackson, you have watched him and how he does things. You noticed the way people behaved towards you after you gave so much of yourself. After you suffered so much for them they shunned you. As you suffered they cried for you, they cried with you. The very next day they threw stones at you. Why Jackson?

"When you were finally released from the Tree of Life and Roddy brought you to your tent, David had a meeting with all of the other dancers under the arbor. As you lay sleeping he instructed the other dancers you lied, that the Tree of Life speaks only to him, never to anyone else. Does that make any sense to you Jackson? Isn't that why we go to the tree? So it will speak to us?

"Chases met with Junior before you went back to your camp. I assume Junior was in your camp when you got back? Junior was told you failed, was told you quit, that you walked out of the Sundance circle. David told him specifically. By doing so David knew he would talk about it with Nate and the others and eventually the word would spread throughout the camp.

"David sees you as a threat Jackson. I know and I am aware you think you aren't, but he sees what he could have been in you. Now he feels he has to destroy you. Of course, he never forgot you defying him your first year here. He never forgave that one either. You stood up to him and very few do. You looked deep inside yourself and did what was right. You did what most could not do, you said no. He knows he can't say the same thing and he is jealous of you."

Jackson was listening intently. He thought he understood how devious a man Chases was but he never gave much thought to why. He began to feel pity for the man who was so insecure, so weak, so desperate to be seen as someone special, and who wanted to maintain the carefully built shadow of what he wanted to be. He was beginning to understand Chases was a sad, pathetic, broken man.

"You see the damage Chases has wrought now, don't you, Jackson?" Mary continues, "How those so lost have come to depend on him. He is leading them deeper into the forest of confusion and many will never find their way out. This is exactly what he wants. Before they wanted him, now they need him. They can't survive without him. Like a parasite he attaches himself to them, until removing him will kill them.

"Their minds and spirits are broken and corrupted by his lies. Whatever he instructs, whatever he says, they immediately believe. Regardless what they see with their own eyes, they prefer to believe what they hear. Watching as you hung in that tree for so long, watching as you came crashing to the ground was something momentous but in less than 24 hours later it was all forgotten.

"This is what killed my grandfather, what broke his heart, knowing there was no way he could fix it. The people consciously choose to be blind, choose to listen to those who feed off them. The predators feast, and the prey doesn't stand a chance. Willingly offering themselves to what is eating them alive.

"You are a mix blood with more white features than native. You're not from the reservation and didn't grow up with your People and as far as anyone is concerned you will always be seen as white. All they know is what they hear, because they choose not to see.

"I see you, Jackson. I have come to know you. With men like Chases out to destroy you it's doubtful many others will really know you. This is why you and those like you will never be accepted among the people. They know Chases, they even know what he does. They don't know you. They don't know your history anymore than you did. You are removed from the people.

"Look closely at the things he teaches them, things like don't ask questions. What a ridiculous thing to say. Yet, they believe him. They hang on to his every word as though he is their god. No longer just a man, he has become practically Jesus himself.

"How is anyone to learn anything if they don't ask questions? Yes, it is best to sit and listen as the Elders speak. In this way you learn so much, but, in this learning, questions will arise. If you listen long enough the answers to many of those questions will be given, but what about those that aren't? How do you find those answers? Isn't that the role of the Elders? Aren't they supposed to guide? Not instruct, other than protocols and procedures of course, but to advise on the individual journey. We each make the journey alone, but the Elders made it first. A little advice can go a long way to creating understanding. Unfortunately, those like Chases see this as an opportunity.

"Some years ago a young man came to see Chases and as usual I was sitting in his living room listening. That young man was much like you, Jackson, growing up away from his people, not knowing where he came from. He, too, had a vision and was looking for direction. He spoke of how one evening as he slept...

...he awakens on a island, way up in the north among the Alaskan people. It is a cold day, the air forming mist as he breaths. On the island are dozens and dozens of totem poles, the grass a bright green, the sky above him blue and clear. He finds himself standing in the center of the totem poles, they are all around him. He hears cracking and splitting as the totem poles begin to come apart. All of the animal figures and creatures carved into the poles separate and they begin to dance around him, to dance for him. They dance to welcome him home, to welcome him back to his People.

"How is that young man ever to find answers to what that vision means, if he doesn't ask.? Chases can't tell him what it means, what he is being shown or instructed to do. The best he can do is make something up, pretend the instructions he gives come from the spirit world, which is exactly what he did, and that young man was instantly lost. No one knows where he is today or what happened to him. I like to think he found his way home to his people and that he is dancing with those totem poles.

"I sit around the fires and camps of many people out there Jackson. I listen as people are told not to talk about these things, as though it's all a big secret you aren't supposed to know. But isn't that why you came here in the first place? Isn't that why you are sitting here?

"Plastic medicine people commanding others not talk about things outside of their council, needy people forced to return to them, as though they are the only source of information available. Keeps them coming back, which is exactly what they want, to have them coming back. Bringing gifts, bringing money. The fakes never really giving or showing anything real. Smoke and mirrors, it's all an illusion built to create need but never to satisfy that need. Like sitting down to a meal, when someone is full they get up from the table. By forcing the people to remain hungry they will never leave the table. They will continue to dine at empty plates and false food.

"Those wounds on your chest, Jackson in several months they will heal and become scars, always reminding you of what you have done for the People. Those who are so sure of themselves will tell you they must be kept hidden, that no one is permitted to see them. In one respect they are right. Those scars are not for public display to flaunt as though you are saying, 'look what I did!' But hiding them is just as bad, as though you are ashamed of what you have done.

"Many have forgotten why they were hidden in the first place, have forgotten it wasn't until the seventies we were allowed to openly practice our beliefs. Men like my grandfather purposefully hid ceremonies because until 1975 it was illegal and we could have gone to prison. For praying! Here in this land they like to call free where they teach their children this society is based on freedom of religion. Teaching their children of how the Puritans were persecuted for their religious beliefs and left England so they could pray like they wanted to without being killed, then turn around and do the exact same thing everywhere they go.

"For a very long time our ceremonies and proof of our ceremonies was hidden, but before the christians came they never were. Our ceremonies were tribal then and many Nations didn't know how we prayed. Not because they were hidden, but because they didn't know us. The scars would be there on the bare chests of our men if they saw them. Our lodges would be standing if they came across them.

"How is it the christians are allowed to build a church on every corner of every street, publicly displaying their religious beliefs, but we must hide ours and pretend it's a big secret? Because of men like Chases and the things he teaches people. They take what he says and spread it like manure and believe it because it came from him and those like him when none of it is true. Practically everybody knows about Sundance, the sweat lodge, most of our ceremonies as well as those of other Nations. Instructing each other that they are not allowed to talk about them is ridiculous. When they are telling each other they can't talk about it don't they realize they are talking about it?

"We aren't a secret society although we do have societies we keep secret. The basics are known about and practiced by other tribes. The same is true that the spiritual ways of other tribes are practiced here.

"The Peyote way, the Midewiwin way, the way of the Longhouse, the way of the Kiva, something is known about all of them. Each is practiced in many places where they originated and among other people. We are no longer our own People with our own country. No longer tribally isolated, praying in individual manners. Our ways as well as other tribal ways have crossed the oceans, as some of their ways have come here. Like christianity, god help us all.

"You, Jackson," Mary said, "you're different and you know that. We have talked about it many times. That difference is part of why you suffer as you do and always will. I don't know enough about your Shawnee People to say how they would handle it, to have the dreams you have had, to lead the life you have. If you were born here as Lakota we would have cried for you, we would have mourned for you. My Grandfather was like you are, and I remember the hard bitter life he lived. A beautiful life in some ways, but such pain and misery also.

"One in ten million children may be born what you are Jackson, entire generations may pass before one like you walks again. Your kind is known to every indigenous culture worldwide through out time, but it's more difficult today, as there is no frame of reference for you in the minds of others, especially within organized religion.

"Yes, you are human, Jackson, as anyone else, but you are not like everyone else. A man isn't a woman and a woman isn't a man although both are human, just different types of human. And you are a different type of human. Those who pretend they are like you are courting disaster. That's a level of insanity beyond words.

"Some may come to this spiritual way of life and learn some things, protocols and procedures. The medicine only comes from the Ancients, the ancestors on the other side.

Maybe at some point in their lives the Ancients will gift a person with a medicine to carry. What you are you were born to be. There is no teaching of this. There are no paths to learning it.

"How can someone who isn't what you are teach you to be what they can't understand? That is like a man trying to teach a woman how to be pregnant. All you can learn is how to live with it, to accept it and with that acceptance learn you will never be fully accepted."

Finishing her cigarette Mary rose from her chair, disappearing into the bowels of her home. Forty five minutes later she reappeared fully clothed and ready to go. More a statement than a question, she said, "You ready, Jackson?"

"Yeah okay, sure, Mary. Ready when you are," was his almost listless reply.

He helped her down the concrete steps to her waiting car and once again they raced down the gravel BIA roads, but he barely noticed her breakneck speed. Turning onto Chases' property she maneuvered deftly around the vehicle swallowing ruts and potholes, tediously making her way to his camp.

All across the Sundance grounds folks were moving and stirring. For some reason the dancers had yet to begin the fourth day, although the sun was already high over the horizon. Pulling up to his camp, Mary stopped long enough for him to get out. "Thank you Mary," he said warmly, as he exited her car.

"You welcome," was her perfunctory response, "call me in a few days and we will talk some more."

"Okay Mary," Jackson said, "enjoy your day."

Not one to sit still for long periods of time, Mary drove away. There were trinkets to sell, white folk to fleece. A lady had to make a living. He watched as Mary drove out of view, then turned and headed over to the camp coffee pot. His gaze wandering over the camp site, Jackson noticed three things immediately. One, the camp was broken down except for the bare essentials. Two, Roddy, without needing to be asked, had broken down Jackson's tent and gear and stored it in a neat pile off to the side. He was still packing gear in his vehicle and looked up, smiling. The third and final thing he noticed was Nate Winter. Well fuck me backward, was the thought the sight of Nate Winter generated in his mind.

Nate Winter was a pain in the ass before he drove Jackson to Sundance. Eight days here, because they had arrived early, Nate had far surpassed his typical level of annoyance. Eight days had turned "Dances with Wolves Nate Winter" into "Great White Savior of All Indian People Nate Winter."

He had spent the last eight days firmly nestled in the ass of Junior Rutledge and was regaled with all Junior knew, all Junior felt Nate should know. Junior was a real Indian after all, he lived on the reservation. Jackson no longer carried any semblance of authenticity as he was from urban society. As far as Nate was concerned Jackson was now a fraud, an imitation of what a real Indian was.

The eight days they had been at Sundance, Junior and Nate had been running the rez. Going to the casino and back, chasing girls, out to Rapid City, all on Nate's dime. Not for one second did the contradiction register with him. Not one night had either of them spent in camp. Leaving immediately after Sundance ended each day they returned in the morning, Junior entering the Sundance arbor to begin a new day.

In eight days Nate had learned all there was to know about life on the reservation. Now he was practically salivating in his hunger to spew everything he knew all over Jackson. As soon as he sat down with his first cup of coffee in camp since yesterday, Nate began throwing up his reams of new found knowledge.

"Where have you been?" Nate inquired of him as though deserving a response, "you aren't supposed to leave here. You're not supposed to leave the Sundance grounds. Everybody has been looking for you. People are pretty pissed off you haven't been around."

Jackson stared at him sipping his coffee and smoking a cigarette, the reason why the fourth day was starting so late suddenly registering. Junior is Chases second in command and the Sundance couldn't begin until he was there. Junior and Nate had arrived only moments before Mary had dropped Jackson off.

150°
CHAPTER FIFTEEN

On the long two-day drive out to Sundance Jackson
had filled Nate in on the history of David Chases, omitting
most of the unsavory. It wasn't Jackson's place to denigrate
Chases in an attempt to somehow protect the sacred. The
sacred protects itself and those who willingly chose to
defile the sacred will eventually pay a heavy toll for their
desecration. Unlike the christian version, the sacred doesn't
wait until death then torment for eternity. For the Ancients,
repercussions are immediate, always severe, and it isn't
necessarily the individual who committed the act that winds
up paying the bill. Most of the time it is their family and
friends, the people they love and care for. There are many
entities that represent the sacred and when they seek to mete
out justice there is nowhere to hide, no chance for forgiveness.
Friends suddenly fell ill, things that shouldn't break do, and
in some cases, family members die. The individual is left to
live and be reminded each day of what they did.

For two days Jackson passed this knowledge on to
Nate as well as attempting to instill some comprehension
in him about what it meant to support someone who would
be entering the Sundance circle. He thought he had done the
best he could with those preparations, but the first day they

pulled into camp Junior introduced himself and it was all down hill from there.

Before camp was set up and prepared, Junior and Nate took off and weren't seen again until later that evening. They stopped by camp for an hour then disappeared for the remainder of the night. Where they went, what they were involved in, only they knew. Jackson didn't care. He was well aware Nate was about to become Junior's prison bitch. Fuck him, he thought, the damn fool can't see when someone is breaking it off in his ass, that's his problem. Ain't like I didn't warn him.

Night after night and day after day their behavior continued. Junior had found his new best friend and Nate was higher than any drug could possibly hope to induce. Jackson doubted Nate had been this giddy since the first time he got laid. Watching him follow Junior around, doing whatever he demanded, at any time, immediately upon request, kept Jackson chuckling. "The poor stupid bastard" Jackson said to the wind.

Tests came from many directions, tests that were opportunities to grow and to define an individual's character. So many want desperately to prove themselves, to show what they can do, if only they were given the chance.

Many believed the words they were speaking and, though the words may be true, in essence they were only words, nothing more than air being moved. It's one thing to believe you will do what you say, but it's another thing entirely to actually do it. When the bullets start to fly what will be the individual response?

The first day of Sundance was rough on Jackson. On top of piercing the first day with the excruciating pain of his flesh violently wrenched from his chest, he also had the responsibility of Nate Winter to deal with and by the end of the first day, Jackson was suffering like it was the end of the fourth.

His mouth was as dry as the desert on a drought-laden mid-august day with not a drop of moisture to be had. He tried the oldest trick in the book by picking up a round stone and placing it beneath his tongue to encourage his mouth to generate saliva, seeking some small amount of relief, if only for a brief moment.

In the months previously, Nate had vociferously assaulted Jackson with his boundless need to assist native People, to do something, anything, for all native Peoples, to ease their suffering. He swore it was his life's mission and never hesitated to paint pretty pictures with words of all the wonderful things he intended to do. During the long drive to Sundance Jackson tried to impress upon him the formidable responsibility of supporting a Sundancer, what Nate's responsibilities would actually be and Nate consciously agreed to his task. He assured Jackson he understood, that he fully perceived he was there to assist in whatever Jackson needed and that he would be there for him, completely.

Unbeknownst to Nate, or Jackson, or anyone else for that matter, he would get his chance to prove himself. Jackson didn't realize until long after the dance was over that he had been used to test him. All Nate had to do to succeed was support Jackson Themal, to be there for him as he had agreed to willingly. To put aside all he thought, his ideas and preconceptions. If Jackson requested a five-course meal served by geisha girls, Nate was responsible for providing it, any way possible, no questions, no opinions and certainly no instruction. His job was to do whatever Jackson needed. At the end of the first day, he needed water.

Traditionally, dancers do not drink or eat these four days. In days long gone before European invasion this was much easier for those who danced this ceremony. Today, in this society of fast food and air conditioning, food preservatives and sugar-laden diets, very few have the health qualifications necessary to survive the plenary shock to the system of four days with no water.

In this century many of the Sundance's across the reservations permit the dancers to return to their camps at the end of each day. Compassionately many Elders realize that physically we are not what we once were. At the end of his first day Jackson searched for Nate and asked him for a small amount of water. The test was on.

It did not matter what Nate thought of the request, or whether he agreed with it or not. His job, that he had agreed to, was to shut up and do it. Could he prove able to serve the needs of one person? In his all-encompassing desire to serve the needs of all native People could he pass this simple test, meet this simple request?

Put aside, if only for a moment, everything he thought he knew to make this altruistic gesture? One chance to serve someone other than himself. For the first time in his life allow his actions to speak for him, instead of his words? To honestly prove what he assures everyone, including himself, was his heart's desire? Nate Winter failed miserably.

Immediately upon receiving the request from Jackson he made a mad dash straight to Junior Rutledge. With all his opinions and new found knowledge of native people and ceremony, he brought Jackson's simple request to Junior's twisted mind and returned promptly, denying his request. According to Junior and agreed with by Nate, Jackson didn't need it. "Suffer through it, deal with it," Nate said to Jackson arrogantly.

In one fell swoop he proved he couldn't serve the needs of one person, regardless of his opinions. How then could he possibly serve the needs of many? Nate Winter had been weighed and measured, and had come up seriously lacking. Compassionately, Roddy Blackstar did provide Jackson the assistance he needed, without a moment's hesitation, although the Ancients would make him pay dearly for it later.

What no one knew is that moments before Roddy brought relief to Jackson, a cup of water somehow appears under the arbor. By itself, glistening in a dew-laden cup as if placed there by the hand of an unknown entity. No one was around, as all of the supporters had long since departed. Jackson appreciated he was on Sacred Ground, earth sanctified to ensure nothing with evil intent can get through and he accepted so gratefully this gift put before him. He didn't know where this gift had come from and he wasn't questioning it.

Sitting in camp days later after Mary dropped him off, sipping coffee and smoking, Jackson was once again inundated with all of Nate Winter's knowledge and opinions. Knowledge granted unto him by none other than Junior Rutledge.

After everything Jackson had gone through these last few days emotionally, spiritually, physically and mentally the last thing he needed was some white boy with an overblown sense of something he couldn't begin to understand. Choking down the overwhelming urge to rise and reconfigure Nate's face, Jackson stood and walked over to where Roddy was continuing to load his gear. "You got any extra room in there?" he asked him.

"Sure, Jackson," he replied, "what do you need me to store for you?"

"Everything, Roddy. Think you can spare a few hours and run up to Rapid City with me?" he inquired further. Knowing something was up, Roddy immediately agreed and began stowing Jackson's gear.

Without a word to Nate or so much as a glance in his general direction, Jackson assisted Roddy in stowing his gear. Finishing they turned to head for the Sundance circle to pray with and support the remaining dancers until day's end. As before, people steered clear of Jackson and he was one breath away from going off. Inhaling deeply he remembered Mary's words, pushed the annoyance and anger aside and focused on what was so much more important.

The final day of Sundance, the fourth day, was surprisingly short. For whatever reason, Chases brought the ceremony to an end by 2 p.m. An hour of dancing those remaining out the eastern door and all was complete for another year. Another hour as the dancers enjoyed their first full meal at the arbor prepared by the women in camp, then time for the giveaway. Passing on items some spent many dollars on, some giving whatever they could scrounge.

The dollar stores do a hefty business in the months preceding Sundance, and typically, the last day of Sundance brings people from all over the reservation. Faces not seen before that fourth day came to see what could be had for free.

Jackson understands giving as a means to say thank you for all that you have received, but what he doesn't understand is what was being given. Nothing handed out had any emotional or spiritual significance to the recipient or the individual giving the item away. Most of the stuff was simply piled on a blanket where people rummaged through the mound of doodads and whatnots picking what they want. Try as Jackson might he just can't find the sacred in it.

No conversation had yet taken place between Jackson and Roddy. Roddy knew, when it was time, if he chose to, Jackson would tell him what took place at Mary's. Roddy in no way pried, prodded or looked for answers to questions he knew better than to ask. He always maintained a great respect for how things were supposed to be done, whether anyone else chose to do them the right way or not.

Jackson for his part, noticed Roddy was mulling something over in his mind. Something was eating away at him, something he wanted to say, and either he couldn't find the words or simply wasn't prepared, and like Roddy, he won't ask. In time, the right time. Until then, best to not concern oneself with it. All done for the year, with camp packed and ready to go, they casually walked over to Roddy's pickup. "Meet me at Chases?" Jackson asked of Roddy, "I'm going to walk over, say good bye, and we are out of here."

"Absolutely," Roddy's replied.

A quick stop by Chases' house, a dilapidated trailer some 500 yards from the dance arbor, and they would be rolling out. The trailer was set in the southern portion of Chases' property with the Sundance grounds in the west. The east is where the people usually set up camp, as well as between the dance circle and Chases' home.

Chases retains the original 160 acres given by allotment to his family, but he uses less than 50 acres of it, the north portion of his property is leased to a local ranching outfit. The ranchers pay .50 cents to a $1.00 per acre for land they would lease anywhere else for $50 to $100 per acre, so Chases isn't making much money on the deal.

Strolling the 500 yards to Chases house Jackson picked his way through the dozen or so discarded vehicles and mounds of junk scattered here and there, old motorcycles and a half constructed barn no one has found the time to finish in the last ten years.

The first 50 yard perimeter of the trailer is cleared but everything around it, other than a few well worn trails and a road that leads campers around the property, is littered with whatever anyone decided to abandon. The junk cars provided extra storage space, guest rooms and somewhere for the occasional drunk to sleep it off.

The feeling of isolation was becoming more and more apparent, the cold shoulders and icy stares. Everything Jackson had suffered through at the Tree of Life was beginning to feel diminished, as though it no longer mattered, and he didn't like the feelings growing inside of him. Reaching Chases trailer and walking up the steps he knocked and stepped inside. Chases was seated at his usual place at the kitchen table. Seeing Jackson enter, he rose to meet him halfway. "Heading out?" Chases asked.

"Yeah," Jackson replied, trying to be cordial, "wanted to let you know. Seemed rude to just drive away."

Chases chuffed, saying, "What about the guy you rode here with?"

"No idea," Jackson replied, "last I saw he was with Junior. Said he wanted to stay awhile longer. He has his truck so I guess he'll find his way home." Jackson had no intention whatsoever of being in the same zip code with Nate Winter, and certainly not riding twenty-four hours back to southwest Pennsylvania with him. He also had no intention of explaining it to David Chases.

Out of this reverie Jackson heard Chases say, "You know you failed this year." Shocked, Jackson stared.

A few things were becoming abundantly clear. The clearest point of all, that David Chases is a son of a bitch. His comment about Jackson failing reminded him of the stunt Chases pulled when he arrived for Sundance this year.

Earlier in the year Chases had called, lamenting his woes of electricity bills he couldn't pay and food he didn't have. Could Jackson help him once again? Jackson recognized what Chases was doing, basically holding his Sundance commitment hostage, and tried desperately to get out from under.

Realizing he was about to be told no, Chases upped the ante by describing a beautiful buffalo robe he had been gifted. If Jackson could see his way to sending him a mere $200, when he arrived at Sundance, Chases would give him that buffalo robe. Hell yeah! Jackson thought excitedly. He had wandered through many shops looking at buffalo robes, and there was simply no way he could afford one. A nice buffalo robe could be purchased for around eight hundred dollars, so when Chases offered the robe for $200, he jumped on it.

This would be the first buffalo robe Jackson had ever owned. He had slept under a few, using them as a blanket when visiting some of the people he knew, and he could barely contain his anticipation of having one of his own. Jackson should have known better, because Chases was once again running a game. Blinded by his desire, Jackson agreed to send him the money, hung the phone up quickly, contacted Western Union and wired the money. He spent months looking forward to that buffalo robe. The way Chases described it that robe would be beautiful.

When Jackson arrived at Sundance his first stop was Chases trailer where he rushed inside to greet him. He hadn't packed a blanket this year because that buffalo robe would be all he needed to stay warm and cozy on the upcoming chilly South Dakota nights, and he was looking forward to collecting it. After the initial "how are you's" and "good to see you's" he asked about his buffalo robe.

Startled for a brief moment Chases composed himself, then pointed to a bundle in the corner. Lying there was a moth-eaten mass of ancient buffalo hide someone had used to lay on when they changed the oil in their car. Old, mottled and reeking of gasoline. This is the robe he promised me? he thought, This mass of missing hair, matted remains and reeking hide?

Jackson sensed the anger building in him for a brief moment, then let it go, immediately chastising himself for his stupidity. Chases had done it again and Jackson let him do it.

The buffalo robe he had used as bait to con $200 out of Jackson had been a gift to Chases from someone else. The money from Jackson went to the casino, not the electric company or grocery store. The buffalo robe he had been promised had been pawned and then taken possession of by the pawn shop for the loan not being repaid.

Turning his gaze from the reeking mass of what once may have been a buffalo robe Jackson saw Chases watching him, daring him to say anything. He feigned a smile, accepted the heap graciously and walked out. Standing here again just hours after the most difficult Sundance Jackson has participated in to date, Chases had that exact same look on his face, daring him to say a word. Rage seethed just beneath the surface again, but Jackson found a way to keep it from boiling over.

"Excuse me, failed?" Jackson stammered.

"Yes, you failed, Jackson. You didn't keep your commitment. You didn't do what you were supposed to do. You are going to have to return here for at least for two more years. You are weak, Jackson, weak in your heart, weak in your mind," Chases said condescendingly.

Every fiber of Jackson's soul wanted to snap David Chases neck. Every ounce of restraint he could draw was brought to bear, to keep him from coming irrevocably apart. It was pointless to remind Chases of their previous conversation after Jackson fell from the tree in the lean-to. Chases would deny it ever took place. With a strained smile he reluctantly shook Chases outstretched hand, then turned and walked out the door.

Pulling to a stop at that exact moment Roddy was slipping his truck into park and preparing to step out. "Don't bother, Roddy," Jackson said through pinched tight lips, "Lets rock out of this place." Again Roddy, being who he was, never said a word. Closing the driver's door and slipping the transmission into drive, he waited for Jackson to climb into the passenger's seat.

Roddy rarely saw Jackson this violently infuriated, and it's something he preferred not to see. There was always a hint about Jackson, just below the surface. Any individual with a lick of sense could feel it, and it was best to leave him be when he was like this. Don't talk, don't look, just drive.

A half a pack of cigarettes later, chain smoked by Jackson most of the way to Rapid City, he told Roddy what Chases said about him failing. Roddy already knew about the buffalo robe. The highlights of what Mary Bloody Heart shared rolled out soon after. "You said Rapid City, Jackson. Want to tell me why I'm driving two hours out of my way in the opposite direction?"

"Probably be a good idea, hey Roddy?" Jackson responded, "We need to head over to the airport to pick up a rental car."

"Okay," Roddy conceded, "want to tell me what this is all about? You rode out here with that numb-nuts Nate Winter. Not going back with him it seems."

"Fucking hell no!" Jackson retorted ferociously, "I would rather stab myself in the eyes repetitively with dull objects than to ever have to be subjected to that whiny, pussy ass, little bitches voice ever again in my entire life."

Roddy chuckled, "No, Jackson, tell me how you really feel!"

The levity helped to dissipate the remaining anger and soon enough they pulled up to the rental car checkout. Roddy waited while Jackson secured a car and when the paperwork was completed he drove over to where Roddy was smoking, his pickup idling. "All set?" Roddy inquired.

"All set," Jackson responded, and they began transferring Jackson's gear into the trunk of the rental. "What do you think will happen to Nate?" Roddy queried curiously.

"Mother fuck me if I know, Roddy," Jackson quipped, "son of a whore can find his own way back to Pennsylvania. Personally, at this time, I officially do not give a flying fuck. Far as I'm concerned he deserves whatever happens to him."

Roddy chuckled again, "Only you, Jackson, only you. I swear I don't know anyone else who would strand a back-stabbing little prick like Nate Winter on the reservation in the middle of the South Dakota prairie. I know a few who would think about it, who would want to do it. Fucker deserves it, yes, but only you would actually do it."

"Let him blow Junior Rutledge for the answers to his problems," Jackson responded furiously. Roddy doubled over in laughter.

The gear finally loaded, Roddy reached out with his hand and Jackson accepted it warmly. Standing there together, looking each other square in the eyes, no words needed be said. Both understood clearly. Clearing his throat as the moment passed and releasing his hand, Roddy apprehensively said, "Jackson, I got something I have to tell you."

"What's that brother man?" he asked curiously.

"Well, while you were at Mary's," Roddy began, "I hung around camp. Every once in a while Junior and Nate would show up laughing and carrying on. Some pretty ugly things got said that night, shit I really don't want to tell you, some I ain't gonna tell you. This however you gotta know. It's been eating me up inside, gnawing on me and I got to let it out." Jackson was all ears. No response from him was needed, his facial expression was all Roddy needed to encourage him to go on.

"Those holes the size of beer cans in your chest and back?" Roddy continued bitterly, "You as well as anyone know the usual procedure is to pinch the flesh between two fingers then pierce that pinch. While you were gone to Mary's, Junior wandered around camp laughing, imitating how he grabbed handfuls of your flesh, bragging about how he mutilated you. You got to know, Jackson, he did it on purpose. He was telling everyone they could 'just call him the butcher.' " Roddy could see Jackson was furious, again. He knew it was time to go, and quickly.

Jackson was stunned one more time, after being stunned so many times in so short a time. These words would echo in his mind as he traveled the eighteen hundred mile journey back to southwest Pennsylvania.

Hope he has enough cigarettes, Roddy thought.

They shook hands once more. No words passed between them as Roddy climbed back into his pickup and pointed his truck south towards Nashville. Jackson watched until he was out of sight and checked the map, setting a course he turned for the interstate.

160°
CHAPTER SIXTEEN

Jackson was driving and the miles clicked away. There was a long way to go but he was in no hurry to get there. Nothing waited for him except an empty room in the back of a tire shop. No family to return to, no home. A few acquaintances he had met but no real friends. Certainly no wife or girlfriend. All that waited was emptiness and loneliness.

The life his mother dreamed of for him never came to fruition, the future, the security. More than what life on the reservation offered had never materialized. Jackson had no desire to be something he wasn't. The "find a job in a factory, work forty hours a week, retire at fifty five" life held no interest for him.

"Just call me the butcher" bounced in his head like a mental game of ping pong, Junior Rutledge the opponent, any respect Jackson had for the man now gone. Mary's words rang dully in his mind as he desperately tried to see the point. He had gone to Sundance to complete what was asked of him, to fulfill his commitment and to keep his promise, to return to what? Pennsylvania now seemed pointless. There were a few things in his room Jackson wanted to retrieve, but

if not for those few items, there was absolutely no reason to go there rather than anywhere else.

Chases had left him feeling as though he had failed, that everything he had endured was meaningless. He wanted to believe he had suffered for the people, but the people didn't care, as evidenced by their behavior. Maybe what Jackson had endured wasn't for the people at all, maybe it was for another reason entirely, for something he had yet to understand, the final pieces not yet falling into place. Considering everything Jackson had gone through these last two weeks, everything he had lived through getting to these last few weeks, he didn't want to imagine what was next.

Alone with no one to talk to on the long drive, and no interest in listening to the radio, his mind began gnawing on the bones of information he'd been collecting over the last few days. He began to ask himself questions. Things like is Evil a physical thing? Can Evil take form, shape and substance? Can true Evil be more than just a concept, more than an action? These are questions that have plagued humans since the dawn of civilization, questions he had often tossed about. Men much wiser than he had attempted to answer these questions, and he certainly had no answers.

What Jackson has are memories, so many memories and not many of them good. As he drove, his mind began to drift through the years-long journey to Sundance, through the experiences of those years, like a scab he cannot stop picking at.

Much of Jackson's lack of desire came from the chain of events he lived through and survived as a child growing into a boy, the utter and complete lack of any guidance or direction that might have steered him on a completely different path in life.

Jackson is a few years short of his thirtieth birthday, but a casual glance into his eyes reveals he is so much older. His soul had aged. Very few perceived the soul peering out of a face so young. Blindly they stumbled about in their attempt to connect to someone they could never comprehend, which was probably why he spent the majority of his time alone. This old soul, that attracted, and at the same time, repelled women.

All women want a bad boy, if only for an evening. Women are naturally intuitive and that intuition sounded warnings relatively quickly. Time was short for any woman who found herself with Jackson. The first night, days or weeks were everything she desired, as all her fantasies came out to play, her contrived excuse to be a bad girl, to let that freak flag fly, to do all the things she secretly wanted to do, things that shame, guilt, or her usual partner wouldn't let her. With Jackson she felt no shame, no guilt, if only for a few hours or days. He encouraged her to be whatever she wanted to be and soon what drew her to him began to push her away.

Revulsion at her behavior, guilt over her actions. Desperate to reassure herself she was a good girl, as though it was his fault the animal inside her had found release from its cage. She also began to sense the lurking danger beneath the surface of Jackson, and concluded it was best to leave quickly before those warnings began to bear fruit.

Jackson began his forays into the physical at around the age of nine, placed in yet another foster home along with a street urchin of fourteen. This young girl was picked up off the streets by the local police for prostitution, and Children Services, with their all encompassing desire to save all the children, never for one moment saw the creature she really was. Manipulative and cunning, she could talk almost anyone into almost anything. A budding sociopath, who had a sweet face and a pretty smile. Few recognized the unadulterated evil they were seeing within her. Placed into the same foster home Jackson was residing in, she taught him a few things he didn't know. While other boys his age were playing with GI Joe and Tonka Trucks he was introduced to a new toy.

In a few short weeks she began to sexually abuse Jackson, although he didn't recognize it as abuse. At the time he didn't know what to call it, but he was most definitely enjoying it. The things she was doing to him felt good and he couldn't get enough. Their first encounter created a hunger in him he couldn't satisfy, and Jackson quickly became more than a willing pupil.

She was only looking for another soul to crush, someone to hurt as she has been hurt. A few months or so into their perverted trysts, the woman whose charge they had been placed in began to recognize what was happening beneath her roof. A quick phone call to Children Services and that young girl was out the door, probably back on the streets.

But the damage had been done. Missing what had been so routinely given from her for months Jackson began to turn his new found sexual appetites in other directions. Nothing seemed to quell the hunger aching in him, to feed the dragon he had been impregnated with, until his first kill.

Early on a warm spring afternoon a squirrel was performing its high wire trapeze act across the power lines crisscrossing the streets. Balanced precariously, while at the same time watching intently for a raptor, seeking to snatch it into oblivion. For no apparent reason Jackson reached down at his feet and picked up a stone and, with a mighty heave, he whipped that rock as hard as he could.

It was a perfect throw, straight into the skull of the unsuspecting squirrel, causing it to crash to the ground dead. Jackson rushed over to retrieve it from where it had fallen, and had an instant orgasm. As he did, the dragon deep inside suddenly went quiet, and Jackson received a dark epiphany.

But the dragon was never satisfied for long. The hunger always returned, more incessant than the last time, always needing, craving and demanding. Jackson fed the dragon, time and time again, with neighborhood pets and stray animals whenever he found them, birds, squirrels, even things already dead. Jackson would sit for long hours playing in the blood, enraptured by the stickiness of it. He reveled in how it coated his fingers, his hands and other places on his still young undeveloped body.

For almost a year he fed the dragon, not every day, sometimes not every week. Only when the hunger became a throbbing his mind, a voice he could no longer drown, did something die, did Jackson play. His behavior began to change, and those changes soon become apparent. The woman he was living with no longer felt comfortable with him in her home. She called Children Services and demanded he be removed, the sooner the better, and back into the system he went.

This cycle continued on and on until he was eleven years of age. Somehow he knew his behavior was wrong. There was no one to tell him not to, only a presence somewhere deep inside. The wrongness of what he was doing continued to grow as he continued to kill, as he continued to play, regardless of the revulsion he felt later. At eleven years of age he learned a new way to control the dragon.

He was introduced to alcohol and found his personal stairway to heaven. With the discovery of alcohol he was granted a temporary reprieve after each incident, a welcome respite from his self-loathing until the dragon woke again. Regardless how determinedly Jackson endeavored to drown the dragon, it always found a way to resurface, because dragons can swim. It would rise angrily, voraciously hungry, demanding sustenance.

By fourteen he was a full blown alcoholic, complete with blackouts lasting for days. He drank whatever he could find, determined to suppress the dragon. He was desperate to hide from his burgeoning self-hatred, eating him from the inside. As long as he remained intoxicated he couldn't hear the dragon. He couldn't hear it's yearning pleas to be fed. Inevitably the alcoholic haze soon faded and the hunger returned, so much more tenacious than before, yammering and howling in his young mind, and there was no one to assist Jackson in his attempts to assuage the horror inside.

Whatever home he happened to be in soon realized there was something not quite right with this boy, but no real concern was shown. There were no "after school moments" to inquire as to what the problem might be, to help. The solution used constantly for this dangerous boy, was to get rid of him, to send him onto the next home, to eventually land in a woman's home with three daughters. Jackson's stay in that home would be very, very brief as her intuition recognized, maybe from her own abusive childhood, what lurked beneath the surface of this highly disturbed young boy.

Fifteen years old, standing six foot tall in his socks, with eyes that didn't belong in the skull of one so young, he scared her. He was the first foster child she had ever accepted. She opened her home because she wanted to do something for poor children, for those who need. It's all her circle of middle class friends can talk about, the poor children. What she didn't want to do is live with a monster in the making.

Someone obviously forgot to tell her it was never a good idea to attempt to make oneself feel better by opening your home to a carnivore. Juvenile detention centers are not petting zoos or humane shelters where a new puppy or kitty can be found – the animals in these places bite.

Jackson's time in juvenile centers was not from any act on his part, but because it was somewhere to drop him off when he became too old for the sexual predators to play with, then he became old enough for those who like to play with teen age boys. Realizing the danger she and her daughters were in, the woman contacted an elderly friend of hers, Dorothy Magnate. She didn't want to send him back as if she was returning a bad present and asked if Dorothy could see her way to giving this young boy a home?

For the first time in his young life Jackson found peace. Dorothy Magnate was a kind woman, the quintessential grandmother figure, her gray hair in the same style she had had since the fifties. She was five foot four, average build, of English and Irish descent, undemanding and kept mostly to herself. Never before had she opened her home to a child, but one look at Jackson broke her heart. She knew something was broken inside this young boy becoming a man, and thought maybe she could help him, if only a little. Dorothy tried so hard, but all her attempts were in vain, failure long since predetermined.

Dorothy grew up deep in the farm country of Kansas. She was an only child and had spent her days playing with her dolls. She often daydreamed of the future when she would have real living dolls to play with, when she would have children of her own. She eased her loneliness in the company of her dolls, finding escape in their porcelain and plastic faces.

Some days she would wander around her father's farm playing tag with the goats and chickens for company. On an ordinary late September morning Dorothy was in her father's barn climbing the nailed blocks of wood to the hayloft above. Reaching the edge of the loft she looked out into the open space before her. Beneath her, stacked thickly on the bare ground that was the floor of the barn, was a pile of fresh hay not yet bailed, waiting invitingly. A soft fluffy cloud she could plunge herself into and for a brief moment, Dorothy could fly.

What she didn't know and didn't see was the pitchfork haphazardly forgotten in the straw below. Jump, climb, jump, climb. A dozen times, each more exhilarating than the last, each moving the pitchfork closer and closer, until the fateful jump. Landing on the tines the pitchfork pierced her abdomen. An emergency hysterectomy was performed to save her young life and the dreams of children she so fervently imagined was shattered.

Answering her phone that fateful day her long-quieted fantasies of motherhood came crashing back as she listened to her friend paint the picture of a child so desperately in need. How, if she could just see her way to, she might save this young boy.

Her friend played on desires Dorothy shared with only a few, but she never once referred to the danger she felt. She bemoaned of how her three daughters needed her, that she has made a mistake and that she simply could not afford another mouth to feed. Could Dorothy help this young boy who needed so much? How could she possibly say no?

Dorothy agreed to help and gave Jackson what she thought he needed. She gave him space and room to grow to become a man. All the while she desperately tried to instill some understanding of love, but it was much too late for Jackson. By the time he reached her home he was broken in too many pieces and his only escape was alcohol.

During the day he drank. On some nights he crept out of her home, the dragon rapacious. Another kill, always animals to satiate the hunger inside. Whether Dorothy knew or not she never said, she never revealed. Quietly, with compassion, she loved Jackson, praying he would one day feel that love and respond to it, but he never did.

At seventeen he left Dorothy's home. Alcohol had become more than a daily excursion for him, alcohol had become hourly. He could no longer tolerate the visage seen by him in any reflective surface, his countenance repulsed him. The simple act of inadvertently catching his reflection in a fresh rain filled puddle incited retching.

Incapable of settling anymore, Jackson hit the road. Something was wrong deep inside him and he was fully aware his behavior was not acceptable in any fashion. Reading copiously he strove to come to understand himself. Tomes of murder and death, novel after novel of true crime, as he desperately sought to come to an understanding of the dragon within.

Maybe away from this one place where he had found a modicum of peace he could find an answer. Maybe he could find relief from the exhaustion of daily donning his dented, rusty armor to do battle with the dragon. This creature inside him some days didn't come out of its cave, while on others it came out with a vengeance.

Jackson set out to find the sword to slay the dragon, to find the dragon's heart, and to learn how to plunge the sword deeply.

170°
CHAPTER SEVENTEEN

Dorothy provided him a home for three short years. She did all she could, but Jackson was so emotionally crippled he was unable and unwilling to accept her unconditional love for him. When he left her home it broke Dorothy's heart, but Jackson was unaware of the pain he caused her. He wouldn't have cared if he had known.

At seventeen years old he was cold, hard and callous. That he may have been hurting someone else never entered his mind. Dorothy was a good woman, a good person. Never overly religious, strict or dominant, she tried gently to be a guiding hand for Jackson. She never forced, but granted him the luxury of finding himself. She had no idea what he was finding.

Dorothy married in her teens. Moving from Kansas to coastal Virginia with her husband Mac they made a good life for themselves, a normal life, a typical life. Mac passed away some ten years previous, and when Jackson moved into her home she was 76 years old. Her faded maternal desires not withstanding, she enjoyed his company, he provided another presence in her quiet, lonely home. For three years she did the best she could for a boy becoming a man, as Jackson slowly realized what he was doing was wrong, that what he was becoming was wrong.

Desperate for answers, for some direction, he walked from coastal Virginia to the coast of California. He carried a few changes of clothes and copies of books he treasured above others stuffed into Mac's old duffel bag, given to him by Dorothy. Something she hoped would remind him of her, of a home he could have if he chose it.

Hitchhiking he stopped a few days here or a few days there. Performing odd jobs to earn a couple of dollars, he was always fighting off the predators and closet homosexuals who tried in vain to pick him up. Jackson was all too cognizant of the predators and he could spot one instantly. For years he wandered, drifting and drinking, sleeping wherever he could find a space, using every drug offered, legal or illegal. Not a thought was given to the passing of days and months.

Jackson sealed the dragon within himself behind a dam he carefully crafted in his mind. Every so often the dragon would scratch behind his eyes, a prisoner in solitary confinement. Tapping the walls it sought the soft spot to initiate digging its way to freedom. Jackson was very aware of its quest for escape as a small portion of his mind remained on constant vigil, to keep the dragon at bay.

During one of his brief moments of sobriety, not because he wanted to be sober, but because he was out of funds, his life changed completely. There was no one around who had anything to offer so Jackson slept instead. As he napped in the afternoon, from where he couldn't say, his Ancestors came calling…

…He senses it is early afternoon and he is somewhere out west. No words come to him, only thoughts, intuition, suggestion. Where he is or how he got there he can't say. This has never happened to him before and he has no frame of reference.

Jackson is looking around him and quickly he discerns he is standing on the vast open prairie. All around him is desolate as the buffalo grass gently sways and ever so slightly a cool breeze caresses his skin. Turning in circles he struggles to understand what he sees before him but no comprehension dawns. As he takes account of his surroundings his gaze unconsciously settles on the western horizon. In front of him is a terrifying sight.

In the west, where earth and sky meet at the horizon, encompassing everything that is the west, is a cloud blacker than the blackest night. Jackson can't see over it or under it and this blackness, seeming itself alive, stretches unending from side to side. No passage through can be detected as lightning crashes in this darkness, sudden bursts of excruciating brightness that are accompanied by hail, wind and rain.

In front of this swirling blackness is a bird. A winged creature that is impossibly blacker than the storm behind it, the largest raptor he can never have imagined. Knowledge registers that the lightning from the storm is not only reflected in its eyes but is generated by them and Jackson observes the creatures talons are sunk deep into the flesh of the storm, into the undulating meat of it.

Dragged as if on a leash by this immense black raptor, the storm is coming straight for him, to envelope him. Upon perilous recognition of his impending doom, the storm crashes into him...

...Jackson slammed back into his body. From a deep sleep he was on his feet instantly, fully awake and shaken to the very core of his being. He had no understanding of what had happened to him as he stood and trembled. Lighting a cigarette with shaking hands he made his way to the computer in the corner.

The apartment he was at belonged to some woman he met in the bar a few days previous. He was hungry, not having eaten in a few days, and she was horny. A perfect match and for three days he had been crashing at her apartment. During the day she left for work while he lazed around until she returned later in the evening. The nights he spent satisfying her lust, although he felt nothing emotional for her. All that was between them was purely physical and he knew it. He knew too it wouldn't last but a few more days. Soon it would be time to move on.

Shaking and trying to smoke he hastily gulped a glass of water while he searched for some information about what had transpired. He knew he was of native descent, but he had never done anything about it. In typical fashion, at least for him, he was the opposite of what was so prevalent. Jackson was an Indian pretending to be a white guy, and he had his charade down to perfection.

With a cursory glance anyone can see his heritage, mix blood certainly but the native showed through. It was this look about him that was the main reason he was so successful at picking up women. They saw him as exotic, as something different. He wasn't like the usual crop of blonde haired men so desperate for their attentions. Jackson knew it and used it to his advantage. A man had to eat and with no job he learned quickly a smile and the right words or a careful touch, and dinner is served. He had no problem exchanging sex for a meal.

Searching the internet he stumbled on the story describing the events unfolding in Tennessee. Explaining how the local natives and others from around the country had come together to stand up against the desecration of a sacred site. The light bulb went off in his mind. No answers would be found in Nashville where Jackson first met Roddy, Randy Hall and butterflies. But he would find direction, along with many more questions, and meet many other mix bloods much like himself.

Spiritual paraplegics desperate to find that lost connection to the blood pounding in their veins. As if they were seeking some miraculous regeneration of long atrophied limbs, longing for when they would rise of their own volition from their beds of despair. Lost souls who had traversed the convoluted hallways of organized religion, where they found no healing, no release from their long-held suffering. Left to be confused, contorted and tortured until eventually they found their way to this indigenous interpretation of life.

There was a time, a few hundred years ago when there was help for the visions, the dreams and the voices in the night. When the First Nations People of this country lived together in tightly knit communities, when they understood the one survived only as part of the whole. Individualism destroyed the community, and although it was encouraged in many aspects, it was equally discouraged in others. Only together did the Nation survive and by ensuring all had the necessities required, none were left out or cast aside. Abuse in any form was not tolerated. Greed was an act punishable by death.

In that time, those who could, watched the children and paid close attention to their behaviors. These Elders guided the children and led them in the direction that would best ensure the survival of the Nation. Some were led to specific societies, as revealed by entities older than comprehension, in dreams and visions. Before these children reached ten years of age they would be directed to the warrior societies, maybe the medicine societies, maybe the spiritual.

The dominant culture that exits today no longer provides this to the descendants of these once mighty people. These discarded descendants, three and four generations removed from their people, are scattered as leaves on a brisk fall day.

No Elders remain to guide in the direction they so desperately seek. Instead they come together when and where they can to find some comfort.

But where there are those who need, always the predator would find its way, to feed on the broken masses and massage their egos. Charlatans who would instill rumor and encourage far-fetched imaginations, self-titled, self-governing and all powerful. They presented themselves as the authority, as the chosen few. The masses so hungry, they flocked to these false faces and drank deeply at their trough of lies.

No longer do the breeds and bloods come together in unison, to assist in the survival of the People. Now, its bloods feeding off the breeds. Breeds so confused and lost they mixed and matched anything they could find, to somehow provide solace and consolation with no sense of unity, no direction, no instruction.

There are hundreds of "Indian Clubs" with federal non-profit status and the majority accomplish nothing more than lining a few pockets, mostly their own. All of them utterly incapable of understanding the "Indian way" they so fervently proselytized. Not for a second do they understand the Chief, the medicine people, spiritual leaders and clan mothers are not the heads of the People, they are the foundation. The unfortunate few whose lives had been sacrificed for the good of others, their wants and needs now totally irrelevant.

Individuals who possess these character traits are also sought after. They are ardently pursued to provide some direction, but when the direction given isn't presented in the manner arrogantly presumed it should be, they are attacked and denigrated, touted as fake and plastic. Those who can teach, finding themselves callously informed they were not behaving the way the movie showed or the way the book said they should.

So many conversations beginning with *"I heard"* or *"so and so said,"* as though the person who imparted the information was telling the gods honest truth. These lies are then propagated, because the confused never take the time needed to check the source or the information for accuracy or authenticity.

The traditional way of life, lived for generations, is gone. The only ones appearing interested in maintaining it are those who are faking it, or looking to get paid. Full bloods who dropped off the reservations and use their place of origin, whatever reservation they are from, to profess title and position, as if this is all that is necessary to be accepted as authentic. The deluded failing to see these declarations are the first clue to imitation. Humility is paramount in any who have been given a position of leadership within an indigenous society. Once the individual begins proclaiming their own dominance, these assertions immediately nullify their position.

Anyone who is, doesn't have to proclaim. They quietly go about their day doing what they do. If they are what they never claimed to be, the Nation and others would attest to their positions. Often they will deny who they are. With what little understanding they are capable of, they know the responsibility they live with, and do not seek to draw attention to it. They understand it is what they do that is important, not who is doing it.

180°
CHAPTER EIGHTEEN

All of this and more wound its way through Jackson's mind as he traveled the two-day road trip from South Dakota to Pennsylvania. As he drove he desperately tried to come to an explanation of why he should keep going, with all that had been shared with him by Mary Bloody Heart, and all he had endured for so long, before and during. Echoing through every thought were the words of Junior Rutledge, *"just call me the butcher."*

The cold distance of the supporters, the continuous betrayal by David Chases. Inexorably, as the miles rolled by, Jackson Themal was coming apart. He stopped for an hour to rest, pulling off the highway just before Davenport, Iowa. Curling up in the backseat he drifted off and dreamt. He found himself back in South Dakota chatting with an Elder he had never met before…

…They are standing at an old, rusty barbed wire fence near a gate held in place with bailing wire. Talking, smoking, they seem to be casually passing time in front of a sun-scorched field of buffalo grass interspersed with prairie sage.

Across the field in front of them, off in the distance, a massive male buffalo appears and slowly walks slowly toward them. Jackson and the Elder continue their conversation as the old male buffalo, easily 3000 pounds, walks toward them shaking his big shaggy head from side to side. Several moments later he stands in front of Jackson, eye level on four feet. He is the dominant male of the herd, his head wider than a truck. Thick, chocolate brown, he blows huge gusts of hot air from his wide flared nostrils straight into Jackson's face.

With no hesitation Jackson opens the gate and steps through to stand beside this massive creature. As he steps up beside the giant the Elder turns to leave and Jackson takes note of his home in the distance. The buffalo uses his enormous head and gently turns him toward the center of the field as the Elder walks to his home.

Jackson and the huge buffalo walk into the center of the field to be joined by the remainder of the herd. Reaching an obviously well worn spot the buffalo Chief folds his legs and lies down, his head inches from the ground. As he does he invites Jackson to lie with him.

Complying, his head resting against the buffalo's flank, the remainder of the herd assume places around them. The afternoon passes and he falls asleep in the field surrounded by the buffalo. The night passes and as the sun crests the horizon its warmth causes him to wake. Rising he notices the buffalo are gone. Unaffected by their disappearance Jackson makes his way across the field back to the gate he used to enter, opens the gate...

...and woke up in the back seat of his rental car. Sitting up absently he banged his head on the roof. After a quick perusal to see that he wasn't bleeding, and rubbing the sore spot, he lit a smoke, wondering what the dream was about. He thought he should probably call Mary and ask her about it when he reaches Pennsylvania. Finishing his cigarette, he climbed out of the rental and stretched. After a quick trip to the facilities, he was back in the car, back on the highway, heading southeast. As the miles are eaten away, his mind drifts back in time to places he had been, people he had met.

Jackson began this journey to the Tree of Life in Nashville, his first steps that would lead him to where he was now. Those first steps helped him to find the courage to put away the crutch of alcohol he had leaned on for so long, so pertinaciously. Somehow he found the strength to trust the voices of his Ancestors, those who walked before him, who gave so much.

Jackson had long since starved the dragon. It found repose in hibernation, but was not dead by any measure. The dragon merely slept. It was waiting, biding its time, aroused only when he became angered. When someone went too far, the dragon stretched its wings, sensing weakness and the possibility of release from the dungeon it had been thrown into so long ago. When angered, Jackson struggled to regain his composure. Successful, always just in time to retain that tenuous hold, he forced the dragon back in its cage. Patiently, the dragon waited, ever alert to every creak and groan of his subconscious.

In his travels Jackson had shared many a cigarette with Elders from many Nations. He was always learning, always seeking to find answers. Books of murder and death had long since been replaced with volumes of history and spiritual understanding. He attempted to find some suggestions, some credible explanations, but he soon discovered no one had answers to the questions that perplexed him. He realized no one knew any more than he did. Some created fanciful interpretations but these it appeared were to satisfy themselves and their over-inflated egos.

Throughout the brief time humans had walked this pulsating blue ball spinning in space these very same answers to these very same questions have been sought. Entire civilizations rose and fell based on someone's interpretation of what lies in the vast unknown. Humans seeking to define existence, attempting to humanize what could never be understood, that attempt insulting at worst, futile at best. The cult-like mentality of organized religion so sure it knew, so sure it was the answer. Force feeding dogma and doctrine down the throat of the unsuspecting and destroying all who refused to capitulate.

How could a creature as insignificant as a human ever comprehend what lay beyond the sun? How arrogant it is to give it a name, then base an understanding around that name. How pretentious to demand that all adhere to that understanding. Undoubtedly, humans have the capability to be the most beautiful of all creations. Unfortunately, they also had the tendency to be the worst.

Along the powwow trail the moccasin telegraph is always tapping. Invitations are extended and received, and toward the end of his wandering years, Jackson was again drawn to Tennessee. He never understood the draw this region had on him, but it seemed he eventually found himself there in one part of the state or another. Jackson had been visiting Roddy Blackstar when they were informed about a gathering outside of Cookeville, organized and hosted by Terry Bishop from the burial mound encampment.

They traveled two hours to Cookeville from Nashville and spent five days with people from all over the country. Among them Alvin Redstone, who had come down from Pine Ridge to oversee and lead the ceremonies. The third evening Jackson was invited to attend a spirit calling ceremony set in the basement of Terry Bishop's home.

Jackson and all attending gathered in the basement and when all were settled the door was sealed shut. Redstone was brought to the center, wrapped and tied in a blanket and then laid on his altar. As the lights were extinguished the basement became pitch black. It was so dark in the basement a hand couldn't be seen if it was held in front of a face. The Ancestors came, whispered to some, touched others, as Jackson watched lights flash in front of him.

Half of the time he denied what he was seeing and the other half was in total awe. At the conclusion of the ceremony the lights were turned on and Alvin Redstone was seated in the corner. The ropes and blankets that had bound him were folded in the center of the room. Not a single person in the room had untied him and Jackson was seriously impressed.

The evening of the fourth day found Jackson and Redstone seated at the campfire together. Jackson had been sitting alone when Redstone walked up and offered him a cup of coffee asking to sit with him. Jackson immediately, almost embarrassingly, welcomed him. He was not fully aware of who the man seated beside him was, but having seen what he could do firsthand he knew there was something special about him and he intended to listen intently to every word. Drinking coffee and smoking they conversed and bantered over nothing important.

Anyone who presents themselves as Jesus or Napoleon would immediately be escorted to a comfortable resting place where people with degrees and white coats would prescribe their daily abdications. Conversely, refer to the self as a medicine man, a headman, spiritual leader of one sort or another, and the urban confused can't find their wallets fast enough. This is absurdity in action, a tragic comedy if ever such a thing existed.

In his travels Jackson had met dozens who professed to be but Alvin Redstone was the real thing. He wasn't faking it and he wasn't proclaiming anything. There was no denying what Jackson had seen the previous evening.

As the evening wore on they spoke and tentatively, hesitantly, Jackson began to speak of the things he had been shown in his dreams. He expected an immediate rebuff as surely this man had heard it all before. Much to his surprise, with no malice or cunning, Redstone encouraged him. When all was said and done Jackson received an invitation to Sundance.

The only place he would ever find the answers to the questions so doggedly pursuing him was in the advice given to him that night. Their conversation concluded after a few hours. Jackson remained where he was while Redstone wandered off and eventually he turned in for the night. Smoking before he fell asleep he ruminated over the words given to him this night at the fire. As he slept he dreamt he was sitting with Alvin Redstone and Roddy Blackstar...

...and they are gathered around a red blanket lain carefully on the ground. Roddy is to his right and Redstone is to his left. In front of Redstone is a medicine bundle. He opens the bundle in such a way that does not permit Jackson to see what is inside and reaching into the contents of the bundle he shuffles about a few seconds then extracts a black and white lightning bolt. He hands it to Jackson...

When he woke the next day Redstone was gone. With no one around he felt comfortable talking to about the dream, Jackson began packing his gear. Nine sweats in five days had left him shaky and weak. The dream left him dazed. As he loaded his gear a young man made his way over to Jackson's beat up old van. "Where ya headed now?" he questioned Jackson.

Not really knowing the guy, Jackson cautiously replied, "Not sure, why do you ask?"

"Well, I understand you might know a few folks up on Qualla," the young man said.

"Do you now?" Jackson asked casually, while paying very close attention. When someone issued a statement like that, to someone they didn't know, answers quickly became evasive. Jackson didn't know who this person was. He couldn't recall his name. He had run into him time to time, over the previous five days, may had even shared a meal with him, but he had shared a lot of meals with a lot of people this week, and he didn't know who they were either. The young man must have sensed he had crossed a line somewhere.

"Not being nosy, just wanted to let you know," he began cautiously, "there are some ceremonies going on right now out on the Boundary. Seems Jack Yellow Bird's wife has cancer and is dying. What I hear, some heyoka medicine guy is there from Rosebud. He is helping to do some healing ceremonies. Thought you might be interested in the information, in case you were heading that way."

Jackson was definitely interested. He knew Jack Yellow Bird from a few years past. In his travels he had been to Cherokee several times. At one point he had been north with the Oneida's helping them with some problems and the Oneidas sent him to Cherokee with an eagle feather. They hoped to get a message to some of the Elders there and one of those Elders had been Jack Yellow Bird. Jackson really had nowhere else to go so he thanked the young man for the information and returned to loading his gear.

He was beginning to feel the effects of being on the road. Most folks when they travel typically had somewhere to travel from, thereby giving them a place to return to. Jackson didn't have any place he was from. He certainly didn't have any place he could return to. The conclusion to every camp ended with a guess as to where he would wind up next and Cherokee sounded as good as any. He hadn't seen Jack Yellow Bird in a few years and knew his family so he figured why not?

After making his goodbyes he climbed into his beaten van and headed for the Qualla Boundary. Having stayed for different periods of time on many different reservations Jackson was aware his uninvited arrival would be seen as suspicious. He accepted he would be questioned when he got there.

One of the questions commonly asked in Indian Country was "where ya from?" and although the question appeared innocuous was actually a land mine because much more than geographic information is being requested. The individual posing the question wants to know who your family is.

The reservations are small closed communities where everybody knows everyone else and a simple name could tell people your entire family history. Jackson, not knowing who he was at the time, not knowing his own personal history, always found the question difficult to answer. His usual response was "nowhere", which generated instant suspicion and distrust.

Jackson didn't like replying to the question in such a manner, but he wasn't going to make up an answer like so many did. He figured that was the truth, if they didn't like the answer, it wasn't his problem. At least he had already been to Cherokee and knew Yellow Bird personally so that should make things a little easier.

190°
CHAPTER NINETEEN

Jackson made his way out of Cookeville. He steered onto I-40 and headed east then pulled up in front of Jack Yellow Bird's house four hours later. A lot of people were already there. Some were gathered around the front porch while others were milling about Yellow Bird's sweat lodge set deep in the back of his property.

As Jackson stepped out of his van and stretched, he gazed about as he looked for Yellow Bird. Seeing him, he walked to meet him. He needed to reintroduce himself and insure it was okay for him to be there. They met halfway to Yellow Bird's house and there was a look of confusion on Yellow Bird's face as he tried to place Jackson.

Yellow Bird is of average height, thick, with shoulder length black hair and very, very dark skin. A jovial man, he is usually smiling and laughing about something. Jackson reminded him of the eagle feather he carried for the Oneida, and respectfully requested permission to join in the prayer ceremonies. Recognition slowly dawned on Yellow Bird's face. He shook Jackson's hand firmly and he assured him he was more than welcome.

"I'm really grateful you showed up, son," Yellow Bird said, "Thank you, for coming to be here for my family."

That was all Jackson had been trying to do for the last few years. He had been desperately trying to find a way to be a good person, to learn what it meant to be altruistic and to truly live it. Jackson had heard many people talk of living this traditional way, referring to it as the "Indian way," but he had seen very few who actually did. Here with Jack Yellow Bird he could be altruistic, he could suffer for one who needs, and he had arrived at precisely the right moment. Those in attendance were preparing to enter yet another sweat lodge, the tenth sweat for Jackson in six days. He gave the ordeal no thought, he recognized only his desire to enter, to begin, to give.

The information he had been given previously by the young man he didn't know proved to be correct. The man pouring water for this lodge was introduced as a Heyoka from Rosebud. Unfamiliar with the society, and having heard only vague descriptions Jackson left it alone. He didn't want to insult anyone or present himself with too high a profile. Quietly he joined the procession when it began to make its way forward to the sweat lodge grounds.

Entering the lodge Jackson found himself seated in the west which is commonly known as the hottest seat in the lodge. The lodge was full of men, as the women would perform a sweat of their own afterwards. He adjusted the towel he carried in with him after arranging himself as best he could. Attempting to get comfortable he breathed in the thick, moist air while those in attendance squeezed their way into the available space left. The man from Rosebud crawled in last and seated himself to the immediate right of the entrance way.

He called to the men tending the fire and over a period of several moments 48 glowing red stones, just under soccer ball size, were brought into the lodge and placed tenderly in the center. After all the grandfather stones were inside with the men the blankets and canvas were tightly secured over the door and the singers began to sing.

Water splashed onto the grandfather stones and they immediately began to sizzle and crackle. As Jackson sweated profusely he prayed, saying thank you for all that had been given, and for strength to continue to live in this good right way. At the conclusion of each round the canvas and blankets were pulled aside to allow a small amount of cool air to enter, and an even smaller amount of moisture-laden air to escape. The moments passed slowly as the men toweled off excess sweat matting hair to flesh. Soon the canvas and blankets were returned and another round began. On the third round for Jackson alone the sweat lodge suddenly expanded exponentially…

…as the size of the lodge increases the universe is suddenly revealed to him. Jackson's eyes expand; all around him is black, as though he is floating in space. With this realization of being in the void his soul promptly rushes back to reality and he finds he is no longer in the sweat lodge. Somehow he is at Sundance.

He is dancing in the southern door as the water song is beaten feverishly upon the drum while singer's shrill voices cleave the hot, dry air. Pierced through his back, facing the supporters, Jackson is clothed entirely in black with a mask covering his face. He is wearing a black Sundance skirt with a black ribbon shirt that is decorated with white hail spots. Jackson sees himself Sundancing, something he swore he would never do. Looking through his mask he notices the supporters are crying...

... and the sweat lodge once again regained its original size. Jackson perceived again the heat, steam and singing as the fourth round came and went quickly. Setting aside the canvas and blankets covering the opening for the last time the men inside crawled out. They scattered about within close proximity of the lodge as they cooled down and toweled excess sweat off their overheated bodies, gulped drafts of desperately sought water.

Jackson's gaze quickly found Yellow Bird seated off to the side along with the man who poured the water. Both were quietly speaking together, and reflecting on what they endured during the brief two hours inside the lodge. As he slowly made his way over to them Jackson overheard Yellow Bird say thank you to the man, addressing him as Stump.

As protocol demanded he stood slightly off to Yellow Bird's right, barely in his peripheral vision. Silently he waited patiently to be acknowledged. The conversation continued between Yellow Bird and Stump for several moments longer, until Yellow Bird eventually gazed up at him and acknowledged his presence. "Thank you, Jackson," he said affectionately, "for coming to pray, to suffer, for my wife."

"You're more than welcome Jack," he responded, "it is always an honor, a privilege, to be here for you and your family. If there is ever anything you may need from me......" he left the statement dangling.

"Everything okay, Jackson?" Yellow Bird asked.

"Sure," he said, "If you guys have a minute I was hoping I could talk to you. Something happened inside the lodge and maybe you might understand it, or help me to understand it. You and, Stump is it?" Jackson extended his hand respectfully in greeting to Stump.

Stump accepted his outstretched hand although it was quite apparent he would have preferred not to. With a quick perfunctory pump he let go.

Stump was a short, fat, little man with thinning hair and no teeth. Something about him felt greasy to Jackson, like fry bread, which Stump obviously ate too much of, which had been sitting out too long. Yellow Bird gave Stump a quick overview of who Jackson was. He told him of how he had brought the eagle feather among the Elders at the request of the Clan Mothers.

In a manner of speaking, Yellow Bird was vouching for Jackson. Turning again to Jackson he invited him to explain what had taken place moments before in the lodge. Jackson quickly acquiesced and upon completing his explanation he sat back and waited patiently, quietly.

Stump had a look of deep irritation on his face as he stared at him for long moments. Jackson had no previous experience with heyoka's and he had never had a conversation with someone who was referred to as one. He had learned from the Elders he had met that many people confuse a heyoka with a contrary. The two medicines carried by individuals chosen to live these ways are vastly different from each other.

A contrary is just that, someone who behaves and speaks in a contrary manner. Someone who says one thing and means the opposite of what they are saying. Contrary men will often wear woman's clothes and vice versa. In the winter, the contrary will complain of the heat and in the summer complain of the cold. The medicine of a contrary is learned over a person's life as they spend years practicing how to recognize and then approach a situation as needed. This medicine is used only in ceremonial situations and not in general everyday life.

The heyoka is born to be. Every waking moment is spent being what they came into this existence as. The heyoka can behave as a contrary, but the contrary can never be a heyoka. They are two completely different creatures entirely.

Known by every indigenous society to have ever existed, The Sacred Clown carries many names. To the Lakota he is known as a heyoka. Others call him a koshare, koyemshi and many other names. These are the thunder dreamers and without a doubt they are the most annoying creatures on the planet. A mosquito or a buzzing fly on a hot summer day can only aspire to be as painstakingly bothersome as a true heyoka.

Every waking moment, with no pretense or effort, the heyoka naturally grinds and gnaws on every nerve of the unsuspecting victim before them. If there is an issue buried deep in the psyche, pain, scars; the heyoka will bring that pain to the surface. They will force the person who has made the unfortunate decision to have a conversation with them to deal with it. The heyoka is a mirror and reflects back whatever is in front of them. Living with a medicine similar to that of a thunderstorm, they bring the crashing thunder, whipping winds and beating hail upon those who need it. They clear away the detritus and undergrowth from someone's life and in the aftermath new life begins. The sun will rise once again and break dawn on a new beginning.

Very few true heyokas ever have or ever will exist. Those born into this way of life are a miserable, suffering people. A true heyoka has no friends and most people prefer not to have anything to do with them. Very few love them and even those that do can only tolerate them for so long. Most despise them and abhor their very presence.

Few people figure out what is taking place when they are around a true heyoka. Typically they don't realize they are with a clown until they suddenly find themselves incensed and then blame the here-to-for unknown clown in front of them. The accuser had probably never met this person before, but somehow the clown is responsible for every horrible thing that had ever happened to the accuser. The heyoka's were to blame for all the accuser's ills and woes. No one in their right or wrong mind would ever want to be heyoka. Heyoka's didn't want to be heyoka's, as if they had a choice.

The medicine they live with is very similar to chemotherapy. Like chemo they destroy to heal, breaking down and eating away the emotional cancer within. Painfully they extract the spiritual tumor until the patient slowly begins to recuperate. Listening to Jackson explain what had transpired only moments before, Stump heatedly lost his temper. "What the hell is it with you white people?" Stump inquired belligerently, "You show up here, there and everywhere playing Indian. Everyone wants to be the medicine man. Where do you people come from?"

While he ranted Jackson stared at the ground. He didn't want to look up and allow this man to see the rage building in him. Stump had been introduced as a Sacred Clown and Jackson wanted to believe this was what was taking place. Unfortunately, it wasn't.

In an effort to teach Jackson that Stump was full of shit and only playing at being a heyoka, the Ancients caused a wolf spider, its circumference as large as the bottom of a coffee cup, to cross in front of Stump's vision. The spider is also seen as a trickster and is considered a cousin of sorts to the heyoka. The two medicines are similar and each maintain a mutual respect for the other. Often they are used in conjunction with each other and neither would ever purposefully kill the other. With no hesitation Stump reached down and crushed the spider. Jackson observed Stump do this, saw that the man had no remorse for his action, and instantly realized Stump was completely serious in his rant. No spiritual medicine was coming into play.

"I am Lakota," Stump continued in a rage, "This is my way of life. I grew up in this. My parents grew up in this. I speak the language. I know the ceremonies and the songs. Why is it everywhere I go some white guy like you has to show up talking about crap they know nothing about? Trying to be something they never will be. You're not Lakota. You will never be Lakota. You don't know these ways and you never will. Where did you hear that story? Who made that crap up that you are talking about?"

Jackson calmly accepted Stump's rant and refused to answer Stump's questions. Standing he ended the conversation. He ineffectually thanked Stump and Yellow Bird then wandered off to be by himself to breathe. He needed to be alone before he did something he could never undo. The dragon, slumbering deeply in its cage, opened one eye and sensed opportunity. Struggling, Jackson denied it, again.

He had heard this same argument many times from many others. Supposedly, unless someone spoke the language of whatever specific Nation they were involved with, that person could not possibly understand anything spiritual about that Nation – their point being the Ancients speak only their specific language.

That was the very same conversation he had days before with Alvin Redstone in Cookeville but Alvin had shed a different light on things for Jackson. He said that the Ancients spoke in a way each individual knew – that they speak in a way each has the individual ability to comprehend. The Ancients don't speak one language, they speak every language.

In actuality, Stump was an alcoholic and ex drug addict. The only thing he grew up with was running with the gangs on the reservation, not the warrior or medicine societies. In Stump's younger years he had no interest in anything vaguely traditional or spiritual. His grandparents were traditional and practiced regularly, but Stump as a young man practiced rebellion. His parents were alcoholics and both his mother and father died from alcohol abuse. Not until later in life did he begin to do anything that resembled traditional Lakota. He assumed the role he now portrayed as a means to provide for himself, not from any real desire to live traditionally.

Two more days passed at Yellow Bird's place, Jackson attended a few more sweats and enjoyed a few meals with those in attendance. On the third day he prepared to leave and as he was warming up his van, smoking a cigarette and finishing his morning coffee, Yellow Bird came out of his house. He walked up to Jackson asked, "Got a minute before you leave?"

"Certainly," he said. Weak from two weeks of ceremony Jackson quickly dismissed his exhaustion and composed himself, "What's up Jack?"

"Someone I want you to meet," Yellow Bird replied. Turning away he headed for his lodge grounds, expecting Jackson to follow. Arriving where the sweat lodge was constructed he introduced an older man sitting there. "Jackson, this is Tony Baker," he said, "Tony lives up in southwestern Pennsylvania. We were talking about what you saw in the lodge the other day."

Jackson fired up a cigarette and waited. He was still seething over the way he had been treated by Stump although he refused to show it. Appearing to be captivated he encouraged Yellow Bird to continue. "Tony has a tire shop up there," he said, "He also has a small trailer for rent. Nothing fancy, but it's a roof. I understand you probably feel like Stump was pretty hard on you the other day. Sometimes the folks from out there they can get really upset at people. Especially those they think are stealing their stuff. So much has already been taken and continues to be taken every day. There isn't much left.

"Many out here in the east play games with things they have no understanding of. Setting themselves up as something they can never be. Putting themselves behind the bucket so to speak. Running lodges and pipe ceremonies. I'm not saying that is what you are doing Jackson, and I don't necessarily agree with what Stump did. I invited him here because another Elder I know couldn't make it, and Stump brought some medicine that had been prepared for my wife. Obviously something happened to you in that lodge. Something is trying to get your attention and is telling you to do something.

"Tony has a friend on Pine Ridge who has a Sundance and he is willing to call to see if he can get you an invitation to go there. Tony is also willing to give you a job at his shop and rent you his trailer. What do you think Jackson?"

A bit taken aback at the generosity shown, especially after the first day, he needed a moment to compose himself. "Sounds great," he said, "exactly what I need to do."

He gratefully shook Yellow Bird's hand and then Tony Baker's. "Guess I'm heading for Pennsylvania," he commented, "as good as anywhere else, I suppose."

After giving Jackson the address Tony Baker began to describe the town he lived in. He said it was small and mountainous with lots of trees. There were people scattered sparsely about and it was mostly a farm community. Yellow Bird said his goodbyes knowing they would be leaving shortly.

Jackson and Tony continued to talk over coffee for the next hour and when they were ready to leave he pulled his van behind Tony's car. With Tony leading the way they headed for Pennsylvania. True to his word Tony gave Jackson a job in his shop and rented the trailer to him, a small camping trailer with one bedroom he had originally set up to give him somewhere to crash after one beer too many in the shop.

Tony Baker was fifty seven, and had retired from the steel mill a few years earlier. He is stocky with gray hair in a buzz cut and a thick gray moustache. Married for over forty years, but his wife didn't come by the shop very often. The tire shop was something to do, something to keep him busy and out of the house. Not native by any means and certainly not an Indian fan, for whatever reason even Tony didn't understand he connected to native people. Having met a few native people earlier in life, their way of life resonated with him. He never Sundanced or performed any ceremonies. He considered that an insult to an honorable People. He simply helped out where and when he could.

Jackson was quite content. He had running water and electricity, luxuries he often had to do without. The bed was small but the toilet worked and so did the shower. For the last few years he had been living out of a van, his toilet the woods or a bucket. Heating water to wash with by filling one gallon plastic milk jugs and setting them in the sun.

In the morning all he needed to do was walk a few hundred yards and he was at work. The rent was low and the wages were more than enough to cover groceries and expenses. Tony contacted his friend, David Chases, and secured an invitation to Sundance for Jackson later that year. Tony wouldn't be going and he advised Jackson to save his money and prepare himself for what he knew would be an extremely difficult thing for him to do.

200°
CHAPTER TWENTY

Finally, the twenty four hour drive from South Dakota, as well as Jackson's reverie, came to an end. He was looking forward to passing out in his cramped room in the tire shop. After the trailer burned to the ground, Jackson had nowhere else to go. He couldn't afford an apartment and didn't have a car any longer. There was a small room in the back of Tony's shop he had been using for storage and Tony offered the room to him if he was willing to clean it out.

Needing only a place to sleep, Jackson was more than willing. He glanced around the room and noticed several cases of road flares amidst the junk, as well as a couple of old flare guns. For whatever reason they held his attention for a moment then he let them go. After a little cleaning, the room was habitable, the junk, including the flares (although for some reason he can't explain he insured they were accessible) have been moved to the sides and covered with some old tarps. The next morning Tony followed Jackson to Uniontown to return the rental car. "Going to have to find a new car now, eh, Jackson?" Tony remarked.

"Yeah," Jackson agreed, then asked, "What are you going to do with that '84 Gran Prix, Tony?"

"The shop car?" he inquired, "Nothing, really. Needs a tune up, some front end parts, maybe a couple of tires. Interior ain't that great. I've been using it the last few years to haul stuff. Was the wife's car, why, you want it?"

"Sure," Jackson said, "think it will take much to put it right?"

"Naaa," Tony replied, "Couple of hundred bucks should do it. I'll give it to ya, you can work on it in the shop. You have to buy the parts for it though."

"Sounds like a deal," Jackson agreed enthusiastically.

With everything they talked about, Sundance was never a part of the conversation. Tony and Chases had a major falling out because Chases never eased up the pressure on Tony. He constantly demanded Tony supply him with more and more. Enough was eventually enough and Tony walked away. Tony suggested that Jackson might want to do the same, but as much as he would like to, he couldn't. Jackson had made a promise, a commitment, and come hell or high water he fully intended to keep that commitment. Intended to fulfill that promise regardless of what Chases did to him. Tony respected Jackson's decision although he regretted ever having made the initial introduction. He was well aware of what Chases was doing to Jackson but he also realized there was nothing he could do about it. Whatever happened, whatever Jackson did, was up to Jackson now.

Jackson returned to his daily routine as the wounds deep in his chest and back slowly healed. Without the aid of painkillers or antibiotics they began to close of their own accord, and some months on the wounds would leave immense scars. Whenever Jackson looked at them, the words of Junior Rutledge echo in his mind, *just call me the butcher.*

During the evenings Jackson worked on the Pontiac. Tony helped him out and soon they had it drivable. A few months after returning, Mary Bloody Heart called to check to see how Jackson was doing. He reassured her everything was fine, although he could tell something was nagging at her.

Mary was never one to tell tales, start rumors or spread gossip; so whatever was on her mind Jackson would have to discover on his own. She certainly wasn't going to say anything. Toward the end of their conversation she asked if he had heard about Junior Rutledge and Nate Winter. Having been treated so heartlessly at Sundance, he hadn't kept in touch with anyone so he had no clue as to what was taking place on the reservation or what she was talking about.

"No, Mary," he answered, "What have those two fools done now?"

"Some of the local boys were out riding their ponies a few days back and came across their bodies in the Badlands. Junior shot dead and what they could find of Nate Winter."

Jackson didn't know what to say. Mary obviously knew a great deal more than she was willing to reveal. He also knew it was pointless trying to get the story out of her. In typical Mary Bloody Heart fashion, she gave just enough information to arouse curiosity then left it to the individual to decide if they wanted to satisfy that curiosity. A few more banal comments and directionless sentences and she said good bye. It was to be the last time Jackson would speak with Mary Bloody Heart.

The next morning Jackson saw Tony. "Morning Tony," Jackson said, "Hey, you hear anything about anyone getting shot in the Badlands?"

"No," Tony answered, "I'll make a few phone calls, see what's going on."

Later that day he asked Jackson to step into his office. As Tony slid behind his beaten gray metal desk, Jackson pulled up one of the straight backed chairs in front. "Talked to a few friends out on the Ridge after our conversation this morning," Tony began, "and yeah, couple of guys were found dead in the Badlands. Junior Rutledge and that idiot white guy you went to Sundance with."

Jackson didn't say anything and listened attentively. Tony had heard Jackson left Nate stranded on the reservation, but Tony wasn't a busy body and figured if Jackson wanted to tell him about what happened, he would. Tony understood some things were best left alone and he didn't pry. As far as he was concerned whatever happened wasn't any of his business. Knowing Chases all too well, having been a victim of his ploys and cons for too many years, Tony wasn't too surprised about what happened. If Jackson had done it he probably had a damn good reason to.

"You knew Junior was involved in running drugs, didn't you, Jackson?" Tony asked.

"Yeah, I knew about it," he said, somewhat distractedly, "I didn't agree with it and certainly never got involved, although he did ask me to. Seemed hypocritical, selling poison to his own people. I heard he used some of that money to buy firewood and propane for a few of the older folks but all in all the whole thing never tasted right to me. I figured Junior was doing what he was doing and it was best for me to stay the hell out of it."

"That was a good call," Tony said, nodding his head in agreement, "Seems Nate wasn't so smart about it. From what I was told this morning Junior convinced Nate selling drugs was a good idea and it didn't take him long to get deeply involved with Junior. Whenever a shipment would come, instead of driving all the way east, Junior would meet him half way then Nate would deliver it to Junior's contacts out here. Worked out pretty good for Junior. Half the distance, all the money. Except Nate just couldn't keep his mouth shut. He got to talking about shit he never should have. Overnight he began to envision himself as a drug kingpin. Suddenly he knew everything there was to know about drug running.

"He divided his time between here and Pine Ridge. When he was here he was either in the bars telling everything he knew about how to be a drug smuggler, or at the local powwows and gatherings telling everyone about how you failed at Sundance. How you asked him for water your first day and didn't finish your commitment.

"Nate got to flapping his lips around the wrong people and word got back because everyone, even Junior, has a boss. Junior involving Nate without permission pissed off some very nasty people and a few hitters got sent to Junior's place. They hung around and waited for Nate to show up. I guess Nate collected the money from here then drove out and delivered it to Junior.

"Those enforcers from that bike club used a new shipment as a decoy and showed up at Junior's place the same time Nate did. They gagged and bound them then drove them off into the Badlands. Shot Junior in the head immediately. Nate, well, he didn't fare so good. A couple of those guys, they went old school all over his face. Grabbed a couple of worn out bike chains and wrapped the chains around their fists. They commenced to beating him until even dental records couldn't prove who he was. When they were done they tied him between a couple of their bikes and tore him in two for nothing more than shits and giggles. They used a shotgun to blast apart what was left. Only way anyone knew it was Nate Winter was his car parked at Junior's place."

Slowly Jackson leaned back into his chair. He fired up a cigarette and took several long drags as he allowed the information sink in. "Well butter my butt and call me a biscuit," he said sarcastically. Jackson couldn't say he was too surprised at this chain of events and Tony didn't look all that surprised, either.

"Few things else you probably need to hear about, Jackson," Tony said.

"What's that?" he asked with mild confusion, not having any idea where Tony was going with the conversation.

"I understand you had some problems out there this year besides Nate and Junior," Tony said, "I heard about the butcher thing and how Junior was bragging he did that to you on purpose. Seems he spread that layer of shit all over the rez along with a few other things, too."

Tony now had him on the edge of his seat. Staring intently Jackson encouraged Tony, "Go on."

"Well," he started, "you are well aware of the shit I dealt with from Chases. You know he harassed me for ten grand, supposedly for his Sundance. Tried to convince me I had to give it him. Like I have ten grand. Anyway, you know he and I got into a pretty nasty argument about it?

"Chases is blaming you for the argument. He says you convinced me not to give him the money. Chases is also saying you never finished your commitment, that you asked him to allow you to quit on the second day. He's telling folks that's the reason why you didn't return." Jackson stares. The dragon peeked.

"You weren't on the grounds that third day, I understand?" Tony continued, "Headed over to Mary Bloody Heart's place?"

"Yeah," Jackson replied, "Mary invited me to come to her place that third day and I went with her."

"Well, Chases took all the dancers aside that third day you were gone," Tony said, "In the arbor after the morning rounds he informed the other dancers you quit. He told them about you saying the Sundance Tree had spoken to you. He said the tree only speaks to him and no one else especially not someone who quits. Between Junior and Chases there are some pretty ugly rumors going on about you on the Ridge right now, Jackson. You are being referred to as 'Jack Ass,' 'Jack Shit,' and 'Jack Off.'

"I have come to know you pretty well Jackson and I have to say this doesn't sound like you at all. Of course I know Chases as well. Knew Junior pretty good, too. You want to tell me what the hell happened out there? Totally up to you but I'm in your corner. You know I'll help if I can."

After several moments the room slowly stopped spinning and Jackson regained control of himself. The depth of betrayal he was feeling seemed to coat every inch of him. For the next few hours, with Tony drinking his beer and Jackson chain smoking cigarettes, he related the actual events to Tony. When all was said and done, Tony stood up and maneuvered around his desk. Silently he shook Jackson's hand.

"About what I figured," Tony said angrily. Belching as he turned to walk back into the shop Tony said, "Well, back to work." The conversation was over. Nothing more was said about it over the next few weeks. Time droned on, day into night.

Late on a Sunday evening a sudden knock on the door interrupted Jackson's routine. The final catalyst that would alter his life forever was moments away. He opened the door and standing in the doorway was a distraught and apparently extremely upset Tony Baker. Not waiting for a salutation Tony looked up at him and said, "Mary Bloody Heart died today. Heart complications. Something went wrong with her pacemaker. Before they could get to her in time she was gone."

A professional pugilist can only fantasize about delivering such a blow as precisely, with as much force. Jackson's only refuge, the one person who guided him, cared so deeply about him, for him, was gone. The mother he had never known. The only maternal influence in his life that had any effect had been stripped away. Dorothy Magnate had tried but like latex over oil what she attempted to instill never seemed to stick. "You okay, Jackson?" Tony inquired with deep concern.

Jackson had gone pale and it seemed he wasn't breathing. Without a word he shut the door. For a few moments Tony stared at the door then walked away. He knew how much Mary meant to Jackson. He knew the depth of their relationship. Obviously Jackson needed some time alone to process this news.

Jackson turned from the door and crashed into the nearest chair, his vacant eyes unfocused. Staring, he saw only the past. The years they spent together. Mary's laugh echoing in his mind; her soft voice, so quiet, yet so easily grasping one's immediate attention.

Jackson was lost and adrift on a sea of despair. The ship of sanity he sailed on, relied on, was unexpectedly blown out of the water. Sunk to the bottom with no life saving debris. He floated as the sharks circled, the drop of blood in the water sensed from miles away. The dragon, ensconced for so long, was acutely aware of the change. The mortar and stones of its tomb once so firmly held in place, began to flake and decay.

210°
CHAPTER TWENTY ONE

A day later Jackson stumbled from his room and, in a fog, attempted to navigate through disjointed days. Working in Tony's shop he paid barely the slightest attention to what he was doing. He almost tore his fingers off working the tire machine. A car he didn't secure properly almost fell off the rack while another vehicle, the lugs nuts not tightened correctly, lost its rear wheel within a mile of leaving the tire shop.

Tony soon pulled him aside and relieved him of his responsibilities. Jackson couldn't seem to focus and before he got hurt, or worse, killed, Tony had to let him go for a while; although he compassionately allowed him to continue to use the room in the back of the shop. Tony realized Jackson had been shaken pretty hard but he expected in a few days he would be back to himself and life would go on.

Jackson accepted his temporary dismissal without question, the dismissal seeming not to register. He spent days in a lawn chair outside behind the tire shop, well into the evenings until the cold, crisp night air drove him inside, only to find him in another chair. Sleeping irregularly, eating only the occasional cold hot dog or fistful of luncheon meat.

Year after year of betrayal, abuse and neglect resounding in him as 'lost in pain' defined his existence. Wave after unrelenting wave, with no one to provide solace. No one to say, "Hey, it's going to be alright." No one there to catch him as he fell from this tree he had tenuously been clinging to. As he unconsciously reached and picked up the phone, intending to call Mary Bloody Heart, he swiftly collided with reality. Viciously he was reminded, as if he could possibly forget, she was gone.

The dragon buried so deeply within him closely monitored every emotion, guiding some emotions, creating others. Tapping against the walls of its prison, it sought one small crack. Finding it, the mental mortar began to free beneath its yellowed, crusted claws.

Jackson was alone. He had always been alone, except for the few precious years he spent in Mary's company. Everything he had to endure, all that he had lived through, he did it alone. Every ounce of pain he suffered through, he suffered alone. It appeared he would suffer though this alone, too.

It wasn't that he hadn't tried to create and maintain relationships. He had, diligently, but they all seemed to crumble in his hands. He had many liaisons with women, each one an attempt to create a lasting relationship between them. Each physical encounter he drank deeply from like a man lost in the desert desperate for a drop of cool, sweet water.

Lost in the desert of loneliness, love was the liquid sustenance he sought. But how could he find something he wouldn't recognize if he did find it? Jackson couldn't define love, couldn't give love a form. Love was something he had absolutely no understanding of and every attempt at a relationship ended miserably. Except with Mary Bloody Heart, and now she was gone. His heart ached for a mother's love, for the comfort only Mary had been able to give him. Never again would he feel the comfort of her words.

When pure love was stripped away what remained was a warped imitation and no lack of women to provide it. The biggest obstacle to maintaining a relationship was Jackson's inability to give something back emotionally, which was what these women believed he should. In mere months the fluttering wisps of desire, the illusionary gratification of physical union, was wiped away to be replaced with revulsion. The initial sparks of interest devolved into vindictiveness and cruelty because he wouldn't give them what they craved, because he was unable to connect to a need within them. They were as emotionally mangled as he was and needed their own version of emotional sustenance. Dismally the crippled were drawn to and found each other as moths to a putrid flame, only to eventually abuse each other.

There were some good women who lived in the area but they were either married or not interested. Most of the women Jackson met were femi-nazi man-haters from prior abusive relationships seeking to castrate every swinging dick they could find. He had as difficult a time becoming friends with the local men, especially the self-proclaimed "warriors." A few were genetically native, but most were non natives playing out their fantasies; and all were as culturally white as the society they lived in. They were pacified little boys in men's bodies who submissively begged permission to use their balls and allowed themselves to be pushed around like unwanted, albeit necessary, pets.

Other than a select few, none had ever attended a real ceremony in their lives. Regardless, that lack of any real knowledge didn't stop them. Given the slightest provocation they enlightened Jackson on all they thought they knew, the worst being some of the women – self titled 'Clan Mothers' who demanded the east coast assume a matriarchal position with absolutely no appreciation for the emotional price that was paid daily by those who actually lived matriarchal.

Crystal twinkies, bliss bunnies, and paid-in-full members of the love'n light brigade – a veritable smorgasbord of wannabe medicine men and spiritual leaders paraded through; every one of them as fake as the fairy wings duct taped to their backs and the pixie dust they sprinkled all over each other. They came together around their made up ceremonies, or slapped together powwows to gratify each other with the latest book or movie.

Everywhere were the miscarried of organized religion, wicca, reiki, witchcraft or any other concocted new age spiritual rubbish they could come up with. When all those forms of make believe failed them, they decided to play Indian, and were as embarrassing as any cast of characters from F-Troop's band of Fugawe. Forlorn and abandoned, they desperately pursued the Indian show, blindly accepting the newest rendition from days of old, the wise benevolent Elder, or the stoic, emotionless warrior.

Just as fervently, they invited full bloods to their half-baked ceremonies where they opened the door to being devoured, because the best at playing Indian are, of course, Indians themselves. Manipulative and cunning, raised in the culture, they see the culture as a something to be used. Well aware of what is expected of them, and fully prepared to provide it, for a price, their fee paid by the individual or latest "friends of the Indians," with their coffee cans for "love offerings."

The urban confused were unable or unwilling to consider that most of the "societies" that come off the reservation are as made up as anything out in suburbia. Some full blood idjit hung a title on himself, undeserved and unearned, from a Society that either never existed, is extinct or they aren't a member of. Brought that fabricated society from the reservation to the imaginations of the willingly subservient, and were instantly accepted as authentic. One phone call to the cultural office would prove it was fictitious, but no one wanted to make that phone call.

This behavior only served to make life that much more of a daily endurance, and any real natives in the area kept to themselves. Jackson and those like him often found themselves decried as fake because they had no desire or interest in tolerating the latest twisted rendition of "the red road." Somehow what was real wound up labeled as arrogant and insolent by what wasn't real, and what wasn't real was accepted as truth. How this worked was beyond explanation, but there you had it.

Inadvertently a chuckle escaped his lips, though doubtlessly he was vaguely aware. He was remembering some of the women he had tried to form relationships with, those who at first blush appeared to have some sensibility about them, but he quickly ascertained he was fishing in a septic tank. He had never been adept at choosing female companions. It's something he seemed to have absolutely no natural talent for. The crazier they were, the more likely he was going to wind up dating them. A mix blood friend liked to tell him that he could be in a room with 1,000 women where 999 were perfectly sane, but that one out of 1,000 – bat shit insane out of her mind – she was the one he'd end up with. If there was a woman within a hundred miles whose baggage had baggage, whose issues had issues of their own, he would probably wake up next to her.

There was the mix blood Nanticoke who insisted native ceremonies were for natives only. Mentally challenged didn't begin to describe that modern day Medusa. At the time, Jackson was bored and hadn't been involved with anyone for awhile. Inadvisably, he agreed when she suggested a physical relationship between them. She had ulterior motives and knew he was completely unaware of them. After she managed to aggravate and annoy everyone Jackson introduced her to he showed her the door. It took six weeks but he eventually figured out she encouraged a sexual relationship with him only as a means to ensnare him. When he refused to concede to her demands for marriage she became enraged and bitter.

After contacting a distant militant group of mix bloods she lied to them and inferred Jackson was a rapist, just to screw him one more time. Days after that fiasco she launched a rumor that Jackson didn't want her because he was having a ménage a trois with Mary Bloody Heart and another native Grandmother. He heard through the moccasin telegraph she ultimately wound up in Canada where, after starting her insolent behavior with someone else, the women in that community enthusiastically kicked her ass.

There was the mix blood Shawnee woman, although calling her Shawnee was stretching it more than a tad. More white than anything else, what blood she had needed to be carefully preserved, as the smallest cut shaving her legs would send all her native heritage flowing down the drain. A walking, talking fuck monster of the highest order, Jackson didn't have it in him to don the swim fins and snorkel any longer. Long after he quit dating that lunatic he continued to try to help her. He bought her a car, paid her bills and assisted when her daughter got pregnant at fifteen, by her fourteen year old boyfriend. What Jackson got in return for his generosity was a knife between the ribs.

Every once in awhile he would hear from someone who knew her and they would inform him she continued to go out of her way to crucify him at every possible opportunity. She was so sure they were soul mates and they had to be together for all eternity. Her thought was if she couldn't have him she would make sure no one else wanted him either. She really was a sad, twisted little freak.

The latest in a long string of attempts to quench his thirst at a mirage was Mandy, a demented diva and nothing short of a super freak. A full blood white chick, the only Indian she ever had in her was Jackson. As impossible as it sounds little miss Mandy was also an ordained minister. Jackson in a relationship with a bible thumping sky pilot – the very idea is absurd in its recounting.

She was older than Jackson, but age meant nothing to him. Mandy was a cougar and he was more than willing to play cub for awhile. She wore the mask of prim and proper, but put that woman in fuck-me-pumps and stockings, and the things that come out of her mouth would make a porn star blush.

Although she was raised in a strict catholic family her religious upbringing did little to quench the hungers within her. She had desires that were not easily satiated by the men she chose as partners. While she was willing to try almost anything her partners proved to be either completely inept or thoroughly disinterested in fulfilling her needs. She was, however, expected to fulfill theirs. If hers were met in the process, well, good for her. If not, that was her problem to deal with.

Mandy married a few times, the first time to a sexually deviant man who couldn't seem to satisfy the dark things inside him. His interests lay in inflicting pain. Within weeks of her marriage she was gift wrapped and hung from whatever apparatus he imagined. He wasn't a man of great financial means but he was creative. As a man with significant mechanical skills he built whatever he needed, devising all sorts of new contraptions to tie her to, in as many positions as his tangled, perverted imagination could conjure. After several years she grew bored with their sadomasochistic lifestyle and divorced him, moving on to new adventures.

Always a daddy's girl, she remarried quickly as she was uncomfortable remaining on her own. Still young and attractive then, it was relatively easy to hook another husband. The first she married to satiate sexual appetite, the next she married for money. Whether or not love played a role in either relationship only Mandy could say and she wasn't talking.

Her second marriage was shorter than her first and although her new husband was wealthy he bored easily. He had a few appetites of his own and they involved as many partners as he could find. Often orgies and swinger parties were held in their upper class home with Mandy being used by several men while her husband watched. She enjoyed it, couldn't get enough of it, and was a quick student. Soon desiring the dominant role she began scheduling the parties where she could find the men and women she wanted to play with. But, as Mandy tired of being a sex toy her new husband tired of her.

Her previous catholic upbringing unexpectedly began ringing the church bells in her memory with slight pangs of guilt and she decided to end their marriage, but she wasn't going away that easily. After the divorce settlement she owned all of their physical property and half of the bank account. Mandy immediately threw herself into her religion to ease her conscience over what she had been a part of, had initiated and enjoyed, for several years.

She began presenting herself as an upstanding, middle class woman of means, driving a sensible car and wearing clothes that didn't call attention to her more than ample assets. What men she led to her bed were young surrogates, boy toys and play things. It was not that she didn't want to date men her age it was that men her age weren't interested in dating her. Viagra wasn't created so old men could have sex with old women.

Mandy also grew up enthralled with Native American romance novels. Within months of her latest divorce she was attending local powwows and meeting some of the people. She learned and took to heart whatever twisted version of spirituality was currently being touted as "the way" and latched onto any unsuspecting Elder she could find to suck them dry of their knowledge.

Her next step was to superimpose native spirituality over christianity. That absurdity devolved to where she was teaching convoluted christian theology with native overtones. Any attempt to follow what she believed left someone scratching their head wondering what the hell they were listening too. The unfortunate and erroneous decision was made by somebody to introduce Mandy to the needs of prisoners, men locked up in facilities across the state. Using a baffling complex agglomeration of christianity, Lakota, Haudenasaunee, Ojibwa and Cherokee; she began teaching the men in prisons all about Jesus the Lakota and Mary the Powhatan. Each prison received their own personal version, each a different medicine wheel, each their own spirit animal.

They met at a powwow where Jackson happened to be. He was bored and had nothing better to do that particular day so he spent the afternoon watching the local crop of weekend warriors bring their imaginations to life. As he entertained himself with their antics Mandy walked up, introduced herself, and they spent the day together laughing and flirting. At the conclusion of the day's activities she invited him to return with her to her home. Relatively attractive for her age, understanding she was probably nuts, Jackson decided, why not?

He found himself speechless immediately upon entering her home. Mandy had adorned the walls of her home with religious depictions. Every picture, painting and statue was a native in a christian setting –the thirteen apostles as thirteen Lakota, Jesus as Chief Joseph of the Nez Perce and Mary Magdalene as the White Buffalo Calf Woman. Her home was a museum of the surreal with the fantasies of every pull-and-play, "aho" sputtering, aspiring goddess of the great celestial beyond, realized in full Technicolor.

Jackson stared in stupefied awe. He was directed to a couch where he sat down as she babbled some inane nonsense about Jesus coming to America. As she droned on incessantly Jackson was wondering what ring of hell he would be in if Dante had written a version for the delusional. Just how looney tunes is this chick?

His gaze returned to surveying her décor – Martha Stewart on crack with a side of modern new age spiritualism infused with christianity, all overlain by native spirituality. It was amazing to behold. Noticing she didn't have his undivided attention Mandy excused herself and returned moments later in g-string and stockings. Throughout the day she had attempted to beguile Jackson with her christian/native blended ideology, but this evening she couldn't get on her knees fast enough. Amen sister and pass the penis.

For six months they continued to see each other and Mandy visited only on the weekends. Some nights she arrived at Jackson's door in nothing more than an ankle length fur coat and a smile. Considering she was high society made their involvement that much more ludicrous.

Adding to the insanity, as if it could possibly get any worse, she was a 25 year veteran of the mental health field. Mandy worked as a counselor for people so twisted in their minds they were not sure who they were much less what planet they were on. God must have been on a bad acid trip when he came up with her.

Occasionally the two of them would venture out on the town for dinner and invariably people stared as if they were witnessing a train wreck, their eyes denying what was so obviously before them, unable or unwilling to turn away.

Mandy eventually began to insist she was married to Jesus and she vigilantly informed everyone he was her true husband. Her conviction went as far as she could take it, even to the point of wearing a wedding ring to symbolize their beatific union. When asked about the ring she related to the inquisitor gushingly all about how Jesus was her one, true love. Crayons weren't necessary, she brought her own form of crazy to the table.

With all her attestations of the celestial union between Jesus and Mandy, she had one small problem. Jesus wouldn't bend her over and slap her ass, telling her she had been a bad girl. Jackson would, and did, many times. Many a Monday morning found Mandy squirming in her padded office chair with his hand branded temporarily, by sheer force, on the cheeks of her ass.

Often Jackson would get a phone call Tuesday or Wednesday mornings because Mandy was distracted from her duties as a counselor. All she could think of was the coming weekend's activities. Jackson willingly played the role of pool boy or tennis coach, basically cuckolding Jesus Christ himself and the very thought left him convulsing in fits of laughter. Especially considering her last husband liked to watch. Jackson hoped Jesus was enjoying himself.

The dragon, locked deeply away in Jackson's subconscious, was all too well aware of her hypocrisy, elongating its forked tongue and sliding it into the crack beneath the door of its cage to lick up and savor each delicious drop of perversion Mandy's Oedipus appetites were creating; like decadent chocolates, each so exquisite and divine.

Jackson soon realized Mandy's demands for sexual violence were escalating and he became consciously aware of the effect it was having on him, that it was awakening desires and needs Jackson had long since buried. Mandy and her twisted need for punishment, along with her voyeuristic celestial husband, had to go. The last he heard of her she had sucked up to another Elder and after stealing his altar and mimicking his medicine she was presenting herself as some great spiritual leader goddess. As perplexing as it was, the fools lined up to follow her.

She did leave Jackson with more than memories of satiated lust. As a mental health professional she regularly quoted to him from the DSM, the bible for psychiatrists, psychologists and counselors like her. In her mind she had to come up with a diagnosis for him to at least explain to herself what was wrong with him. Mandy also loved to read every version of native Spirituality she could get her hands on and often quoted from biographies of famous Native American healers and prophets, as though those biographies were instruction manuals illustrating the proper behavior Jackson was expected to emulate.

Based on her professional diagnosis, Jackson was a border line sociopath with a severe case of PTSD, fueled by homicidal tendencies. Based on her native knowledge he was a medicine man in the making. She was obviously out of her mind, interpretations aside. He paid no attention to her inane ramblings and waited patiently for her to satisfy her justifications so they could retire to the nearest piece of furniture or floor space and do what Mandy really came to see him for.

Reaching inside himself Jackson pulled back to reality and released his grasp on fading memories. He had to do something. He couldn't sit in this chair or that chair day after day numb. Having leaned on the ceremonies of his Ancestors to guide and assist him to the point he was at now he again turned to those ceremonies.

Jackson decided to do it himself, with no assistance. He gathered a few items and set out for the nearest secluded, forested area he could find. An hour later after securing a position of guaranteed isolation he made himself comfortable and began to pray.

These ceremonies are ancient in nature and should never be conducted unless under close supervision and guidance – certainly never when someone is in the state of despair he was in. Performing these alone with no protection or direction is foolhardy at best. Doors are opened. Cracks between worlds and dimensions are revealed. Invitations are extended that invite admission to entities of all shades both beneficial and destructive.

Whatever happened, if anything happened, would need to be interpreted. Doing so by oneself is inviting disaster because no one can or should interpret these things on their own. Self interpretation is always biased to the individual's expectations and those expectations could lead to substantially devastating results.

Jackson sat alone watching as the sun slowly faded into the horizon. Something was coming. He could feel it. The creatures of the forest sensed a rising storm and sought shelter. When this excursion was complete he would no longer be who, or what, he had endeavored for so many years to become.

220°
CHAPTER TWENTY TWO

This was not the first night on the hill for Jackson. Each year at Sundance and prior to it, he made a journey off alone to prepare himself emotionally and mentally for what he was about to do. The first hours alone are typically uneventful as he noticed the forest animals meandering about in their daily routines of seeking food and shelter. He recalled a story given to him the first time he set out on one of these sojourns to humble himself before all of creation. An Elder of deep wisdom and vast compassion, and several in their first year as well as Jackson, were gathered around an open fire. This Elder was instructing them on what to expect and on how to handle what was about to happen.

"Some time ago, but not too long ago, a young man much like those of you seated here began his journey on this very same road. That evening is also to be his first alone in the dark. With determination and feigned courage he willingly follows his escorts as they guide him to his place on the hill and he is prayed for. The sacred songs are sung and he is promptly left there to begin his ordeal.

Sometime late in the evening he hears something crash though the woods in the distance. As fear creeps up his spine this thing, whatever it may be, crashes and careens through the forest. As it comes closer and closer he becomes terrified. More and more the fear paralyzes him with each passing second. Desperate to run yet unable to live with shaming his family, he quickly grabs his c'anupa and begins to pray.

Closer and closer whatever it is comes. Thundering, branches breaking, the brush trampled. He buries his face deep in the earth and grips his c'anupa tightly. Squeezing the stem with all his strength, he is beside himself with terror. Terror threatens to explode within him as the thing in the night he cannot see makes its way to stand in front of him. Hot breath sears the back of his neck and suddenly this creature hovering above him bellows......moo!"

All at the fire collapsed in laughter. A cow! Each had been imagining their own personal hellhound walking the earth, preparing to devour the young man. That Elder was an excellent storyteller, and through his compassion he created an ease and acceptance among those leaving for their places to pray. Many would find that story all they needed to alleviate their fear and assist them in completing their individual commitments.

Each time the dark encouraged the slightest trepidation in Jackson's mind he returned to that fire and that story. He thought again of that Elder and his compassion. The fear he felt attempting to overwhelm him evaporated instantaneously and the endeavor ultimately culminated in success.

Jackson's first Hanblecia, or humbling, is something he would never forget. Unlike those who were out in the dark his first was conducted inside a sweat lodge. With his fear of the dark he convinced himself that somehow this ordeal would be easier if he performed this ritual inside the lodge instead of out in the darkness alone – as if reverse psychology had any hope of working on the Ancients. The lodge was exactly where they wanted him.

Before entering the lodge for the ceremony, Painted Lady butterflies by the hundreds arrived again, in the same manner as they did for the first ceremony that he attended at Randy Hall's place. The butterflies landed and blessed each individual in attendance as the people gathered around the ceremonial fire, then the butterflies danced into the licking flames of the ceremonial fire and alighted on the glowing embers of the burning wood only to fly back out again unscathed.

When all was prepared and the initiates were ready they left for their chosen places. Jackson was escorted to the sweat lodge and the altar was laid out with the buffalo skull in the center, situated so it faced west approximately three feet in front of the door to the lodge which faced east.

Jackson was instructed to make 1,000 prayer ties for that ceremony; in black, white and red. For reasons never explained, he was instructed not to make any yellow. He was also instructed to carve four forked sticks and fashion six colored robes four feet in length, one each of black, yellow, red and white, with one blue and one green.

As ready as he could be he crawled into the lodge and settled himself in the west with his c'anupa in front of him on a bed of sage. Gazing out the door he saw nine orange butterflies with black and white spots, more Painted Ladies, sitting on the buffalo skull looking at him. One of them took flight and entered the lodge with him. It sailed directly to him where it landed at his c'anupa and died.

The first night he slept and dreamt he was in a cave with blue lights dancing around him. Every night after that was torture. Four days inside a sweat lodge is similar to being locked inside a closet for four days – a closet four feet high with thick, heavy, moist air. The entire time he was inside the lodge Jackson swore he had entered a beehive. A loud buzzing sound continuously filled the interior space. Occasionally the door to the sweat lodge was thrown back as a new grandfather stone that had been heated in the ceremonial fire was added to the pit in the center. During one of these brief moments a black and white spider came to visit.

When the ceremony was complete the door to the lodge was opened and the Painted Lady butterfly that flew in at the beginning of the ceremony resurrected itself and flew away. Jackson watched as it happened and was astonished. Later in the evening as he was talking with the man who had tended his fire he mentioned the buzzing sound. His fireman said he wasn't surprised it sounded like a beehive to Jackson. While he was inside the lodge its exterior had been covered by thousands of dragonflies. No explanation for the events that transpired at that ceremony had ever been offered and to this day Jackson has no idea what they could possibly mean.

Tonight, like that night and many other nights, he sat alone and watched as the sun slowly faded into the horizon. Something was coming. He could feel it. Slowly grief began to envelope him as great torrents of tears flowed across his face.

Jackson remembered reading there are degrees of pain. At some point the pain becomes more than any one person can endure and they lose consciousness. He remembered the pain hanging from the Tree of Life. He felt again the breath rush from him when he was informed of Mary's death. He was reliving every moment of pain he had survived up to this evening. Somebody lied because he was quite conscious.

Life was raw, never ending pain before he began this journey. He had traveled so far within himself as well as in the physical world in the immense battle he fought within himself to be more, to be better. He was determined not to succumb to the beast within and become what he loathed, to somehow drag himself from the need for alcohol-induced amnesia and find the courage to accept himself, the strength to begin the journey to know himself.

Having needed someone for so long he unpredictably found Mary Bloody Heart. Affectionately he remembered assisting her as she walked. Opening her door and helping her from the car. He remembered long days under the hot sun as they poked fun at the latest absurd rumor or the newest adaptation of native spirituality by the love and light brigade. Little things came to mind like her phone calls in the middle of the night only to ask if he was awake. Mary rarely slept and she gave no thought to the difference in time zones. If a thought had been given she wouldn't have cared and certainly wouldn't have hesitated.

He recalled their long conversations over the phone and in person, at her home and in ceremony. Laughing and learning as she delicately instructed, her lessons sometimes going unnoticed, their point not revealed for hours or sometimes days later, leaving him laughing at revelation at the most inappropriate moments. Whoever he was with at those moments gazed at him as though he has lost his mind.

He had found peace at the end of the long journey in their companionship. She became a mother, a friend and a confidant – the one person who accepted him regardless of his mixed blood or past experiences. She was the only person willing to look into the depth of him and offer forgiveness and love.

She taught him how to forgive himself and how to receive and return love. Now she was gone and there was no one to assume her place. With no warning she was torn out of his life, the pain nothing less than amputation without anesthesia.

He was roiling in anguish and agony as wave after wave of raw emotion smashed into him, crushed him with a sense of loss he had never known before. He adamantly denied this was happening. Not after all he had already survived. Not after all the years of loneliness and ostracism. This pain could not be real.

His desire had always been to go home, to be a part of a family, to know love and to understand love. He remembered Dorothy Magnate and how she tried to give him love. She tried to instill within him a sense of security and peace, a place he could call home, somewhere he could say "I belong."

She offered love freely with no strings or expectations but he had been completely unprepared to accept what she had to offer.

He, instead, spent those years wallowing in dark turmoil with the life saving rope unseen before his eyes, lost to the nearest source of alcohol or mind numbing substance. Too involved in self destruction to perceive salvation existed in Dorothy's embrace. Incapable of understanding that the longing he so diligently drowned, was a self created delusion, unable to accept that each day he awakened in her home he was absolved. Blinded by pain, abuse and neglect he lived exactly where he dreamed of someday being and the obviousness of it was utterly lost on him.

Tonight he was looking into the past, seeing what had been, and how he had thrown it all away. He understood now that he had stepped over all that was so freely given in search of what he already had.

Had Fate chosen to intervene in his life at a much younger age maybe he would have found himself raised by Dorothy in her loving home where he would have been cared for and nurtured. With her guidance he may have become a completely different person. Maybe he would have been educated with his interests fulfilled. Maybe some direction would have been found. At best, this was wishful thinking in Jackson's mind as he sat alone on this dark hill and suffered.

He began cursing himself for ever beginning this journey so long ago. Why had he continued? What had he been searching for? This pain, this suffering the reward?

Loneliness became a weighted robe of despair and settled heavily about him.

He had reached the conclusion that love was nothing more than an illusion, an emotional concept created to manipulate and constrict. But somehow he maintained an ember of hope for love and finally he was granted what had previously been only fantasy.

Jackson was coming to full comprehension of what love really was – the absurd giddiness of it, the overwhelming joy of sharing someone's company. The pleasure of sharing silence. A simple cup of coffee and conversation able to provide total happiness knowing the person before you accepts you with all your flaws and imperfections.

He was permitted to have fantasy become tangible, then suffer unimaginably when the tangible disintegrated before his eyes, watching as love crumbled in his fingers as though his hands held sand. Time could never heal this wound, time could only make it worse.

The final lesson he came to know is the lesson of loss, the soul shattering paroxysm of loss, writhing inside him as if it were a living creature.

Jackson would never experience the luxury of another chance as he began to fully understand and appreciate love, to regretfully accept loss. Pierced by loss as though it were echoing through the night across the eons. His memory recalled the stories told to him of the long journey of his people, the loss his ancestors felt generation after generation, far longer than anyone alive could remember. Loss when they were offered to a blood thirsty God they had no belief in. Loss of home on a journey to foreign lands. Loss at the hands of the greedy and self involved with their demand for more, reaping only destruction; another blood thirsty God, this one consumed by the people instead of the people being consumed by it.

He believed he had found peace in the companionship he shared with Mary Bloody Heart. That a long journey has been traversed and he had finally found serenity after years spent alone. With no home to come from or return to, after years of desperately seeking acceptance in a world that refused to grant him any.

He now recognized himself for all he was, all he could have been and all he would ever be. He began again the circle of loss as his ancestors did before him, the journey repeated.

230°
CHAPTER TWENTY THREE

No sleep came through the long night. Exhausted from emotional release Jackson dozed as the second day passed. He roused momentarily and was quickly granted reprieve from pain through unconsciousness. Slowly daylight faded and dusk settled in.

Feeling somewhat rejuvenated he awakened in the twilight before real dark began. Beyond the periphery of his vision he sensed something was out there in the dark. Something was watching him.

Jackson forced peace to settle upon him as the grief that threatened to tear him apart through the previous evening gave way to rejection. A sense of rejection not understood before by him, he comprehended how absolutely, utterly alone he was. No one remained in his life for more than a few months. Cruelly, they discarded him immediately upon draining him of all they could.

He knew he could easily disappear and just as easily die in an apartment anywhere in the world and it would be months, even years, before anyone knew. Having witnessed that happen to other unfortunate people Jackson could picture it happening to him. Who would care? Who would make an effort to find out if he was alive? Who would come to the funeral services to remember him and pay their respects? Settling as a great weight the answer, no one, resounded deep within him.

He had spent his life knowing he was different, knowing the blood in his veins was not that of the dominant culture. Jackson, a mix blood, white and native, but try as he might he couldn't make the connection to his white blood.

Right or wrong he connected all the hurt that had been done to him by his White blood. Each and every one who had raised him, raped him, tortured and brutalized him had been White, both male and female.

Eventually, gratefully, he found his way to the red side of his ancestry. He believed this was what he had been searching for. This was where he would find salvation, where the pain would end. This was where he would find the sword to slay the dragon.

The pieces seemed to fit like a giant puzzle but he learned this, too, was a lie; and he was raped as emotionally, as spiritually, as anyone had ever done physically. With this realization the pain returned and it was so much greater, so much heavier than it had been when it was merely his body that had been damaged. This pain was crushing in its enormity.

With the death of Mary Bloody Heart he realized no one else would accept him as she had. Where would he go now? Who could he turn to? As he reflected on the history she passed to him about his own people, so few months ago, he wondered if it would make any difference? If those who so callously rejected him knew? If anything it would probably make things worse.

Although there is a distinct difference between being Indian with White blood and White with Indian blood, as far as most First Nations people were concerned Jackson was white. Regardless what he did he would be seen as just another white guy playing Indian. Breeds like Jackson are never extended the privileges of membership but they are expected to follow the rules and not say a word about the contradictions. Anyone not born on the reservation is expected to allow themselves to be used by anyone at anytime. They are also expected not to complain. If you have something and someone wants it, the expectation is to give it away to whomever asks for it then say thank you and move along.

Jackson learned early in his journey to discern the difference between doing for and being done by. He didn't fall so easily for their games, neither did he buy into the propaganda that they were born there and that fact alone is what designates them as real, while Jackson and those like him are merely the false pretense of wanting to be.

Jackson remembered with great pride the ancient Kiowa war bonnet that had been gifted to him midway through his journey. Many days during those years Jackson went hungry and he could have sold that war bonnet at any time but he refused to. He would rather starve then to desecrate something so precious. He learned when he returned the war bonnet to the Kiowa that early in the 19th century Chief Lone

Wolf had commissioned thirteen of them to be made and all were lost over the years. Twelve of them eventually found their way back to the tribe, the one Jackson returned was the last. Many on the rez, the self declared and recognized "real Indians," would have sold it in a moment. Jackson never did, yet his character was questioned. He was reprimanded for being disrespectful of traditional ways.

Jackson often thought he should write a book about the things he had done, then dismissed the thought outright. No one would believe him. Two hundred years ago songs would have been sung about his sacrifices, today nobody cared. No songs will be sung in this century. No ceremonies to honor him.

He had traveled to so many places, met so many people and participated in so many ceremonies across so many First Nations. He didn't do what he did because he was trying to be like any one Nation anymore than he was trying to become or emulate the Lakota. He is Shawnee and is proud of his Shawnee blood. But the Shawnee Nation does not accept him as one of them. He is considered an outsider and he isn't permitted to take part in Shawnee ceremonies.

With all he had experienced, with what would allow him to pray in an indigenous manner, what made most sense to him was the c'anupa. He agreed with the giving of himself, as required following this way of life, even when he was requested to have the flesh ripped from his body. This too, appears irrelevant; the concept of all related has become twisted and contorted. Its definition has become deformed, lost in mutual destruction. Anyone foolish enough to attempt to make their own way is dragged back into the quagmire like crabs in a bucket. No one gets away from the despair and desperation. All must suffer the same fate that eats away at the soul of each other.

Each are encouraged to dream, to fantasize about a better way; but once those dreams became real they are instantly set upon like wolves to a kill to be ravished and devoured. Continuously attacked until they are brought back into line, to behave as the conquered people present today. Individuality crushed beneath the overwhelming anguish endured by all. Within the Nations misery not only loves company but demands it. No longer are all related. Now all are miserable and that misery is brutally enforced.

Jackson concluded the state of affairs in Indian Country today is nothing less than absurd. So many tribes desperately trying to maintain some integrity, yet seeming to forget the reservations were originally designed as a temporary solution to the "Indian problem." Included in that system, designed by the greedy and power hungry, is the subsystem of blood quotient.

Tribal law stipulates that someone must have a specific blood quotient to be recognized. Anything less than what each individual tribe specifies, and the individual is not considered a tribal member. It made sense, sort of; certainly from a protective point of view as well as a financial one.

The system, however, is seriously flawed. Accordingly, unless you have "x" amount of Indian blood you are no longer Indian. This is a system designed by white people, adopted by red people and implemented by corrupt tribal councils.

Used today by many tribes as a hammer; used in a way that promotes self destruction and causes further separation.

Tribal law among the Anishinaabe said if a woman of the Nation married someone outside the Nation, they are no longer considered part of the Nation. The same is true among the Oneida of New York. Jackson personally knew a family of Oneida where the husband was the immediate son of their Chief but because he married a woman outside of the Oneida his children could no longer refer to themselves as Oneida. He was full blood Oneida and his children were obviously First Nations but based on the system, they aren't.

Jackson knew many families who forbade their children to date anyone who isn't native and God help their asses if they brought home a white boy. It didn't matter what tribe they were from but they damn well better be from some tribe and preferably not their own because the Nations have been isolated for too many years and the gene pool is about as deep as a mud puddle. Anyone on the reservation has to be real careful about who they are dating. Most of the time they turn out to be a cousin.

Doesn't anyone see this is the continuation of assimilation? Another way to record how effective annihilation is? The slow, painstaking eradication of the indigenous peoples will continue until none remain, until no one is left to claim the land and what is beneath it, until the government and the corporations that pay their salaries can move in and assume complete control.

The whole idea becomes even more revolting when many of the greatest native leaders were mostly, if not totally,

White – the Brant's from the Six Nations, the Ross's from the Cherokee, Bluejacket from the Shawnee; some even say Crazy Horse.

Jackson remembered an afternoon under the hot South Dakota sun years back, drinking coffee and passing time with Mary. She was telling him what the old timers said about Crazy Horse, about how his nickname had been Curly. "Think about that," she said, "ever seen an Indian with curly hair? They called him that because he was found on the prairie by a hunting party. A white foundling child raised among the Lakota as one of their own. That's why he never let anyone take his picture. He didn't want people to see he was white."

Sitting in the dark with all of this in his mind, Jackson recalled native history and the original occupation of these lands. He speculated about those who had been so readily accepted into the Nations regardless their original ancestry. If someone was willing to suffer through the ceremonies, for all intents and purposes, they were considered as much a part of the Nation as anyone else, Whites and Blacks that were brought into the Nation who refused to go back to "civilized society." What an amazing psychological statement that made.

Stories abounded about the many women who were captured throughout the early history of this country. They made wonderful dime store novels about how those savage Indians captured those poor white women. The truth is some never came back even after they were given a chance to do so.

Some of the women were returned and ran back again the first chance they got. Men walked away from military posts and out of frontier towns never to be heard from again. Years later they were seen flying eagle feathers with their faces covered in war paint stomping a hole in the invaders. These were individuals who could no longer stomach their own people's destructive, oppressive way of life. They left to live among the First Nations people and were accepted by the First Nations People as their own.

Today if you don't look right, you aren't accepted, period. If you aren't from the reservation and can't quote your family line back seven generations all you are is white playing Indian and unfortunately, many are just that.

Some, however, aren't. Some are dead serious about what they are doing and are not trying to play Indian or be something they weren't. None of that matters – if you aren't from the rez then you are not welcome unless you have something that can be taken. When you have been bled dry, you are just as quickly invited to leave.

What happened to the families of French traders and the northern tribes? What remains of those who left the boarding schools and faded into the cities? Full tribal members who, with the passage of the Indian Relocation Act in 1956, were "encouraged" to leave their homes "for education and economic advantages" only to find themselves lost among the ghettos in cities like Cleveland, Detroit, or Philadelphia? Where did their descendants go? Some did find their way back to their Nations, but most simply disappeared. Jackson began to realize it didn't matter. They, as well as he, would never be accepted.

What was Jackson to do? Find a church? Become a christian? After everything he had witnessed? After religion was used against him and he watched that religion used against others? After what Jackson's own mother suffered at the hands of "a good christian man?" He learned long ago the fallacy and hypocrisy of organized religion – that it is just another shining example of "do as I say, not as I do."

Religion is a cloak so many wrap themselves in like a child, with a favorite blanket, the fervent are so afraid of what may be in the dark they prefer to hide beneath the fabric of lies and misdirection. Anything is accepted to keep the creatures of the night at bay and so few find the strength to step out into that night and face whatever was out there. Few found the courage to demand it prepare for battle as they choose their weapons, willing to die honorably instead of as a weak kneed child. None of these zealots seemed to realize the very idea of creating a son figure in and of itself is contradictory even though this belief is so passionately proselytized.

Granted, the original concept of the Three being the One and the One being the Three is actually pretty astute, but centuries of interpretation and manipulation was used to control the masses. Add fanatics, forming their god into their own image and claiming it to be Truth, and the sheer hallucinating whack jobs who mix in fairytales, history and fantasy to create their own belief system, and the whole idea has been turned into a bad joke.

They suggest that if God broke off a finger then formed that finger into human and granted unto that finger consciousness, that finger would suddenly be individual. But how could it be? That finger would remain God. Granted the finger would be self sustaining but it would still be God. To state and then enforce the individuality of that finger and pervert that perception into dogma and doctrine with the expectation that all must follow seems the utmost betrayal of any God figure as well as human arrogance gone mad.

Would not the very existence of such a son figure immediately nullify the omniscience of God? Regardless how spiritually devoid, how thick headed any individual may be, if God is God, omnipresent and omniscient, will God then not be able to in some way reach the individual? Insisting God must first speak through one individual to instruct another presents God as fallible, thereby nullifying the existence of God. Why doesn't God simply give the instructions immediately to the one needing instruction?

Jackson could not support the lie that was organized religion, certainly never promote it, but how could he support and promote the lie he was coming to understand he was following? The way of the c'anupa is dead, at least in what he understood it to be. Although it is quite capable of performing it is now used as another means to "prey" instead of "pray."

Who alive actually lives the principles of red clay and wood? Whose life is altruistic? Who lives what they know would be detrimental to the self yet beneficial to the whole? Who guides without biased instruction? Who listens with compassion? The last person, the only person Jackson had ever known to live this way is now gone. His one ally, dead on the blood soaked field of battle.

240°
CHAPTER TWENTY FOUR

This long second night gave way to morning and the sun rose again in the eastern sky. Jackson exhausted, weak and hungry but with no desire to eat. He laid down to rest and dreamed...

...that he is in a jail cell. Not a new jail but an old one. Something one would expect to see in an old western or maybe in Mayberry. That's it, he acknowledged. He is in Mayberry, R.F.D. What the hell? How did he get to Mayberry and why is he in jail? Jackson is waiting for Sheriff Andy and Deputy Fife to come around the corner, but he isn't prepared for what does.

An Elder Grandmother, a really, really old Grandmother, her age somewhere between dirt and time, comes into view. When she reaches his cell she unlocks the barred door and invites him to step out and follow her. Quickly he falls in behind her as she leads him to a chair in the main part of the sheriff's office where the characters from the Andy Griffith Show used to sit. He notes the steps leading up from the sunken room to the main door.

An old, straight backed metal chair with red padded arm rests, seat and backrest is in the center of the room.

As he sits he notices that he and the Elder Grandmother aren't alone. There are several other Grandmothers and Grandfathers all as old or older than the one who let him out of his cell.

Jackson can see someone is sitting in the corner just on the edge of his peripheral vision. A blanket is wrapped completely around them. Only their eyes peek out and those eyes appear to glow as they radiate unspeakable power. Jackson cannot discern if the person is male or female but he senses it is best not to look directly at that one. When he glances at whoever it is they emit a throbbing sense of foreboding.

His attention reverts back to the other Ancients gathered about him as they encircle him and the Grandmother who opened his cell door begins to speak. "We have been watching you Jackson," she says in a quiet and gentle voice that seems capable of altering the very fabric of time and space. "We have watched as you have helped the children, the sick and the old. Not once did you consider yourself. You always gave to those who need. At times we see how this is very hard for you and we watch as you suffer, but you continue to give. We are proud of you Jackson. Proud of what you have done and of how you have lived. At anytime you could have quit. At anytime you could have refused to live this way but you never did. We gave you the strength to continue. Strength you accepted willingly but so painfully. You are now one of us," the Ancient Grandmother says as a deep blue/black blanket was wrapped around him.

The Ancient in the corner never speaks, only watches, condoning the Grandmother's actions. They imprint their names on his mind, five names he is told never to forget...

...Jackson woke in the afternoon of this third day with those five names in his mind repeating as if on a loop. He searched his memory trying to recall if he had ever heard those names before, trying to remember if he had ever met anyone with those names. He realized that even with the hundreds and hundreds of people he had met, he didn't know anybody nor had he ever met anybody with those names. Before this moment those names had been completely unknown to him.

Fully awake he also realized there was no one he could talk to about this dream. He hadn't had the opportunity to talk with Mary about his sleeping with the buffalo or what happened when he passed out in his tent after crashing out of the tree. He had absolutely no idea what to do with this new information bestowed upon him, so he simply accepted it.

With this acceptance Jackson also accepted that the lost would remain lost. The road home had long since been destroyed in the aftermath of apocalypse. The European Invasion, begun such a short time ago, succeeded in accomplishing exactly what it set out to do. All that remains are the survivors and the walking wounded. Little if any memory is left of the civilization that existed before the nuclear bomb of organized religion, supposed civility and capitalism was mercilessly dropped on their unsuspecting heads.

Like many who continued to be, Jackson began this journey self deluded. As a child he watched with rapt attention the television programs starring David Carradine and Bruce Lee. He wanted to believe all he needed do was seek out a teacher, to find someone who would show him the way, someone to teach him how to become what he should be instead of the monster he was raised to be.

It took but a few short years for him to see the absurdity. Now he understood the futility. Unfortunately, most never did. They preferred to believe, needed to believe, in their delusions. They insist that somewhere a wise old Elder waited for them and if they were patient long enough, if they learned their lessons well enough through the years, they, too, would someday become the wise old Elder.

Jackson has no real knowledge as to how Asian spirituality works, its processes and means. All he has to rely on for information is movies and considering what he had come to understand that is probably bullshit, too. Asian and First Nations spiritual understandings resemble each other only in so far as being Ancestral in base. From there they diverge.

In the First Nations' way of life there is no elder or teacher to show someone the way. There are no long years of solitude in a monastery reflecting on the subtle difference of individual cherry blossom leaves. No one ever finds that wise old elder.

What they do find is themselves kneeling at the feet of the nephilim and what they are learning isn't the secrets of the universe. They find men and women like David Chases waiting for them, to feed off of and drain them of all they can ever hope to be.

Very few are willing to accept this realization and the lost and confused continue to vehemently demand those like Chases are the embodiment of all they imagined, regardless what they witness their demigod do. With no strength or courage to stand up to these predators they consciously chose to remain afraid of the dark.

Elders are supposed to be there for guidance and advice because they already lived it. They have already experienced it. When something happens to someone, they could say "I did this" or "you could do that." They left it up to the individual to decide which direction to go.

At least that's how it was, how it was supposed to be. Elders like that no longer exist. Now it is Olders waiting in their webs, not to advise but to direct – that direction given not to assist but to provide; not to provide for the one seeking assistance, but for themselves.

Jackson had come to understand the real teachers are the Ancestors, those who walked long before christian corruption. If an individual can find peace within themselves, the Ancients will speak in many ways, so much more than verbal, in a language of individual understanding if the person can find the patience.

Comprehension dawns in Their time, not ours. So many want to believe they will suddenly, instantly be, that they will just as suddenly, instantly know. Not for one second do they understand if they did, their minds would shatter. Like attempting to fill a water glass with an ocean all at once. The process moves slowly, as a child's instruction, a tiny piece at a time. Always small at first then growing larger and larger as the individual learns to listen, learns to heed, to comprehend. Open that window, pick up those keys, stand in that corner, move that object. This is the Ancients testing the individual to see if they are listening. Jackson is finally seeing those instructions.

He watched and personally suffered for an individual who professed his undying need. He watched as that person failed miserably while their true persona was revealed, as their mask was unceremoniously ripped away and the monster they truly were is exposed in the full light of day.

It is so much easier to be a sheep and follow. It is much easier to adhere to the instructions of another human. So many claim to be so spiritual, but possess no understanding of how to live what they so adamantly profess.

They are unwilling to suffer the ordeals, to suffer the trials and tribulations necessary to achieve that understanding. They are unwilling to accept the guidance given from Spirit and prefer instead to heed the instructions of a person, exactly like the young man who journeyed to the Tree of Life under instruction from a man and paid so dearly for his submissiveness.

So many are so quick to deify a human while all around them the Ancients cry. They never see the Ancestors' tears of despair or hear their echoing laments of disappointment as the seeker falsely stumbles through the motions. So convinced they know the Truth. So quick to support someone who is usually in it for the satisfaction of their own ego or sense of entitlement.

The lost, with so little self esteem or courage, were entirely convinced they must be something special, become someone special. All so sure they are enlightened medicine people, great Chiefs and Clan Mothers in the making, as though life itself isn't enough. The simple yet beautiful gift of being unable to satisfy their lust for recognition. There must be more. They must be more. It is not enough to live a good life and to be a good person, not enough to learn and to live true altruism.

The blind eating the blind spending years prostrated before the likes of David Chases so sure that in time they will become. Off to see the wizard, but the wizard is standing before them. Not Oz they find, but themselves in Charlie's Chocolate Factory. Hypocritical spiritual justification used to initiate verbal defecation as they employ the spiritual to attack the spiritual.

Like Jackson's mutilation at the hands of Junior Rutledge the flock supporting the mutilation. Accepting it because they were told he deserved it. How dare he, with unmitigated gall and audacity, stand before David Chases and say no? Defiance comes at a steep price, and the acolytes of Chases are more than willing and able to denigrate and defile.

Chases was convinced he was using Jackson, when what was really happening was that Chases was being used to create Jackson. Chases may have even understood yet would never admit it. His admittance might reveal to those who follow, the crack in his facade. The flow of money and support might dry up. Chases might fall and those like him as well.

Obviously those like Chases don't want this to happen, and just as obviously, the followers of the predators aren't willing to allow it to happen. Their world would implode and that logic allowed them to accept that Jackson had failed in his commitments and obligations because Chases said so. Chases had spoken, therefore God had spoken. Let there be light.

With their absolute devotion to the false, no one would see what had happened was exactly what was supposed to happen. From the depths of time beyond mere human comprehension a being was created. All that is pain formed into one to become retribution, revenge and admonishment.

Years Jackson had traveled, creeping through the foliage of deception, ever alert to the predator lurking above. Occasionally he feigned the guise of where he was and what he had attached himself to in self preservation. Led to the Tree of Life he was offered to what lay beyond the sun. Cocooned in raw, mind searing pain he metamorphosed as he hung. The hands of all of his Ancestors formed into a single hand and grasped the choke cherry pegs. Those small twigs erupting from his chest as he crashed to the earth reborn to become what he unknowingly was created to be.

What was dragged into the tree is not what fell from it, nor what sat here tonight. All Jackson was, was replaced with all he would become. His acceptance of the death of Mary Bloody Heart was the final piece of the puzzle to fall into place. That acceptance reverberated deeply in the recesses of his mind.

Jackson is still Jackson. He still looks like himself and has his memories and thoughts. There are no bikini bottoms and go-go boots under his clothes. He hasn't attained any magical powers with the ability to change into a super hero. He accepted and found peace.

With no one to assist him, Jackson began to interpret all that had been revealed to him during these last three arduous days. He concluded it isn't the dragon that is evil. Evil is what he allows the dragon to do. Killing to satisfy sexual appetites is wrong, as wrong as killing for the sheer pleasure of watching something die. As he stood before the cave in his mind where the dragon dwelled Jackson dropped his armor, laid down his sword and surrendered. He accepted in this moment that denying the dragon meant he must deny himself. Because Jackson is the dragon.

But in order to inflict loss he must first understand loss and now he believed he did. Not loss on the order of "Where are my keys?" or "Has anyone seen the dog?" He must understand loss to a degree even greater than that of someone loved and cherished. He must understand loss as a living thing. Loss on the scale of cultural genocide. Loss of country and identity. Loss that the original People feel as a whole. Their consciousness as loss. The day to excruciating day of existing in the abyss knowing there is no escape.

Hell was once a concept carelessly used as a means to control the populace at large, used as a threat of "if you don't." That concept had become reality. Hell had assumed shape and form.

The Ancestors waited patiently as they watched as their descendants were forced to live that hell. They waited until Hell became accepted as normal and evil became accepted as common place. They watched as their grand children were so completely lost to them. These same children were given explicit instructions for return, the instructions ignored. No one capable of interpreting the instructions any longer.

The Ancients waited and watched as foreign invaders reigned down devastation in less than 300 years. Waited and watched as the invaders turned a pristine utopia into a fetid pool of decay and the Ancients' descendants became replicas of the invaders; as their descendants wreaked the same havoc and destruction upon each other. For millennia the Ancients existed, watching what was given so freely become a commodity whereby the greedy demanded payment for what was never theirs to sell.

The Ancients seethed with immeasurable enmity and they set Jackson into motion. His responsibility is to inflict loss for loss, destruction for destruction, abuse for abuse. All that he had suffered, all of the pain, the abuse, all of the evil he had endured while that very same evil tried so desperately to destroy what had been created.

Years he suffered at the hands of those who reveled in that evil. Never knowing he was protected at all times. Never knowing the Ancients were matching him step for step. Not until this moment did he understand this was how he had survived what would normally have killed most. Now he knew that the Ancients were the fount where he drew the strength he needed to overcome.

His mind drifted to his first vision of the immense black bird leading him to the great storm. He saw now that when it crashed into him it didn't do so to destroy him, but to initiate him. The immense bird was the switch that turned on what he was to become.

Jackson had journeyed through his life like an amnesia patient not knowing who or what he was. He sought with desperate need the answer to what he knew he should be with no understanding of how to become that. Pain became the Creator, guided by unseen hands; pain, the physician, slowly peeling away the layers to reveal what had been forgotten.

Led to the Tree of Life and leaving his body when they dragged him into the searing South Dakota sky; offering him to the Sun to crash to the earth with their assisted release, to be reborn the destroyer, to become the weapon of the Ancients. The weapon they would use to extol their revenge on those who so undeniably deserved it.

Jackson is created to become Shiva, Kali, Perseus, the Four Horsemen – created to be the living embodiment of Thunder and Lightning. As the storm, he will rain down devastation. As raging wind, he will clear away the choked underbrush and the fallen detritus. As crashing hail, he will break through their false protective coverings.

He will thunder into the minds of the deaf and split the sky of the blind. When this storm passed, this storm that is Jackson, new life will begin. The epiphany of a circle closed and a circle begun overwhelmed him.

He thought of the words Mary Bloody Heart shared with him of his family and all they suffered through. His mind immediately returned to the volumes of history on this country and all it should have been were it not for the greedy. Historical events began to return to his memory.

The horrors visited upon the unsuspecting original peoples of this country tumbled through his brain in slow motion. In his mind he saw all that the People could have been, a People once so strong. A People overflowing with honor and compassion reduced to mere shadows of what they once were. Their willingness to share, that gratuity, perceived as weakness, and used against them.

Genocidal destruction wrought at the hands of those absolutely convinced they were right, who used their Doctrine of Discovery and Manifest Destiny as justification, so utterly convinced the hand of God itself guided their every move. In the name of their God they committed acts of rape, murder, and torture. They initiated the wanton destruction of all that was beautiful and good while using the words of their God, transcribed and bound between leather, to beat any and all survivors into submission. Using their religious conviction to reduce the original inhabitants of this country to what they consider the lowest of animals, nothing more than beasts and savages.

Men so consumed by greed and hunger for power they enacted laws and rules of behavior they themselves were not held accountable to and never expected to be. Hundreds of years later their continued behavior of destruction has become global.

Sadly the lessons of violence, greed and power mongering were learned well by the original peoples who leveled the effects of those lessons of brutality against their own. The native Nations in effect became their own self sustaining, all consuming, greedy corporations. Whites turned Indian into a hobby while Indians turn Indian into a business.

Jackson obviously couldn't go back in time. If he could have, no human mind would be able to comprehend the level of pain he would inflict on Richard Whitman. Unfortunately Whitman himself died over a hundred years ago. The current state of affairs in Indian Country are a direct result of his greed, his desperate need for power, and his all consuming ego. If not for Whitman this country might very well be a completely different better place. Those born outside of the Nations might actually have someplace to return to and the predators might not exist.

Whitman's behavior set into motion all that is. This is the legacy he left behind which continues to live on. Whitman is obviously not able to pay for his actions personally but his descendants can. The sins of the father will be visited vociferously on the son. This devastation began with Whitman and would end with Whitman...or what was left of him.

As the sun set on Jackson's third day alone he slowly stood. Gathering all he had brought he packed these items gently with great reverence for the power they held. Returning to his room he gathered what few belongings he had and stowed his things in the old Pontiac Tony Baker helped him put back on the road. He packed the flare guns and several cases of phosphorus flares as well. Jackson closed the door on the final pieces of a life now gone.

Knocking at the door of Jackson's room in the morning, Tony would find him gone. No note or details of where or why. Tony was well aware of how the news of Mary's death has shaken Jackson but has no idea of the depth. Tony will have no idea where Jackson has gone or what will become of him. As Jackson expected, Tony took no notice of the missing cases of flares. He had forgotten about them long ago.

Jackson left southwest Pennsylvania to begin a new journey, making his way to Detroit, Michigan. Jackson is coming, but unlike his mother before him hell isn't coming with him. Hell is in hiding, fearing for its life.

250°
CHAPTER TWENTY FIVE

Jackson is fully aware of the myriad of things he is expected to do. He could ask two dozen people their opinion and he would get back two dozen distinctly different answers. Unfortunately, the only people available to ask are either suburban pretendians who adorned themselves with whatever title or name their imaginations could create, or off the rez predators looking to get paid – full bloods who travel the country collecting followers in the process so they can continue to get paid.

Of all of the people he had met Jackson can not think of a single Elder or Leader he could trust. Every one of them sold out for the satisfaction of their ego or the first movie or book deal. Worse are those attempting to relive their glory days with no concern for the epic battles that are currently being waged among the People. What they had done was heroic, but it was time to let that go and concentrate on something else.

Jackson can't return to Indian Country and the reservations, not with the rumors started about him by Chases. Indian Country is worse than a small town and everyone gossips prodigiously. In the few months that had passed since Sundance, Jackson's name is now worthless. Chases also knows many people off the rez and he has spent his time wisely in that arena as well. He has made sure everyone far and wide is well aware of all of Jackson's faults as perceived and defined by Chases. His many acolytes fulfilled their duties of disparaging with scalpel-like precision leaving Jackson basically screwed.

He could stay in Pennsylvania at Tony's place, changing tires, maybe eventually convince Tony to sell him the business and run it for himself. He could try to turn the place into a profitable business instead of the part time hobby Tony used it for. For the first time, Jackson could join society and start paying taxes. If he was lucky – really, really lucky – someday he might even earn enough to pay off a piece of the substantial debt he would incur trying to make the business run. Then he could retire on a minimum pension, living day-to-day in an assisted living community, and finally give up on this nightmare he had chased until he died.

But what about all the dreams and visions he had? What was he to do with them? He couldn't interpret them and he had no clue what they meant. There were hundreds of idiots who believed they could interpret them, and would, given the first chance. The best they could do would be to come up with some eastern philosophical nonsensical answer that wasn't an answer at all. They didn't know any more than Jackson did.

Those who did things as they used to be done, had long since faded into the background or were dead and no one was stepping up to take their place as guides to the few who are even vaguely interested in being guided. Most natives are as ambivalent to their way of life as any backsliding, wayward christian is to their religion.

Jackson couldn't call Alvin Redstone, the Elder who had helped him all those years ago at Terry Bishop's place. His first year of Sundance Jackson had left a little early to visit with Redstone. When Jackson arrived at his place Alvin had turned a full 180 degrees and behaved as though he couldn't get away from Jackson fast enough. After all he had assisted Jackson with and instructed him on Redstone behaved as though he had never met Jackson before that day, as though he had never even had a conversation with him.

Redstone even attempted to embarrass Jackson in front of everybody in a sweat lodge. He demanded Jackson sing specific songs right then and there to prove if he was or wasn't what he assumed Jackson thought himself to be. Of course Jackson wasn't able to and Redstone was shown to be right in front of everyone in attendance. By appearances Redstone made it look like Jackson was only faking it, whatever "it" was. Maybe Redstone was upset that Jackson chose to go to Chases dance instead of his. Jackson would never know because he left Redstone's place and has never spoken to him again.

Obviously Jackson needs to do something. Quitting doesn't seem right, although he would be more than justified in doing so. After the last vision where the Grandmother stated *"He is one of them now,"* quitting isn't even an option. Obviously some very powerful entities are watching so he'd better figure something out and figure it out quick.

But what? After everywhere he had been and all he had done, all he had to show for it was to have his ass handed to him over and over again. What was the point, to build character? No one is interested in someone's character anymore. They are only interested in what can be done for them. Where was their pay off? He could talk to Mary Bloody Heart but, oh yeah, she is dead. She isn't saying anything. Unlike what the twinkies so desperately need to believe, she hasn't come back as Casper the Friendly Ghost to assist and guide him in his daily travails. He didn't hear her voice in the wind. He didn't see her shape in the mist. She's dead. D.E.A.D. Dead. Buried. Gone.

He thought for a moment about Nashville. Maybe he could settle down somewhere near Roddy Blackstar. Then again, no. Roddy has his own life and his own problems. He certainly didn't need Jackson's to add to his. Roddy's wife bailed on him and left him to raise two daughters on his own. Roddy's immediate family is as emotionally screwed up as any other, if not more so, and although Roddy has some support it is minimal at best.

Roddy is doing a great job being a dad to his two girls, raising them the best he can in a white world with red influence. He isn't rich by any stretch of the imagination. He is barely getting by and it is everything Roddy can do to make it day by day. The responsibility of his daughters hangs heavy on him, but there is no way in hell he will let himself fail in their upbringing. He will do whatever it takes to ensure they have whatever they need. He can't give them everything they want but he can do the best job possible with what he has; which is exactly what he is doing and doing quite well. The last thing he needs now is Jackson dropping into his life. That will only make things harder for Roddy and after all he had done for him Jackson would remove limbs before he made Roddy's life any more difficult.

Jackson knows he could simply disappear. It would be the easiest thing to do. Maybe find a little cabin on several hundred acres he could rent for cheap. Maybe find a place to be a caretaker. He could hang out in the woods alone and stare at the walls, watching as the paint dried. After all the places he had traveled it wouldn't be too hard to find someplace. He could hang a map on the wall and throw a dart. Wherever it landed would be as good as anywhere else. Then he could cut off all his hair, grow a beard and live in disguise.

The best choice would probably be a small town where no one knew him, somewhere he could hide from society. But how does one hide from the Ancients? Where does someone go to escape from them? He knew the answer to that question and knew a few months in a small town or out in desolation would find him swimming in the vodka again. Every day with all he had experienced thumping around in his head? The voices of those who visited him in the night? The five names he could not forget always hounding him? No one to talk to but himself for weeks upon weeks? He would shoot himself for sure.

Of course Jackson could always set up the Indian Show. He knew more than enough to pull it off. There were thousands of idjits out there who would believe anything he said to them. One look at the scars on his chest and back would provide all the validity they required.

He could make up a fake contact on the rez, but then again, he didn't have to make someone up. He knew enough predators that would support him if he kicked back a few dollars. He could have them come out a few times a year and put on some fake initiation ceremonies into a made up warrior society. Maybe get some woman to help him create something for the women to be a part of.

He could portray himself as Chief with some made up family history, then everyone could be a part of yet another Indian club and dress up on holidays in their invented finest where they could impress each other with how little they understand. He could even give presentations at elementary schools to teach children and share the Indian Show with them.

Maybe Jackson could start an Indian business. He could be the one person doing things the right way and show that it can be done the right way. Prove that we can still live an altruistic life and prove that no one has to spend their days feeding off everyone else, emotionally and spiritually. He knows the songs and the years he spent with Mary helped him to come to many understandings. He could pour water for the people and help them with some of their problems. With the knowledge he had earned through the years from some of the good people he had met he could assist in guiding them.

But the genetically native residents in urban environments away from the reservations would never accept the truth. Unless what he did coincided with how he was expected to present himself, in the manner the books and movies said he should present himself, he would be told what he was doing was wrong. From out of every crack and crevice would come some annoying pain in the ass who knows how Indians really are and would want to instruct him on what he should be doing. It would be just as bad if he started yet one more non-profit to help the people. How long before that became corrupted? Besides, who would he get to help him? What did he have to choose from – a pool of half baked, mentally challenged and imagination induced wannabes? Just what Indian Country doesn't need, another non-profit.

Maybe he could turn the other cheek and accept all the abuse that was continually thrown his way, and continue trying to move forward? He could learn to become, what? Why? Who really cared? And what would be the point? Back on the road dealing with the urban confused and all they thought was right? More super Indians and off the rez gods? More rape and abuse? Jackson had more than his fill of both.

Maybe he could find an apartment, get a factory job and a wife. Then he could follow the laws of the land and be a good citizen in this land of the free where freedom was an illusion, a lie so many were willing to accept. The only freedom in this country is the freedom to do as you are told.

Ninety percent of the dynasties of this country, the super wealthy families, started by breaking the law. Trace the family back far enough and there was one guy, usually a regular guy, who had had enough. After organizing other members of his family and some friends, they broke the law and together they ran drugs, whiskey, weapons or whatever it took at the time. They turned a few hundred into a few thousand, and a few thousand into a few million, none of it legal. Later they washed themselves of their dirty past and began presenting themselves as high society when in truth they were no better than any other cut throat or bandit.

As high society they could control the law. Instead of local or national law breaking they now broke laws on a global scale. All the laws they broke to get to where they were they rewrote with their power and money. They bought into office who they wanted, when they wanted, and had the laws they wanted written. Somehow this is legal and Jackson is supposed to behave according to it? This is the life Jackson is expected to live? These are the rules he is expected to follow? For whose benefit? Certainly not his, or anyone else he knew. Jackson had a few other ideas about what to do and they aren't anything like what is expected of him. He pondered the morality of what he was thinking and decided quickly morality didn't play a part, any more than the law of the land did.

This land, once so pristine, has become a den of corruption. Corrupt laws enacted by corrupt people to provide protection for a corrupt way of life. If someone has enough money they can do anything they want, to anyone they want to, at anytime.

Corporations poison the food, the air and the water. If anyone doesn't like it and doesn't have the money to stop them they have one simple choice – sit down and shut the fuck up or die.

Every once in awhile the socially infuriated came together for sit-ins, protests, and occupy movements while the rich and powerful watch from their ivory towers, laughing their nuts off. Those with power and money are the bullies, and those without power and money are the bullied. And those in power know there is nothing anyone can do about it. The elite know no one is actually willing to start a revolution. No one is willing to spill blood. Not one individual is willing to die or kill for the basic human rights that have been so diabolically stripped from them.

Sit-ins and protests are as effective as asking a rapist to stop raping you in the process of raping you. No one has the strength to pull the dick out of their ass, turn around, and punch the offending walking cumstain in the mouth. The vast majority prefer instead to blubber like a pudgy nine year old girl after scraping her knee. In unison they cry, "Please mister bad man, stop punching me in the face and I promise I'll be a good little bitch."

When this was Indian Country from sea to shining sea, there were laws and those laws demanded retribution. For generations communities lived by simple laws. They lived by natural laws and life flourished. Children grew healthy and strong. Communities prospered. The Nation thrived. Everyone knew the one law that covered every Nation... don't fuck with anyone.

Native law used to be real simple. Behave like a greedy bastard...dead. Rape, abuse, molest...dead. Hurt the community, the family, the sick, the elderly....dead. Murder, steal, lie, cheat...dead. Quick, simple and straight to the point. No drawn out expensive trials, no lengthy incarceration at the people's expense. Maybe it's high time someone's head is on a stick. Maybe someone needs to travel a few thousand miles and start killing some sons of bitches. Maybe it is time native law took precedence.

Jackson is about to initiate some native law.

260°
CHAPTER TWENTY SIX

There are no records that Jackson existed, as far as the system is concerned he is a ghost. His driver's license was assigned to a long ago address with no forward address or trail. He has no bank account and no telephone. The car he drives is titled and registered to Tony as a shop vehicle. His fingerprints and DNA had never been documented. He never served in the military or did any time in prison. What files that did exist were juvenile and they were sealed. If they were broken Jackson would appear to be a victim and not a perpetrator. He is essentially off the grid.

Can he do what he is thinking about doing? How much will he be able to do? As "Happy?" performed by Mudvayne blares through the speakers he turns onto the Pennsylvania Turnpike and follows it up to I-80 where he stops outside of Cleveland. From there I-75 will lead him into Detroit, the other armpit of the world. The only other place Jackson can think of that is as bad as Detroit is Philadelphia, where the Declaration of Independence was signed, the formation of a democracy begins and the doctrine that all natives are Canaanites was instituted. Jackson will get there soon enough.

Detroit was once part of the Three Fires Confederacy, the Odawa, Ojibwa and Pottawatomie, collectively known as the Anishinaabe. Before European Occupation they controlled the Great Lakes region and were buffered from the Haudenasaunee Confederacy by a loose mix of unassociated tribes including the Erie, the Mingo and the Kickapoo. The Anishinaabe continue to exist although the Three Fires Confederacy is not what it was. Jackson visited with all three Nations earlier in his travels and attended some of their Midewiwin ceremonies.

After he had left northern Ohio, fed up with the ego driven madness there, Jackson had wandered the east coast. One of the places he visited was a Sundance in Maryland. Rumor had it that Sundance was started by Mary Bloody Heart's grandfather. Interesting, considering Mary and Jackson hadn't met yet.

He never danced there, although he did attend their spring ceremonies where he was invited to their Sundance and he went early to help if he could. For two weeks he cut grass, gathered firewood and performed whatever labors were asked of him. They provided him with a log splitter and he spent all day splitting and stacking firewood for their upcoming Sundance. This was the first Sundance he had ever been to and after supporting, he concluded it was something he would never do – or so he thought at the time.

Jackson prayed with the people gathered at the dance as a young man of no more than sixteen years of age hung in the Tree of Life. His younger brother below him on the ground, barely fourteen years old, was dragging a train of nine buffalo skulls. A soul wracking experience the likes of which Jackson had never witnessed before.

The older brother was high in the Tree and pierced through his back. Jackson watched as the boy danced in the air with fans made from eagle wings in each hand. At the same time his younger brother was below him struggling and straining to complete four passes around the Sundance circle. When the signal was given to break, the brother in the tree was lowered enough to allow assistants to grab onto him and tear him from his harness. While this took place the younger brother, after having completed four circles, stopped at the western door. Children from among the supporters climbed onto the train of buffalo skulls and when they were all settled the fourteen year old boy pulled as hard as he could, painfully rending the pegs from his back.

That dance was also where he was permitted to experience the peyote ceremony for the first and only time. A family had traveled from the Four Corners region, guests of the dance, and they conducted the ceremony. When he reflected on that ceremony Jackson saw it as one of the hardest things he had ever done in his life. Beginning around 11 a.m. he had entered the teepee set up for the ceremony with the other men. Over a twenty four hour period he would drink the peyote tea and eat the peyote medicine. Unlike how the movies portrayed the experience he had no wild hallucinations or dramatic effects. He did experience a cleansing, a sense of healing – of what he remains unsure.

During a break in the ceremony, late into the early morning hours, Jackson and several of the other men were permitted to step outside of the teepee to get some fresh air. Lying on the cold grass staring into the deep space above he began to see white lights in the blackness, large balls of white light high above him that slowly began to come closer. Neither satellites nor planets they began barely outside of breathable atmosphere and stopped within feet of his vision. The balls of white light performed a beautiful dance as he watched and when the other men moved he returned to the ceremonies that were recommencing inside.

Jackson met several people at that dance, Archie Campbell for one. Archie had launched a coup to take over the native spiritual programs being presented in the State Prisons – the very same programs Mandy the sex freak/hypocritical christian zealot would later be running. Archie decided Jackson would be his apprentice. He came to the conclusion he would give Jackson a job and responsibility for the future. Archie, involved with native protests for many years and accepted in many circles, never asked Jackson – he told him.

Archie Campbell was in his late sixties with gray hair, gray beard, a gray moustache and an attitude of one who knew it all. He was also a one hundred percent white guy. Archie insisted he would teach Jackson everything he needed to know about being an Indian and benevolently Archie would permit him to work on his projects. He instructed Jackson that the man running the dance had already done everything anyone would ever need to, therefore Jackson would never have to do anything else. His only responsibility would be to follow Archie around and do what he was told. When Jackson didn't immediately concede to his demands Archie became angry.

A rumor began floating around camp that Jackson was a federal agent, preposterous but somehow believed. Archie, in all his graciousness, knowing all about native spirituality, was willing to bestow all his knowledge onto Jackson. Jackson wouldn't concede to his generous offer so Jackson was an ungrateful bastard and Archie ensured he was treated like shit through that entire gathering, and he was ignored and spoken to as if he were a dog.

After Jackson spent weeks working his ass off for them the best they could do was kick him in the teeth. He never returned to that dance although he did run into Archie accidentally when they inadvertently attended the same event. Archie made it a point to be as much of an ass as possible. He went out of his way to inform anyone how useless and insincere Jackson was. According to Archie, Jackson wouldn't know spirituality if it jumped up and bit him in the ass. As much as Jackson would have liked to stomp a hole in him, he didn't. He understands there will be an Archie Campbell everywhere he goes.

He was fortunate to meet and spend time with an Athabascan Elder from Chickaloon, Alaska at that dance. They spent the last few nights of the dance smoking and drinking coffee with Jackson listening to the Elder's stories. This Elder was referred to only as Wolf and Jackson never did learn his full name. Wolf is in his seventies and still spry. A full blood with his hair tied in two braids, Jackson often wondered what happened to Wolf and where he went. While together, Wolf gave Jackson a message to take to the Odawa Nation.

In Petoskey, Michigan a yearly gathering was scheduled to take place two weeks after Jackson and Wolf talked. Wolf had a vision some months back and this was why he was traveling the country. He was doing what he was instructed in that vision and sharing what had been given to him. He wouldn't be able to make the Odawa gathering and asked if Jackson would carry his words for him.

Unfortunately Wolf had his dates wrong and Jackson arrived a week too late. Jackson was able to meet with the Chief of the Odawa and pass on the words Wolf gave him. The Chief invited Jackson to stay with the Odawa Nation and introduced him to a sub Chief of their Thunder Clan. Jackson stayed with them for a few months, sleeping in his van and attending ceremonies when he invited.

A young Odawa man showed up at the sub Chief's house one evening a week into Jackson's visit after he heard Jackson was there. When that young man saw Jackson he turned instantly pale. Curt hello's were exchanged and the young man sat down on the couch and listened quietly to the conversation going on. Eventually he requested permission to speak. Something was on his mind and he had to get it out.

When permission was granted he began to tell the story of how several years ago, while participating in Midewiwin ceremonies with a healer of high order, he was given an eagle bone whistle. He was instructed he must never lose it, that he must keep it safe and sacred until the right person came to claim it. A week before Jackson arrived, this young man had a dream...

...that he is standing on an asphalt covered playground with basketball hoops and chain link fences. In the dream he is talking with someone he has never met before and toward the end of their dream conversation he hands the eagle bone whistle to the man he is talking to. The man in the dream he is talking with is Jackson...

The room was immediately, eerily silent. No one dared breathe too hard for fear of breaking the silence. For seven years this young man had honored that eagle bone whistle. Whenever a stranger arrived in Odawa Territory he went to see them and always brought the whistle with him just in case.

The young man stood and took the eagle bone whistle from his pocket. He walked over and passed it to Jackson. "My job is done," he said to Jackson, "now yours begins." Jackson would carry that eagle bone whistle through three of his Sundances, and would mourn its passing when it is lost in the fire that consumed his trailer.

As the days and months passed casually Jackson learned as much of the Odawa history as they were willing to teach him. He was told how Detroit was once considered Sacred Ground and about a stone altar that had once stood there. For generations the Anishinaabe made yearly pilgrimages to perform ceremony at the place of the stone altar.

In the late 1600s two French missionaries stopped at

the stone altar on their way to Sault St. Marie and destroyed it. They threw the broken pieces of stone into the river where they were lost forever. French settlers soon followed and planted twelve pear trees in place of the altar to instead honor their twelve apostles. A settlement was constructed where the altar had stood and the French name it Fort Pontchartrain du Detroit.

Pontiac of the Odawa laid siege to the Fort in the mid 1700s. The fort transferred to British hands and the name was shortened to Detroit then returned back to French control. The Battle of Fallen Timbers was fought at Detroit in the late 1700s and after signing the Jay Treaty the fort was finally turned over to the United States. In the early 1800s Detroit burned to the ground.

After being rebuilt Detroit became the center of commerce and industry and the miles and miles of virgin timber brought the loggers. The Anishinaabe refused to sign away their timber rights and this left the Government and their cronies desperate to devise a new plan. According to the Odawa Jackson spoke with, the United States decided the easiest way to get around the Anishinaabe was to create its very own Indian Tribe.

There were many full blood native women in the area who were married to or kidnapped by French traders. These women were no longer considered part of the tribes or the Three Fires Confederacy. The United States gathered these displaced women and provided them with full federal recognition. This action instantly allowed businesses, supported by the government, to ratify treaties with this new tribe and thereby sign away the timber rights as well as all other natural resources.

The process of destruction and all out greed began immediately upon acquisition. Long before New York, capitalism grew to astounding proportions in Detroit, and all on land once held sacred by a Nation who had lived there for generations. Detroit would continue to grow and create vast fortunes for many a good christian white man.

The Three Fires Confederacy, once the stewards of vast holdings including parts of northern Ohio into Illinois, Michigan, Wisconsin and Minnesota and well up in to Canada, were broken into small reservations and never regained its stature. Their timber and other natural resources were stolen to provide lumber for housing and furniture and they never saw a penny of the vast wealth generated by those who stole their resources.

The small tracts of land so graciously allotted to them by the greedy and corrupt were no longer home to ancient oaks and elms. Today they appear no different than any other bedroom community and no one would ever suspect they were standing on a reservation if not for the physical features of the residents and the boundary signs. There are super centers and fast food restaurants, auto parts places and convenience stores, including stores that sell alcohol.

While the mix blood urban confused bemoaned the state of affairs in Indian Country and cried crocodile tears over alcohol abuse, many of the Nations sell that alcohol to their own people. It's just a bit difficult to break the cycle of addiction when what feeds the addiction is so readily supplied by their own. For the few dry Nations, just beyond the perimeter of the reservation are border towns more than willing to provide. A review of deed and land title for many of those establishments would show they are also owned by natives.

As if alcohol isn't enough the establishment of casinos and allotment checks introduced a new form of self annihilation. Once a certain age is reached, usually eighteen, the full member of the Nation on many of the reservations receives a lump sum payment. Some of these payments exceed ten thousand dollars or more.

What happens when an eighteen year old receives that much money? Very few buy a home and set themselves up for the future. Most have spent their youth up to then dreaming of that check while they roam the streets drunk and stoned. With the sudden windfall of a huge chunk of cash, they buy the fastest car they can find, proceed to get blown out of their minds and wrap that vehicle around the nearest light post or tree. One more dead Indian.

In stark contrast to what the general public believes and the media purports, casinos are not a boon to native Nations. Indian Gaming laws are passed by those who wanted those laws passed. Casinos are said to be a means of providing financial stability to the Nations, and this is complete and utter bullshit.

The casinos are typically owned by a cabal of families and a government supported coven of businessmen. The overwhelming majority of monies made goes to those cabals not the people. Some of the casinos give their people a pittance of the profits made, no more than the scraps they throw to the rez dogs. Casinos and the life they create are a microcosm of dominant urban society. The traditionalists don't like it and never wanted it to begin with. They knew what would happen and they aren't surprised that it did.

Because of this many Nations like the Anishinaabe are aloof, standoffish people. No one gets in unless invited. They never speak of their traditional ways to anyone outside of their Nation and many detest Americans although they would never say anything to someone's face. Much like an old black man from the south who grew up in the forties and fifties they may smile to your face and say things like, "Yes suh, no suh, of course suh," but inside what they really want to do is put a bullet in your head. Their smile is as fugacious as they can manage.

Within the Anishinaabe many of the more traditionalists see the world at large as themselves, and then everybody else. Either you are Anishinaabe or you're not and tracing someone's linage helps very few. One matrilineal misstep, unintentional or not, and you're out forever. As far as they are concerned once the line is broken there is no amount of repair possible. The guidelines for acceptance are strict and they do not blur those lines for any reason. You may be native and they may recognize you as such but you aren't Anishinaabe and you never will be.

Decades of destruction and genocide later, Detroit today is a hell hole. Where once was great power, on land perceived as Sacred Ground, now stands decay and rot. Most of the businesses have closed up shop and moved to other countries. The remaining few are barely a shadow of the giant corporate conglomerates that once existed there.

Like anyone who moves from anywhere, things got left behind. In the factories and mills are solvents and chemicals. The ground and buildings were saturated with centuries of flammable liquids. In some of the basements beneath the basements, hidden where no one can find them, are 55 gallons drums of fuel and explosive materials, all left to rot and poison the ground. Thousands and thousand of gallons just waiting for a spark.

As there is very little money coming out of Detroit to support itself, and there is even less coming in. Two thirds of the police department personnel are gone because there is not enough money to pay wages. Fire and rescue squads were scaled back to skeleton crews and former residents abandoned their homes. They walked away and left them to rot. Entire city blocks are empty. Homes can be bought in Detroit for less than the cost of a late model used vehicle if someone actually dared to live there.

Detroit is mile after mile of desiccated steel and tin, skeletal houses with no glass, collapsing roofs and porches. There are potholed streets, cracked and broken sidewalks and long burned out street lamps. It is home to every drug and social disease known to man and the city created a few of its own. As though Armageddon began months earlier, unknown to society at large, in Detroit's industrial district and was eeking and slithering its way into the suburbs one block at a time. Driving into this cesspool of human filth,

Jackson Themal felt like the Destroyer. He had thought this through as carefully as he could.

Coming in off I-75 around 3 a.m. Jackson dropped onto Michigan Avenue, then turned left onto Third street. Pulling over, he retrieved some of the flares and flare guns packed in his trunk. A drug addicted street thug watched casually and Jackson saw him pull out a cell phone. He expected the gang member was about to call his thug buddies and quickly got back in his car. Driving slowly he began firing flares into the buildings around him. An empty block here, a set of houses there, all deserted with no one around. He fired, reloaded and fired again. By the time he reached Montcalm Street sirens were raging. The drug thug must have called the police instead of his friends.

Jackson had stopped outside of Cleveland and picked up a portable police scanner and paid cash at a pawn shop to insure no record existed of the purchase. He listened to that radio as frantic calls began going out for police and rescue to respond to the fires he had set and was continuously informed about which direction the police were coming from.

He continued to fire off flare after flare. If anyone saw him as he cruised the dark streets, he was unaware. With the south and the west side burning, he moved north along St. Antoine and turned on to Beaubien, burning as he went. In the distance he saw flashing lights coming straight at him and he pulled quickly into an alley. Jackson went unnoticed as the city police car raced past him. Looking to his left he saw a homeless man sitting on a broken concrete stoop, watching him.

Leaning out his car window with a smile playing on

his lips Jackson said laughingly to the homeless guy, "You might want to run." He reloaded and fired a flare through the vacant glassless window of the building the homeless guy was sitting in front of and the man took off at breakneck speed. Jackson slipped the transmission into reverse, backed up and returned to drive, continuing on. He eventually joined Jefferson, which led him back to I-75 and out of the city.

A few miles down I-75 he pulled off and stepped out of his vehicle. Jackson could see the entire city was now ablaze. The scanner he held reported the fire was completely out of control and everyone must evacuate the area. The fire had found the hidden materials left by the greedy corporations that had existed there for years. The chemically saturated buildings added to the fire's fury. Jackson turned off his scanner, climbed back into his car and headed south as "Hell" by Disturbed began to play on his radio. "That should keep everyone busy for awhile," he said to the dashboard.

In a matter of hours Detroit would burn to the ground, again. Jackson would never know that the homeless guy he scared the shit out of survived and that he had found his way to the river, hiding until the raging inferno died down to embers. Crawling out of his hiding place he made his way to the police barricades and described Jackson and his car. His report is buried among the hundreds of others for months because there weren't enough detectives to review and follow up every lead.

270°
CHAPTER TWENTY SEVEN

Within hours Jackson was well out of Michigan and deep into Illinois. He followed I-94 west to Joliet and turned south on I-55 toward Springfield, Illinois. In the distance he saw a dead owl off to the side of the road and suddenly had a wicked idea. He pulled off quickly and sprinted to the dead bird, plucking the tail feathers, returned to his car and continued on.

By the late 1700s the United States was firmly established. So was the federally instituted Indian Policy of assimilate or annihilate and the First Nations People were allotted those tracts of land the new Americans weren't interested in – land that was either deforested, unable to be farmed or considered inhabitable and worthless.

Before white settlement, in the northern territories, the Naudowessie or River People, later to become known as the Dakota, lived in flourishing villages and at one time they were considered by many to be the greatest of all native Nations.

Originally they were composed of twelve bands, and they dominated their ancestral territories in Northern Minnesota. In 1815 a treaty was signed between the Dakota and the United States and by 1825 the boundary lines between the tribes and the newly formed United States were defined. Just as quickly, the new Americans begin their process of devastation.

By hook and by crook, greed and corruption, the new Americans immediately took possession of every natural resource and did with these resources what they saw fit. The River People were decimated and wanted nothing more than an end to the genocide. All they asked for in return for all that was taken was food, shelter, health care and education. It didn't seem too much to ask for an entire country.

Agents of the government were assigned to monitor and distribute food supplies and these agents, far removed from government oversight in Washington, disagreed with the terms of the treaties. The government may have agreed to give the food away but they certainly didn't, and within weeks the greedy began starving whoever managed to survive the American Holocaust.

As far as the agents were concerned, simply giving that food away was an utterly absurd notion. They believed it made much better sense for them to sell that food to their own people. That way they could make a dollar or two for themselves and in the process ensure good christian white folk had enough to eat. The savages could fuck off. If something rotted before it could be sold, well, the injuns could have that.

The Dakota were forced off their ancestral lands, their resources were stolen and they were confined to postage stamp sized reservations. Everybody started freezing to death and to add insult to injury the food they were promised was stolen as well. After all they had already suffered they were given scraps the dogs wouldn't eat to feed their starving children. Enough was enough and in 1862 Little Crow gathered as many men as he could that were willing to join him and they commenced killing settlers and the soldiers protecting them.

Unfortunately his actions played directly into the plans of then Governor Alexander Ramsey. Ramsey publicly stated that every Sioux Indian in Minnesota must be exterminated or at the least driven out of the state. Adding to that insult Ramsey placed bounties of up to $200 for the scalp of anyone not yet captured, a sum equal to $4,450.00 today. With the average yearly income in the 1800s at roughly $500, it didn't take much more than that to convince volunteers to sign up.

In charge of the entire murderous menagerie was Colonel Crooks. He was an arrogant career military man and the commander of the garrisons. He was also answerable only to Ramsey. He, too, was more than happy to oblige when ordered to begin the mass slaughter. Before the blood was dry three hundred and three Dakota would be imprisoned in the stockades at Fort Snelling.

The case was brought before President Abraham Lincoln who reduced the number of convicted to 38. On December 26, 1862, the day after Christmas, all 38 were hanged at the same time under orders from Lincoln. Days later he would sign the Emancipation Proclamation.

This was the largest mass hanging in the history of this country. Amidst Christmas decorations, while the white settlers sang Oh Come All Ye Faithful and Silent Night, these native men were murdered by order of the United States President for having the insolence to rise up against oppression, rape, abuse and starvation.

Through the unbearable winter of 1862 and 1863 the remaining 265 plus those that could be rounded up were forced to exist in the brutal concentration camps of Fort Snelling. In May of 1863 those left alive were shipped to Davenport, Iowa where they remained imprisoned for another three years. In 1866 the survivors were finally shipped to the newly formed Crow Creek Indian Reservation in South Dakota. Today, Crow Creek remains one of the most inhospitable places on the planet.

Jackson is well aware of the history of Mankato and the Dakota 38. He is also aware that Fort Snelling stands today as a museum, that it has been renovated and is recognized as a State Park. It physically honors those who self righteously slaughtered in the name of their God and reminds the world that although it may be Jesus' birthday that don't mean we can't kill a few folks. Jackson would be visiting the museum soon.

With history boiling in his mind Jackson reached Springfield, exited I-55 at Clear Lake Avenue, and merged onto Jefferson. At a little past six in the morning he turned left on Seventh and pulled up to the visitor center of the Lincoln House. Noting the park attendants had not yet arrived and the place was deserted, he quickly jumped from his car and sprinted to the main entrance. He secured an owl feather to the door of the visitor's center and scrambled back to his car where he quickly exited the parking lot and maneuvered as close as he could to the Lincoln House.

Reaching over to the passenger's seat, he picked up three flares and in rapid succession he fired them into the windows closest to him. With the blaze set and tires squealing he raced away. Back on Seventh he made a quick right and then another quick right on Sixth. Reaching East Monroe he doubled back on Seventh and screeched to a halt in front of the Lincoln Library. Jackson fired three more flares into those windows and stomped the accelerator. Quickly he turned left on East Capitol, then right on South Eleventh, and another right on South Grand.

In under ten minutes Jackson initiated the complete destruction of two historical structures dedicated to a man regularly presented as "ole' Honest Abe" who, in truth, remained the consummate politician. His policies weren't enacted because of his personal beliefs but because it was what his constituency wanted at the period. Maybe if the man had some balls and did what he wanted to do instead of what others told him to do he might not have been shot in the head.

From South Grand, Jackson merged with I-72 and quickly pulled off. He turned on his scanner and listened to the urgently broadcast calls. Up ahead he saw an Illinois State Trooper rushing to respond and he waited for the trooper to pass, appearing to be just another traveler who had stopped for a few moments to rest. When the trooper was out of sight he turned off the scanner and eased into traffic heading east to I-74.

Flipping on the car stereo he listened to the reports already coming in across the local news stations of the fire at the Lincoln House and Library. Those stories were interspersed with others about Detroit burning to the ground. So far no one had made the connection between the two and according to the news stories the police had no suspects or leads. There was no mention of the owl feather. That piece of information was probably being held back to insure conviction. Jackson smiled and drove east. An hour later he blended with the traffic on I-70 which led him across to the eastern seaboard. Following I-70 for several hours he reflected on the places he had been and the people he had met.

When Jackson left the Odawa he headed east to attend the yearly powwow at Allegheny in New York. While there he met a few Seneca's from Tonawanda and received an invitation to visit. That was where Jackson would learn of and receive the Kiowa war bonnet.

In 1848 the Allegheny and Cattaraugus broke away to form the Seneca Nation of Indians. The families that created Tonawanda retrieved their horns of authority from the deposed Chiefs and Clan Mothers with the intent to govern themselves. Tonawanda became a federally recognized Seneca reservation in 1857 when a treaty was signed between themselves and the United States. Previously Ogden Land Company had fraudulently stolen the land using the Buffalo Creek Treaty of 1838 and the Compromise Treaty of 1842. The United States graciously permitted the Tonawanda Seneca's to buy it back.

While visiting with them Jackson was introduced to a Seneca Elder, William Leaf. A full blood Tonawanda Seneca, and easily 80 years old. He is a short, stout man with a round face and short, close cropped hair that he had maintained since he served in the Marines. He is also one of the crankiest people Jackson has ever met.

Grandfather Leaf's family was one of the original Seneca families that set up Tonawanda. He continued to live on the same land his family purchased and he dared anyone to disturb him. Leaf told Jackson the story of when the Council came out to give him a hard time about some violation or another. Fluent in each of the languages of the Six Nations Confederacy, Leaf told them, in all six languages, the land was his and he would do with it what he damn well wanted to, when he damn well wanted to. When he finished his oratory he told them in English that they could all go fuck themselves if they didn't understand what he said. Leaving them standing there with their mouths agape he turned his back on the Council and walked into his house. Not many bothered Grandfather Leaf after that.

Jackson attended a sweat lodge with Grandfather Leaf and a few other Seneca, by invitation. Jackson and four others were gathered at Leaf's home around dusk in late February in upstate New York and it was as cold as the balls on a brass monkey. They were sitting in his home when the phone rang. Leaf answered and with a quick reply of okay he stood up from his chair and announced all was ready. Jackson was a bit confused as he looked around the immediate property outside the windows. No glow from a fire could be seen. Shrugging his shoulders he followed everybody else as they headed outside.

Leaf climbed on to a four wheeler. Tied behind him on the luggage rack was a packed gym bag. He drove off purposefully into the woods behind his house and left everyone else to follow him using the well worn trail on foot. Forty five minutes later, deep in the woods about a mile back, they finally came to the sweat lodge fire. Leaf was already inside the lodge impatiently waiting on those walking. "Let's go girls," he shouted haughtily, "I'm getting cold in here!"

While they walked rain and sleet began to fall and the temperature was easily 10 degrees or less with a blowing, blustery wind. They quickly shed their clothes and stripped down to their underwear. In a hurry they crawled into the lodge. Thirteen stones were brought into that lodge and Jackson swears his skin was coming off. Never before had he been in a lodge with so few grandfather stones that got so hot, so fast. Four excruciating rounds later the lodge mercifully ended.

Leaf had brought a change of clothes with him in the gym bag tied to his four wheeler. No one else had thought to do the same. While all were participating in the lodge their clothes remained outside and the rain soaked them thoroughly. When the rain stopped the clothes froze. Now everyone, except Leaf, after spending two hours being cooked, must dress in frozen clothes. Leaf climbed aboard his four wheeler in his fresh dry clothes, cast a glance at the shivering men and cackled hysterically. "Dumbasses," he called to them, "See you at the house. I bet the coffee is nice and hot!"

With a quick turn of the throttle and not even a backwards glance he roared off, still cackling, back to his house leaving everyone else to walk. The temperature was below zero, it was raining and sleeting, they were wearing frozen clothes and they had a mile to walk. Jackson didn't know what hurt more, the walk or the lodge.

Chuckling over the memory Jackson pulled himself back to the present. Turning on the radio again the news casts continued about Detroit and Springfield. The stories cried over the loss of the great city of Detroit, home of Motown and the auto industry. Not one mention was made of the atrocities committed to erect the hellhole. Great city, my left nut, Jackson thought.

Newscasters lamented the loss of history with the total destruction of the Lincoln House and Library. They extolled its virtues as a national treasure that was now totally destroyed by fire with historical documents that could never be replaced. Only ashes and the foundations remained. "Historical lies would be a bit more accurate, don't you think?" Jackson asked the radio.

Who could do such a thing the newscasters asked? What would compel a person to commit such a horrid act of terrorism on the poor people of the United States? "Uh, me?" Jackson answered as he continued addressing the radio, "and I bet there are a few more who would like to. Talk to a couple of Indians, assholes. Might explain a few things."

Turing off the radio Jackson was comfortable that they had no idea who to look for and absolutely no idea of where to begin looking. Around 3 p.m. he turned off I-70 outside of

Wheeling, West Virginia and stopped for a few hours of rest in the back seat of his car. He felt no guilt over what he had done and no trepidation over what he was going to do. When he woke he craved coffee and quickly found a fast food joint. Smoking and sipping he reviewed his map.

Settling on the directions he decided best, he climbed back behind the wheel and finding the I-470 bypass he swung around Wheeling and picked up I-70 again outside of Washington, Pennsylvania. Rested and refreshed he checked the radio. More of the same. Nothing new and still no leads. He followed I-70 east until he picked up I-79 heading south and continued on to join I-68 east. He continued on the interstate until he picked up I-95 south and when he reached the Capital Beltway, exited at 176-A and headed south on North Kings Highway. At around 9 p.m. Jackson searched for and found the nearest super center where he could park and wait. Smoking and thinking he remembered again William Leaf in Tonawanda.

On the last day he was there they were smoking and talking, just the two of them in Leaf's home, while warmth from the pot belly stove in the corner radiated throughout his little house. Leaf informed Jackson about events that were taking place on the Oneida Reservation over by Syracuse. He said some years back the Clan Mothers had chosen a few men to represent them at Grand Council as the Oneida didn't have a Chief anymore because the last one died several years prior. These men were appointed temporary representatives until a new Chief was given his horns of authority but one of the men wasn't satisfied with his temporary position. He decided to take it upon himself to make his position permanent.

He presented himself to the Governor of New York after he came up with a grand plan to create a casino. He said if the Governor would help him get the laws he needed passed and built the casino he would see that the State of New York received immense compensation. In return he would run the casino and would be recognized by the United States as the head of the Oneida Nation which he incorporated. The Governor agreed, the laws were passed, the casino was built and the people got screwed, yet again, by one of their own.

The officially recognized Oneida Clan Mothers formally presented themselves to the Governor and explicitly explained the guy was self appointed, but no one listened. He eventually un-enrolled everyone who stood against him and bulldozed the houses on what remained of the reservation. He locked up their longhouse, lorded himself over his people, and those who stood up to him were crushed under his heavy hand. Assisting him were those he personally appointed as Clan Mothers and Headsmen.

At Leaf's request Jackson traveled to stand with the traditional Oneida. He spent several winters with them off and on, coming and going. At one point he drove the Grandmothers to Canada to speak with their relatives in Southwold and Six Nations.

At a Clan Mother's request Jackson carried an eagle feather from the Oneida to the Cherokee in North Carolina where he first met Jack Yellow Bird. From there he traveled to Oklahoma and delivered the Kiowa war bonnet. Leaving Oklahoma he returned to Roddy's place outside of Nashville where they traveled together to Terry Bishop's place outside of Cookeville.

Jackson awakened in his car, back in the present. At some point he must have dozed off. Looking around he spotted a convenience store gas station and he drove over. Sore and stiff from the long drive he climbed out of his car and after stretching he walked inside to find the largest cup of coffee he could. Glancing at the clock he noticed it was a little after midnight. Perfect, he thought. Returning to his car he lit a cigarette while sipping his coffee and mentally reviewed what he was about to do.

Finishing the smoke he flipped the butt out the window and steered back on to Kings Highway. He followed Kings Highway south, reaching Mt. Vernon around 1 a.m. Driving past Mt. Vernon he headed over to Riverside Park and hid his car in a wooded section. He knew security guards were patrolling the property so he had to be very careful not to get caught.

None of the guards were as alert as they should be. All had heard what happened at the Lincoln House and Library over the radio and television news programs but in no way did they believe anyone will dare try something like that here.

With a flare gun and a bag of flares in hand Jackson trotted the Mount Vernon trail and came in behind the main mansion. From the river side he launched as many flares as possible through as many windows as he could see of George Washington's Mt. Vernon Estate. Out of flares he turned and raced back into the woods as sirens immediately began to alarm the grounds keepers and security guards.

The heavily polished furniture and oil soaked floors quickly ignited while custom draperies and velvet helped to feed the flames. By the time he reached his car the main mansion was engulfed and the fire was spreading to other buildings. He had mere seconds to climb into his car and get away but before exiting his hiding place he rolled down the window and tied an owl feather to an accessible branch.

Hurriedly he sped down George Washington Memorial Parkway and turned left onto State Route 629. The scream of sirens filled the air and Jackson saw a helicopter far off in the distance coming straight for him. With no time to spare, he just made it to Inova Mount Vernon Hospital and pulled into the parking garage where he disappeared from sight. While the helicopter made several passes he sat in his car and breathlessly waited. The helicopter turned and left, flying to the inferno that was Mt. Vernon. The old timber of the mansion and the outbuildings provided ample fuel for the flames and the estate would burn and burn until very little was left.

Jackson remained in the parking garage for the rest of the evening. The afternoon of the next day he left his car and entered the hospital. As far as anyone was concerned he was either a patient or visiting a patient. He wandered the halls of the hospital for a few hours and occasionally picked up on conversations between workers or caught news programs in waiting rooms. Mt. Vernon, the home of Washington, father of these great United States, was destroyed. It was all he could do not to smile and into the evening he returned to his car.

Driving out of the parking lot and finding again Route 628 he turned left onto 626 and right on Richmond Highway. He noticed a road sign for Huntley Meadows Park and followed the signs to the park. Jackson found a secluded spot, unloaded and then buried all the flares and the flare guns. He returned to his car and checked it thoroughly to ensure nothing was in it to incriminate him then gathered the owl feathers and tucked them up under the dash.

Turning on the radio he listened as reporters described the aftermath of Mt. Vernon. The reporters informed the public there was little left of the first President's glorious home. They describe it as the most horrendous thing to have ever happened in the history of this great country. "Not even fucking close," Jackson said vehemently, still talking to the radio. Back on Richmond Highway he headed toward the Capitol Beltway and immediately ran into a road block.

State Troopers were searching every vehicle and he knew there wasn't anywhere he could go so he patiently waited for his turn to be searched. As traffic slowly inched forward he calmed himself and prepared. If he was caught, so be it, although he preferred not to be. There was so much more he wanted to do. Jackson's turn arrived quickly and the trooper, with a no nonsense grimace on his face, motioned for him to roll down his window and he immediately complied.

"License and registration please," the trooper instructed.

"Yes sir," Jackson replied respectfully. Reaching into his glove box with his free hand remaining in plain sight of the trooper he obtained his documents and handed them to the trooper who immediately began inspecting them. "Is this about what was happening on the radio?" Jackson asked inquisitively.

Cocking his head sideways, as if imitating a dog hearing an unusual sound the trooper, obviously annoyed, retorted, "Do I look like a news reporter to you, son? Do you think I'm standing here to answer your questions, that I pulled you over to give you information? Some smart ass son of a bitch thinks he can commit terrorist acts in this country and until I know better, as far as I'm concerned, you're him." Staring intently at Jackson's registration he asks suspiciously, "Says here you're from Pennsylvania. What're you doing in Virginia?"

"I was over at Inova visiting with a friend of mine who is dying," Jackson responded with as much honesty as he could fake. Having spent the last few hours wandering the hallways, Jackson easily described the cancer ward and floors, doctors and patients. During his explanation another trooper brought a scent dog over to his car. When they reached the trunk the scent dog immediately alerted to the smell of the flares that until a little over an hour ago were stored there. With the dogs alert the trooper and his partner were immediately at full attention and he demanded authoritatively, "You want to step out of the vehicle sir?"

Jackson again complied immediately. "Is there a problem officer?" he asked meekly.

"Please open the trunk sir. Now." was all the trooper would say, one hand on his weapon. Jackson did so and with its nose the scent dog pointed exactly to where the flares had been. The trooper spun furiously to address him and demanded in a commanding voice, "What was in here?"

Jackson was waiting for this and was fully prepared. "I'm not sure, officer," he stammered submissively, "Could be anything. If you look again at the registration, sir, you will see this car is a shop vehicle. We haul all kinds of crap in it. Tires, gas cans for people who break down, tools and stuff to fix tires. All kinds of things."

The trooper carefully reviewed his documents again and paid close attention to the registration. "Wait here a moment," he demanded and returned to his cruiser where he hastily made a phone call to check Jackson's story. Moments later he walked back and handed him his documents. "Story checks out, sir," the trooper said almost but not quite apologetically, "Sorry for any inconvenience. We're all a little stressed over what has happened. Had us thinking you were our guy for a second there."

"Thank god!" Jackson exclaimed enthusiastically, "I gotta say, you scared the poo outta me."

"It's all okay now, sir," the trooper responded dismissively, "if you will return to your vehicle and move on we have other cars we have to check."

For the final time at the checkpoint he complied. If the officers in Detroit had paid attention to the homeless guy they would have known what make and model car to be looking for. The exact make and model Jackson was driving. If they had done more than file his story they would have had a description to work with. A description Jackson fit perfectly.

He positioned himself behind the wheel of his car and drove off. Merging with traffic on the Capital Beltway he headed south on I-95 using the interstates to connect to I-64 south to Norfolk. He had intended to swing over to

Charlottesville and take out Monticello but it was way too hot with police to try it now. He suspected as much listening to the stories in the hospital which was why he buried the flares.

He heard the radio reporters, in a fury, describe everything that had happened over the last few days. First Detroit, then Lincoln's House and Library and now Mt. Vernon. My god, the Father of the Country! The greatest of all great men who ever breathed just short of Jesus himself!

Jackson noticed every radio station had someone who was an expert on George Washington and each one was his number one fan. Each tried to outdo the other on informing the public about all the wonderful things George had done. Each was more devastated than the other over what had happened. Occasionally there was an expert on Lincoln, but he was greatly overshadowed by George. Jackson listened and thought about how he would seriously enjoy punching each expert right in the mouth.

Not once did they mention that the French and Indian War was George Washington's fault. Nowhere did anyone say anything about his ill conceived and piss-poor attempt to assault Lafayette at Jumonville. No mention was made of how he was pushed back to Fort Necessity, where George had his ass handed to him. The name itself should have been a clue but obviously wasn't.

No mention was made of the Haudenasaunee women who brought food and blankets to George's men as they were starving and freezing to death at Valley Forge. Not a word about the Seneca man who stood in the bow of the boat and guided George across the Potomac. "Fuck Washington," Jackson said viciously, again addressing the radio, "and fuck these idiot assholes who are defending him."

As far as Jackson was concerned, George Washington was a narcissistic, arrogant, egotistical asshole. His rank, privileges and wealth were amassed through the rape, murder and torture of the First Nations People – activities he either participated in, encouraged or condoned. What someone becomes later in life in no way excuses what they did to get there, regardless the whole "Do what you want, when you want, to whomever you want, the repercussions don't matter" ideology. Then simply say I'm sorry and all is forgiven? Exactly how does that work?

Hell isn't somewhere someone winds up after they die, hell is right now. Hell is the life being lived and the effects it has on everyone else. Washington was a perfect example of the former, Jackson the latter. The only thing that asshole fathered is greed, corruption, and the genocide that followed, Jackson thinks as he drove on.

There was so much more to do.

280°
CHAPTER TWENTY EIGHT

Jackson traveled south on I-64 headed for Norfolk, Virginia. Several hours of driving later he found a rest stop to pull into and get some much needed rest. No dreams plagued him that night as he slept like the dead. Rousing early the next morning he located the nearest restaurant, walked in and ordered black coffee. He asked the waitress, "Is there a local library around here?"

"Sure," she replied, quickly sharing the address and directions to find it. He found an empty booth in the back to sit and have breakfast and invariably he was stared at. It happened everywhere he went, all the time, as though he was a zoo animal that had somehow escaped its cage, and it really annoyed the hell out of him.

White people, Asian people, even Black people stared at him like he was an alien from another planet. They had never seen an Indian before and he was a novelty. While in grade school they learned all about Indians in their textbooks. Some have even seen the Indian movies on TV or dress their children up as an Indians on Halloween. But to see a real one? They thought they were all dead. At least that's what they tell him when they incredulously asked if he was Indian.

A black woman walked up and asked with blatant amazement, "Are you an Indian?"

Jackson responded sarcastically, "Are you black?" She walked away in a huff, as if he had just insulted her. Not for one second did the thought pass through her mind just how insulting she was to him.

It's as though Jackson is Indian first and human second; and he is a mix blood. The full bloods have it much worse. He recalled walking through a Wal-Mart some years back picking up supplies for something or other. Turning down an aisle he almost ran into a white woman with her child in the seat of the shopping cart. As Jackson stepped back to facilitate not crashing into her, the child excitedly pointed at him and exclaimed, "Look Mom! A real Indian!"

Feigning a surprised look on his face Jackson pointed in return at the child and exclaimed, "Look! A real white boy!" The kid started to cry and his mother got mad and stomped off like somehow it was all Jackson's fault. And you can merrily go fuck yourself, too, Jackson thought irascibly.

Then there is the whole "How!" thing. He swore the next son of a bitch who said "How!" to him would die on the spot. Even more infuriating were the idiots who thought they were somehow being respectful. Jackson's usual response was, "I already know how, ask your girlfriend when."

Previous generation's behavior aside, as revolting as that was, the current generation is abhorrent. By the 1960s the use of black face was recognized as insulting, but pretend to be native, replete with chicken feather headdresses and polyester buckskin, that is somehow seen as being okay.

Reducing an entire race of people to the status of imaginary creatures is beyond insulting. Adding to the insult, what was held Sacred has been commercialized to identify products. Everything from feminine hygiene to lawnmowers, elementary school sports teams to professional athletes. The adults admonish their children and instruct them not to be racists while professing utter incredulity to their children when asked why Indians are so angry all the time. Maybe it is time a native Nation started building cars. Then we can have a Jeep Jesus, maybe a Buick Baptist or even a Chrysler Crucifixion.

The whole thing really isn't that hard to understand. Let someone they don't know move into their house and in a few weeks the tenant, so graciously assisted, of their own accord, pretentiously assumes ownership of all their stuff. Including their car, their bank accounts and maybe even their wife. The original occupant would then be given a corner in the garage or basement with no heat and only a concrete floor with the rats and cockroaches.

The original rightful occupant would be expected to say thank you when the garbage was occasionally thrown to them so they may pick through it to possibly find something to eat. If lucky, a worn out t-shirt or used pair of tennis shoes may be tossed at them so the new tenant can be seen as being charitable. The new tenant, of course, insists it was theirs all along and the original occupant was nothing more than a squatter. Further infuriating the situation the new tenants uses a foreign religious belief as justification for their actions. Jackson wonders how long it would take for someone to get furious enough to start killing?

Shaking his head in disgust he finished his coffee and light breakfast and noticed he had an hour to kill before the library opened. He paid his bill and walked to his car. Climbing in and setting the transmission into drive he pulled out of the parking lot. The library was barely a few miles away so he cruised downtown and watched the people come and go. Ants rushing to work to begin another day of fruitless consumption, all whispering amongst themselves about the events over these last few days. It was all anyone could discuss. Around the water coolers and gathered at picnic benches they extrapolated and hypothesized over who could be committing these unspeakable acts. What was their motive? What was the reasoning behind it all?

Jackson watched them all with a faint smile on his face. If they only knew he was among them. Soon growing tired of people watching he went in search of the library. A few wrong turns and he eventually found it. Walking in, looking for the librarian, he noticed a couple of matronly looking women behind a kiosk. He arrived at the desk as a woman, probably in her thirties he thinks, glanced up from cataloging loose books and met his gaze, "Y'all have the internet here?" he inquired as he stepped towards the kiosk.

"Yes, we do," she answered pleasantly with a sincere smile.

"Is there a fee to use it?" Jackson asked.

"Not at all," she said in a genial manner, "We have a large computer room here. Many of the students come by to use the computers. Are you a student at the college?" He thought about lying and confirming he was then changed his mind and instead said, "I'm thinking about it. All I really need to do is some quick research."

"That's okay," she encouraged, "all I need is your ID and we can set you up." Jackson handed her his driver's license and, after she recorded his information, she cordially escorted him to the computer room. With a quick smile she turned and left him to do what he needed to.

Jackson was researching Richard Whitman. As a former President, many had researched him before and there were reams and reams of information. Everything about the man, including rumors and suggestions; and most of what he finds supports Whitman's Presidency. After this many years the man is considered a hero, regardless the death and destruction he reigned down on the indigenous people. Next thing you know his face will be on the twenty dollar bill.

Jackson began to trace Whitman's family tree and began to see they were never a prodigious family. None of the families had many children. Richard Whitman himself only had two daughters. They married and each gave birth to a son. Those sons married – one of them never had children and the other son had two daughters. They married, one had a son and the other a daughter. They and their parents were the only ones left alive today, both of the children were in their early twenties, both were in college. The Whitman fortune was handed down generation after generation, and, as the family remained small, the fortune remained vast.

Jackson thought about the many families living hand-to-mouth in government housing on the reservations; in homes infested with roaches, mold and decay – children who had nothing more for dinner than sleep. Some children who hadn't eaten for days.

The Whitman's, thanks to their Presidential ancestor, never experienced hunger. Not for one moment did they want for anything. Their wealth and power provided all they would ever need at any time they needed it. The world and everyone who lived in it perceived as their servants, to be tolerated until dismissed.

"Finding what you are looking for?" the woman who escorted Jackson asked. Startled, he jumped and she laughed as she turned slightly away with a small smile playing at the corners of her mouth, "You were so engrossed. I wanted to be sure everything was alright," she continued. Actually, she noticed Jackson was native and felt she simply had to talk to him.

"Kind of," he replied as vague annoyance tinged his voice.

"I'm sorry," she stammered, apologizing as she quickly turned to walk away, "I didn't mean to interrupt."

An idea suddenly came to Jackson and he shyly replied, "It's okay," looking deeply into her eyes and seeing pain reflected back. Someone hurt this woman, Jackson thought with sudden awareness, someone hurt her real bad.

"Maybe you can help," he offered seductively.

Like a dog with a thrown bone, she instantly turned back to him, "Certainly," she replied while enthusiastically smiling, "What are you looking for?"

"Information on President Richard Whitman," he answered quietly, "He is kind of a hobby of mine."

"Well, you are in luck," she exclaimed, almost giggling, "I studied President Whitman extensively. Genealogy was a hobby of mine back when I was in college. You're Native American, aren't you?" she added suggestively.

"Yeah," Jackson said as he tried to keep the aggravation at the question out of his tone.

"Cool," she replied bubbly, and extended her hand in greeting, "I'm part Indian, too. My mother is Native American, we're Cherokee. I'm Jenny Randall, but everyone calls me Jenny Lynne."

Yippee fucking skippy, Jackson thought with annoyance. Another blonde haired, blue eyed Cherokee. But he didn't say what he is thinking. Instead, he smiled to encourage her and to make her feel comfortable. Shaking her hand he replied politely, "I'm Jackson. You know Indians don't come in parts, don't you?"

A stunned Jenny Lynne stared, then twittered a bird-like laugh, "Wow! I never thought of it like that before. I guess it is a bit of a ridiculous statement. Something tells me you know a lot more than I do."

Jackson thought acrimoniously, *Really? How astute of you,* but again didn't say what he was thinking. He replied,

"I'm going to be here for awhile, maybe a few weeks or so. If you want, I can share what little I have picked up with you and maybe you can share what you know about Whitman?"

"That would be so great!" Jenny Lynne vociferated, no longer attempting to mask her excitement or interest, "My shift finishes in a couple of hours. If you aren't doing anything later this afternoon maybe you would like to meet me for coffee? I have so much stuff on the Whitman's; everything about his family – what happened to them and where they are now." As if imparting a secret, she whispered surreptitiously, "There are even some rumors I found out about!"

Jackson's smile broadened. How absolutely perfect. Instead of hours pouring through dusty books or making his eyes scream after staring at a computer, here was someone who had everything he needed. He quickly accepted Jenny Lynne's invitation for coffee and after a few awkward comments between them he turned to leave.

"See you at the coffee shop?" Jenny Lynne called expectantly as he walked for the door.

"Absolutely," he called back in agreement, "No way I would miss it." Jenny Lynn blushed so brightly Jackson could see it across the room. *Gotcha,* he thought to himself.

Jackson had a few hours to waste. He slipped into the nearby college and found a men's locker room where he could shower and change clothes. Back in his car he napped and around 2 p.m. made his way to the coffee shop to meet Jenny

Lynne. Walking in he saw her in the corner. She apparently arrived early and was anxiously looking for Jackson.

"Hey there!" she called, as vibrantly as before, as if he hadn't seen her. Jackson sauntered over, gazing directly into her eyes as he moved toward her. His eyes invited her to come closer, assured her everything would be alright. His eyes told her she was safe with Jackson and she could trust him. Without a whimper Jenny Lynne succumbed. "It's really great to see you," she continued shyly, "I have to say I thought for a moment you weren't going to show."

"Not even a thought," Jackson purred, "I have been looking forward to this all day."

Jenny Lynne wasn't overly pretty but certainly not ugly either. She was chubby but not overweight with long strawberry blonde hair, green eyes and an oval face. Her obvious Scandinavian features shown through. She was tall for a woman, about five foot nine or so. Her clothes appeared to have been expensive at one time but were dulled with age and too many hard washings. With no perfume or extensive make up she looked like what she once was – an average, everyday, suburban housewife. They began making small talk and the conversation immediately turned to currents events.

"Have you been listening to the radio?" she asked.

"The stuff about Detroit and all?" he responded inquisitively.

"Yeah," she exclaimed, "Can you believe it? Detroit, nothing left. Then the Lincoln thing and Mt. Vernon. Oh my God, Mt. Vernon."

Obviously Jenny Lynne was eating up all the crap the media was dishing out to the public. Jackson could see she almost had tears in her eyes and he didn't know whether to laugh or throw up. Effusively Jenny Lynne continued, "I can't imagine why someone would do such a thing. Those great men, all their history. So much is gone now. It was probably digitized, but the originals? They can never be replaced. Do you think it was terrorists, Jackson?"

"Might be," he agreed, placating her, "Just might be, Jenny Lynne."

"The news stories all say they have no idea who is doing it and that they have no suspects. The FBI is involved now, did you hear?" she asked.

"No," he said, not feigning surprise, "I didn't know that. Wow, the FBI! Whoever it is, they are in serious trouble now. The FBI will get them for sure." This was new information for Jackson. He turned the radio off after leaving Richmond because he wasn't able to stomach another Presidential expert whine about the loss of history.

"Absolutely," Jenny Lynne agreed, "They will get them for sure. The news says the fires are connected and that they were all started the same way. Something about flares used to burn everything down."

Interesting, Jackson thought as he sipped his coffee, they are making the connections.

As if needing to unburden herself Jenny Lynne began to tell him her story, egged on unknowingly by Jackson. Married at 25 with two children by 30, a house in the suburbs with an inattentive husband, a decent job and the usual debt.

Four years earlier on New Year's Eve Jenny Lynne and her former husband, Bob, were attending the usual office party. Bob, as usual, drank way too much and caused a terrible accident when they were driving home. She suffered the brunt of the accident and broke both her legs and her pelvis while Bob walked away with barely a scratch. After months in the hospital Jenny Lynne returned home. Bob, unable to ease his sexual needs with her, began having an affair and Jenny Lynne became addicted to pain killers. A few months after Jenny Lynne had returned home from the hospital Bob left her for the other woman and took their children with him.

Citing her addiction to pain medication Bob sued for full custody of their children and won. He claimed Jenny Lynne was an unfit mother. The judge agreed with Bob and her former life ended. Someone forgot to mention the entire thing was Bob's fault and it didn't matter because no one cared. Jenny Lynne spiraled out of control, soon crashing and burning and eventually found herself in a detox program.

Her decent job gone she now worked at the public library. The pay wasn't much but with help from welfare she got by and she visited her children on the weekends. Jenny Lynne was a wrecked, vulnerable woman and perfect for Jackson's needs.

Having acquired all the information about her he needed he deftly steered the conversation to Richard Whitman.

Jenny Lynne had brought all her notebooks with her. She must have left the library a little early to go home and get them and he smiled at the thought of her rushing about. He could picture her getting everything in order to be prepared to see him. She thought the smile was for her.

"Here is what I have," she began, "seems the Whitman's never had many kids like you noticed at the library Jackson. Today there are only two families left, the Gardner's and the Jensen's. The Gardner's have a daughter, 23, and she is currently attending college in Raleigh Durham. The Jensen's have a son, 24, and he is in South Carolina. These are the only people left alive today that are related to President Whitman." Jackson was ecstatic as the plan formulating in his mind began to take on shape and form. "There is one other thing," Jenny Lynne abruptly interjected into his musings.

"Yeah, what's that?" he asked curiously.

"You know the things President Whitman did to the Native American People, right, Jackson?" she stated more than asked, "He really was a horrible man. Seems he was also a liar and a philanderer. There is a rumor he had a child out of wedlock to one of his servants. So far I haven't been able to track down any information on the child so maybe it is only a rumor. To be honest I never really looked into it very deeply."

A wrinkle, Jackson thought to himself, *a very curious wrinkle indeed.*

Cooing, whispering, and teasing he slowly brought Jenny Lynne along telling her all she wanted to hear. He agreed with her when she told him how terrible her ex-husband was. He consoled her as she cried about her children. In earlier days Jackson often traded sex for food. He had no problem now trading sex for information and in a matter of hours he was at her apartment tenderly making love to her. Jenny Lynne thought she had died and gone to heaven.

The following morning over coffee at her table they continued their conversation from the day before, "This rumor about Whitman," Jackson coaxed, "you think there is any credibility to it?"

"I think so. It's mentioned in several texts although usually only in passing. Don't want to besmirch the name of a great man, huh?" she said sarcastically.

"Oh, but of course not," Jackson replied, just as sarcastically. "What do you think the chances are of finding out more about it, Jenny Lynne?" he inquired.

"I guess pretty good," she answered, "It would take some digging but if anyone can do it I'm pretty sure I can. I have access to the files and information at the library and of course the internet here at home. Might take a little while but if it's real, the rumor that is, I bet I can track it down."

"That would be amazing," he said. Gratitude at her willingness to help him coated every syllable. Jenny Lynne turned on her television and soon they were both engrossed in the latest news stories about Detroit, Springfield and Mt. Vernon. They discussed what the reporters revealed and Jackson agreed with her, it was all so terrible. Reporters informed the people that the fires were connected, although police continued to have no leads as to why or who. They said local, state and federal agencies were setting up surveillance at all historical presidential museums, libraries and homes. Good to know, Jackson thinks, good to know.

The attention of the country was focused on the catastrophic destruction he had brought to bear. What the country didn't know, as well as the authorities both state and federal, was that everything he had done so far was nothing more than diversionary. Their attention was focused exactly where Jackson wanted it to be focused. Now he could move ahead with what he really wanted to do, his intentions from the beginning. Jackson posed an impromptu scenario to Jenny Lynne, "I have an uncle who died recently and I have to travel to be at the funeral tomorrow."

"That's so sad Jackson," she said with sincere remorse in her voice.

"I would love to see you again. Maybe dinner or something? Plus look deeper into this rumor about Whitman. I just love a great mystery," he teased.

Jenny Lynne looked as though he was telling her she won the lottery and hurriedly replied, "I would love to see you again, too, Jackson. Dinner sounds great. And I love a mystery too. I've often thought about finding out if the rumor is true or not, to satisfy my own curiosity if nothing else. You go to the funeral and do what you need to do. I will begin the research and see where it leads us. When you get back you can help me and together we can get to the bottom of this. Besides, it will help take my mind of these horrible things that are happening."

Jackson smiled the smile of the cat who ate the canary and Jenny Lynne again thought it was for her. A few hours later when she left for another day of work he left for Raleigh Durham.

290°
CHAPTER TWENTY NINE

Following the local highways until he reached I-95 Jackson turned south. Three hours later he turned onto 40 and drove into Raleigh, North Carolina, known as 'The Triangle' by the locals. He learned of this reference as he and Jenny Lynne researched the area last night. Everything anyone could want to know was on the internet and they had been searching for Sherry Gardner. Finding her easily they discovered she was currently studying cultural anthropology at Duke University. With a little time and research, aided by Jenny Lynne's notebooks, Jackson knew exactly what dorm Sherry lived in, her complete course schedule, as well as her hobbies and interests. Jenny Lynne was a thorough researcher.

He searched for the YMCA closest to Duke University and after noting its location, he found a nearby barber shop. Entering the barber shop he observed the barber was relaxing in his chair and reading a local paper. No other patrons were in attendance.

"Got time for a quick cut?" Jackson asked politely.

Looking up from his paper and rising from the chair simultaneously the barber invited him to take his place. The barber quickly noticed Jackson's long, straight hair that was practically to his waist. "Quick, huh?" the barber asked curiously, "Guess you only need a trim?"

Settling himself in the chair Jackson replied, "Nope, want to make it short."

"That ain't going to be quick," the barber retorted, "Sure you want me to do that?"

"Yeah," he said forlornly, "I guess it's about time. I'm not a teenager anymore and I probably should start thinking about looking like an adult."

"Can't argue with you there, son. I'm John," the barber introduced himself and asked, "How short do you want it?"

Jackson shook John's offered hand. "Jackson," he informed, "Off the face, above the ears and collar," he instructed.

John the barber raised his eyebrows and queried, "You sure about this? Last chance to change your mind."

Jackson's hair had been long his entire life and he never considered cutting it previously. Realizing the need to blend in and to go unnoticed he knew he would have to cut it. He wasn't happy about it but he was willing to do what he had to do.

Jackson confirmed confidently, "I'm sure," and the cutting began.

"Been following the news?" John the barber asked, making conversation as he snipped.

"A little. Shame what all is going on," Jackson responded in an inviting tone.

"Ain't it though?" John said, obviously more than a little peeved. "Probably those freaking terrorists again, trying to wipe out our history. As though we can forget ourselves. Pardon my French, but those guys are fucking idiots. How can we forget who we are?"

"Really," Jackson agreed, "How can an entire Nation of People simply forget their own history? As though everything that has ever been done can simply be wiped away like it never happened. Gotta agree with ya John, fucking idiots."

"I tell ya," John continued as though Jackson hadn't said a word, "It ain't gonna happen. We worked our asses off to control this country and built it to be just what we want it to be. Just the way we want it to be. I'm a good christian man, and good christian men built this country, made it what it is today. This country is home to good christian men and it's damn well gonna stay that way. We got government programs to help people in need, business, a chance for people to become anything they want to be if they work hard enough. No terrorist is gonna destroy that ever."

"I guess it does seem kind of stupid," Jackson duplicitously agreed, "Trying to erase someone's history. Think there could be any other reason?"

"Naaaa," John said, "For the life of me I couldn't tell you what it would be. Just doesn't make any sense. Granted, Detroit was a shit hole. Went there once and swore I'd never go back. But museums and history places? That's just weird."

"Weird," Jackson repeated. *Idiot*, he thought.

In thirty minutes, his shiny copper brown locks covered the floor and Jackson was light headed from the weight suddenly gone off the back of his neck. It was an unexpected side effect he was unprepared for. Looking in the mirror he barely recognized himself.

"Looking all socially acceptable now," John the barber quipped.

"Yeah," Jackson hissed, "That's me, Mr. Socially Acceptable."

Paying John the barber Jackson inquired as to the location of the nearest Goodwill Store and he left the barber shop following the directions he was given. At the Goodwill Store he found a short sleeved, lightweight, plaid, button down shirt; khakis; and a well worn pair of topsiders. Paying cash for his items, he left the Goodwill Store and returned to the YMCA he noted earlier.

The YMCA provides shelter to many homeless men and a place to shower. This was all Jackson needed as he did not expect to be in town more than a week or two. After insuring a bed was available he showered and changed into his Goodwill clothes. Using his fingers he smoothed his hair down so it hung around his face, then he returned to his car and drove over to the Duke campus.

Jackson had learned Sherry Gardner could usually be found in one or two of the campus parks when not in class. Searching the first and not finding her he drove to the second and she was there. She was seated on the grass beneath an old box elder tree, deep in her anthropology texts, paying little to no attention to her surroundings.

Sherry was working hard toward earning her Ph.D. in social anthropology. Her goal was to eventually study indigenous societies and their cultural impact on today's societies. She wanted to learn how they came to be and where they were today. She was trying to understand the impact historical events had on those societies and how those societies adapted to fit in.

Jackson watched her for a brief span of time and noted how, although not attractive, she wasn't exactly unattractive either. Short and stubby was the best way to describe her. Obviously Sherry didn't give much time or thought to her appearance. It was apparent she needed a haircut and she was somewhat overweight. It was also apparent she wasn't wearing any make up.

Jackson could see from his vantage point that her clothes were of a good quality, but she didn't seem comfortable in them, as if they belonged to someone else and she was borrowing them. Sherry revealed all the traits of a social outcast, alone and submissive, she never met the eyes of those who walked past and glanced at her.

Jackson quickly unbuttoned his shirt and re-buttoned it incorrectly. Head down and appearing to be another bedraggled student he made his way over to her. With his hands in his pockets, as if lost in thought, Jackson behaved as though he hadn't seen her sitting there. As if, had she not been there, he would walk head first into the tree. Sherry squealed when he almost stepped on her and Jackson feigned being startled.

"I'm sorry," Jackson said.

"No," Sherry replied, "It's my fault. I was in the way. I'm sorry, I didn't mean to, I was just sitting, and I didn't see you and…"

"No, no, no," Jackson said, "It's my fault. I wasn't paying attention to where I was going. I'm so stupid. I never look where I'm going. Jeesh, I could have hurt you. I almost stepped right on you. Dumb, dumb, dumb. What is wrong with me?"

Sherry cast her eyes to the ground while Jackson appeared to shake momentarily. He offered his hand weakly in greeting and Sherry timidly accepted it as introductions were made.

"Jackson Themal," he began.

"I'm Sherry Gardner," she responded.

Introductions complete he began making small talk. "Are you from Raleigh?" Jackson asked, "How long have you been attending Duke? What field of study are you in?"

Sherry had always been a loner and was not accustomed to anyone showing the slightest interest in her. She was hesitant to respond. "Yes, I'm from Raleigh," she replied as she timidly pushed the grass with her toes.

Jackson slowly worked and encouraged her to open up more and more. He never looked too deeply or too long at her. He cast furtive glances as though he, too, was a social reject. Slowly he began to build her confidence and in a relatively short time she was chatting away over the most irrelevant of topics. He patiently sat and listened, behaving as though he was paying rapt attention.

Their conversation soon turned to Mt. Vernon and the Lincoln House. "Can you imagine?" she queried.

"Not at all," he insisted.

"I listen to the experts and all their opinions," Sherry continued, "but something seems to be missing. There is more to this than anyone is saying – the impact those men had on society, the effects of their actions, how they guided this country to where it is."

"You think?" Jackson encouraged.

"Absolutely," she confirmed, "This country stands today because of those men. Everything this country is, including our commerce and government. Our entire way of life – they started it all. Imagine what the Native Americans must think. They must be partying on the reservations."

"Why do you say that?" Jackson inquired cautiously.

"Because silly, those guys weren't anything like the history books wrote them to be. A lot of Indian people died because of them. They destroyed entire societies and tribes in their days. Whole groups of people are gone because of their actions. Kind of makes me nervous," Sherry confided.

"Why would you be nervous?" he asked.

"You must be new here," she said, laughing, "I'm the great, great, whatever granddaughter of President Richard Whitman. He more than anyone else caused the most damage in the construction of this country and my family is still here. So is his home. I'm scared we are next on the terrorist's list."

"Wow," Jackson exclaimed, "I had no idea. That's amazing. How cool to be a descendant of his. You must be really proud. You don't have to worry though. I'll protect you."

Sherry blushed and looked down, playing with the grass again, "Would you, Jackson? Would you protect me from the big, bad man?"

"Absolutely, Sherry," he responded convincingly, "Absolutely."

Time passed and the afternoon waned. Sherry noticed the time and quickly leapt to her feet. "Damn!" she exclaimed, "Did time get past me! I have a class I need to get to." Glancing at her expensive watch Sherry realized she missed the class. She had never missed a class in her life! Somehow a few hours had passed totally unnoticed. This was the first time a boy, any boy, had paid any attention to her and Sherry was feeling a bit giddy.

Jackson, in a hesitant voice, stopped her before she could walk away, "Um, can I ask you something?" he said in a mouse-like whisper.

Sherry almost had to lean into Jackson to hear him, "Of course," she replied.

"I'm new here," Jackson said, "and I really don't know the area very well. That, and I don't really get along with many of the other students here on campus. I was wondering if maybe...," he let the question trail off.

"Maybe what?" Sherry asked hopefully.

Shyly, as if the very idea caused him pain, Jackson said, "Well, um, maybe, if you would like to, if you might be interested, but only if you want to...,"

"What are you trying to say Jackson?" she encouraged.

"If maybe you would like to see each other again? Coffee, a sandwich in the cafeteria, only if you want to, not that you would want to, but maybe if you did then we could," he stammered.

Sherry felt her heart skip a beat. A date! This cute boy was asking her on a date! Sherry had never been on a date before. Her father would never permit it. By the time she reached college she was much too timid.

She often dreamed of going on a date with a cute boy. Maybe to a movie, maybe a quiet drink in a smoky bar. Just like the romance novels she poured over. "Yes!" exploded from Sherry so quickly she was afraid she had spoken too soon.

Jackson seemed to lighten almost as if he suddenly weighed a few pounds less. Adjusting his posture, he stood a little straighter. To Sherry he glowed.

Having studied at Duke a few years now and well accustomed to dining out alone she knew the perfect place they could go. They agreed on a time for him to pick her up the next evening and parted company. Sherry practically floated to her dorm.

The evening was restless for Jackson as well as Sherry, albeit for quite different reasons. Jackson was mentally sculpting while Sherry was anticipating her first date. At 24 she was still a virgin and in her mind fantasies were playing over and over. They became one thing then faded to become something more beautiful than the last.

Sherry was the ugly duckling who never became a swan. She always had the potential to be a swan, but any initiative or interest to facilitate the changes required to do so had long since faded. Sherry spent the night tossing and turning on her lumpy, uncomfortable dormitory mattress. She rose in the morning to attend class for the day and was unable to focus on the simplest of tasks.

When the long, tortuous day of study finally ended she returned to her dorm room and prepared herself for a night she had dreamt of for so long. As ready as she believed she could be, she cast a surreptitious glance out her one window. She spied Jackson waiting on the walk, pacing wide loops that she believed was because he was anticipating the evening as much as she was. Practically racing down the stairs to throw open the dormitory door she stopped at the door to check herself, to try to achieve some semblance of calm and assured; inside her the storm raged. She opened the door and met his gaze then hesitantly walked to him as calmly as her heart would allow.

"Hi!" Sherry whispered, her voice almost cracking.

Jackson cast a quick glance to her, as if embarrassed and unsure of himself. "Hello," he replied and allowed his voice to stumble as he said, "Where would you like to go?

My car is over there," he pointed hesitantly.

Sherry giggled and said, "Your car isn't necessary. I know the perfect place to go. Follow me."

They walk to a small bistro off campus that she visited often. It was a place that had become a favorite haunt of hers where she often sat alone and in her mind lived out the fantasies of her romance novels, all about how she would meet a cute boy and they would come to this very bistro. They would make small talk and fall in love with each other immediately and live happily ever after. It's happening! she thought. Exactly as she pictured so many times.

The evening moved on slowly, ecstasy for Sherry and torment for Jackson. The conversation twisted and turned with Jackson divulging very little and Sherry flowing like a broken dam. She had already convinced herself this was the boy she had dreamed of. Her mind was conjuring introductions as Sherry Themal in less than twenty four hours.

As her story unfolded she quickly made him privy to all her secrets. Almost impatiently she told him her life story. "Well, my mom died when I was born," Sherry began, "and my dad never let me forget it. As far as he is concerned it was all my fault. Every day growing up he reminded I'm only alive because she gave her life for me."

"That's really sad," Jackson said.

"Yeah," she agreed, "my dad is like that. He's really controlling and it seems like he is mad all the time. It's really hard to talk with him. He really is short tempered. Always snapping and snarling at me."

"That must have been rough," Jackson said.

"It is what it is," she responded, "Hey! I'm telling you all my secrets!"

"Oh Sherry," Jackson encouraged, "You can tell me anything."

"I really feel like I can, Jackson. I'm so comfortable around you. You make me feel good. Did I tell you my Dad is named after President Whitman? He really is. How neat is that?"

"Really neat," Jackson agreed, "Yep, that's really neat alright."

"I tell you, Jackson, I was so happy to finally get out of my Dad's house. It is really exciting to be in college. Plus, he would never permit me to be here with you. He never let me date."

"Then I'm your first date?" Jackson asked, "Your first date, ever? Wow, that's pretty neat, too. I feel so special."

Blushing and bowing her head Sherry replied, "You are special Jackson. Special to me."

Several mind numbing hours later the evening ended. As Jackson attempted to pay the bill Sherry said, "No, Jackson, let me get it. My Dad keeps me on a very strict allowance but I never spend any money anyway. What would I spend it on? Dad is like this super frugal man. Doesn't want to waste the family fortune and all that. Like that's even possible. I think I can handle a couple of cups of coffee." He agreed and after she paid he escorted her back to her dorm.

Hugging her for a brief moment he said good night and turned to leave. Sherry was taken aback as fears of rejection began to replace fantasies. He hadn't even tried to kiss her! At the end of the walk he turned and sheepishly said, "Can I see you again, Sherry?"

Once more her heart soared. He was only shy! He wasn't rejecting her. He was as nervous as she was. She believed that Jackson was trying his best to be a gentleman. More and more he portrayed every attribute she imagined her dream boy would have.

"Of course, Jackson, I would love to," she said.

Rushing to stand beside him she hastily scribbled her phone number on his palm.

"Call me tomorrow?" she asked expectantly.

"Of course I will," he said. Head down again he walked away and Sherry didn't push. Watching him climb into his car and drive off she tried desperately to smother the unrequited embers of lust burning in her. She was so sure Jackson was moving slowly and trying not to frighten her off, which, of course, was exactly what he was doing. Not, however, for the reasons she thought.

300°
CHAPTER THIRTY

The next week passed in much the same manner. Jackson saw Sherry every other day, an occasional peck on the cheek, a hug, then he left. Those impersonal visits left Sherry diving and soaring like a kite on emotional winds, so high one moment only to come so close to crashing into the earth the next. Each intense moment with Jackson fueled her unrequited passion and the moments away from him were spent with her desperate need for him to return. She wanted so much for him to touch her, to hold her. She needed with all she was to be with him, feeling such excruciating longing, but she also feared if she pushed too hard he might slip away.

The days Jackson didn't see Sherry he returned to visit Jenny Lynne, the three hour trip to Norfolk providing him ample opportunity to keep up with the latest developments. The news reports about Detroit, Springfield and Mt. Vernon were beginning to taper off. With no new leads the FBI was not sure which direction to go.

Why would someone burn a city and then burn historical places? If this was terrorists why wouldn't they continue attempting to burn cities? Why go after Detroit in the first place? If historical sites were the focus why not stick with historical sites? They connected the fires physically through chemical analysis of the flare residue but had yet to connect them beyond that. The FBI knew the same person or persons had burned all three, but why? None of this was making any sense to the authorities.

Driving up to Jenny Lynne's apartment Jackson parked and stepped out of his car. He noticed she was standing at the door and as usual was happy to see him. Diligently she continued to work on the unconfirmed rumor of the child between Richard Whitman and a servant. They spent the nights together working on the leads and chasing false information. After hours of tedious searching they retired to her bed and he left in the morning. Jenny Lynne had no idea where Jackson disappeared to but she wasn't complaining. It was nice to have his company and she was satisfied, for now, content not to ask for more.

Shocked when she saw him after their first night together Jenny Lynne gasped, "Jackson, your hair!"

He ran his fingers through his now short hair and ruffled it, "Yeah," he said, "I felt like I needed a change. What do you think?"

Laughing, but obviously pleased with his new look, nodding to show she thought cutting it was a good idea, Jenny Lynne said, "I like it, but you look so young now. People are going to think I'm dating my son or something! Me, a cougar? How ridiculous!" Jackson laughed with her at the absurdity of the thought.

In the morning he returned to Raleigh. At Duke, Sherry was unable to concentrate. She attended classes and listened to lectures but didn't seem to hear a word and studying was impossible. She found herself drawing little hearts with Jackson's initials and doodling his name. Unable to take the pressure any more when Jackson called late into the seventh day she invited him to her family home immediately outside of Raleigh and Jackson agreed hesitantly. He didn't want to appear over eager.

The Gardner family never left Raleigh and currently resided in the former estate of President Richard Whitman, passed down through the family. The land was originally part of the Cherokee Nation, a community of businesses and homes. Once a thriving, prosperous town, Richard Whitman burned it to the ground. Immediately upon acquiring the land he built his estate.

Sherry needed for her father to meet Jackson. She concluded that if Jackson could see how much she had to offer he would come to her bed. They agreed to meet in the early afternoon. Arriving, Jackson saw her waiting for him. He walked up to give her a quick hug. At her feet was a package.

Accepting his hug and practically vibrating with anticipation Sherry said, "I have a present for you, Jackson."

"Really?" he said, as he cast a curious gaze at the package at her feet. "A present for me? Wow, that's really nice of you, Sherry."

"I hope it doesn't make you mad but my father is a very picky man. He seems to notice every little detail of something," she said, picking up the package and almost throwing it at him, anxious that he see what's inside.

Sherry had bought him a new set of clothes that included an expensive pair of black casual pants; a soft, pale, yellow, polo shirt; and a pair of black loafers with dark socks. It was a monumental effort but he somehow managed to keep the fury out of his voice when he said, "This is really nice of you, Sherry," then asked, "How did you know my sizes?"

Sherry, hands on her hips haughtily, looked as though the question was totally absurd to her, "I don't. I guessed. I hope they fit. Do you like them?"

"They are really nice," he replied as he looked down at the pavement. Through clenched teeth he said, "Let me slip into the dorm stairwell and change." In her excitement Sherry didn't notice the storm building in him. In her desperation she didn't notice much of anything.

Jackson used the opportunity to change to calm himself and bury his anger. This game wasn't over yet and he needed to be in complete control of all his emotions. Moments later he returned, resplendent in his new clothes and asked, "What do you think?"

"Wonderful!" Sherry exclaimed, "You look amazing."

Jackson smiled, calm now, and Sherry extended her hand to be held as together they walked over to the student parking area. Sherry drove a late model SUV, nothing fancy and American made. The car was purchased by her father and, as always, was just enough. Climbing in, with Sherry driving, they travel to meet Richard Gardner.

Consciously, Sherry believed she was doing this to impress upon Jackson all he could have if he would only take her. She was well aware her father always wanted a son, as this was something else Richard Gardner never failed to remind her of. Sherry would bring him a son. She would bring him Jackson. She yearned to lead him to the buffet table, to sit him down and say "feast."

Unconsciously, she was also vying for her father's affection, so desperate was she to be Daddy's girl. Her offering of Jackson was to appease her father. After her father accepted him, she just knew the three of them could move into the future as one happy family. Eventually Jackson would give her children, sons, of course – more offerings on the altar to her father/god Richard Gardner.

Twenty minutes outside of Raleigh Sherry found the access road to the estate. At the bottom of the road was a dark government sedan and inside were two FBI agents maintaining surveillance. Noticing her turn signal, the driver opened the door. Before they are out of their vehicle Sherry pulls up to them, rolls down her window and warmly called, "Hi guys!"

They recognized Richard Gardner's daughter and they paid no attention to Jackson in the passenger seat, didn't even glance at him. Slamming the car door again, they allowed her to pass. It had been over a week since Mt. Vernon and they were bored. They had spent twelve hours a day in a hot car in the middle of the countryside in Raleigh, North Carolina, with nothing to do but watch the grass grow, and they had become seriously lax in their security. Initially they were instructed to a post immediately adjacent to the house.

Gardner tolerated that for a couple of days then moved them to the end of the access road almost half a mile away.

Sherry maneuvered up the long and winding access road to the main house. She parked in what was originally the space where the horses were tied to shit and piss on the ground as a group of mixed breed dogs that roamed the estate rushed to greet her vehicle. On a hot August afternoon the scent of horse shit occasionally still wafted through the air though no horses remained on the estate. The scent left visitors to wonder where it came from.

The family estate is a vast tract of land that composed several hundred acres. Many a slave had toiled these fields; sunup to sundown, sowing, planting and harvesting the crops of tobacco, cotton and hemp, their labors adding to the family's wealth year by year.

The original house and outbuildings remained and were cared for by the local historical society. The Gardner's maintain all property and occupancy rights tax free due to a legal loop hole put into place by Sherry's grandfather. Occasionally the historical society brought curiosity seekers or admirers of Whitman who believed the history written about the man and who were staunch supporters of the former President. The historical society also meticulously maintained the rooms inside the mansion. Each was decorated precisely to show how Whitman lived, in the decor of the time.

Stepping from the vehicle Sherry used her foot to push aside the mingling dogs. "Pests," she said.

"Oh, they just want a little attention," Jackson said, as he stopped for a few minutes with them.

As Sherry and Jackson ascended the wide veranda the door was thrown open vigorously by her father, Richard Gardner; a tall, thin, pugnacious man with thin, almost balding hair. He was well groomed in an expensive suit and had sharp, hawkish features. He wanted to meet this boy his daughter was bringing to his home.

Probably pregnant, Gardener thinks, and now they have come to tell me about it.

Carefully walking towards her father, Sherry introduced Jackson. Not shaking his hand, as if to insinuate, if I must, Gardner turned and retreated into his home. They followed him and stopped in the foyer where he instructed Sherry to bring tea from the kitchen. Motioning expectantly Gardner moved towards his study with Jackson in tow. As he seated himself behind his broad, expansive desk he gestured to a leather covered, antique, straight back chair in front of him. Jackson seated himself and gazed at this domineering man.

"So you are my daughter's boyfriend?" Gardner initiated while staring at Jackson as though someone had taken a crap on the chair in front of him.

"Yes sir. I expect I am," Jackson responded, not taking the bait and no longer feigning the air of inferiority he maintained around Sherry.

Gardner stared down his hooked nose as if to say Jackson was not worthy to be in this home and immediately began verbally assaulting Jackson. "Well, what are your intentions then? Is this a casual fling for you? Is my daughter just another conquest? Maybe you think this is your ticket to wealth and fame? Worse, she is probably pregnant, isn't she? Is that why you two have come here today? To tell me she is pregnant, it happened accidentally and now you two just have to get married. Probably your plan all along, wasn't it?"

"No, sir," Jackson replied as the rant trailed off. Obviously, Richard Gardner was confidant he knew everything there was to know about what Jackson was planning. Gardner not only inherited his ancestor's name, he also inherited his bigotry and arrogance.

Another thing he inherited was Whitman's fervent belief in Manifest Destiny. While Whitman applied the concept continentally, Gardner applied it globally, with the same drive and initiative from South America to Africa to the Middle East. Anywhere an indigenous society existed that wasn't using their natural resources fully, Gardner insured he was involved. If the indigenous people couldn't see the vast wealth available, he certainly did, and obviously someone needed to step in. In Gardner's mind it was irrelevant that the original people of a country may have been there for generations, that didn't infer they belonged there.

Using the wealth left to him Gardner expanded the family fortune and was making money from both sides of the table. With the advent of privatized military resources his commercial interests maintained a fully supplied arsenal and the men who knew how to use it. Gardner was the silent partner in the largest privatized military corporation in the world, as well as the philanthropic public figure whose corporations assisted in rebuilding war torn countries.

Privately Gardner's corporate army entered a country and eliminated any opposition. With the full support of the government and at the taxpayer's expense, small third world countries were invaded and the population was annihilated. This allowed him access to whatever resources may exist there. Once the indigenous peoples of those countries were eradicated or removed his public companies returned to the devastation to rebuild.

Gardner also owned the lumber mills and concrete plants as well as employed the individuals rebuilding the countries that his private army had leveled. To finalize the process christianity was used to enforce conformity. Gardner was a christian by title only and occasionally attended a Sunday service for his public image. He used the christian concepts of "do unto others" and "thou shalt not" as tools to implement and maintain his appearance.

Jackson cautiously allowed this man to reveal himself. He understood the wealthy do not maintain their wealth by being stupid and he knew he was treading dangerous waters. After assuming his normal authoritarian presence Gardner said, "This home you see here, these lands, they have been in my family for many years, handed down generation to generation. A lot of blood has been spilled by my ancestors to acquire and maintain these lands, Whitman blood."

"I'm certain you have been following what has been happening these last few weeks, some ungrateful ass burning down historical sites. Presidential homes and the like. Not here boy, not here. There have been a lot of people who have tried over the centuries to take this land from us. We haven't lost if yet and we certainly aren't about to do so now. Who are you boy? Where do you come from?"

Jackson wasn't caught off guard and he knew exactly how to answer this question. He had been studying this man for weeks, studying his corporate as well as personal portfolios. He was fully aware Gardner was an ardent supporter of white, Anglo Saxon superiority. Jackson also knew that Gardner was just as vehement in his acquisition of wealth. Much like his famous predecessor, enough was never enough and Jackson's story was well rehearsed.

310°
CHAPTER THIRTY ONE

"My family is from out west, sir," Jackson began, "For over two hundred years we have maintained a vast ranching empire in Oklahoma that encompasses well over five thousand acres with most of our interests in cattle operations. We supply the majority of the beef to this nation's supermarkets and are working with other operations like ourselves from the Dakotas throughout Texas. In this way my father managed to acquired a great deal of wealth.

"From those holdings our investors work with some of the Indian Tribal Councils in their respective geographic regions. My father and his investors have worked diligently to assure the general public that the natural resources of this country are gone, but, as I am sure are well aware sir, they aren't. There are vast reserves of plutonium, coal, and gold beneath many of the reservations and the current residents, of course, aren't using it.

"We work behind the scenes, unknown to the public, and are actively involved in the tribal elections. Once we have key members in place we encourage the Councils from those various regions to secure large financial liens on what is left of their lands through the banks we own. We then ensure they default on those loans. It's a slow process but we have greatly reduced their land holdings over the last century.

"We allow the key members to keep the monies for themselves. It's a small amount, really, and the price of doing business. Makes them feel like they are getting something and keeps them placid. Once the loans are defaulted we repossess the land and assume immediate ownership. We then mine what is available and after those resources are exhausted we commercially develop the land. We also employ the workforce we use to rebuild the regions into viable commercial locations.

"I'm sure a man as actively involved in global development as you are, sir, is well aware of the natural gas deposits currently being exploited and the vast wealth they have the potential to provide. We are also heavily invested in several of those mining operations. We use a proprietary blend of chemical compounds, inject them into the ground and drain the deposits. With a new technology we have developed, its irrelevant if someone refuses to allow us to drill directly on their property. We can easily access the reserves from adjacent properties.

"We have a reservation in Wyoming right now that is attempting to fight us, although their fight is pointless We have complete access to those lands either from above or below. Publicly we appear to be supporting their grass roots movements through people we have placed within them. Privately we have our own people in their organizations and control what information is given to the media. We also control how it is distributed."

All the while Gardner has been listening intently to Jackson and he liked what he was hearing. He, too, was invested heavily in the drilling operations of the eastern seaboard, primarily the Chesapeake Bay Watershed. Gardner was one of a group of private investors currently lobbying Congress to construct the pipeline from Canada to the Gulf of Mexico, something Jackson was also fully aware of.

Gardner sensed a perfect opportunity in the making. He thought, if this young man has the contacts he says he does this could work out perfectly. One of the investment group's largest obstacles had been the Indian Tribes. The so called traditionalists who were making his and his investor's lives an absolute hell. Construction was halted at this moment because of them. The traditionalists were insisting the Government had no right to access those lands. Only last week a convoy of trucks carrying materials was delayed by them for several hours while they bitched and moaned about it being their land.

Maybe my daughter has finally done something worth a damn in her life bringing this young man here, he thinks, with his father's contacts and my investors working together we can quietly put an end to all these protests and finally get the damn pipeline built.

As Gardner played over the scenario in his head, Jackson stood up. He walked over to a photo on Gardner's credenza and paid close attention to the photo's details. He noted the authoritative posture Gardner assumed in the photo as well as the cowered and cringing posture of his wife. Jackson asked, "Is this your wife, sir?"

"Yes, that was my wife," Gardner answered as he distractedly rose from his desk to meet Jackson at the credenza, picking up the photo and gazing disdainfully at his dead wife.

Richard Gardner had married Cecilia Townsend, a local debutante, and all of the local wealthy families agreed it was a perfect union – Richard, an up and coming business man, and Cecilia, the perfect southern belle.

Although he never abused her physically, he was never a good husband. No affection and very little interest was ever shown to her. She was expected to play a role, to present herself correctly at functions and gatherings and was expected to be seen as totally supportive of her husband's achievements.

Gardner appeared to have been remembering this and pinching his face like he just bit a lemon he said, "She died giving birth to our daughter. Cecelia was her name. A weak woman made weaker by the pregnancy. I'm not sure why I married her. I assume it was expected of me at the time. Cecilia came from a wealthy local family and back then we were expected to marry within our social classes.

"Damn woman went and had the audacity to give me a daughter and then die doing it," he continued, "What the hell am I supposed to do with a daughter?" Sherry chose that moment to walk in, bringing with her the tea her father requested earlier. She overheard what her father said and obviously she had heard it before. Meekly she set down the serving tray, pulling at her hair and looking at the floor.

"Here's your tea Daddy, Jackson. Everything okay in here?" she asked.

With obvious disgust on his face Gardner peered at her as if she were a cockroach that had somehow found its way into these venerated chambers. "Everything is fine. Don't you have something you can do?" Gardner demanded of her. "Go clean something, play with the damn dogs, I don't care. Leave us be, we're talking. You don't belong in here and you know it." Sherry immediately turned to leave and walked out of the study with her head down and her feet shuffling as Jackson watched intently. This was a scene that had obviously played out many times before and was well rehearsed. He paid close attention to her behavior and to Gardner's mannerisms.

"Damn fool girl," Gardner said, "about useless."

Like his father and his father's father before him, Gardner sees women as nothing more than property. An accoutrement to be displayed when necessary like a tie or cuff links, then tucked away. He believed the place for a woman was in the home, caring for the home and ensuring her husband had all his needs met. She was to be seen but not necessarily heard. Jackson intuitively sensed Gardner had taken the bait of his invented financial scenario and verbally completed setting the hook.

Sure that Sherry was well out of hearing he cleared his throat slightly and said, "To answer your earlier question sir, my intention is to marry your daughter. Not for your wealth obviously. My family is already quite wealthy. I believe Sherry will make a fine addition to my future plans and she will be quite capable of portraying herself correctly in situations she is allowed to attend."

"Well, good luck with that," Gardner responded but it was all he needed to hear. He was convinced this young man had the right attitude and was sure he would be able to work with him. Setting the photo back in its place, he returned to his seat behind his desk as Jackson continued to peruse the study, feigning an interest in the masculine paraphernalia. Gardner was watching him every moment.

Deer antlers were prominently displayed on the walls and a mounted cougar was in the corner. In another corner was a huge bear, fully preserved and displayed in an angry attack posture. Next to the bear was a rack of guns. "Shot them all myself," he said when Jackson noticed the stuffed and mounted creatures, "That damned bear almost ate me but I got him at the last moment."

Before Gardner could launch into his bear story, which he had obviously told many times before, Jackson moved past it and stopped to stand before the gun case. Where he had intended to be all along. "Nice gun collection, sir," he says, "My father would be very impressed. We do a lot of hunting, too."

Gardner rose again and moved to join Jackson in front of the gun display. Speaking as he walked he said, "Used everyone of them myself at one time or another. Here, let me show you something."

Next to the case of rifles, set on its own table, was a display case with two matching Army Colt revolvers from the early 1700s. When Gardner reached where Jackson was standing he leaned down and picked up the darkly stained wood and glass display case. He held the case as though its contents were priceless and returned to his desk. Setting it down in front of him reverently he invited Jackson to return to his original chair.

As Jackson sat down Gardner launched into an elated dissertation over his ancestral hero and the weapons. "These guns belonged to the great man himself, President Richard Whitman. He even wore them in the White House, wore them everywhere he went. Many a red devil died at the business end of these guns."

Jackson flinched uncomfortably for a second, the flinch unnoticed by Gardner as he gazed longingly at the revolvers, petting the case as though it was alive. "These guns even protected this very land. At one time a band of local Indians even tried to storm this plantation, but President Whitman stood out on that very veranda and gunned them all down." A repulsive smile crossed Gardner's face as the pride at what his ancestor had done so enthusiastically spewed from his lips. It was all Jackson could do not to vomit. Composing himself Jackson portrayed a look of sheer amazement.

"They look heavy, sir," Jackson said.

"They are," Gardner assures him. "Very heavy. President Whitman must have been a strong man to wield these weapons." He opened the display case and affectionately extracted one of the Army Colts, holding the weapon as though it were the son his inconsiderate wife never gave him. The son he believed he deserved. Doing what he normally wouldn't, Gardner invited Jackson to stand and unconsciously handed the weapon to him, maybe thinking as if by touch the weapon would impart on to Jackson its awe and power.

Jackson slowly accepted the weapon and allowed its heft to settle into his hand. Looking closely at the revolver, insuring it was loaded. "They still work?" Jackson asks.

Haughtily, Gardner laughed and smirked. "Of course! These revolvers have been taken care of by everyone they have been passed down to. Every month I clean them and make sure they are in perfect working order. They are exactly like they just came out of the factory, after I clean them I reload them. What good is a gun that isn't loaded? Like having a car without an engine." Continuing to laugh arrogantly Gardner gestured at the fully loaded weapon Jackson was holding and said, "Every once in awhile I shoot them. Damn things go off like cannons. Scared the shit out of that security detail down the road. They pissed me off being outside like that, running into the house at every sound. These guns give me all the protection I will ever need."

Standing across the desk from Gardner Jackson looked up from the Army Colt and met Gardner's eyes. Raising his eyebrows slightly, with dripping contempt he said, "Do they now?"

Slowly he raised the old revolver, pointed it directly at Richard Gardner's forehead, eases back the hammer and pulled the trigger. Spraying Richard Gardner's brains all over the wall.

Hearing the thundering boom of the old revolver Sherry ran into the room. Jackson turned, stepped toward her and without hesitation knocked her unconscious. At the end of the long, winding drive the two federal agents hear the boom of the old revolver but they didn't move. "Damn fool is playing with those guns again," one said to the other. "Probably," the other agreed. Readjusting themselves they went back to watching the grass grow.

Jackson raced to the front of the house and waited to see if the agents would come tearing up the road. Tense moments passed but they didn't show. Satisfied they wouldn't he returned to the study and half carried, half dragged Sherry outside and deposited her in the rear of her SUV. Returning to the house he made his way into the kitchen where he quickly found a carving knife, some paper, duct tape and matches. Exiting the house again he climbed into the driver's seat, fired the engine up and drove off across the fields to a heavily wooded section beyond the outbuildings.

In the distance stood an ancient oak tree, solitary and forlorn. Jackson could almost see the men and women who had been hung from that tree. He drove straight for it and upon arriving he hurriedly exited the vehicle and rid himself of the clothes Sherry bought for him, ripping them off as if they were attacking him.

Naked, while what she had spent so many days craving and fantasizing about limply slapped against the inside of his thigh, he retrieved Sherry and dragged her to the tree. Lifting and heaving, grunting and groaning he positioned her in an erect posture and used the duct tape to secure her to the trunk. Leaving most of her body exposed he wrapped the tape around her forehead, waist and ankles; firmly fastening her hands backwards around the tree.

When they had driven up to the estate earlier in the day and parked, the dogs, around ten or so that roamed the old plantation, had come over to greet them. Jackson had made sure to affectionately pet each one, affection they never received from Richard Gardner or anyone else. Sherry, never a dog person, ignored them. She waited while he petted them, annoyed he was getting their scent all over the new clothes she had bought him. When he drove into the woods the dogs had followed. Sitting in a semi circle they watched as he secured Sherry to the old hanging tree.

Forcefully he slapped her in the face and brought her back to consciousness. Coming to, dazed and confused, Sherry had no idea where she was or what was happening. Slowly she began to understand that she was taped to the tree and could not move. Terrified, she comprehended Jackson standing before her, naked. Her eyes were wide with fear but unable to speak because he had covered her mouth with duct tape.

Sherry watched as Jackson, now sure she is fully awake, turned and began to gather small sticks and twigs. Fifteen yards or so from her he began to build a small fire, mounding the kindling together over the paper he had brought from the house. Slowly the flame began to appear and grow larger as the paper was consumed and the twigs began to burn. Jackson kept the flames low so as not to draw the attention of the half asleep federal agents parked at the end of the road. Returning to Sherry's SUV he retrieved the carving knife, the dogs watching his every step.

Gardner hadn't taken very good care of the dogs. He permitted them to run his property to keep the rodents at bay but didn't take much time to feed them. Occasionally he tossed them scraps but mostly they fended for themselves and the dogs were hungry. Very, very hungry.

Returning to Sherry's side Jackson began carving strips of flesh off of her, careful not to cut anything vital. Careful not to sever an artery. He cut in exactly the same way his ancestors had done to those who had pillaged their villages, raped their women and murdered their children. In the same manner he pierced those strips of flesh with a green stick and slowly roasted them over the fire. The smell of cooking meat agitated the dog's ravenous hunger and they began to salivate carnivorously.

When the flesh was barely singed but still bloody Jackson waited a moment and allowed the strips of flesh to cool slightly. When the meat that is Sherry had cooled enough he casually threw the pieces to the dogs and they snapped them up greedily. Methodically Jackson carved arms and legs, wherever he could find loose flesh. He roasted. He fed. Then repeated.

Sherry witnessed every moment, every second. Tied to the tree she watched as she was carved and cooked by Jackson. Watched as her flesh was cooled and devoured by the starving dogs. For hours, until her mind snapped.

When nothing remained of her sanity Jackson cut her throat. He soaked one of the owl feathers he had tucked into his sock before meeting her earlier in the day in her blood and tied it to a low hanging branch. Walking to the SUV and he redressed himself in the Goodwill clothes he had stored in her car then returned to the house.

In the study at the back of the house where Jackson and Gardner had been talking he carefully piled together what he could find in furniture and belongings and on top of the pile he placed the clothes Sherry bought him. Rummaging through the kitchen he found a can of lighter fluid and returned to the study where he started a small fire.

Jackson walked out of the house and climbed back into Sherry's SUV and casually drove down the long access road, passing the agents. One glanced up, hearing the car coming, and recognizing it as the daughter's car, he returned to his half doze. Jackson drove by unnoticed.

By the time he reached Raleigh the small fire was an inferno. The old wooden structure fed the rapacious flames and the agents at the end of the road were too late in responding. By the time they noticed the house was already engulfed. Because they barely noticed Jackson with Sherry earlier they would have a hard time describing him.

The federal agents released an all points alert for Sherry's SUV, but by the time it was released over the air the vehicle was at student parking, carefully wiped down, and Jackson was back in his own car, heading for Norfolk.

320°
CHAPTER THIRTY TWO

The FBI was in an uproar and the public was outraged. How could this be happening? What the hell was going on? Burning down historical sites was one thing, burning down an entire city something else, but murder? While two federal agents sat not more than a half a mile way?

Based on their agents' reports the FBI was now aware one man was responsible. They knew this wasn't a terrorist cell from overseas, that this was domestic. But how can one man wreak this much havoc? Cause this much devastation? Who was he? More to the point where was he?

Richard Gardner had many highly placed government friends and many perceived him as a pillar of the community with an entire wing of Duke University dedicated to him. Powerful people wanted answers and they wanted them now. They refused to simply accept his death or his daughter's brutal mutilation and murder.

Sherry had been an outcast. She had no friends and no close associates. Many were shocked to learn she was the descendant of former President Richard Whitman. They assumed when seeing her she was just another ordinary student on campus and they never suspected.

The FBI canvas of Raleigh produced no new leads and it seemed as though no one knew anything. No one remembered seeing her with anybody and this wasn't making any sense to those investigating. There was no connection they could see.

As the FBI spun in circles, Jackson arrived in Norfolk early the next morning and, as usual, Jenny Lynne was happy to see him. She was on her way to work and just leaving her apartment when he pulled up. "Can you believe what is happening?" she exclaimed as she rushed over to greet him.

"Not at all," Jackson replied, "and while we are researching Whitman. What a freaky coincidence. It's why I came back. To see you, to talk with you about this. What is going on, Jenny Lynne?"

"I have no idea," she answered, " and it is weird. I was thinking the exact same thing this morning in the shower. Here we are working on Whitman's ancestry and then Gardner and his daughter are murdered and their estate is burned to the ground. The FBI are clueless and they are saying it is one person. How can one person do something like this, Jackson?"

"I don't know Jenny Lynne," he replied soothingly, "I just don't know. Maybe it has something to do with their past? Should we keep going? Maybe find a clue we can share with the FBI? Help find out who is doing these horrible things?"

"That's a great idea Jackson!" she responded enthusiastically, "Here is the key to the front door. I have to go to work for a few hours but my research is on the desk.

You can pick up where I left off and when I get home we can work on it together. Who knows what we may find?"

"Okay, hun," Jackson agreed, kissing her gently, "Would you like me to stay with you while we work on this or would you prefer I find a room?"

"Find a room?" Jenny Lynne says, pinching her eyebrows, "Why would you do that Jackson? Of course you can stay with me."

Leaving after another long kiss Jackson stretched out on the couch, taking a nap. Returning a few hours later she called, "Jackson, I'm home," as she entered her apartment. He roused quickly to meet her in the living room. "Get any research done?" she asked.

"No," Jackson replied, "I started looking over things but decided it would probably be best to wait for you."

"Let me take a quick shower and we will get started," she said, "Unless you want to join me?"

"But of course," he agreed seductively, "You know how much I like to conserve water." Laughing together they made their way to the shower for an hour of wet, slow, passionate love making. They retired to the living room where Jenny Lynne updated him on what has been happening.

"Bob is being a dick again," she said, her face contorted in anger.

"What's going on?" Jackson inquired as he gently rubbed her shoulders.

"Mr. Fuck Ass has decided he and his slut are going to get married," she said, "Now they want me to sign the papers that relinquish my rights as the kid's mom so that whore can adopt my kids. I swear to God I wish it was legal to kill some people because those two need killing."

Jackson chuckled at her outrage, softly and encouraging. He continued to rub her shoulders and occasionally nuzzled her neck. Obviously exasperated, with her hands gesturing and making every point, she continued her rant, "Adding to all of this the only thing anyone can talk about is what's going on. Cities being burned along with historical places. Now people, famous people, are being murdered. What the fuck, Jackson? Isn't anyone safe anywhere?"

"It's okay, Jenny Lynne," Jackson consoled, "I'm here with you. You're safe now. Relax baby, it's all okay."

"I tell ya, Jackson, I am beat. All of this has worn me the hell out. I'm just not up to research tonight. Do you think we can continue it tomorrow?" Jenny Lynne asked.

"Absolutely hun, absolutely. Let's get some sleep," Jackson said. He stayed with Jenny Lynne for the next three days and the research into Richard Whitman began to pay off. They found documents that proved he had fathered a child with one of his servants. Although it was well known he was a prodigious slaveholder, going so far as to hold auctions at his estate, as well as a bigoted racist, this information had been buried deeply. But every lie finds a way to resurface and this lie had, too. Jenny Lynne's patient research revealed the name of the woman who gave birth and now all she had to do was follow that name to see if anyone was alive from that line.

Jackson left in the afternoon for the University of South Carolina in Columbia where Benjamin Jensen was enrolled. When Jenny Lynne returned home and noticed he was gone, yet again, she began to get annoyed. She had enough shit in her life and she certainly didn't need some man drifting in and out at his leisure. She enjoyed the sex but there should be more to it than sex. The only reason she hadn't shown him the door was the research. The work of unlocking the mystery had become an obsession for her and Jenny Lynne's appetite for more information continued to grow. She would keep going, keep looking, to see for herself where the trail led. At a minimum maybe she could call someone when it was all over and let them know their ancestry. As she and Jackson had discussed maybe even help out with the ongoing investigation.

Arriving in Columbia, South Carolina, Jackson again searched for a YMCA and a local Goodwill. Finding what he needed he stopped at a local convenience store, picked up a disposable cell phone and returned to the Y to get some sleep. This looked to be a long evening and he wanted to be well rested.

This excursion would rely on him dredging deep pain and putting it to work, because Benjamin Jensen is gay. Not that Jackson had an aversion to homosexuality, at least not anymore. At one time he found homosexual behavior revolting, basing his feelings on a complete lack of understanding. Jackson had seen many who suddenly found themselves homosexual at 50. Most were bored, their sexual perversions having become mundane, so they urgently sought something new and exciting. He listened to their public protestations and shook his head. He decided some time ago both sides of the argument were absurd.

On the one side of the argument, homosexuals, men and women who demanded the world at large see them and accept them based solely on their sexual proclivities. There are many in homosexual relationships across the world who simply lived their lives, enjoying themselves and being who they were. It was those who so ardently sought out attention that drove Jackson nuts.

Parades, protests and social gatherings appeared to be designed solely to wield homosexuality as a club to beat the general public into submission. Flagrantly they flaunted themselves and placed themselves above everyone else as though they were better than the rest of society based on who they choose to have sex with. What they seemed incapable of understanding was that what they were doing is simply the other side of the coin, that their demanding behavior is just as wrong as what is being done to them.

On the other side of argument, the right wing christian advocates who insist gay and lesbianism is the act of the Devil himself. They insinuate homosexuality is a disease and can somehow be cured. They are all divinely convinced that homosexual behavior is so perverted that God himself will punish the wicked severely, thereby reducing God to the status of a peeping Tom. God probably has better things to do than look in someone's window to see who they were having sex with.

Lying on his bed at the YMCA in Columbia, Jackson inadvertently recalled the special individuals who, upon meeting him, felt they simply must impart to him all they knew about homosexuals in native Societies. He can't count how many times someone had attempted to explain to him the role of gay people in native tradition. Usually it was some white guy with feathers from the "I'm too sexy bird" stuck in his hair on a roach clip. Many times Jackson had to walk away before dealing out severe physical punishment.

Some years ago Jackson had the opportunity to sit with a leader of a Winkte Society. The man was openly gay but not annoyingly gay and he provided a window into a world Jackson had not understood before, because he wasn't gay.

He said to Jackson, "Homosexuality is a medicine, a way to provide healing. Men behave as women, women behave as men, for very specific reasons. As with any traditional spiritual medicine it should never be flaunted or displayed. It definitely isn't supposed to be waved in the face of every individual on the planet as though it is the flag of a separate country all must pay homage to.

"The medicine should be used quietly for those who need it, to assist where it is needed. Maybe for men it is to learn how to be compassionate and gentle. Maybe for women it is to learn strength. Not to hide the medicine as though it is something that must be kept secret but not to attach a neon sign to it either."

Continuing on with his instructions the Winkte Society Leader shared a unique and quite different perspective on creation as Jackson sipped coffee and smoked. He said, "That which created the universe began with one thing. Think of a giant cookie. A cookie as big as the universe. Now, imagine that Creation breaks that cookie into two pieces. One piece contains everything male and the other piece contains everything female. Creation then crumbles each of those two pieces and brings to life everything male and everything female.

"In the process of breaking the original cookie pieces crumble off the center of the cookie that are both male and female at the same time, hence, homosexuals." As Jackson sits back stunned the Winkte Society Leader asked. "Now I want you to do something, Jackson. It's probably going to be hard for you, but try it. Try to imagine yourself as homosexual."

Jackson did as he was instructed and was instantly uncomfortable. Homosexuality was something he had never considered before. Something about sex with another man caused instant revulsion in him, but beyond the obvious physical connotations, he can't explain why.

Long moments into consideration he realized there was absolutely no way he could be homosexual except to hurt; to cause abuse, to create destruction or to inflict pain. The spiritual medicine he was in proximity of was beginning to manifest itself. Jackson started to understand why he found revulsion in homosexuality. Why the idea of homosexuality created in him the desire to hurt.

Subconsciously he was returning to being a little boy, back to when he had been used, abused and raped by those paid by the State to care for him. Now he saw how the thought of homosexuality returned him to the physical abuse he suffered at the hands of sexually twisted and perverted men and women.

"Thank you," Jackson said to the Society Leader, "You have really helped me to understand something I didn't before." Shaking the leader's hand, Jackson turned to leave. His entire life up to then he had been terrified of the dark and he didn't understand why. He decided it was time to face this demon.

The next morning he left the camp he was in, the gathering he was attending, to be alone. The gathering was in the desert in Arizona at the end of the summer he spent with the Kiowa after returning their grandfather. This would be his first night in the dark, alone.

A mile from camp he climbed over huge boulders to the edge of a sandstone cliff. Peering over the edge of the precipice he saw a ledge a few feet below him, approximately ten feet wide and thirty feet long. Jackson eased himself over the edge and on to the ledge.

As he settled himself into a comfortable position he suddenly heard the distinctive flap of wings. The shadow of a bird crossed over him, it banked and then hovered on the drafts directly in front of Jackson's face and stared at him. The largest, blackest raven he had ever seen was mere inches from his face. For long moments they held each other's gaze until, with a loud caw, it flapped its wings again and flew off. "This is going to be an interesting night," he said to the rocks around him.

The sun set and Jackson was by himself in the dark. He was seated on a ledge three hundred feet in the air with no way to climb out and no way to climb down – forced to sit and to face his fear. In the course of the evening he came to understand it wasn't the darkness itself that he was afraid of, his fear was of what lurks in the darkness.

As a young boy he was forced to live in the homes of sexual predators and deviants, men and women who, by day, appeared to be the kindest of souls; but when the lights went off they came out to play. In the dark no one could see them or see what they did. The medicine of the winkte had done its job well and a few hours before the sun rose he laid down to get some rest. It had been a long and exhausting night and as he sleeps, he traveled…

…and returns to Sundance. He is dancing in the North, pierced through his chest. He is wearing a black skirt without a shirt and his chest really, really hurts. A grimace of pain is etched across his face. Behind him an old Grandfather stands, and Jackson notices its Mary's Grandfather! He had seen pictures of the man at her home…

When the sun rises Jackson is never afraid of the dark again. He let the memories fade and focused on the task at hand.

330°
CHAPTER THIRTY THREE

Once he completed things here he would check with Jenny Lynne to see if she had discovered anything new. For now he needed sleep and as he did in Raleigh he searched for and found a local YMCA. When he woke he called her and he could hear the irritation in her voice but there was nothing he could do about it at the moment. Leaving the conversation with a promise to call in a few days he hung up the phone and went in search of Benjamin Jensen.

Benjamin Jensen attended South Carolina specifically. It was the only school he would attend, the only school he was interested in attending. Benjamin's grandparents were originally from South Carolina. They relocated to California where he was born but this wasn't why he chose this school or why he insisted on it. Fully aware he was the descendant of President Richard Whitman, he didn't care.

Known as Benji, his decision to attend South Carolina was based solely on the school's mascot, perverting the mascot's image to fit his needs. South Carolina's mascot is the Gamecocks and Benji considered himself a game cock, too. Obviously not what the University intended, but Benji didn't care. It suited his purposes.

Benji Jensen is a tall young boy with tussled blonde hair and a light complexion. A bit on the thin side, he is very attractive and very, very gay. Benji isn't simply gay, he is super gay, he is ultra gay. He is so gay that advocates of gay rights find themselves uncomfortable in his presence.

Born and raised around homosexuals, he watched as they hid themselves away and they always seemed ashamed. How they only revealed themselves within their own communities. Benji decided at a young age he would not hide and was often seen on campus in a t-shirt emblazoned with slogans like "Of course I swallow," or "My ass or yours."

Living in a supportive fraternity his wealthy parents gave him anything he wanted at any time he wanted it and Benji lived life as though he was on a mission. His mission was to insure every male on the planet had at least one homosexual experience in their lives, preferably with him.

In his frat house bedroom stood a grossly oversized, hard, plastic phallus. Not to be used, although if Benji could have found a way he would have, the giant plastic cock had notches carved in it. One for every man Benji has had sex with and there were a lot of notches. The game for Benji was to find a straight man and try to turn him, or at the least to have sex with him. Nightly he could be found trolling the gay dives, seeking the unsuspecting fool who stumbled into the wrong bar. Tonight Jackson stumbled into the right bar.

At the local Goodwill he acquired a gray button down shirt along with a charcoal pair of chinos and hard soled, casual shoes. With his hair slicked back he appeared to be at least of upper middle class. Benji was already at the bar when he arrived and was fully engaged in his routine. His t-shirt read simply, "Do me."

Jackson watched as Benji flagrantly displayed his sexual preferences and waited. Already several drinks into the night Benji made his way to the restroom and Jackson followed, standing next to him at the urinals and pretending not to notice him. Benji, absorbed in peeing, didn't notice Jackson either. Looking up, finally he did see Jackson, and Benji's face lit up as if someone had stuck a light bulb up his ass. "Well HI!" he exclaimed as a feminine lilt tinted his soprano voice, "I haven't seen you in here before."

Jackson returned Benji's smile and shyly looked away, which was all the bait needed for Benji to once again commence his mission. He stared intently at Jackson for several long seconds as though receiving new orders over a two-way radio only he could see and hear, *Butt pirate to base, butt pirate to base, we have contact! Base to butt pirate, initiate conversion!*

"Found yourself in the wrong bar, have you?" Benji inquired slyly.

"Not really," Jackson said dismissively and he instantly had Benji's immediate attention.

Well, what's the story with this handsome young man? Benji inquired of himself. Unable to contain his curiosity, he said in a surprised voice, "Really? You don't seem gay."

"I'm not," Jackson answered, "well, I haven't been. Let's just say I'm curious."

This was the invitation Benji was waiting for. If this young man, so absolutely gorgeous, needed help understanding his sexual confusion, well, Benji was just the person to help him! He grabbed Jackson by the arm and steered him out of the restroom and led him to his table. Benji's friends, seeing he has found another plaything, quickly dispersed and left them alone.

"Curious are you?" Benji inquired further after they had taken their seats. Jackson tried to sit on one side of the table but Benji quickly pulled up a chair beside him.

"Yes," Jackson said, "I've been straight my whole life. I've dated several women but they always leave me feeling like I am missing something, like maybe there is something else. I don't necessarily like having sex with women, it always seems to be what is expected of me, what I am supposed to do. Recently I have been questioning myself. Then I heard about this place being a gay bar and all so I thought, what the hell. I will come down here, maybe meet somebody, see where things go."

Benji now had a very painful erection and he hastily convinced himself that before this night was over he would have this young man in his frat room bent over begging for more. Benji on his knees satisfying him. Oh the things he would show him as he guided him to a life of happy homosexuality. As the night wore on the conversation continued.

Benji was aware of recent events including the murder of his cousin and Uncle but he didn't care. All he could think of was this man in front of him. He was almost drooling while

Jackson hesitantly described his curiosity. Benji adamantly assured him of how wonderful it all would be. A few hours into the evening Jackson stood up to leave, saying, "Well, I have to go. I have a huge presentation at the office tomorrow and I need to be rested for it."

Benji just couldn't let this beautiful plaything walk out the door. "Please Jackson," he said, "Just one more. It's so early! Surely you can stay for one more drink?" Jackson assured him he just couldn't, and after prying Benji's fingers from his arm, he turned to leave. Benji, crestfallen, looked as though he was going to cry. He was so sure of the night's successful outcome.

"Can I see you again, Jackson?" Benji implored as Jackson was walking away. Stopping, as if pondering the question, Jackson spied a pen lying on the table. He reached for it and picking it up, he turned to Benji. Lightly holding Benji's arm Jackson wrote his number, gently ran his fingers across Benji's face, then turned and walked out of the bar.

Benji collapsed into his chair and within moments his friends came to join him. "What happened, Benji? We thought for sure you were going to score with him," his friends asked.

Benji smiled his best smile and revealed the phone number hastily scratched on his arm. "The game isn't over yet," he said with certainty.

He finished the evening with his friends and returned to his frat house where he masturbated himself to sleep with thoughts of sex with Jackson. The next morning Benji woke and called Jackson. The phone rang and rang but Jackson didn't pick up. Every few hours throughout the day he would call, but he continued to get no answer. On and on this went for two days and Benji became more and more exasperated. On the third day, when Benji was at his breaking point, Jackson finally picked up the phone.

"I have been desperately trying to reach you, Jackson! Where have you been!" Benji spouted like a jilted lover, "You walk into my favorite bar, drink with me and chat, tell me the most delicious things, then leave me wanting. Only to not be available for three days! All I've done is think about you Jackson! I really must see you again!"

Allowing Benji to squirm a little longer, Jackson finally agreed to meet him later in the evening at the same bar for drinks. Benji was overjoyed and the remainder of the day he practically skipped to his classes. His friends noticed how much giddier than usual he was and inquired as to his current state of blissfulness. He told them he had a date with the same beautiful, homosexually curious young man they had seen him with three nights ago. He said excitedly, "I told you the game wasn't over yet."

Later that evening Benji prepared himself to meet Jackson. He found his best shirt and slacks with the perfect shoes. Just a dash of cologne and styled his hair just so. Ready as he could be for an evening he just knew would be unforgettable. Arriving at the bar he found Jackson seated by himself at the table they shared before. Benji walked over to him and leaned in to kiss him.

"Whoa there, Spanky Mchappy pants! You wanna back the fuck off?" Jackson said threateningly as he jerked backward violently. Benji, sensing the crack in Jackson's facade, stared at him, horrified. Jackson realized he had almost made a fatal mistake and he moved quickly to repair the damage and placate Benji.

"I'm sorry, Benji," he said soothingly, "You took me by surprise there. I told you I'm curious. You think you might be coming on a bit strong? You're moving faster than I am comfortable with." Benji, rejected, accepted his apology and foolishly allowed his fear to dissipate. He pulled up a chair and sat down at a more respectable distance.

"I can't stay long," Jackson said to him, "I have a prior engagement I have to be at and I'm already late." Benji was instantly crushed. He was so sure tonight would be the night.

Pouting, he barely spoke as Jackson rambled on about nonexistent, boring office work. Finishing his drink Jackson got up to leave. "Call me in a couple of days, okay Benji?" he asked and left the bar. Benji departed soon after him and returned to his frat room to cry himself to sleep, curled up with his giant oversized plastic cock, his fingers tripping over the notches, caressing the spot he had chosen for Jackson.

Benji was coming apart at the seams. He couldn't study or pay attention in class. He barely ate. All he could think of was Jackson and being with him. Everyone he saw reminded him of Jackson. Everyone he talked to. He tried to call him but got no answer. Benji left long, imploring messages; begging Jackson to call him back. Each message more pained than the last. Benji's father called after two torturous days and a few moments into their conversation his father Walter noticed the depression in his son's voice. "Are you okay Benji boy? Is everything alright?" he asked his son, deeply concerned.

"No daddy," Benji cried, "I'm sad."

"Why are you sad Benji boy?" Walter questioned, again with deep concern for his son, "What can I do to help you?"

Benji explained to his father about meeting Jackson in the bar a few days earlier. He told his father about how beautiful he was and how desperate Benji had become to get to know this young man. How all he could do was think about him day and night. Sobbing, he said Jackson wouldn't return his phone calls and that he had called so many times! "Why isn't he calling me back, daddy?" he wailed as if his father must have had the answer.

Walter assured him he just didn't know. He said his son was such a special, wonderful boy and how any man would be lucky to spend even a moment with him. Walter asked, "Benji, would you like to fly home for the weekend? The family jet can pick you up at the airport and you would be home in only hours." With this invitation an idea spontaneously came to Benji's mind. "Absolutely Daddy. Have the driver pick me up and bring me to the airport. I have a call I have to make now. Thank you so much Daddy!" he said and hung up with his father, immediately dialing Jackson's number.

Jackson didn't answer so Benji left another message. "I'm flying home to California on the family jet for the weekend, Jackson. It would be so fabulous if you joined me! We can visit my parents, you can meet them, and it will all be so wonderful! Call me back right away you delicious man and tell me you will come with me. Call me…please, please, please." Hanging up the phone he practically floated down the steps to the frat house kitchen for a sandwich. He just knew Jackson would call now and a few hours later he wasn't disappointed.

Jackson had received every message Benji left on his voice mail then promptly deleted them. With the invitation to California to meet Benji's parents, the perfect opportunity presented itself. Jackson called him back and agreed to go with him, and Benji was higher than he had ever been on any drug he had ever taken.

The next morning a local taxi company dropped Jackson off at the airport where Benji's private jet was fueled and ready to go. He ran up to Jackson and hugged him as tightly as he could, not trying to kiss him this time. Benji was fully prepared to go slowly, to bring Jackson along slowly. There is no way he can get away now, Benji thought to himself as they boarded the family jet, what a weekend this is going to be!

340°
CHAPTER THIRTY FOUR

Weeks have passed and the FBI are as clueless as to motive as to when this whole thing began. DNA evidence was found in Sherry Gardner's SUV but it is useless with no one to match it to. No suspects and no one had seen a thing. Without a complete understanding of what was happening, no one thought to assign a security detail to the Jenson family. They were contacted and informed of Richard and Sherry Gardner's deaths but that was as far as things had been taken. Slowly the agents were working through the eye witness accounts gathered in Detroit and in a few days they would come to the homeless man's report. Pieces of the puzzle would begin to fall into place.

Seated on the Jensen's private jet Jackson got comfortable and said, "Hey Benji, can I ask you something?"

Benji exclaimed, "Of course, silly! Ask me anything."

Jackson had brought a briefcase with him. Setting the briefcase in his lap he popped the clasps and extracted the Army Colt revolver he used to shoot Richard Gardner, "Is this going to be okay on the flight?"

Taken aback, his face showing alarm, with a shriek Benji said, "Put that away Jackson! Oh my God, a gun!" Quickly a wicked smile crossed Benji's face as he assumed a coquettish posture, "Really, you won't need a gun for me this weekend." A grimace flashed across Jackson's face which Benji either didn't see or chose to ignore. Benji continued, "Where did you get that? Is it an antique?"

"Yes," Jackson replied, trying to hide his annoyance, "You don't understand. This past week while you were trying to reach me I was out looking for this. From what I understand it belonged to your great whatever grandfather, the one who used to be President? I bought it and thought it would make a wonderful gift for your father."

Benji leapt from his seat. Hugging Jackson he squealed, "That will be so perfect! My daddy will just love it!"

The flight was mercifully short and a few hours later they landed at Santa Paula Airport on a private airstrip where a limo was waiting to pick them up. High into the Ventura Hills they drove to the lavish estate of Benji's parents. Benji bounced from the limo and rushed to hug his father. Releasing his father he turned to his mother and quickly hugged her, then ecstatically introduced Jackson, Benji bubbling like a school girl.

Entering their home Jackson was greeted by the sight of very expensive furniture and paintings, all originals. Each one hung strategically and precisely on the walls, the Jensen home the very model of high society California elite. As they ushered him in Benji followed, grinning as though he has just received everything he asked for at Christmas plus more.

In the living room Jackson again met Benji's mother, Margaret. A tall, thin woman with a vaporous way about her, almost as if she had lived her entire life confused. Her brown hair styled perfectly, shoulder length, in the latest style of the movie stars she so voraciously followed. Offered a seat, Jackson found a place on one of two matching $10,000 couches and set the briefcase down beside him.

Walter Jensen, Benji's father, noticed the briefcase but didn't say anything about it. Quickly exchanging pleasantries Walter adjusted his $5,000 suit and found a comfortable spot on the other $10,000 couch. Walter, an affable man with a really bad toupee he didn't seem to notice. Short and fat with a well-chewed cigar stuck in his mouth that had obviously been there a few hours he cleared his throat and said, "So, tell us about yourself, Jackson," Walter encouraged, "Where are you from? Who is your family?"

Stopping his query suddenly Walter gazed at Jackson quizzically. As if a start button had been pressed he suddenly blushed and exclaimed, "You're Native American, aren't you Jackson! I knew there was something about you when you stepped out of the car!"

Benji squealed as though Jackson had pinched him, "I knew there was something super sexy about you Jackson! Native Americans are so sexy! Isn't he sexy Daddy?" Benji leapt from the couch and disappeared into the recesses of the Jensen's expansive home. Walter and Margaret were practically glowing as Walter raised his right hand and said, "How."

Jackson glanced down at the briefcase.

Walter continued, "We love Native Americans! Margaret and I are part of a drum and chanting circle that meets every month. Sometimes we drum and chant here. There is a room in the back of the house we call our Indian Room. It's where we have all our costumes and stuff. Margaret found us two wonderful drums on the internet. They were $3,000 each so we know they are authentic. We can show you all our Indian stuff after dinner."

Benji returned and burst into the living room clutching a plastic tomahawk and wearing a headdress with green and yellow dyed chicken feathers. He immediately began dancing around the center of the living room and pantomimed perfectly the patented Hollywood 'woo woo woo,' patting his hand over his lips in unison.

Jackson continued to stare at his briefcase.

"Benji! You are going to make Jackson nervous," Walter said, "This isn't the time for Indian dancing and chanting. We only do that on special occasions, isn't that correct, Jackson?" he said, looking to him for confirmation.

Jackson continued to stare at his briefcase.

"I just had the most splendid idea!" Margaret chimed into the conversation, "Chelsea, on the other side of the Valley? Her Pekinese will be giving birth soon and we have been asked to perform a blessing chant for the puppies. Maybe if Jackson is in town he could lead it for us! How spectacular would that be!"

Benji had stopped his war whoop and mouth slapping to resume his position practically in Jackson's lap. The chicken feather headdress remained perched on his head. "You know, Jackson, I always wanted to be an Indian," he said demurely, "I was in the Boy Scouts, The Order of the Arrow, where we learned all about how to be Indians. Isn't that just the neatest thing, Jackson?"

Gratefully not giving him time to answer Walter interrupted and said, "Margaret and I both have Indian names. I call myself 'Two Spirits' because when I was younger I was bisexual, so I thought it would be perfect." Jackson noted Walter's obvious effeminate mannerisms. Walter was still openly, if not actively, bisexual. Margaret never blinked, obviously fully aware of Walter's dalliances into homosexuality. "Margaret's name is 'Dancing Rainbow' because she is so sparkly and colorful when she does the Indian dances," Walter continued.

Stoned faced and silent, Jackson listened. Unnoticed, he had been clenching his jaw, and feeling the sudden pressure, he smiled to ease the pain. Taking the smile as an invitation, Walter continued, "Margaret just mentioned Chelsea? Well, she is who got us involved in the drum and chanting circle. Chelsea has a friend, Debi. Some years ago a man lived here in the valley and Debi met him at one of those sweating ceremony thingy's.

"He went to the reservation for the summer and they trained him in everything he needed to know about how to be a medicine man. Well, they adopted him, then he adopted Debi who he later named 'Dolphin Dancing Eagle.' He trained her to be a Shaman and she leads all of our drum and chant circles now with her husband Chaz. She named him 'Crying Wolf.' Chaz is training to be a medicine man, too.

He was Indian in a former life. A psychic told him he was a Chief back then."

Jackson was barely holding it together. As if granted a reprieve, Maria the house servant stepped into the living room and announced dinner. The explanations of how spiritual the Jensen's were stopped as they all make their way to the dining room.

Seated around the table, a veritable feast before them, with Walter Jensen at the head of the table and Margaret to his right,. Jackson was given Benji's normal seat at Walters left and Benji sat immediately to Jackson's left. As Maria finished laying out the food Walter said, "You know, I feel so bad for Indians today. I would love to help them but I just don't know how. At least we honor them with our drum and chanting circles."

Margaret quickly agreed with him, "We certainly would. But what could we do? You know I always thought it was rather silly for the Indians to abandon all their land in the East. Just walk away and leave their homes like that. If they had kept them they would probably be doing a whole lot better by now. Good thing my family bought up all that land and started using it. Do you know why the Indians left their land like that Jackson?"

Jackson wasn't sure how much more of this he could take.

Walter dismissed Maria after she completed setting all the food on the table saying, "You can leave for the evening, Maria. We won't be needing you any more tonight." She turned to leave the room and in moments Jackson heard her open the front door and leave. He waited and listened impatiently for the sound of her car driving away.

Sure he was alone with the last of Richard Whitman's descendants, Jackson reached for his briefcase. As he did Benji began to clap his hands with excitement. "Jackson has brought you a gift daddy!" Benji exclaimed, "You won't believe what he found. You are just going to love it! Love it! Love it!" clapping his hands to each "Love it," beside himself with glee.

Moving his plate aside, Jackson set the briefcase on the table in front of him. Opening it slowly he reached inside and removed the Army Colt revolver. Walter's eyes went wide when he saw what Jackson was holding. What a beautiful piece! Walter thought, admiring the craftsmanship and the authenticity as the Army Colt was slowly revealed.

Jackson adjusted the weight of the revolver in his hand, slowly pulled back the hammer, pointed the barrel at Walter's head and pulled the trigger. From almost point blank range his head exploded like a ripe melon and his body was blown out of his chair from the power of that old Army Colt.

Jackson immediately turned his attention to Margaret Jensen before the octaves of her screams could begin to rise. She was staring at him as though what just happened was only a movie. Pointing the old Army Colt right between her eyes, retracting the hammer, he pulled the trigger and blew her out of her chair. She was dead before she hit the floor.

By now Benji was screaming like a little girl, not moving, other than his hands which were waving in the air as though they were no longer attached to his arms. Sitting, squealing, screeching. Jackson reached over and grasped

Benji by the back of his neck and bounced his head off the hard mahogany dining table.

As Benji began to whimper Jackson looked out the sliding glass window where he could see a park-like setting that has been landscaped into the back yard with small trees and a fire pit. Perfect, Jackson thought. Standing, Jackson roughly jerked Benji from his chair and pushed him outside. Benji stumbled willingly, cowered and afraid; whimpering, sniffling and crying. Jackson had also stowed a roll of duct tape in his briefcase as well as a small folding knife. He taped Benji's hands behind him, then duct taped his face, covering his eyes and mouth, leaving only his nostrils so he could breath.

Jackson stripped him naked and forced him to the ground. Benji, unable to see, barely able to breath, was terrified at what was being done to him. Unsure of what would happen next, urine trickled down his leg. Jackson turned him over onto his back and using the knife he quickly cut a small hole in Benji's abdomen then reached into the hole he made and extracted a small amount of Benji's intestine. The pain minimal Benji only felt a peculiar tugging in his groin. Standing him back on his feet Jackson led Benji over to the fire pit and a small tree with no limbs at its base. Grasping the dangling end of intestine he secured it to the small tree.

Jackson quickly collected kindling and started a small fire. As the fire came to life he reached high into the tree and broke off several green branches, stripping their leaves. Holding the bundle together he placed one end into the in the fire. In moments the ends of the green sticks began to glow red hot.

Benji, was on the verge of losing his mind. His eyes still taped so he couldn't see what was happening. He wanted to run except every move caused that peculiar tug at his groin. Picking up a glowing stick Jackson leaned over to Benji and, speaking loud enough to be heard through his duct tape covered ear said, "You wanted me to poke you Benji boy, well then, let's get to poking."

Jabbing him with the glowing red hot stick Benji jumped, then began to move forward to avoid the stick. As the stick cooled Jackson retrieved another and another. Benji walked in circles around that small tree slowly pulling his own intestines out. Hours later, around 4 a.m., Benji lay dead in a pile of his own reeking guts. From his back pocket Jackson pulled an owl's feather, also previously in the briefcase, and dipped it in Benji's blood. He secured it to the remaining branches, leaving the feather to gently sway and drip in the breeze.

Returning to the house and he piled together what he could move. Searching and locating a can of charcoal starter fluid he soaked everything thoroughly and created a trail out the front door where he lit, then threw, a match. The last of President Richard Whitman's descendants now dead. All, found and killed, except for a child, born out of wedlock to a slave a few hundred years ago.

Jackson turned and began the long, walking descent out of the Ventura Hills. As he walked he slowly tore apart the ancient Army Colt and scattered the pieces. Never again will this gun be used to kill another native.

Ten minutes into the walk he could hear the fire and police sirens racing up the hills as they responded to the blaze.

The roads of the Ventura Hills are steep and winding and he had plenty of warning from their flashing lights before they reached him. When the sirens got close enough he ducked out of sight and let them pass. The first responders would be too late because Jackson had done a good job. Before the night was over there would be nothing left of the Jensen home but ashes.

Jackson had spent the days between meeting Benji the first and second time, selling his car. He knew before long the FBI would have a bead on it and he needed to get rid of it. Good thing he did because now he needed the money for the return trip. All he had to do was make it to the airport.

Reaching a well lit convenience store he stepped inside and called a taxi. Back outside he sipped a cup of coffee, a smile playing at his lips, Jackson listened as the fire department sent more responders. The fire must be a good one, he thought to himself, sounds like they are sending everybody.

The store clerk, gazing out the window, watched as the police, fire and ambulance vehicles rushed past. Jackson turned and caught his gaze. The clerk looked to him as if to say, "I wonder what's happening?" and Jackson shrugged in return, suggesting he had no idea. When the taxi arrived he climbed in.

Arriving at LAX he searched the terminal for a flight back to Norfolk. Noticing one would be leaving in fifteen minutes he quickly paid for a ticket and boarded. He was the last passenger, the flight attendant ready to secure the door. "Just in time," she exclaimed, smiling.

"Just in time," he repeated.

350°
CHAPTER THIRTY FIVE

The early morning mid week flight was sparsely attended with the usual mix of business people and miscellaneous travelers returning home after a vacation to the west coast. All year they slaved in a factory for pennies to eventually receive two glorious weeks in Hollywood, or Disneyland, or some other ridiculous vacation spot. Now it was back to the daily grind to scratch out a living in a society where they are worth more dead than alive, spending their lives making someone else wealthy so they could pass their leash and collar on to their children. What a happy, fulfilling way to live.

Jackson found an empty seat off to himself and settled in. He made himself as comfortable as possible and promptly fell asleep. While he slept police and fire crews feverishly tried to keep the fire he set from burning down Ventura County. Finding Benji's body and the owl feather tied to a branch the FBI was called immediately. This had gone on long enough.

The FBI was furious. How was it possible that one man, completely unknown, could travel the country, reign utter terror, and not be caught? The full force of the FBI was brought to bear in the investigation. They quickly connected the dots from California, back to South Carolina and a contingent of federal agents were dispatched to canvas at Duke University. Within hours they found Benji's friends.

Several interviews later the FBI had a composite of the man they were looking for. Copies were forwarded to every police agency in the country and Jackson's roughly drawn image was plastered across every television set in the country. The FBI might not yet know why, but they almost know who. They are closing in.

As the FBI compiled information, a gentle shaking roused Jackson. Groggily he came to and remembered quickly where he was. Thanking the stewardess for waking him he departed the airplane and walked off to the long term parking area. He checked camera locations and insured there were no roving security guards or dogs are around. Confident he won't be seen, he broke into a late model sedan. He flipped the visor down and sure enough, there was the parking ticket. He drove to the booth and paid the attendant, then turned off into the night.

Jackson stopped at the first Wal-Mart Super center he could find and again checked to see no one was watching him. To be safe he switched plates with another vehicle parked off to the side, climbed back into his stolen car and headed for the highway. A few miles down the road he pulled off to call Jenny Lynne and she picked up on the third ring. Fortuitously for him she had taken the day off.

Earlier in the morning she rose to prepare for work and, suddenly queasy, she found herself on her knees in front of the toilet. She thought she was coming down with something and with all the children who visited the library she wasn't too surprised. Little walking petri dishes, she thought to herself.

Returning to bed she heard the phone ring and didn't check to see who was calling as she groggily answered, "Hello?"

"Hey, Jenny Lynne, it's Jackson. Doing anything?" he spoke into the phone.

She sat bolt upright and exclaimed, "Jackson! Wow, two weeks go by and not a word. Now out of the blue, here you are. Thank you, kind sir, for graciously extending unto me, your humble sex servant, a brief audience over the phone."

"Come on, Jenny Lynne, that's not necessary," he said. It had been a long flight, he was tired and cranky and really didn't need her attitude.

"No," she replied, "What isn't necessary is me picking up the phone. What isn't necessary is me even talking to you. I swear if I didn't feel like shit on a stick this morning…if I knew it was you calling I would never have answered the damn thing!"

Jackson began to apologize. He said he was so sorry he had been gone and that he hadn't called. Suddenly an excuse came to mind. As he continued to apologize he said, "Jenny Lynne, I wanted to call but I couldn't. I received a last second invitation to ceremonies and I just went. I know I should have called you before I left, hell, you probably would have wanted to go with me. Guess I thought you wouldn't be able to get the time off from work. Plus with all the shit Bob is putting you through, well, I expected you wouldn't be able to make it."

Instantly mollified she let her anger slide. She couldn't really say she gave a good crap about it anyway. It was not like he owed her an explanation. Jenny Lynne had been touchy and irritable these last few days and she thought she was catching a cold.

"How is the research going? Finding anything?" Jackson asked into the silence on the phone.

"As a matter of fact, my favorite bastard, I have great news," she said as she slowly eased herself from her bed. Groaning a little she said, "Damn I feel like crap. Kids. I tell you Jackson, I love them dearly but I don't love all the germs and bugs they bring with them. I swear if there is a new bug I'm the first to get it."

Jackson apologized again to her saying he was sorry that she felt so bad. "If you felt so bad you would be here with me," she retorted, "Hang on a second. Let me get my notes." Setting the phone down she retrieved them and returned to her bed. Finding the phone, she inquired, "You there, Jackson?"

"Yeah, I'm here, Jenny Lynne. What do you have?" he asked sweetly.

"As we saw the last time you graced me with your presence, Sir Jackson," she began sarcastically, "President Whitman did have a child with one of his servants. The mother eventually left his estate, probably sent away by

Whitman so no one would find out. Anyway, she winds up in Kansas of all places. She married a white guy and has the baby. Time goes on but the family line never got bigger than one child, always a daughter. How strange, huh?"

"Anyway, I traced the line up to the last family and they, too, gave birth to one daughter. That family is named Rogers and this is where things got a little tricky because that daughter had an accident as a child and when she was sixteen she disappeared. I'm thinking she's dead until I stumbled across her marriage certificate. Her maiden name is Dorothy Rogers and she marries a young Marine named Maxwell Magnate. They moved here to Norfolk, Jackson! Can you believe it? Dorothy is still alive and lives less than 50 miles from here."

"Jackson? Jackson?" Jenny Lynne realized she was talking to dead air, "Son of a bitch!" she exclaimed.

Jackson dropped the phone and stared at it as though it were a viper preparing to strike. Lightheaded and dizzy, short of breath, thunderstruck and speechless, Jackson composed himself after several minutes and shook off the sense of something wrapped around him. He walked back to the car, jumped the wires in the stolen vehicle, and took off for Seashore State Park.

The park is a place he often visited as a teenager. It was somewhere he could go to walk and think. An hour later Jackson arrived, found an empty space and pulled in. Stepping from the vehicle he crossed the wooden bridge that wound deep into the foliage and fauna. Arriving at the shoreline he sat and watched as the sun slowly dragged itself through the sky, finally setting as it burned orange the remaining daylight. His mind numb. Hours later the moon rose and he rose with it. He knew what he had to do. Heading back to the parking lot he found the stolen car still there and climbing in he headed to Dorothy Magnate's home.

While he sat on the beach in Seashore State Park, Jenny Lynne was turning on the television. Earlier, after Jackson had hung up on her, she threw the phone at the wall. The phone had landed on her bed undamaged, but the wall wasn't so lucky. "Asshole!" she shouted, "Let's see that prick show up at my door again. Call me, you prick. Go ahead, I dare you to call me." But the phone didn't ring, no matter how hard she stared at it. Jenny Lynne retrieved her phone and set it back in the cradle, noticing the hole in her wall. "Fuck it," she said and went back to sleep.

Around sunset Jenny Lynne got up and walked into her living room. The television still on for background noise, she slowly shuffled her way into the kitchen to prepare a cup of tea. The television was tuned to a national news station and as the water brewed she vaguely heard the news reporter say something about President Richard Whitman. Her curiosity piqued, with tea in hand, she returned to the living room and seated herself on the edge of an ottoman as she watched and listened intently.

The newscaster was relating a story of how both of the remaining families descended from former President Richard Whitman had been found slaughtered. That their homes, as well as the Whitman Estate, were burned to the ground. How the bodies of the children were found horribly mutilated. *No,*

Jenny Lynne thought, *oh my God, no.*

She sat on her ottoman as realization of what Jackson had been doing when he disappeared slowly burned into her mind. Seconds later a roughly drawn sketch filled the television screen, a roughly drawn sketch of Jackson. The tea cup in her hand crashed to the floor unnoticed.

While her world was crashing down around her Jackson pulled up to Dorothy Magnates house. The final strains of "The Animal," performed by Disturbed faded from the speakers as he turned off the vehicle and stared out the windshield. A story told to him by an Elder some years ago returned to his mind...

...Some time ago, long before humans walked this earth, the animals controlled everything and all was in perfect balance. Each knows its place and responsibility and there was no guilt of evil behavior. Each did as each was born to do and accepted this is what they were. One day in that time a lone wolf pup becomes separated from its pack.

A mother deer stumbles across that little lost pup. She feels sorry for it as she has no children of her own, and she brings the wolf pup back to the Deer Nation. Presenting the wolf pup to the Chief of the Deer Nation, a huge buck with eighteen point antlers, the mother deer cries to her Chief. She cries of how she has no children to raise. Will the Chief permit her to raise this lost and lonely pup?

"How can you raise a wolf pup?" demands the Chief of the Deer Nation, "He is a wolf and you are a deer."

The mother deer cries and cries. She pleads until

the Deer Chief finally consents. "Fine," he says turning abruptly and stamping his front hooves, "You raise him. He is your responsibility."

So the wolf pup is raised among the Deer People believing he, too, is a deer. Time passes and the pup eventually grows into a young wolf. One day while the Deer Nation is in the forest foraging, unknown to them, an old wolf is watching. Suddenly the old wolf jumps up on to all four of its feet. There among the Deer People is a young wolf! Playing with the deer! Eating grass and behaving as a deer! The old wolf can't believe his eyes.

Surging forward the old wolf scatters the deer and corners the young wolf. "What are you doing?" The old wolf demands of the young wolf.

The young wolf cries, "I am a deer, old wolf. I am only foraging for my dinner."

The old wolf laughs and says, "Oh no, you are not."

"Follow me," the old wolf commands and the young wolf does as the old wolf instructs. Reaching a creek the old wolf asks the young wolf, "Do you know what a deer looks like?"

"Of course," the young wolf says.

"And do you know what a wolf looks like?" the old wolf asks.

Again the young wolf replies, "Of course."

"Well then," says the old wolf, "I want you to look into this creek and tell me what you see."

The young wolf again does as commanded and is shocked to see himself! As a young wolf! Looking back at himself! The young wolf realizes he isn't a deer after all. He is a wolf! After speaking with the old wolf for several hours the young wolf asks what he must do to become a real wolf. What is his true nature?

"Come again with me young one," the old wolf commands once more.

The old wolf leads the young wolf back to where the Deer Nation is bedding down for the night. Locating the mother deer that tried to raise the young wolf, the old wolf explains what the young wolf must to do.

The young wolf hesitates a brief moment, the old wolf snaps at the young wolfs hind legs and the young wolf races forward, ripping the throat from the mother deer...

Tonight the young pup, Jackson, raised by a deer, Dorothy, would become the wolf he was born to be. Stepping out of the stolen car he stepped on to Dorothy Magnate's porch, knocked, and opened the door.

360°
CHAPTER THIRTY SIX

For the second time today Jenny Lynne picked up the phone. This time she called the FBI and within hours a team of agents are at her door. After several hours of interviewing her they had all they needed as she told them everything she knew about Jackson.

When she first met Jackson the scars on his chest were still raw. Their first night together she was very tender and cautious, understanding they must hurt him. Asking Jackson about the wounds he told her about the Sundance he attended on Pine Ridge weeks before they met. Jenny Lynne passed this information on to the FBI.

They left her apartment and drove first to the library to retrieve Jackson's information from the identification he gave to her when they first met. The agents then drove to the nearest field office where they began to put their information to work.

Gathering a team of agents in South Dakota they began canvassing the Reservation and within hours were driving up to David Chases' trailer. They spent a few hours with Chases who was all too happy and willing to do his civic duty. He fully informed the FBI about everything he knew and directed them to Tony Baker's place in Pennsylvania. A quick phone call and agents were at Tony's shop, interviewing him. They learned of the vehicle they thought Jackson was driving but they didn't know he sold it. "Well, that explains that," Tony said to the agents.

"Explains what?" they inquired.

"Got the weirdest freaking phone call a few weeks back," Tony said, "Some state trooper asking me about Jackson at a road side vehicle inspection in northern Virginia. Was wondering what the hell that was about. Damn, I just never put the pieces together. I been following the news but never thought it was Jackson. Hang on a second." Hurrying to the back of the tire shop with the agents in tow Tony opened the door on what had been Jackson's room. He hurriedly entered and threw back the coverings on the stacked boxes of junk. No flares. No flare guns.

"Looking for something?" the agents ask.

"Yeah, I was," Tony answered dejectedly, "Few years ago I got a good deal on several cases of road flares. Was going to sell them to my customers. I stored them in here then forgot all about them and they ain't here no more." The agents traded glances as one immediately reached for his phone and called in a forensics team for chemical analysis.

Laboratory results would match the flares from Tony's shop to those used to burn down Detroit, the Lincoln House and Mt. Vernon. Those same chemical results were found in the trunk of Jackson's car. The 1984 Pontiac Gran Prix Tony helped him put back on the road. A search of the VIN number, which Tony still had, led them to the buyer. The FBI now know exactly who they are looking for. What they didn't know was where or why.

While the FBI scrambled Jackson left Dorothy's home in his stolen vehicle. Serendipity played her part as he turned on the stereo and the CD player kicked in. "Finding Beauty in Negative Spaces" by Seether began to thunder through the speakers as he drove to the interstate, heading for Pine Ridge.

The blood line of the few, in Jackson's mind, who initiated the demise of the First Nations People was now completely wiped off the face of time. Every descendant dead. The future reserved for those who perpetuate that demise.

There are so many predators in Indian Country, sustaining their arrogance by feeding off the people in order to satisfy their egos. Topping the list – David Chases. Jackson is fully aware others will step up to take his place. He is also aware he can't do anything about them. What he can do is start the fire.

This country is so much like a petulant child; spinning the most outlandish of tales, ashamed of what it has done and not having the courage to admit the truth and face due punishment. The God of Greed demanded sustenance and men like Richard Whitman were all too eager to bow before the altar and serve. They worshipped the mighty dollar, always demanding more with no fear of retribution. Jackson had become retribution.

When all is said and done would any of it matter? Probably not. When Jackson's reasons are revealed, his purpose, will anyone care? Probably not. The Nations will disavow him and Jackson will be labeled as a domestic terrorist. A mad man with his own agenda, nothing he had done will be condoned by any authority figure. Publicly it will be stated he acted alone.

Those who tell him he couldn't talk about what he knows? They can all go pound sand. The memories are his and if he decides to run them up a flagpole that is his prerogative. Damn the consequences and thank you Mary Bloody Heart.

Jackson is completely aware he is trying to empty the ocean with a teaspoon and he doesn't care. He accepts his actions, what he has done, regardless the outcome. He knows the twinkies will continue playing with their crystals and the bliss bunnies will continue living with their heads in the clouds, so stoned on the spiritual that they forget they are human as well. Those who think they know, think they are, will continue to instruct uninvited. Predators will rise and fall and others will take their place. Nothing will change.

For those who were truly seekers, seeking direction and an understanding, good luck. For as many Ancients that exist to assist there are as many that exist to distract. These Tricksters have persisted for eons, applying their well-designed psychological tactics and are all too willingly assisted by the arrogant and egotistical. The mind is their playground and the petitioner risks their soul on this perilous journey.

If nothing else, Jackson has spoken. Loudly and clearly. Whether anyone chooses to listen or chooses to ignore is not his problem. What is done with what he has done is each individual's choice.

Jackson thought momentarily of Jenny Lynne. He never loved her, only used her for what he needed. He doesn't feel bad about it, doesn't feel anything at all. He thinks she is a good person and hopes it all works out for her.

Unknown to Jenny Lynne, certainly not to Jackson who will never know, she isn't sick. She doesn't have a bug picked up from one of the children visiting the library, Jenny Lynne is pregnant. In nine months she will give birth to a healthy baby boy and the child will be raised by her. She will never reveal to him who his father is. All this child will ever know is love and adoration from a deeply caring mother. He will be raised in a loving home with attention and affection as all children are supposed to be. As Jackson should have been.

Jackson drove onto the Pine Ridge Indian Reservation while the FBI and every police agency country wide were looking for him. He traveled only at night and during the day he found secluded places deep in the country to hide, refueling at the most dimly lit service stations, eating what little he could scrounge.

When he crossed the Reservation boundary Jackson saw a road side stand up ahead where a local family was selling pretties and hand crafted items to those who passed by. A glint of sunlight on steel grabbed his attention so he pulled over and got out of his car, casually taking in all they had to offer.

His eyes settle on a handmade war axe that had been crafted from the remains of a vehicle leaf spring. Heavy and extremely sharp, the handle beaded in orange, black and white with fringe hanging off the end. Haggling with the old native woman at the stand he purchased it for the last $100 in his pocket. Back on the road he drove through Wounded Knee and over to Chases property.

He pulled onto Chases' land as "The Enemy," performed by Godsmack threatened to permanently disfigure the car speakers and there was Chases, sitting by himself in the front yard. The Sundance Tree Jackson hung from mere months ago is still standing, the prayer flags flying in the wind. Chases did not recognize the car pulling up and doesn't rise.

When the bass completed its final heavy thuds he turned off the stereo and pulled up to the broken split rail fence someone had installed for aesthetics. Stepping from the vehicle his eyes met Chases. Recognition instantaneous as a sly smirk tilts Chases' lips. "How you doing, Jackson?" Chases asked knowingly.

"Best I can," he responded, "best I can. Wanted to come by and visit for a moment while I was here on the rez. Brought you a gift."

"Did you now?" Chases inquired as he noticed the war axe in Jackson's hand.

Standing from his chair he walked over to him, extended his hand and from all around him Jackson hears, "Freeze Motherfucker! Don't you fucking move!"

Unknown to Jackson and fully known to David Chases the FBI had set up a surveillance team on the property. Someone in the FBI thought Jackson might show up there and the agents were on full alert. They didn't want to make the same mistake their cohorts had in South Carolina. The federal agents had pulled back when he drove onto the property, hiding themselves among the junk vehicles and scattered debris. Jackson never noticed they were there.

They had watched as Jackson drove up and parked. They had watched as he exited his vehicle and walked towards Chases. Waiting seconds too long for the signal from their SAC, they are seconds too late. As the signal was given to apprehend, Jackson struck. When Chases walked to meet him and achieved the perfect distance, a second before the agents told him not to move, Jackson buried the war axe deep in David Chases' skull.

Pouncing on Jackson the agents pinned him to the ground. Handcuffed, jerked roughly to his feet and thrown into the nearest federal vehicle. At their feet Chases lay dead in a pool of blood, fringe splayed across his face.

Jackson was driven to Rapid City and escorted to a cell. The FBI had their man. The news is trumpeted throughout the land and the people are satisfied.

For four days he sat in a cell as the FBI agents grilled him, implementing every interrogation technique they knew. They want to know why. But it is hard to get someone to incriminate themselves when that person won't speak.

For four days Jackson didn't say a word and on the fourth day the routine began again. Walking into the interrogation room the agent asks, "You ready to speak, son?"

"You want my confession?" Jackson replied.

The agent, instantly at full attention, exuberantly responded, "Absolutely! What would you like to tell us?"

"Bring me a few notebooks and a pencil and I will tell you everything you want to know," Jackson replied. The agent couldn't run fast enough. Within moments he returned to the interrogation room with notebooks and pencils as requested. "Here you go, son," the agent said as he placed them in front of Jackson.

"Hey, you know what the date is?" Jackson asked the agent.

"Yeah," the agent said, "December 29th. Why? Any special reason?"

"Huh," was Jackson's only response as he chuckled at the joke the Agent so obviously missed. He said, "You might want to get some coffee. This is going to take awhile." As the agent left and closed the door he turned to watch through the one way glass as Jackson began to write…

"I was hanging around my campsite drinking coffee and waiting. I arrived five days earlier and was waiting for the camp crier to announce it was time. It was Tree Day, the day Sundance would officially begin…"

ABOUT THE AUTHOR

Michael "hawk" Spisak is a 49 year old mix blood, White/First Nations who has been on his own since he was 13. Living his life traveling the world, he has seen and done what most never will. After 48 States, almost every Indian Reservation and 13 countries, he settled down in Tennessee with his orange dog, S'unka the Superdog. He is single and lives alone, far away from suburbia.

Printed in Great Britain
by Amazon